C000147768

SLELETON
KEY

SKELETON KEY

Reed Bunzel

coffeetownpress

Kenmore, WA

coffeetownpress

Epicenter Press
6524 NE 181st St.
Suite 2
Kenmore, WA 98028
www. Epicenterpress.com
www. Coffeetownpress.com
www. Camelpress.com

For more information go to: www.coffeetownpress.com

All rights reserved. No part of this book may be reproduced or transmitted in any form or by any means, electronic or mechanical, including photocopying, recording, or any information storage and retrieval system, without permission in writing from the publisher.

This is a work of fiction. Names, characters, places, brands, media, and incidents are the product of the author's imagination or are used fictitiously.

Cover Design: Anthony Sands

Skeleton Key
2019 © Reed Bunzel

Library of Congress Control Number:2019943852

ISBN: 9781603817769 (trade paper)
ISBN: 9781603817752 (ebook)

Printed in the United States of America

•

In memory of Pierre Nantell
Sept. 30, 1976 – Sept. 30, 2018

•

ACKNOWLEDGMENTS:

As I was writing Skeleton Key I lost my son-in-law Pierre Nantell—the person on whom the character Jack Connor is based—to service-related PTSD.

Pierre was a kind and caring soul who endured the torment and misery of battle, and who returned home after leaving so much of his heart and spirit in the lonely sands of the Iraq desert. As British author Terry Pratchett once said, "No one is actually dead until the ripples they cause in the world die away," and I choose to believe that—through the words and deeds of Jack Connor—Pierre will remain in our world for many years to come.

RIP, my friend.

This book came about with the welcome assistance of a great number of people, and I would like to recognize a few of them here:

My amazing and tireless agent, Kimberley Cameron.

Jennifer McCord, and the rest of the marvelous editorial and publishing team at Epicenter Press/Coffeetown Press, for believing in Jack and providing him a warm and loving home.

My daughter, Jennifer Nantell, for her invaluable philosophical insight and spiritual input.

Last, and in no way least, my extraordinary wife Diana, for her ongoing inspiration, reassurance, love, and support. Thank you so much for accompanying me on this ongoing journey and—as I've said before—for sharing this bold and dashing adventure with me.

CHAPTER 1

Salt, sand, tourists, and tequila: all the aromas and sounds, the causes and effects of summer were in the air tonight. A wisp of a breeze trickled in from the dunes, the scent of rum and sunscreen hung in the air, and the rhythmic thrum of reggae and rock and country drifted in on the thick veil of summer heat. The faraway strobe of an airplane heading south to Miami or St. Somewhere blinked in the indigo sky overhead, and the glow of Charleston lit up the sky to the north. It was nightfall on the Carolina shore, the easterly winds were blowing up from the Bahamas, and the open-air drinking establishment known as The Sandbar in Folly Beach was careening headlong into another Friday evening.

And not a drunk or sober soul in the place had a clue that Death was lurking in the shadows of the night, aiming to crash the party.

"Hey, bartender—that was one killer trick. Do it again, will you—?"

Jack Connor took the lid off the blender, poured one perfectly measured piña colada into a plastic cup. Then he turned to face the voice that had just spoken as he popped a wedge of pineapple into the drink and set it on the counter.

"And just what trick would that be?" he asked the girl who was standing on the other side of the bar, slowly running a finger around the lip of her cup. Man-oh-man, did she have beautiful eyes. And a smile to match.

"The one with the limes," the girl said.

"That narrows it down to two," he told her. And as he really looked at her now, it was difficult thinking of her as a girl—she must have been late-twenties at least. Her hair had a hint of henna in it, rather than the "ho"-blonde look that so many girls were into these days. Still, he was he was pretty sure the color came from a bottle—just like everything else at The Sandbar.

He grabbed a beer from the cooler, popped the cap and set it next to the piña colada. The man who had ordered the drinks flashed him a thumbs-up and said, "Put it on my tab."

"You got it," Connor replied.

"I've only seen the one trick," the young woman told him.

"Stick around," he grinned as he reached for a box of cheap white wine and pressed the plastic spigot.

He stole a glance at his watch: just a little after nine. He'd already gone through one round of his bar magic tonight, and he wanted to give it a rest before starting in on his second routine of the night. He had a dozen tricks in all, simple sleight of hand stuff he'd learned at the V.A. treatment program last winter. One of his fellow former grunts—a kid in his twenties named Dragon—had hit the hardest of hard times after coming home from Afghanistan, minus a foot and a kidney and haunted by the ghosts of war twenty-four/seven. When it came time for him to talk during group, he would say nothing, just run a quarter across his knuckles or perform a magic trick from a childhood act he'd done with his older brother. Also, a veteran of the war, and also now part of the V.A. rehab system.

Connor was there because he'd been slogging through his own personal hell and had been mandated by the court to attend the group meetings, face up to the grief and guilt he still carried from the war. A month after that horrific night along the banks of Pelican Creek just a year ago he'd crashed his prize 1969 Plymouth Fury into a bridge abutment out near the airport, trying to outrun the ghosts of the past that had come back to haunt him. That led to three weeks in the PTSD program, at the end of which a thin membrane of scar tissue had begun to form over his festering wounds. He still walked a fine line between salvation and relapse, light and dark. Hope and despair. But he was dealing.

A week after leaving the V.A. center he'd landed in Folly Beach. It was a stretch of surf and sun just a few miles south of Charleston, a place the locals liked to call The Edge of America. Every flashing beer sign and neon martini hanging over a doorway beckoned to him that day, and on that particular afternoon he trudged up the stairs into one of the joints across from the road from the ocean and hoisted himself up on a stool with wobbly legs. His and the stool's. The place was just recovering from the hurricane that had ripped through the Lowcountry a few months before, and his eyes zeroed in on the selection of bottles lined up against the mirror along the wall.

He'd looked at the bartender, chewed on his lip for a second, and said, "Might you have a job for a veteran with a good work ethic who doesn't mind getting his hands dirty?"

That first night he swept peanut shells off the floor, and the next night he hoisted cases of booze in a back room that felt like a steam bath. Same thing for the next week, and the week after that. He slept on a sleeping bag on the floor and took cold showers at a scuba shop a couple doors down the street. Then one night one of the bartenders didn't show up, and the other one asked him if he knew how to make an extra dry martini. Back in the day gin had been one of his four main food groups, and by the end of the night he was slinging painkillers and cosmopolitans like a pro.

At the same time, Dragon's card tricks helped him to divert his thoughts from the relentless blamestorming that filled every waking second, and many while he was asleep. He found that shuffling cork coasters or making cocktail onions disappear with just the wave of a tiny napkin took his mind off the skeletons that still rattled in his head. The ladies would belly up to the bar to see this magic man do his thing, while the guys kept a suspicious eye on his hands and pockets. The real trick, of course, was to get his customers to buy a little more booze, get their brains just a little more fuzzy, and drop a little more cash.

"I think you're afraid to do it again," she challenged him now.

Who is this chick? Connor wondered.

"Patience is a virtue," he reminded her. And now that he really looked at her, he figured she was on the plus side of thirty. Tiny lines at the corner of her eyes, a dusting of freckles on her nose. All of which spoke to maturity, which made her even more attractive. "I've got a couple more to go before I get back to that one."

"You mean you do your tricks in order?" she said with a frown.

She was leaning on the rough-hewn wood counter, staring at him with eyes that seemed too green to be completely natural. Eye shadow to match, lips the color of maraschino cherries, and just as slick. Wearing a tight sundress, low-cut, leaving little to the imagination, a look in her eyes that told him she was well on her way to getting drunk. Connor knew the symptoms; he saw it on a nightly basis.

"First rule of magic is to never do the same trick in front of the same audience," he told her. Now he was mixing a rum and Coke, with a twist of lemon.

"But I want to see the lime trick again—"

Connor shook his head while he squeezed a wedge of lemon into the drink. "Just for you I'll make an exception, but you're still going to have to stick around a bit."

"Then you'll just have to make me another one of these," she told him, holding up her plastic cup. "By the way, nice tats."

Connor got that a lot, from admiring gals and envious dudes who were totally awed by the range of body art inked on his arms and neck. Depending on what patch of skin was exposed, the handiwork included a bald eagle, Japanese dragon, up-turned hourglass, compass rose, black leopard, creeping vines, even a Glock nine that looked like it was tucked into his waistband when he took his shirt off. A few of the older patrons shook their heads in dismay, chalking it all up to youthful excess, but typically the reviews were positive.

"A work in progress," he told her as he popped the cap off a hard lemonade.

"All that needlework must have hurt," she replied with a shudder.

"Human pincushion," he said, one of his standard lines.

She pounded the rest of her drink, then slid the empty cup across the bar. "No use wasting a new one," she told him.

"Bay breeze, right?"

"Good memory," she said.

"Too good, sometimes," he said. "Can't tell if it's a gift or a curse."

He tossed the used ice and cherry stem into the trash and set about making a refill. Vodka, grapefruit and cranberry juice, topped off with another maraschino cherry. Just like her lips.

"This was on a tab, wasn't it?" he asked as he placed the fresh drink in front of her.

"Yeah, the guy in the Yankees cap over there." She nodded toward a tall, athletic man with long black hair tied up in a ponytail. He was wearing the cap trendily backwards, with a little slant to the bill. The guy was dressed in baggy cargo shorts that almost came down to his knees, and a black tank top hugged his beefy frame.

"First name Alfonse," Connor remembered. "Last name Romano." He plucked the American Express card out of a small stack on top of the cash register and rang up the charge.

"Very good," she said. She grasped the plastic sword and stirred her drink slowly. "How long, you think, till the lime trick?"

"Ten minutes," he told her. "Give or take." Then he heard someone say, "Sex on the beach and a painkiller," and he instantly went about concocting the drinks, operating on auto pilot.

So far it was a good night. He'd opened the bar right at five, and within minutes the eighteen stools around the counter were full. So were the plastic tables pushed up along the wood railing of the drinking deck, and the rest of the floor was filling up fast. The Sandbar was a no-frills joint whose specialty was liquid refreshment, offering just enough food to slide past the municipal codes and liquor licensure. That meant a genuine New York hot dog wagon, a roasted peanut cart, and a massive basket of chips with a vat of salsa. All of it self-serve, and all offered on the honor system.

The place was across the shore road from the beach and was set up on wood pilings, another necessity because of stringent building codes put in place after Hurricane Eleanor. A set of stairs led up from a small sand-covered parking lot, and a ramp with several switchbacks assured those with disabilities that they had an equal chance to join the party. The roof was nothing, but a patchwork spinnaker fastened tightly to aluminum support stanchions, strings of party lights slung between them.

This time of night most of the customers were tourists, getting a buzz on before staggering back to their hotels, rented condos, or houses along the beach. But there was also a Greek chorus of regulars who habitually showed up night after night, burning through their paychecks and marinating their brain cells in draft beer and cheap vodka.

Around six o'clock a shower had moved through, dumping a load of rain on the Dacron roof and bringing in another wave of day-trippers who'd been lingering on the beach. The rain passed just as quickly as it had come, and in a little while those customers paid up and moved on. Around nine the die-hards started to show up, and that's when The Sandbar became one of the most happening joints in town. Folks of legal drinking age from anywhere in the world could walk in, press up to the bar, order a beer or a gin and tonic, make new friends, fall in love, and move on, remembering only half of it the following morning.

Connor still had a hard time thinking of himself as the manager of a beach bar, wearing shorts and a T-shirt to work instead of the hazmat suit that protected him during his years cleaning up blood and brains and decomposed bodies. No more scrubbing the stink of death out of floors and walls and automobile seats; now he simply measured out generous portions of booze for people who seemed to have no concept of the term "moderation." At times he missed the job and his old team, even the anticipation of what he might find when he pulled up in front of a new work site. Suicide? Murder? An accidental tumble down the attic stairs?

He thought about his old colleagues now—Lionel Hanes, D-Dub, and Jenny, aka the Jenster—and wondered if they still worked at the company or had moved on. The answer was just a phone call away, but it was not a call he'd wanted to make. Jordan James, his old boss, had tried reaching out to him, but Connor had avoided all his attempts. He still blamed the old man for roping him in on that last job for the governor, an investigation that resulted in his entire life being flushed down the crapper. Danielle would still be his gal, they'd probably be married, and there might even be plans for a little Connor running around.

But that devastating night in the pines near the shore of Pelican Creek had become a black hole of memories from which there was no escape. Whenever his mind took him back there all he could think of was watching the EMTs load his new fiancé into the back of the ambulance, an image that quickly flashed forward to seeing her lying in a hospital bed as a breathing tube kept her alive. The bullet that had torn through her body had destroyed a rib, punctured a lung, and shattered her scapula before slamming into the dashboard. She was alive but had slipped into a deep coma, her chest cavity filled with oxygen, her immune system struggling with the threat of severe sepsis. All of it because Connor had ignored her wishes, hadn't been able to leave well enough alone.

He pushed all that to the back of his brain now as he stood behind the bar, gazing out across the darkening water at the billowing clouds that reflected the setting sun to the west. Deepening shades of tangerine and ginger and crimson filled the sky as night fell upon the coast. The drink orders were coming in quickly now: an old fashioned, a martini on the rocks, two rum punches, a bloody Mary, three cosmos, three Buds, two g-and-ts, two white wines, and a double shot of expensive Scotch for a guy who looked like the most interesting man in the world from the beer commercials on TV. The original one, not the actor who replaced him.

Then he realized he was back to the chick with the maraschino lips.

So, he did his magic trick, a simple sleight-of-hand illusion in which he asked her to write her name with a Sharpie on a full lime. He then palmed it, causing it to disappear, only to make it reappear thirty seconds later in a wire basket that hung from a wooden crossbar overhead.

"Is that your name?" he asked her, handing it to her.

She looked at the name "Jessica" scrawled on it and said, "Unbelievable. How do you do that?"

"Lots of practice," he told her. "And lots of limes."

Just then a dog slowly rose to his feet in a corner of the bar, near the rest rooms. The chocolate lab stretched a second, then shambled over to where Miss Bay Breeze was standing and began licking the back of her calf.

"What the…!?" she said, wheeling around. The dog glanced up at her, an impish glint in his eyes and a string of drool trickling from his mouth. "Where did you come from?"

"His name's Clooney, and he comes with the bar," Connor told her.

"Clooney?" she asked. "Like the actor?"

"I didn't name him," Connor replied with an apologetic grin. "In fact, I found him wandering on the side of the road during the hurricane."

The chick named Jessica thought on that for a second, then ran a hand across Clooney's head and down the rough of his neck. "You really found him in a storm?" she asked him.

"Someone was evacuating, didn't have enough room in the car for him," he replied.

"That's barbaric. They just booted him out?"

"That's what the note on his collar said," Connor replied. "I thought about trying to find out who it was, afterwards, but figured they didn't deserve him. He's been with me ever since."

The woman named Jessica hung closer then, grabbing a bit of conversation with Connor whenever he had a second on his way from one end of the bar to the other. Julie, the other bartender, was working the far end of the bar tonight, and she was just as fast as he was. Faster, maybe, and she kept her own schtick going at her end, an improvised routine of "Name That Tune." Her phone was filled with the opening riffs of hundreds of hit songs, and she always had a running contest going with her regulars.

"Two Heinekens," a voice called out from Connor's end of the bar. Without even looking up he dug two iced bottles out of the cooler, popped the caps, and brought them to a man who had pressed through the crowd to get himself heard.

"I can see I'm in the wrong business," the guy observed as he grabbed the beers. He swept his gaze over the dozens of people who had crammed into the place, and another dozen or so who had spilled out into the parking area down below.

"And what business would you be in?" Connor inquired as he wiped a spot of moisture off the bar with a dishrag.

"Software," the man replied. He was a little on the slight side, maybe five-nine, with a rich tan and thick black hair combed back in a retro *Miami Vice* look. Two-day stubble, wide ears, round eyes shaded by a bushy brow that was only broken in the middle by a half-inch. He was dressed in the requisite shorts and tropical shirt, tan with green palm fronds on it, a little faded from too much washing.

"Software runs the world," Connor observed casually.

"A sad commentary on our time," the man said. "Can a man run a tab in this joint?"

"All I need is your card."

The man thought on this for a second, then pulled out his wallet and produced his Visa. "I can trust you not to go running up multiple slips on me now, right?"

Connor could have acted offended at the implied accusation, but the man's question was the second-most asked on a nightly basis, right behind, "Can I get sex on the beach?"

"The Sandbar is a scam-free joint," he assured the guy. He accepted the card, checked the name embossed at the bottom. "Have you been in our lovely town very long, Mr. Carerra?"

"Just got in this afternoon," the man replied. He gave a nod over his shoulder at a woman standing at the railing that kept Connor's patrons from falling over onto the sand. "Me and the missus…sort of a late honeymoon. We got married last month, but couldn't get away until now."

Connor could tell that Mrs. Carerra was a good ten years younger than her husband and, on balance, far more attractive. She had what romance novelists would call a heart-shaped face, flowing black hair with platinum streaks in it, high cheeks and skin that had yet to feel the touch of age. She wore a blue strapless dress with a school of brightly colored tropical fish on it, and a white straw hat was nestled on her head.

"Staying at the Tides?" he guessed, just to make conversation. The Tides was the resort hotel that sat squarely on the sand and anchored the town's shabby-chic business district.

"No, we're renting a cottage at the north tip of the beach," he explained. "Nice place, right on the sand. Found it online. My wife loves it, even the name."

"And that would be?"

"Calypso Cove," he said.

"I know the place," Connor told him. "Turquoise and yellow, with a bright pink roof. Just watch out for the undertow up there. We've already lost a couple kids this summer."

Carerra gave him a wary look, wondering whether Connor was messing with him, finally figured he was for real. "Well, thanks for the brewskis," he said. "I'll check back in a bit."

"Say 'hi' to the missus," Connor replied. Then a call for a screwdriver and another painkiller brought him back to the other side of the bar.

The next few minutes were pretty much a blur. Friday evening, high season, late July really brought people down from the northern climes, and that was good for business. At one time or another virtually everyone who set foot in Folly also ventured into The Sandbar, and between the booze and the souvenir glasses and selfies, they'd go back home with smiles on their faces and memories in their heads.

Connor did his Visa trick—cutting up a man's card only to have it reappear in one piece in his shirt pocket—then poured the distraught owner of the card a shot of tequila on the house. That one always got a great roar of approval and a wave of more drinks—which, after all, was the whole point.

"Cool move," the chick named Jessica cooed.

"Got me a few black eyes before I got it right," he confessed. "First few times I tried it I sliced up the wrong card."

She laughed at that, feeling good about him, thinking this guy was quick and funny. "Who was that man you were talking to?" she asked him.

"Just a customer," he replied with a shrug.

She nodded at that, said, "Have you lived here at the beach for long?"

He was mixing something with melon liqueur, shaking it up to a froth. "Six months, give or take," he said as he poured the mixture into a tall plastic cup. Without hesitation he started in on another drink, this one a frozen margarita, no salt.

"Let me guess," she said, fixing him with her eyes. "You came down on vacation, liked it so much you never left."

"Something like that," Connor said, not wanting to get into it.

He wondered what her gig was. On vacation with friends? Here with her boyfriend? She wasn't married; that was the first thing he looked for. She acted single, and if it wasn't for her pal in the baseball cap, who was paying for her drinks, he'd maybe ask her what time she got off. But from the way Alfonse Romano stood there at the railing, talking to a couple guys but glancing this way every few seconds, he couldn't be sure what the angle was.

So, he asked her.

"So…what's your story?" he said, casually. "You here for work or pleasure?" Small talk, nothing more. It was almost a year after Danielle had summarily expelled him from her life and he still wasn't any good at this.

"Mostly work, actually," she replied as she fiddled with her plastic cocktail sword. He'd stopped using straws a few months back, out of concern for the turtles that laid their eggs in the dunes just up the beach.

"And that would be?"

She glanced up at him, her eyes fixing on his. "A little of this, a little of that," she said, lowering her voice to just above a whisper.

"I see," he said. "Does 'this and that' keep you busy twenty-four hours a day?"

"Sometimes yes, sometimes no," she said.

"Then what do you do when it's 'sometimes no'?" he asked.

She seemed to think that was the funniest thing. "What exactly are you asking?"

For one thing, who's this Alfonse guy you're with?" He nodded his head at the guy with the dark ponytail. "Seems to be one right popular dude."

"He sure thinks so," Jessica said. "And he's part of the mostly work thing. In fact, he's all work, if you get down to it."

There it was: subtle but direct. Whoever the guy was, he was not an obstacle.

"Let me guess he's your boss, and he's got you on a short leash."

"The bartender is a magician *and* a psychic," she smiled. "Do you have any more tricks up your sleeve?"

"Nothing you haven't seen before," he confessed.

Jessica started to say something in response, but Connor didn't hear a word she said, because just then a gunshot rang through the bar. Very sudden and very loud.

Followed by an even louder scream.

CHAPTER 2

Instinctively Connor spun around, drawing his gaze to the far end of the drinking deck. Just in time to see a man crumple to the floor, leaving the shocked look of horror on the face of the woman who had been standing next to him. It was Mrs. Carerra, and her eyes were open wide, her mouth in a terrified "O" like in that famous painting everyone thought was a van Gogh, but wasn't. She stood there unmoving, staring down at her husband lying at her feet.

She screamed again, an ear-numbing wail that rivaled any police siren in town. Connor stared at her for a split second as the entire scene came together in his mind, then vaulted over the bar. "Get back...let me through," he said as he pressed his way into the Friday night crowd. "Give the man some room—"

Out of the corner of his eye he saw a dark figure down on the sand, hovering in the shadow of a palmetto tree. The guy was staring up at the place, watching the commotion, his lips caught in a tight smile. Knit cap, yellow and red and green, pulled tight over his head. For a second Connor could swear that their eyes met; then the man turned and raced up the beach road, scrambling up over a dune and disappearing into the night.

Connor hesitated a second, then then turned his attention back to Mr. Carerra. He was lying on his back with one leg slightly tucked under the other, arms splayed at his sides. His blank eyes seemed fixed on a point beyond the ceiling fan gyrating slowly above him.

At first glance he appeared dead, but then he blinked his eyes—once, very slowly—and a slight draw of breath moved his chest. A large red rose had soaked into the tropical shirt in his upper right shoulder. It was an exit wound, which meant Carerra had been shot in the back. Connor momentarily thought about the slug, where it might have ended up, but that was unimportant right now. The critical thing was to try to save this man's life.

"Mar...ti...na," the man wheezed in a thin, raspy voice, before his eyelids closed.

"Tony...no!" his wife wailed. She had a few red spatters on her face and the top of her dress, as if someone had just tossed a bloody Mary at her. "You...stay with me! Tony—!"

Connor felt the man's wrist for a pulse, found a slight one. He looked over his shoulder and shouted in the direction of the bar, "Julie—call 9-1-1!"

"Already did," called a woman from the edge of the crowd, cell phone glued to her ear. "Ambulance is on its way."

The customers who had been standing next to the Carerras had moved back a few feet, and one or two couples had taken the opportunity to quietly sneak out of the bar. Didn't want to get involved, Connor suspected, momentarily wondering if they'd paid their tabs.

Martina Carerra was now kneeling next to her husband. She started to lift his head, but Connor gently touched her on her arm. "Don't move him," he told her. "It could make his injuries worse."

She looked at Connor, then drew her gaze back to Mr. Carerra. She kissed him on the forehead, then gently lowered him back to the wooden floor. Connor thought he saw the man's eyelids flicker again: he wasn't dead, but he sure seemed close.

"Let me through...I'm a doctor," came a voice from the crowd. Most of the curious customers by now had backed up and were giving Carerra some breathing room.

"E.R., by any chance?" Connor asked.

The woman pressed through the small crowd and said, "Med surg."

He recognized her as the woman who had called 9-1-1 and said, "Good enough."

She pushed forward and knelt down beside Connor. She placed two fingers against Carerra's neck, then listened to his breathing. "Pulse is low, breathing irregular. This man is going to go into shock if he doesn't get help soon."

"EMTs should be here any second," Connor said.

"EMTs might not be enough," the nurse replied shortly. "He's going to need a trauma unit and a surgeon, stat."

"Closest hospital is in Charleston," Connor told her. "The Medical University."

"Then we need to get him there as soon as possible."

Martina Carerra was still kneeling next to her husband, rocking slightly on her ankles. "Who...who would shoot my Tony? Why?"

"I'm afraid I don't know, ma'am," Connor told her before he realized it was just a rhetorical question borne out of panic. Out of the corner of his eye he caught Jessica and her pony-tailed colleague speaking in hushed tones and gesturing wildly, but he was too busy to be envious.

Somewhere in the distance the sound of a siren split the night. Mrs. Carerra gripped her husband's hand and gently squeezed it, silently urging him to hang on. Connor's thoughts again went to the person who'd been standing down by the palmetto tree and then had bolted into the darkness.

Everything happened quickly after that. The ambulance swerved to the edge of the road that separated The Sandbar from the beach, and two paramedics jumped out. There was no question where the emergency was, and they took the stairs two at a time up to the bar. Connor didn't recognize either of them, which wasn't surprising. Even though Folly Beach was a small town he'd only been here a few months. Most faces were still new to him.

"Holy shit," the first EMT said as he searched for Carerra's pulse. He reminded Connor of a medic he'd known in Iraq: round head, large ears, square jaw. Dark eyes, intense and penetrating. He pressed his finger to the victim's neck, just as the med surg doctor had done, then glanced down at where the blood had stained Mr. Carerra's shirt. "This man's been shot clean through."

"He's going into shock," the doctor said. "You have to control the bleeding and minimize breathing trauma."

"And you are?" the second EMT asked her. He was thin, black, short hair and a soul patch on his chin. Wide jaw, small ears, round eyes that right now seemed full of worry.

"Dr. Lessard," the med surg doctor said. "Duke Raleigh Hospital, here for the weekend. The bullet may have nicked a major artery, or it could have a collapsed lung. Either way we need to be worried about airway management."

Both EMTs studied her for a second; then the first one said to the second, "We have to get him on the bus. Doc…can you apply direct pressure to the wound while we carry him down the stairs?"

"Let's go," she replied. "But you're also going to need to pack the wound with hemostatic gauze, since a tourniquet is out of the question. And maybe insert a tube for oxygen flow."

The two EMTs worked fast, taking great care as they slid Mr. Carerra onto a stretcher and strapped him in so his body wouldn't move. The man was in enough trauma as it was, and now he'd have to endure a risky jostling as they carried him down the steps to the ambulance. Connor noticed it was a Ford E350 4x4, the same model he'd driven for Palmetto BioClean in his previous life. Which then caused him to contemplate the vast amount of blood that had spilled on the wooden deck and was dripping through the floorboards into the shadows below. Not something he wanted to deal with right then, but he'd have to clean it up first thing tomorrow. As a former pro he knew just what the job called for.

"Is he going to be okay?" Martina Carerra asked no one in particular as she wiped tears from her face. Her hands were trembling and there was a dark look of fear in her eyes.

"MUSC is one of the best hospitals in the South," Connor assured her. "He's going to get the best care he possibly can."

"No—I'm going with him," she suddenly announced as she raced down the flight of steps after the EMTs.

"Ma'am—" Connor called after her, but it was no use. She had shifted into overdrive and caught up with them as they were hurriedly loading her husband into the back of the ambulance.

"I'm going with him," she repeated to them, direct and very no-nonsense.

"No room," Soul Patch told her.

"I'm his wife," Mrs. Carerra said. "I have a right—"

"No, ma'am, you don't," the med surg doctor from Raleigh stopped her. "The tech is correct…there's only room for your husband and two others."

"Him and me," Mrs. Carerra said, tilting her head toward Soul Patch.

The doctor gently placed her hands-on Mrs. Carerra's shoulders and stared into her eyes. "Your husband is in critical condition, ma'am. He needs a doctor, so I'm going with him. He'll be in good hands."

"But—"

"Trust me," the doctor said.

Mrs. Carerra fixed her with dagger eyes, a dark look that seemed almost threatening. Then she shifted her glance to the med tech and finally to her husband in the back of the ambulance. She hesitated as her instinct fought her brain; then waved her hand and said, "Okay…go. Take care of him. Save him."

"We will," the doctor assured her, then jumped up in the back of the vehicle and pulled the doors closed.

A hundred pairs of eyes followed the ambulance as it made a wide U-turn, then accelerated up the road in a blast of red strobes and sand. Connor had followed Mrs. Carerra down to where it had been parked, and now he came up behind her and lightly touched her shoulder. "He'll be there in less than ten minutes," he assured her.

But Martina Carerra didn't seem to hear. "Please, Tony…don't die," she pleaded softly as she watched the lights fade. "Please, dear God—"

The police had been slow arriving on the scene, but two of them showed up now. Connor had heard the approaching siren as Carerra was being loaded into the ambulance, and he knew they would be pissed off that the victim had been moved before they got there. The police station was a two-minute drive from the bar, but since no one had shown up until now Connor figured everyone must have been out on a call somewhere else in town.

Mrs. Carerra clearly heard the siren, too, because she suddenly pivoted and looked him in the eye. "I need to get to the hospital," she said. "I should have ridden in the front seat."

"The police are going to want to talk to you," Connor told her.

"I've got to be with my husband."

As soon as the SUV from the Folly Beach P.D. came to a stop two doors swung open and a pair of officers piled out, both of them dressed in black over black. Guns and batons and mace and other things were strapped to their waists. The rooftop light bar cast flashes of blue across the drinking deck and its customers, the number of which was beginning to thin out. Typical, once the police show up the party shuts down.

Connor recognized them both as they strode across the road toward the bar. Darnell Evans and Cleveland Wolfe, both of them occasional beach bar customers and part of the regular weekend patrol that kept the town in order. Good guys, relatively good cops, and painfully talkative whenever their vocal chords got going.

Connor knew what was coming, and he didn't much want to hang around answering questions while Evans and Wolfe took names and copious notes. He also knew that the State Law Enforcement Division soon would get involved, which meant endless more questions that would last well into tomorrow. He didn't know if anyone else had seen the man in the shadows, and now he tried to recall whether the guy might have been holding something in his hand. Something like a gun. But Connor had only seen him for a second, hadn't really seen a thing before the man had hightailed it over the dunes. By now he could have been just about anywhere.He knew he should stick around and talk to the cops, but he just wasn't up to the task. The last time he'd done that the love of his life had just been shot, and the sound of the gunshot tonight had yanked Connor back to that night. His brain was still etched with the image of the evil look in the gunman's eyes as he'd pulled the trigger, and Danielle had screamed. Her life had hung on a thread for days, but she had survived, although their engagement did not—and nothing he could do could put Humpty together again. "Come with me," he said as he shook the memory off and grabbed Mrs. Carerra by the arm.

"Where are we going—?"

"The hospital."

She considered this for all of half a second, then said, "But the cops…they'll want to talk to you."

"You and me both. And the second they see us there'll be no escape."

Mrs. Carerra thought on what he was saying, then nodded and said, "Let's do it."

"Your car or mine?"

She hesitated only a second, then said, "My keys are in my purse, up there." She glanced back up at the party deck, where just minutes ago she had been laughing with her husband.

"We'll take my Jeep," he said.

He gave her a gentle nudge and she moved, but again glanced back over her shoulder. "All my money and cards are in it," she suddenly remembered.

"I'll call Julie as soon as we get on the road," Connor told her. "She'll hold it behind the bar until you claim it."

"Sounds good," she said, and then hustled along, a half step behind him.

Connor steered her to where he had parked his Jeep under the deck. The cops would be furious when they learned he had skipped out, but they knew where to find him. Besides, if they got too angry with him, The Sandbar's complimentary beer tap might suddenly dry up for them.

"This is it," Connor whispered as he led her around the old Jeep Wrangler, gray primer over rust. He'd bought it off another buddy in his V.A. group, a two-tour Iraq vet on full PTSD disability who had been arrested trying to drive off the

Talmadge Memorial Bridge outside Savannah. The police had stopped him and seized his vehicle, which he'd sold to Connor for the cost of the impound fees and three thousand cash, which was just about all Connor had from the blood money he'd earned doing that last job for the governor.

"What is this thing?" Mrs. Carerra asked as he helped her up into the passenger seat.

"Dependable," was all he said as he fished his keys out of his pocket. "And your only option at the moment, unless you want to call an Uber."

"Drive," she said, not even hesitating. "Where are the doors?"

"There are no doors," he said as he started the engine. "No air conditioning, either. Hang on to your hair."

"Just get me there."

"Ten minutes," he told her.

It actually took closer to twenty, and Mrs. Carerra didn't say a word the entire ride. Connor knew where he was going because he'd made this same trip the night Danielle had been shot, but he tried to push that line of his thinking from his mind. When they arrived at the hospital a series of signs directed him through a narrow gate to the E.R., and ten seconds later he pulled the Jeep up against the concrete curb. He jumped out from behind the wheel and ran around to Mrs. Carerra's side, but she had already climbed down.

"This way," he told her, sensing she was trembling from shock.

She pushed through the double glass doors and made a beeline for the admissions desk. At least a dozen people were waiting in plastic chairs, some of them looking sick or in pain, while others worried for loved ones who were in the back being examined. Friday night at the busiest hospital on the South Carolina coast was not an ideal time to be here, but Mrs. Carerra had no choice. Nor did she care about those who might be in line ahead of her.

Two nurses were standing behind the counter, and they looked up as Connor and Mrs. Carerra raced toward them.

"An ambulance just came in from Folly Beach," she said with urgency.

"And you are?" one of the nurses asked.

"My husband was in it...his name is Tony Carerra," Martina Carerra explained. "Can you tell me where he is?"

The two nurses stared at them for a moment, then shared a glance between themselves. Finally, one of the nurses, a tall and very dark woman whose name tag identified her as Mona, said, "You're his wife?"

"That's right," Mrs. Carerra said.

"Do you have any I.D.?"

"No...I left it in the bar, where Tony—my husband—was shot. Please...just tell me how he is—"

Mona fixed Mrs. Carerra with a somber expression that made her tense, but said nothing.

"He *is* going to be all right, isn't he—?"

"I...I don't know what..." Mona said, almost stuttering. She glanced briefly at the other nurse; a young girl named Alicia who averted her eyes by looking down at the counter. "I...we...I mean...let me go get Dr. Mitchell. She's authorized... she'll fill you in."

Mona quickly darted from behind the admission desk and disappeared through a pair of automatic doors into the emergency room, leaving Alicia in an anxious position at the desk. She tried to keep busy shuffling papers and not looking at the man and woman standing in front of her, but Connor didn't go for the delay tactics.

"Please, tell us...what's going on?" he demanded.

"Like Mona...Miss Shulman said...the doctor will explain everything."

"Can't anyone tell me if my husband's alive?" Martina Carerra seethed, her eyes narrowing in an angry furrow above her nose.

"That would be me."

Connor and Mrs. Carerra looked up at the E.R. doc, who was pushing her way through a set of swinging doors behind the nurses' station.

"It's about goddamned time!" Mrs. Carerra blurted.

The doctor's scrubs were spattered with blood and other various fluids, and she was pulling a blue nitrile glove off one of her hands. "I'm Dr. Mitchell," she introduced herself. "Please, let's all go over there and have a seat." She motioned toward some empty chairs in a corner, two along one wall and two along the other.

"I don't want to sit down," Mrs. Carerra protested. "I just want to know how my husband is doing!"

The doctor—first name Melanie, as identified by her plastic badge—gave a lot of thought to this, bit her lower lip as she stared down at the bridge of her nose. She was a tall, thin woman, and she seemed to be swimming in her green E.R. scrubs. Young, early thirties, pale, mottled skin that suggested she spent very little time in the great outdoors. She wore a single gold stud in each ear and no color on her thin, almost nonexistent lips that barely framed a set of small, white teeth when she spoke.

"I understand, Mrs. Carerra," she said, trying to conjure up some façade of a bedside manner. "You do not have to sit if you choose not to." She was holding a clipboard in her hand, and studied it to buy herself some time.

"Please, doctor," Martina Carerra pressed her.

"There's no easy way to tell you this, ma'am. But your husband...well, the EMTs and the doctor who rode here with him...they did everything they could to save him. But the bullet nicked an artery, possibly the upper axillary or, less likely, the descending aorta—the autopsy will show which one—and he suffered severe internal bleeding. We prepped an operating room, but he passed away before he got here. I am so sorry."

CHAPTER 3

In the next two seconds Connor realized why Dr. Mitchell had suggested they sit down. Mrs. Carerra turned a ghostly white and buckled at the knees, then collapsed to the cold floor as if every bone in her body had turned to rubber. Except for her head, which hit the hard tile with a resounding thud.

"Oh my God…Mrs. Carerra. Ma'am," Dr. Mitchell said as she dropped to her knees to revive her. She gently shook her, then made an effort to straighten her out so she was lying flat, and raised her legs off the floor about a foot. "Mona—get me some pillows, stat," she called to the nurse at the admin desk.

Fifteen seconds later Mrs. Carerra had come around and was sitting up, rubbing the back of her head. She seemed a bit disoriented as Dr. Mitchell walked her through some basic coordination tests, then checked the dilation of her pupils. In fact, Mrs. Carerra had only begun to regain a sense of consciousness when the worried doctor announced she was going to take her into the E.R. for further examination.

"Nonsense," Mrs. Carerra stated. "I'm perfectly fine."

"You don't have a choice," the doctor said. "Hospital policy. Any injury on the premises must be checked out by a physician."

"I told you, I'm fine—"

"And I told you, you don't get a vote."

Mrs. Carerra looked about ready to cry, and no one would have blamed her if she did. She had just learned that her husband had died, and now she was being forced to undergo an exam by the same doctor who had probably pronounced him dead just a few minutes before. She continued to protest, but the nurse named Mona helped Dr. Mitchell get her into a wheelchair and then rolled her into the back of the emergency department.

Connor hung around, not knowing what to do. He took a seat in the waiting room, picked up a copy of *National Geographic* and read about carnivorous bats and the Dalai Lama and cattle ranchers in Argentina. He really needed to get back to the bar, face the barrage of questions the local and state cops no doubt would hit him with. They'd still be hanging around, and now he felt bad about just running out on them. Julie, too. But he couldn't just abandon Mrs. Carerra here, with no way to get back to Folly Beach or the place she and her husband had rented on the beach for their honeymoon. *Calypso Cove*.

A little over an hour later a different nurse came out of the E.R., looked around, and headed over to where Connor was sitting.

"You're with Mrs. Carerra?" she asked him. Her name tag identified her as Alma, and her pale skin was covered with a constellation of freckles. Her red hair was buzzed close to her scalp, like a Georgia peach, and she wore wiry spectacles that seemed to pinch her nose. Her teeth were straight, but yellowed from too much caffeine. Or nicotine.

"I brought her here," he answered. "She was hysterical—"

"Are you her husband?"

"No. I just drove her up from Folly."

"I'm afraid I'll have to speak with Mr. Carerra, then," Alma said.

"That's going to be a little difficult, seeing as how he's probably down in the morgue by now," Connor said, maybe just a little too smart-ass.

"Pardon me?" the nurse asked, furrowing her brow.

"Mr. Carerra was the victim of a shooting tonight," Connor said. He explained to her how Mr. Carerra had been gunned down at The Sandbar in Folly Beach and apparently died while in transit to the hospital. "I'm sure it's all in your computer."

"I am so sorry…" she said, her words trailing off for a second. "I had no idea."

"So, how's she doing?"

The nurse closed her eyes, looked as if she was trying to collect her thoughts. "I really shouldn't be telling you this, since you're not family. But she may have suffered a concussion and is showing signs of shock. We're going to need to keep her overnight for observation. Strict hospital policy."

Legal liability was more like it. "Is she awake?" he asked.

"Keeps going in and out," she told him. "And she keeps asking for Tony. I guess he would be her husband."

"You'd guess right. Any chance I can see her?"

The nurse thought a moment on this, then raised a shoulder in a slight shrug. "No harm if you poke your head in. But that's all. We gave her a sedative, and she needs to sleep. We're going to transfer her to a room upstairs as soon as it's prepped."

Mrs. Carerra looked pretty much as the nurse had described her. She was lying on a gurney behind a curtain, an IV drip feeding into one arm and a maze of wires that disappeared down the collar of a drab hospital gown. A monitor on a stand displayed her vital signs, and he could tell she was doing as well as could be expected. Heart rate was 72, blood pressure 130 over 86, breathing was 12 per minute. She appeared to be sleeping, but occasionally her eyes would flicker, and her lips would move, as if she were saying something. Just on the subdural side of consciousness, Connor figured. Either that or she was having a dream.

Her face looked pale, her hair limp and almost colorless on the white sheet. There was a redness around her eyes that Connor attributed to the tears that had come earlier. A bandage was taped to the left side of her skull, just above her cheek.

"Is that where she struck her head?" he asked the nurse, who was standing next to him, making sure he didn't try to start a conversation.

She nodded, said, "Everything looks okay, but with these things you want to err on the side of caution."

He flashed back a couple hours to earlier in the evening, when Mr. Carerra—*Tony*—had bellied up to the bar and ordered a couple of cold Heinekens. Late honeymoon, he'd explained before he walked back to where his wife was standing, neither of them realizing how the evening would end. Him shot dead through the back, her fainting from the shock of the news and now lying in a hospital bed, drifting in and out of consciousness.

Some honeymoon, Connor thought.

"Think she'll sleep all night?"

"She should. The sedative we gave her was relatively mild, but it should last quite a while."

Connor massaged his temples, suddenly realized how tired he was. He glanced at his watch, saw it was already a little past one. He suddenly felt his body sag.

"Then I think I'd better get going," he announced. "Is there any way someone can give me a call when Mrs. Carerra gets released?"

"Give me your number, I'll see that it gets on her chart," Alma promised him.

Connor drove home in silence. He didn't want to hear anyone, talk to anyone, see anyone. No late-night rock or country or shock talk on the radio. Not since Danielle had been shot had he felt so unsettled, his soul so gutted. This was so much different from then, of course: Tony Carerra was dead, whereas Danielle had pulled through. Three days in a coma, twelve nights in the hospital before being transferred to a rehab facility across the river in Mount Pleasant. That's where she had unloaded on him, told him that he'd violated her trust. After recovering Jordan James' missing painting just weeks after they'd met, he solemnly promised never to put his or anyone else's life in danger again—and had almost gotten them both killed because of his pointless lunacy.

He'd begged and pleaded and made a raft of new promises, but she wasn't having it. She'd already quit her job at the animal park in Florida and was too banged up to start her new one at the rescue ranch. Her lung was starting to heal but the threat of infection still loomed, and her shattered scapula meant she had to remain as motionless as possible. Same thing with the second vertebrosternal rib, which had been fractured when the slug tore into her chest. Pain was a constant factor, exacerbated by Danielle's refusal to take any medication except for those moments when it got over the top.

Three months after the shooting she went home, to Orlando. Her divorce from her cheating ex-husband had been finalized, but she'd made it clear that

Connor was not to visit her, call her, or text her. All those painful days and nights in rehab had caused her to do a lot of thinking, and she'd decided they were through. Kaput. *Fini*.

"You may be the last honorable man in Charleston, and you mix a mean dirty martini, but I'm done with your death-wish bullshit," was how she'd put it.

At first, he went through the typical stages of rejection, which weren't all that different from the stages of grief: disbelief, denial, anger, understanding, bargaining, depression, and acceptance. He sank into despair and desolation, a toxic blend that led to the V.A. program in Georgia and a recovery process that allowed his heart to mend. His life slowly got back on track, and he'd managed to hit the reset button and steer himself in a different direction. The only reminder he carried with him was the chafing wound in his heart that he feared would never close completely, and which was still messing with his mind.

He pulled the Jeep into his space beneath The Sandbar and let the engine sputter into silence. As he trudged up the stairs to the deck, he spotted a half-dozen hearty drinkers still positioned around the bar, sucking down beers and puffing on cigarettes. Then he smelled a distinct odor in the air and realized it wasn't just tobacco.

Julie the bartender glanced up as he walked in, cocked her finger at him. "The prodigal bartender returns," she said.

"I left a voicemail, telling you where I was going," Connor replied. He stepped around the yellow police tape that had been stretched from one rail of the drinking deck to another, marking off where Mr. Carerra had gone down.

Julie eyed him skeptically. "Well, you missed out on all the fun," she said. "Cops were here till about a half hour ago."

"Looks like it," he said, nodding at all the tape. He shook his head slowly as he walked up to the bar. "Got any cold ones still in the cooler?"

"A couple," Julie said. She took out two bottles, popped the tops, handed one to him. "I heard the guy died."

Connor took a long sip and nodded. "Never had a chance, I guess." The cold foam felt good going down his parched throat, so he did it again.

"How did she take it?" she asked. "The dead guy's wife, I mean."

"She fainted. Irony is, they're keeping her there for the night. Did you stash her purse?"

"In the cubby under the cash register, just like you asked," Julie said. "Cops weren't too happy you skedaddled like that."

He nodded again, stared out at a speck of light out on the dark horizon. "They know where to find me."

"And they told me to remind you of that fact," Julie told him. "I wouldn't plan on sleeping in."

Connor said nothing for a bit. The way he saw it, the shooting wasn't his business. None of it. Sure, a man had been shot in the bar, but the guy who did it had been standing down on the sand, outside the place, shooting upwards. And the more he thought about it, he figured it had to have been the man who had been standing in the shadow of the palmetto tree, then took off into the night.

Fact was, he knew how cops worked. They'd want to know what Connor had seen, what he'd done. Even more important, they'd want to know why he'd left the scene. And while they eventually might accept his gesture of driving the dying man's wife up to the hospital, it wouldn't make them happy.

"I hate to ask, under these circumstances, but how'd we do tonight?" he finally said, gazing out at the night.

"Pretty good, considering," Julie sighed. She shook the crumbs out of her dishcloth, then hung it on a rack behind the bar. "Business slacked off for a bit, then word of the shooting got around and we had a good run there for a while. Even with the cops here the crowd didn't taper off until maybe twenty minutes ago, except for the pros over there." She nodded at the remaining lost souls who seemed glued to their stools.

"They're here every night," Connor said. "I'm beginning to think they live here."

"So, do they," she shrugged. "By the way, that chick you were talking to earlier, she took off with her pal not long after you did."

"What chick?"

"The one who was drooling all over you," she said with a wink. "Just in case you didn't notice."

Until that moment Connor had forgotten all about the girl with the green eyes. What was her name? Jessica. No last name, no known address. All he knew about her was that she seemed really into his lame bar tricks.

"Is that all?" he asked.

"No," Julie said, a grin forming on her lips. "Before she left, she said to tell you she really liked your magic, wondered what you might be able to pull out of a hat."

"She said that?"

"No," Julie said with a grin. "But she did tell me her last name is Snow."

"Not exactly a warm weather sort of name," Connor observed. He glanced down the bar at the last remaining customers. "You give 'em last call?" he asked.

"More than once," Julie said. "You know how that goes."

He did, and he wasn't worried about them. "Okay," he replied. "Let's close it up. Once the booze is sealed off, they'll take off. I'll stash the receipts upstairs and be right back."

Because The Sandbar was open to the elements, Connor locked down the alcohol every evening with thick pressure-treated sheets of plywood secured by a series of hardened steel padlocks. Tonight, he and Julie tackled the job together, working around the two patrons who were still hunched over their beers. He recognized them from a kayak rental joint out near the marsh, but paid them no mind. They couldn't get past the locks and, as long as they didn't get into a fight and start busting up the bar stools and plastic furniture, he didn't care if they stayed here until dawn.

"Quite a night," Julie said as she pulled a wooden peg from her hair, shook it until it fell over her shoulders.

"Yeah, and thanks again for holding down the fort while I was gone," he said, exhaustion suddenly settling in.

A kaleidoscope of shit was flashing through his mind, old shit he hadn't wanted to think about ever again. Months of therapy with Dr. Pinch, and then the V.A. program, had cleared out most of the cobwebs and he'd mostly been able to push the bad memories from his brain. Unfortunately, many of the good ones remained, and they caused almost as much pain.

One of the things he liked about Folly Beach was its anonymity. No one here seemed to know who he was, knew that his actions had inadvertently brought down a sitting governor and had gotten his fiancé shot in a dark Carolina forest. He kept quiet about his time in Iraq, too, and the nagging post-traumatic shock that still gripped him when he heard a truck backfire, or a string of firecrackers explode on the fourth of July. No one here knew about the men he had killed, or the suicide bomber who had blown up his Humvee, or even the masked gunman who had shot his niece Lily in cold blood—the original sin that had tipped the line of dominoes and caused him to sign up for war in the first place.

Everyone here in Folly seemed to have back story, their own reason for being there and not somewhere else. Some were here because they were running *from* something, others were here because they were looking *for* something. Either way, if you were looking to be lost or found, Folly Beach was the place to be. As a local bumper sticker said, "We're all here because we're not all there."

Connor grinned at that as he picked up his beer, walked over to the wall switch and turned off the lights. Then he mounted the stairs that led to his attic apartment, giving one last look to see if the two kayak rental guys were still sitting at the locked-down bar.

They were.

CHAPTER 4

Connor slept until eight, when the divers showed up at the scuba shop two doors down.

Every morning of the week they stomped around beneath his window, laying out their masks and fins and clanking their aluminum tanks as they readied themselves for the van that would shuttle them to the boat in the marina. Divers as a rule were an early rising, noisy bunch, and there was no reason to expect anything different today. For the first few weeks after he'd moved into the attic apartment, he'd tried wearing ear plugs, but he felt a cloying sense of claustrophobia when he couldn't hear the noises of the night. Or morning. He'd thought about finding another place to rest his head, but this small pad came with the job and the commute to work was easy.

Connor rolled over and tried to go back to sleep, but it was no use: the day had begun. Down on the sand tourists were setting up beach umbrellas and lounge chairs, and along the potholed streets delivery drivers were offloading crates of food and drink so the town could do it all over again tonight. The aroma of shrimp and grits and biscuits and gravy drifted through the jalousie windows, churned up by the overhead fan before it reached Connor's nose. But the smell of freshly brewed coffee was what did it, and Connor lazily swung his legs over the edge of his bed and ran his ragged fingernails across his bald scalp.

That's when he heard the banging on his door, which opened out onto a small landing that faced the sea to the east. A set of stairs led up from the drinking deck below, and Connor could see someone standing out there. Face pressed to the glass, peering inside. The guy waited a moment, then knocked again.

The banging awakened Clooney, who raised his head and let out a throaty *woof* at the sight of this tall, dark stranger standing at the door. But Connor recognized him: Lincoln Polk, one of the local cops who regularly helped him roust folks from the bar who didn't want rousting. Polk had explained once that his mother had wished for her first-born son to grow up and be president one day and figured that having the names of two former commanders-in-chief couldn't hurt. Initially she'd been disappointed when he'd joined the police department after finishing two years at South Carolina State, but it was a good job and he was helping out the community—especially when it came to domestic violence. Spousal abuse was almost epidemic in South Carolina and, after what Polk's father tried to do to his mother, he wasn't about to take shit from anyone. Which included his old man, who currently was doing three-to-five for assault up in Ridgeville.

"Clooney!" Connor called to his hyper-alert canine protector. "Settle down, boy. You know this guy."

Clooney wasn't so sure about any of this, not yet, but he followed Connor's lead and lay back down on the floor. Connor pulled on some cut-offs and a Sandbar T-shirt, and opened the door.

"Morning, Mr. Polk," he said, as cheerily as five hours' of sleep would allow.

"And a good morning to you, Mr. Jack," Polk replied. "You're up bright and early, considering the events of last night."

"You know what they say about the early bird," Connor grunted.

"You got an appetite for worms?" Polk said, evidently not finding anything humorous this morning. He was lanky, black, late thirties, and always dressed in a loose-fitting white button-down shirt and a pair of dark trousers, despite the hot sun. He was wearing a Braves baseball cap, backwards, the flat bill almost touching his collar. If he was going for plain clothes, he had the look down perfectly. "That dog's got quite a bark on him."

"Worse than his bite," Connor replied. "And I know why you're here. You want to come in?"

"Not particularly," the cop said, sniffing the stale air. "How about you and me, we go and get us a cup of Gilbert's fresh grind?"

A cup of coffee was just what Connor needed, and he'd been in the process of getting one when Polk had knocked on his door. "Sounds good," he said. He felt his pockets, realized he'd left his wallet on the nightstand next to his bed. "Hang on…let me get some cash."

"Never mind…I'm buying," Polk told him.

"Even better. Mind if I bring Clooney? I'm sure he's got to take a leak."

"Never argue with Mother Nature," the police officer said.

Connor slipped on a pair of sandals and locked his door, then followed the cop downstairs and up the street to Gilbert's Grill. It was a small place, just a Formica-topped counter with five chrome stools and a stainless-steel stove, where bacon and onions were sizzling. The joint was spotless, the result of Gilbert fastidiously wiping down every surface over and over again until everything shined like glass. He'd done several hitches in the Coast Guard, where he'd learned to cook, and then did another twelve years in the kitchen of a cruise ship, where he'd learned that cleanliness was next to Godliness. And Godliness, he liked at say with a broad grin, was next to impossible.

No one but Gilbert was in the place, but a young couple was sitting at one of the small tables on the rickety porch, enjoying breakfast in the sun.

"This going to take long?" Connor asked Officer Polk.

"Depends," he replied with a shrug.

Connor considered this, then looked at the skinny old man with tired eyes standing behind the counter. "In that case, Gilbert, I'll have a sausage and egg sandwich on a biscuit," he said. "And a large black coffee."

"And you, sir?" Gilbert asked, turning to the cop.

"Just the coffee," Polk said. He took out his wallet, dropped some cash on the counter. Gilbert started to protest, but Polk shook his head. "New department policy," he explained.

Connor plucked a paper cup off a stack and drew some thick coffee out of a pump thermos. He knew from experience that anything Gilbert cooked on the grill typically took a while to fix, so he went outside to the porch where Clooney was waiting for him. He dropped into one of the white plastic chairs and propped his feet on the peeling rail. Polk followed him out, but instead of sitting he simply leaned against a support post, looking out at the ocean in the distance.

They sipped their coffees in silence, letting the scenery do the talking. Sea the color of sapphires, endless sky, crisp horizon, an underlayer of grease and hash browns hovering in the air. Somewhere reggae music was already thumping, and somewhere else people were shouting. Laughter followed, and Connor felt himself draw in a deep breath of clean, warm air. *Amazing how paradise never gets old*, he thought.

"A man got shot at your place last night," Polk finally said, pushing away from the railing and looking directly into Connor's tired eyes.

"Technically, I suppose you're right," Connor responded.

"Technically? How do you mean?"

Connor raised his brow, shooed a dragonfly away from his coffee. "A man was shot; I'll give you that much. And he was in The Sandbar, so you're right about that, too."

"Then your point would be?" Polk asked.

"Well…from what I could tell, the shooter had to be standing outside, down in the sand, near the road. So technically, even though Mr. Carerra—that was the victim's name, but I'm sure you know that—even though he got plugged in the bar, the shot came from the ground. So, when you say he was shot in my place, it depends on whether you're talking about where the guy was hit, or where the gun was fired."

Officer Polk studied Connor a second, then shook his head. "Before you started slinging drinks is there any chance you passed a different kind of bar exam?"

"You mean, was I a lawyer?" Connor said. "You sure know how to insult a guy."

"Well, you sure as hell sound like one." Polk watched a hummingbird that was nosing its long beak into a honeysuckle bloom, then said, "But yeah, what you just laid out is how we think it happened."

"So, what can I help you with?"

"Well, why don't we start with what you saw?"

"I saw a lot of things, sir," Connor said. "It's kind of my job."

"Then let me be more specific," the cop said. "Did you see the victim get shot?"

Connor shook his head, explained that he was mixing drinks and paying attention to his customers at the bar. "All of a sudden I heard this bang, and when I looked over Mr. Carerra was falling to the floor."

"So, you didn't see who pulled the trigger?"

"Not then, no."

"But at some point?"

"I'm not sure, but maybe," Connor said. He told Polk how he had jumped over the counter and made his way through the gaggle of customers to where the injured man was lying. "That's when I saw this guy standing under a palmetto at the edge of the lot. I'm pretty sure he saw me, and then he ran up over the dunes and disappeared down the beach."

"Running which way?"

"That way," Connor pointed to his right. "But it was dark, and the dunes, there, blocked my view. Plus, there was a man dying on the floor in front of me. I was a little preoccupied."

Polk looked as if he were making mental notes. "Did you know this guy? The man who was shot?"

"No...I'd just met him when he ordered a couple beers. Why do you ask?"

"You called him Mr. Carerra. You knew his name."

"He wanted to run a tab, so he gave me his credit card. I always check the names."

Gilbert took that opportunity to come outside with Connor's sandwich, arranged on colorful waxed paper in a red plastic basket. He set it down on the table without saying anything, then disappeared back inside.

"Did you get a good look at the guy?" Lincoln Polk finally asked. "The one with the gun?"

Connor picked up his sandwich and took a bite. "I'm not even sure I saw a gun," he said as he chewed.

"But you said you saw the shooter."

"No, I said I saw a man who ran away when he caught me looking at him."

"Did you give any thought to why he ran away like that?" Polk wanted to know.

Connor had to think on that one a minute. "Half the people who live in this town ran away from something," he eventually said.

"True, that," Polk agreed. "But this one was doing it last night, at the very same moment someone got shot in your bar."

"Did you find a slug or a casing?" Connor asked him then.

"One piece of brass, down by the tree I think you're talking about. A twenty-two, recently fired. No prints. We searched your place for lead, but you don't have much in the way of walls in there. Plus, the shot was fired upwards, at an angle, so it's anyone's guess where the slug ended up."

A twenty-two? Connor thought. Then he said, "Did you check the spinnaker roof?"

"We did, and when you finish that heap of grease you're eating, we'll go take a look at what we might've found."

The yellow police tape hadn't done much good to keep people away. Fresh footprints had been trudged in the sand where the shooter supposedly had stood under the tree, and Polk kneeled down and poked his finger in it. Clooney joined him, sniffing around the trunk of the palmetto.

"Here's where we found the casing," he said. "And this is where we figure he must've been standing when he fired the shot."

"Almost exactly where I saw him before he took off," Connor told him. Then he pivoted on his heel and pointed up at the railing that ran along the closest end of the drinking deck. "And Mr. Carerra was standing right about there."

"A clear shot, no more than twenty feet."

The two men trudged up the stairs into the open-air bar and moved over to where another length of yellow tape was rippling in the morning breeze. A large brown stain indicated where Tony Carerra had fallen, so Connor didn't have to guess where he'd been standing when he was shot.

Using his finger, Polk drew an imaginary line from where the shooter likely had been aiming the gun to where the bullet had penetrated Carerra's back, high up near his shoulder. Then he continued the line, finally pointing to a hole in the Dacron ceiling where the slug may have traveled. The gap was about the size of a nickel, and the edges looked neat and fresh.

"Is that new?" he asked.

Connor studied the opening a moment, then nodded his head. "Looks like it," he said. "Otherwise I would've known about it during that thunderstorm we had the other night."

"Then that could be where Elvis left the building," Polk said. "Might be out in the street, or someone's yard."

Connor nodded again, then glanced down at the stain where Carerra had fallen. It was irregular, approximately the shape of a kidney swimming pool, maybe four feet by two feet. The deck boards were a light, unstained gray, but the blood had dried to the color of dark brick. Pretty noticeable to anyone who might show up tonight and try to figure out where the murder had taken place. As soon as Officer Polk wrapped up his investigation, he would have to get to work on it, hopefully finish up before the happy hour crowd began to arrive.

Fortunately, Connor was a pro at getting blood out of just about anything.

"So where did you take off to last night?" Polk asked him.

Connor was pretty sure Polk already knew where he was, but he humored the cop with an honest answer. "The victim's wife wanted to go to the hospital, to be with her husband," he said. "I gave her a lift."

"So, you drive an Uber now?"

"No Uber, no taxi," Connor said. "I just gave a ride to a lady in distress."

"You sure you don't know these people? The Carerras?"

Connor rolled his eyes. "Mrs. Carerra's husband got shot in my bar. I drove her to the hospital. Nothing wrong with that."

"Technically," Officer Polk said.

"Technically, what?"

"Like you said, technically he was shot in your bar, but like you also said, the shooter was standing down there."

The two of them exchanged glances, then the cop slapped Connor on the shoulder. "Loosen up, man. I'm just having fun with you."

"Right. And just for the record, it's not my bar."

"I know. But you're the manager, and that's close enough."

"You have any idea at all who the shooter was?"

"No, but our local guys and state detectives are talking to all the usual suspects," Polk said. "Any chance you can help us with that?"

"I doubt it," Connor said. "Like I keep telling you, I didn't get a good look at him."

"But you're sure it was a him?"

Connor thought on that only a half second before nodding. "Hundred percent sure. Young, too. Kinda skinny."

"Black or white?"

"Black."

"It was dark out."

"So was he."

That brought another grin from Polk. "Okay, so we've got a black kid hanging around outside your bar—*or not your bar*—in the shadow of a tree. No one sees him, he's just standing there, biding his time. Maybe he's gunning for this Mr. Carerra in particular, or maybe anyone'll do. Anyways, he sees the guy, pulls out his gun, pops him right through the back. Then he takes off running. That sound, about right?"

Connor nodded at Polk's words, then said, "He was wearing a hat."

"What kind of hat?" Polk asked, suddenly seeming interested. "Like a baseball cap?"

Connor shook his head. "No, it was more like one of those wool caps, like I used to wear up in Michigan in the snow."

"You happen to catch a color?"

"Several of them. Yellow, green, red."

"Rasta colors," Polk said. "What about his eyes?"

"Far as I could tell he had two of them," Connor's attempt at sarcasm went over like cow dung, so he added, "He looked at me for maybe half a second, then took off."

"Over the dunes."

"That's right."

"Would you recognize him if you saw him again?"

Connor turned up his hands in exasperation. "I'm really not much good at that sort of thing."

"How old do you think he was?"

"Sixteen, maybe eighteen years old. I'm not good with kids, either."

"Never had any of your own?

"None that I know of," Connor replied.

Polk stood there a moment, chewed on his lower lip while he thought things through. A gull screeched overhead, then banked and flew out over the water.

"Anything else stand out last night?" the cop asked.

"Nothing that comes to mind," Connor said. "Like I said, the ambulance came, the EMTs packed up the guy, then they were gone."

"And you took off right after that," Polk said, nodding in the direction of the Jeep.

Connor nodded; they'd already hashed out this part earlier. "By the time I got back you guys were long gone and I had a bar to close up. And I guess that brings us up to the present."

"Just one more thing," Polk said. He stroked his chin, from which sprouted a dark stubble that gave a look of coarse sandpaper. "This Mrs. Carerra, the lady you took up to the hospital. Did she come back here with you?"

Connor shook his head, explained how she had fainted and cracked her head on the floor. "They kept her overnight for observation," he said. "My guess is she'll take a cab back when she's released."

The cop said nothing, just pushed off from the railing where he'd parked his butt and started toward the exit. "Well, if you see her, give me a ring," Polk told him. "You never know if maybe she knows something that totally eluded your steel-trap memory."

CHAPTER 5

Once Officer Polk was gone, Connor ducked into the ground-level store room and sorted through the shelves for any kind of solvent that might cleanse blood out of the wooden deck. He knew from his previous employment cleaning up death scenes that blood was a particularly devious substance. It was invasive, it followed the laws of gravity, and it seeped into the deepest cracks and creases of any porous material. The threat of HIV, hepatitis, herpes, hantavirus, and other nasty things loitering in a person's bloodstream was very real, and mere soap and water was hardly sufficient to get rid of it.

In the best-case scenario a good application of oxygen-based bleach or hydrogen peroxide did the trick. Worst-case scenario, which Connor had encountered in some of the nastiest jobs, required the removal of entire sheets of drywall or carpet all the way down to the subfloor. The stain on The Sandbar's drinking deck fortunately was not one of those, and Connor eventually found an assortment of solvents he knew would minimize the stain. He loaded several containers into a plastic bucket and carried them up to the bar, then dragged a hose up the steps and got ready to do his thing.

That's when the F-350 Ford panel truck bearing the name Palmetto BioClean pulled into the narrow drive that separated The Sandbar from the building next door.

Clooney looked up from where he'd been sleeping, appearing more annoyed than curious at the interruption. Connor did a double take, the truck seeming so out of place this morning but totally obvious at the same time. It seemed natural that it would be there, since this was a death scene that definitely needed cleaning. He'd worked dozens of jobs similar to this one and many that were far worse, and he'd always been the contact person when a new customer called to inquire about the company's services. Connor would explain how he and his team would sanitize the site, dispose of any waste materials, then bill the insurance company for all fees. In most cases the client was dealing with autopsies and death certificates and funeral arrangements, and the less they had to worry about claims agents and corporate red tape, the better.

But Connor had not called Palmetto BioClean this morning, and as he scratched his shaved head, he wondered why the truck was there. More specifically, who had sent it, and under whose orders? He had never actually met The Sandbar's owner; officially Connor reported to a senior manager at a food and bev company up in Charleston. It made sense that news of last night's murder would have made it up the command chain to headquarters, but so far, he hadn't talked to anyone from higher up. In his mind he had no need for a professional cleaning service to take care of a task he clearly was capable of doing on his own.

What the hell was going on?

Connor's question was answered a second later when a blue Bentley Continental GT with a W12 supercharged engine pulled in behind the BioClean truck. The luxury car was tastefully fitted with Mulliner interior, contrast stitching, veneer door inserts, and ventilated seats. He knew all of this because he knew the owner, and he'd listened to the man's boastful spiel about his new car at least a dozen times.

Three doors opened all at once: two of them in the cab of the truck, and the driver's side of the Bentley. That's the door Connor was focused on and, sure enough, Jordan James climbed out from behind the wheel and stretched his arms high over his head. He was old and getting older, stiff and getting stiffer. Meanwhile, Connor's old partner in crime-scene clean-up, Lionel Hanes, climbed down from the BioClean truck and now walked back to where James was standing, shielding his eyes from the hot Carolina sun.

Clooney let out a low growl, not sure whether these newcomers were friend or foe. Right about now Connor wasn't sure, either, but he patted the dog on the head and told him, "Stay cool."

The two men talked for a minute, but Connor couldn't hear what they were saying from where he was standing. Mr. James was pointing up at The Sandbar's covered deck, and it was evident that neither of them could see Connor in the shadows. Eventually a young woman who was dressed in a tight tank top and black jeans slid out of the truck's passenger seat. She was sipping from a can of Cheerwine and seemed immersed in deep thought. Her hair was pink, and her lips were blue, and she was wearing massive sunglasses that made her eyes look as big as a horsefly's. And just as green. That was Jenny, who always seemed to have a new look for every day of the week. Connor grinned to himself, remembering how three years ago Jordan James had thought she was a risky hire, predicted she would bolt at the first sight of dried brains. But Connor had made a strong case for bringing her on board, and he was glad to see she was still with the company.

In any event, he wished they would all go away and let him clean up the blood by himself. After Danielle gave him the heave-ho he'd jettisoned Palmetto BioClean and all the things that went with it, and he didn't want any of them to start resurfacing now.

"Well, look at what the shrimp boat dragged up," he called down to them anyway as he reluctantly peered over the deck rail. "What brings y'all to this little corner of paradise?"

"We heard there might be blood," Hanes called back. "What are you doing up there?"

Connor held up his bucket of cleaning solvents and said, "Same thing as you, only it looks like I beat you to it. Good morning, Mr. James."

"Good to see you, Jack," his old boss called back. "Permission to come aboard?"

Connor studied his old colleagues and his former boss, and remembered again that he'd never actually learned who owned The Sandbar. The place had changed hands twice after the hurricane, but both sales had been kept secretive and confidential. Connor had run a property search in the county records, but he'd only come up with a shell company owned by a holding company. Some sort of limited liability corporation with a name like Lowcountry Refreshment Ventures, Inc.

Which Connor now concluded was owned by Jordan James. It was no secret that James was the eighth-richest man in Charleston, as ranked by the local alternative newspaper that published a top ten list of such things every year. That had been last year's chart, so the man may have climbed or fallen in the annual tally. At Connor's last count the native Charlestonian owned about a dozen restaurants across the Lowcountry, a chain of pawn shops, a string of laundromats, a funeral home, several bail bond storefronts, a majority share in a local bank, a private security firm, and Palmetto BioClean. Plus—Connor would bet good money on it—The Sandbar at the Edge of America.

"Permission granted," he replied, wondering why James would have bought this place. Or even whether he'd ever set foot in it. "Have a look around."

A round of handshakes and back-slapping and cordial small talk followed. Lionel Hanes had quit his personal trainer gig at a local fitness gym and had taken over Connor's fulltime job running Palmetto BioClean. He was a former Georgia Tech football star who had played four games with the Atlanta Falcons before a motorcycle crash ended his NFL career. Both of his sons were now in high school, addicted to designer basketball shoes and high-end gaming apps. Meanwhile, Jenny continued to teach yoga part time while cleaning death scenes whenever her schedule permitted, as it did this morning. D-Dub, who had been a part of the team when Connor managed the company, had relocated with his wife to Atlanta. The cupcake business Mrs. D-Dub had started during the recession had finally taken off, and she was now franchising the specialty shops across the southeast.

The conversation eventually drifted around to last night's shooting. Connor explained what had happened, and then showed them the blood stain that had discolored the deck planking. He could feel Jordan James' eyes boring into him the whole time, leaving no question that the old man was itching to speak with him privately, as soon as he got the chance.

"I was just getting ready to clean it up when you guys arrived," he explained when he was finished.

"Is that the dog you found in the storm?" Lionel Hanes asked him.

"You remember Clooney?"

"It's been a while, but who could forget this handsome dude?" That was Jenny, who bent down and gently scratched him behind his ears.

"I appreciate you guys showing up, but seriously—I've got this," Connor told them both. "It's on my resume, or at least it would be if I had one."

"I know, but you're the customer this time, not the employee," Hanes told him.

"I really don't need any help—"

"That's not the point," Jordan James interrupted. He looked at Hanes and Jenny and said, "You two, do whatever you can to get that blood out. And while you're doing that, Jack and I are going to have a little chat."

Connor hesitated, but only for half a second. Jordan James once again had insinuated himself into his life, and a gnat of resentment nibbled at the back of his brain. There was nothing he could do about it, not unless he quit, which he was not prepared to do. His life had settled into a comfortable rhythm, as empty and aimless as it sometimes seemed in the middle of the night when his mind went on rewind. One of the V.A. doctors at the PTSD facility had suggested he step away from the past and focus on the power of now. The doc had told him to look into someone named Eckard Tolle when he got home, but of course Connor never did.

In any event, he had no choice but to do whatever Jordan James said, up to a point. So, he said to him, "It would be good to catch up."

"Have a nice talk," Lionel Hanes said, almost taunting his former colleague. Then he and Jenny went back down to the BioClean truck to gather whatever they needed to take care of the blood.

Once they were gone Jordan James glanced at the locked-down bar and said, "Do you have the key to that?"

"Sure do," Connor replied. He sneaked a quick glance at his watch, saw it was barely past ten o'clock. "Might I get you something?"

"The usual," James told him. "And make one for yourself, while you're at it. It's the weekend."

The usual was a double Beefeater martini, desert dry, straight up with two olives.

"I just finished my morning coffee," Connor replied, holding up the cup that contained the dregs from Gilbert's.

James gave this a second's thought, then said, "It's always five o'clock somewhere."

"So they say. But five o'clock is five o'clock when you run a bar."

"Fair point. But you know me: into every day a little gin must flow."

"Of course, Mr. James," Connor said as he unlocked the bar cover and removed the theft-proof panels. Clooney curled up in a corner of shade, resting his head on crossed paws, as he was prone to do.

"C'mon, Jack. It's always been first names with us."

Connor couldn't remember any time when he had called his boss by his first name, but he said, "Yessir," anyway.

"And none of that yessir shit, either."

"Got it."

He fixed the man's martini and poured it into a plastic cup. "Sorry I don't have a proper glass," he said as he set it on the wooden counter that had been gouged with customers' initials over the years. He knew Mr. James didn't like to drink alone, so he splashed some tonic water on ice and started to take a sip.

"Wait," James said, holding up his drink. He seemed to reflect for a minute, then said, "To old times, and old friends. To new times, and better friends. No judgments, no doubts. Just trust and honesty and respect. *Salud.*"

At that, he tipped his cup back and sucked about a third of the martini down his throat.

Connor had no idea where this was going, but he knew Jordan James well enough to know it was going *somewhere*. Meanwhile Lionel Hanes was hauling a pail full of solvents back up the stairs, and Jenny was following him with a bucket and several mops. While Connor appreciated the assistance in cleaning the blood out of the floor—and was happy to see his old friends again—he couldn't help feeling irritated at the sudden and unannounced intrusion into his day.

"Exemplary martini," Jordan James told him, nodding his head as if there was some sort of private rhythm beating in his head. "And you're probably wondering why we're here."

"I understand why *they're* here," Connor said, cocking his head toward Lionel Hanes and Jenny. "But since you arrived in a caravan, I can only figure that you're behind the shell companies and the corporation that owns this place. Lowcountry Refreshment Ventures, I believe it's called."

"Bullseye," Mr. James said. "Just as smart as you always were. Which is why I bought this place."

"Say what?"

"You know me, Jack. Always looking around for a good place to park a little money so I can make a lot of money. This place had all but blown away in the hurricane, but when I heard you were running it, I wanted in."

Connor knew his words were meant as a compliment, but he was so over that sort of shit. So over Jordan James, who'd had had his hooks in him ever since he moved to the Lowcountry. That wasn't really fair, and Connor knew he owed the man more than he could ever repay. Still, he always felt as if Mr. James had his own private drone hovering in the sky, keeping an eye on Connor's every movement. He understood the man was motivated by a genuine feeling of obligation and debt, since he was convinced Connor had saved his son Eddie from the suicide bomber in Iraq. As a gesture of thanks, he had put him in charge of Palmetto BioClean, a counter-intuitive line of work for a former grunt who was having difficulty extricating his mind from the bloody horror of war. James had also turned over the title and keys to his son's prize '67 Camaro, bright orange, with a 396 supercharged engine under the hood. The same Camaro, named Isabella, that Connor eventually returned to her rightful owner after refitting her with special equipment so Eddie could take her out for a chaperoned spin every once in a while.

He understood these acts of appreciation and accepted them gratefully. But Mr. James also had introduced Connor to Governor Luck, a fateful meeting that had pushed him into the path of death and mayhem. No matter how he looked at it now, or whoever provided words of wisdom or sage counsel, Connor still could not move past the chain of events that led to the shooting in the piney woods that warm August night, and Danielle's icy rejection.

"I'm just starting to pick up the pieces," Connor reminded him. "Not a good investment in the long run."

"I respectfully disagree," Mr. James replied as he took another sip of his martini. "The bar's quarterly numbers are up twelve percent year over year, figuring in the losses from the hurricane, and net earnings are up fifteen. Plus, *Lowcountry Weekly* just named The Sandbar the Number One drinking establishment in Folly Beach. They haven't announced it yet, so don't tell anybody. Anyway, like it or not, that's all on you."

"It's in a good location and has a sweet vibe," Connor conceded with an indifferent shrug. "That's all."

Jordan James plucked an olive out of his drink and popped it in his mouth. "That's the Jack Connor I know; as modest as ever. You may not see it, but you have a talent. A good head for making things work. Figuring things out. Patient and determined. That sort of spirit and energy isn't easy to find in today's workforce."

"You left out co-dependent and self-destructive," Connor countered. "That's according to the V.A."

"Those days are behind you, Jack. Besides, I believe in looking at the good side of a human being, rather than continuing to poke at the nicks and scars." And just like that, there went the rest of his martini. He put the cup on the counter and nudged it toward Connor. "One more of these, for the road."

The words *for the road* gave Connor a bit of encouragement, even though he knew it meant Jordan James would be getting behind the wheel. He quickly threw together another martini with a little less gin and an extra olive, and placed it in front of him. "I appreciate your confidence, Mr. James," he said stiffly as he set the fresh concoction back on its cork coaster.

"*Jordan*," the eighth-richest man in Charleston corrected him, again. He studied his new cocktail like an art patron might eye a painting on a museum wall, then drained half of it in one swallow. "And my confidence is well-placed. Also, just so you know, I didn't come here today just to tell you I own this place."

Connor kind of figured that, so he said, "I kind of figured that."

"I appreciate what you're doing here at The Sandbar, as well as mixing just about the best martini in all of Charleston," Jordan James told him. "Just like I appreciated what you did to grow the BioClean business, and when you located my painting. I know how you like to get in the middle of things, get your hands dirty. But I also see something that I don't think you see, at least not yet."

He let it hang there, forcing Connor to say something. Eventually he did. "And what might that be, Mr. James?" he asked.

"Well, let me put it this way. I came here today to let you know that I always have openings in the company. Openings where you might be able to put your talent, patience, and determination to better use."

"I like what I'm doing here," Connor countered.

"I knew you'd say that, and I respect it," James replied. "No rush on anything. I just wanted to unlock the door to your future, in case you're curious what might lie on the other side of it."

Jordan James was starting to sound as if the martinis were doing their thing, but Connor wasn't about to mention it. As long as the man was able to drive his sapphire blue Bentley Continental GT with the W12 supercharged engine, it was of none of his concern. Whether Mr. James had a busy afternoon or a long nap in his immediate future, Connor wanted to wrap this up and get on with the rest of his Saturday.

These days I'm living in the 'now,'" Connor said.

"Shirley reads Eckard Tolle, too," James said. Shirley was his first ex-wife and mother of the son whose life Connor had saved in Iraq. "Eddie's condition has caused her to live one sunrise to the next."

Connor nodded but said nothing as he absently wiped a rag across the counter.

"Any event, I want you to think about what I said," Jordan James continued as he stared into his plastic cup. "You have great promise, and one of these days you're going to get restless. Or bored. And while I would hate to pull you away from this bar, there will always be a place for you in the company."

"Thank you, Mr. James" Connor said.

"Jordan."

"Sir."

The man sighed with resignation as he checked his watch, then pounded the remains of his martini. He chewed the three olives, then said, "Gotta go. Lunch meeting with the new mayor at noon. Think about what I said, now, won't you?"

"I sure will."

"Excellent," Jordan James said. He turned to go, then looked Connor straight in the eye. "Just promise me one thing?"

"I'll try," Connor replied.

"Stay out of this." James nodded in the direction of where Lionel Hanes and Jenny were vigorously scrubbing the blood out of the deck. "Whatever it was that happened here last night, just leave it alone."

"I learned my lesson last time."

Jordan James offered a throaty grunt and said, "I know you, Jack. Better than you do. And for your sake, whatever last night was about—whatever reason that man was shot—leave it to the police. If anything happened to you, it would be like losing my own son."

CHAPTER 6

After Jordan James had driven away in a cloud of Bentley dust, Connor pitched in to help clean the rest of the blood from the deck. It really wasn't a large stain, so it didn't take very long, and because the planks were actually fabricated from a sealed composite material, the blood hadn't soaked in. With the scorching July heat and humidity in the mid-nineties, it was an odious task that reminded him why he was glad he'd moved on from that line of work.

Once everything had been stashed back in the BioClean truck Connor popped a Corona for Lionel Hanes and a Cheerwine for Jenny. They sat in the shade under the billowing spinnaker roof, watching the waves in the distance and talking about old times. It was all surface-level chatter—*have-you-heard* and *did-you-know* sort of stuff—and eventually it was time for his old teammates to leave. He gave Hanes a hearty man hug and Jenny a quick peck on the cheek, and then they were gone.

Connor spent the next hour in his apartment counting last night's cash and credit receipts. When he was finished, he stuffed everything inside a money bag that he tucked inside a pocket in his cargo sorts, then trudged off to the bank before it closed at one. Not long after he returned the booze truck pulled up, always a good sight on a Saturday when Friday night had all but cleaned him out. The driver, Desmond Green, was a tall, lanky black guy in his late twenties, born and raised on one of the sea islands off the Carolina coast. He was Gullah by heritage and a wizard with a bass guitar, and when he was younger, he'd headed west to Memphis to seek his musical fame and fortune. Like so many others he ended up right where he began, without barely getting started.

The two of them hauled the cases of beer and tequila and vodka into the walk-in cooler on the ground level. Then they knocked off and Connor cracked two cold ones, which they drank on the wooden stairs that led from the sand up to the drinking deck.

"Heard you had a bit of excitement last night," Desmond said. He took a long sip of foam, wiped his mouth on his arm.

"Grisly news travels fast," Connor observed.

"It was all over the TV this morning, man. Tourist gets shot in Folly, that's big news."

Connor nodded as he watched a blue-tailed skink dart across the floor. "Did the TV say anything about who could've done it?" he asked.

Green said nothing for a minute, just probed a gooey spot on the stairs with the tip of his shoe. "Not the TV," he finally said. "But there's talk."

Connor was staring out at a sailboat that was making its way south out near the horizon, but now he shot a curious glance at Green. "What sort of talk?" he asked.

"Just talk. But the shooter...they're saying he's a local kid."

"Local, like from here in Folly?"

Desmond Green lifted a shoulder in a noncommittal gesture. "Somewhere down around here, is what I heard. Don't know much more than that."

"Do the cops know this?"

The booze guy tipped his bottle back, swallowed the rest of its contents. Then he stood up, holding the empty by the neck. "You know how it is," he said as he turned to go. "Despite what they like to think, cops're usually at the end of the donut line."

With that Green lumbered down the stairs and back to where he'd left his truck under a No Parking sign. He'd been parking there for four years, never got a ticket. Never had to worry about one, either. Folks in Folly look after their own.

Connor spent the next hour restocking the bar, making sure there was enough liquid refreshment of every variety close at hand for that evening's business. He inventoried the limes and cherries and the coasters and cocktail napkins, even the little plastic swords for the martini olives. And for an occasional magic trick.

A few minutes before four, thunderheads began to build to the south and the wind began to shift. Connor looked up just in time to see a man coming up the stairs, way too early and well-dressed to be a customer. He was wearing black trousers and a light blue button-down shirt, black shoes and wire-rimmed shades. He came over to the bar and produced an ID card that identified him as an investigator for the State Law Enforcement Division, also known as SLED. Connor knew someone from the state level would show up sooner or later, and that time had now arrived.

The SLED guy was named Jake Crittenden, and he was all business. He asked mostly the same questions Lincoln Polk had hit him with, without the folksy demeanor and deportment. What did Connor see, and when did he see it? Did he observe a suspect with a gun, possibly run over the dunes into the darkness? Did he know the victim prior to the shooting, and why did he give the man's wife a ride to the hospital?

"Don't you guys share information?" Connor finally asked him. "I already went through all this with the local cops."

"A man was killed in this bar," the SLED agent reminded him. "How much of your time do you think it's worth to find him?"

Now was not the time to get into technicalities of the shooting, as he had done with Officer Polk. Instead he simply said, "Whatever it takes, sir," and spent the next ten minutes reviewing the same details over and over again.

Eventually Agent Crittenden seemed ready to wrap up. He'd actually been taking notes in a spiral notebook, which he flipped closed and slipped back into a pocket. He turned to go, then said, "Couple years back you were arrested on felony drug charges, with intend to distribute. Care to mention what that was all about?"

Connor had thought the record from that unfortunate incident had been expunged, but he figured SLED agents had access to all law enforcement records. So, he said, "False charges, brought on by a man with a vendetta. The charge was dropped the next day."

The detective stared at him through his sunglasses for an uncomfortably long time, then said, "You want to keep it that way, Mr. Connor," his voice thick with accusation.

"Yes, sir," Connor said, going back to his Army days when he'd learned that was the best response when you didn't have a clue what your commanding officer was talking about.

Julie showed up just as the SLED agent left. She started slicing mangoes, and Connor helped her out. The Sandbar served several varieties of rum drinks, the favorite being a potent concoction called a tropical tryst, created from four kinds of rum and five fruit juices and served in an oversized plastic bowl. The centerpiece of the drink was a mango island with two plastic figurines—a naked mermaid and merman—taking up somewhat compromising positions under a paper umbrella. The drink had been written up in *Conde Naste* magazine, and the blurb was picked up by several travel blogs and guide books.

"Was that guy a cop?" she asked him as she sliced through a particularly juicy mango.

"State Law Enforcement," Connor confirmed.

"He says if they were close to nailing the guy who did it?"

Connor shook his head, said, "Not very forthcoming with the facts. 'Working on some leads,' was pretty much what he told me."

"Can't have tourists getting shot for no reason."

"What makes you think there's no reason?" Connor asked her.

"Well, it seemed so random. I can't think of any real purpose to it."

Connor had been thinking the same thing, and it didn't sit well with him. "Not for me to figure out," he said.

"What about the local cops?" Julie asked. "What time did they show up?"

"A little after eight this morning."

"Ouch!"

"I was already up," he said. "Hard to sleep through the divers."

"You should find another place to rest your head," she observed.

"It's crossed my mind," Connor replied. "But it's hard to beat free rent."

"Any sign of What's-Her-Name?" Julie asked. Connor shot her a confused glance, so she added, "The dead guy's wife?"

Connor shook his head. He knew Mrs. Carerra eventually would drop by the bar to fetch her purse and her husband's credit card, but he wasn't expecting her any time soon.

"I'm sure she's in no hurry to return to the scene of the crime," he said. "If it was my husband who got killed, this is the last place I'd want to be."

"I guess. But sooner or later she's going to drop by to close out his tab."

Just then the first customers of the afternoon wandered up the stairs into the bar and settled in on a couple of stools. A young man and woman, mid-twenties, smiley and happy and clingy to the point of nausea. Connor pegged them for honeymooners, but he let Julie take their orders, since he was still elbow-deep in mango slime. They ordered frozen margaritas, one with salt and one without. Saturday night at The Sandbar had begun.

For the first few hours business was pretty much normal, the crowd a little larger than normal because word of the shooting had spread, and a lot of looky-loos wanted to see where it had happened. A light rain shower moved through a little before sunset, dousing the beach and everyone on it. This time of night it was usually younger folks—average age early twenties—throwing a football, skimming a Frisbee, making out in the sand, or all of the above. When the rain came, they scurried up from the sand and jammed onto the deck, and the bar had a run on beer and banana daiquiris for a solid twenty minutes. Then the shower passed, and the crowd thinned out again.

It was a little after ten when Jimmy Brinks walked into the bar. It was more of a swagger, really, like a cowhand who had just ridden a hundred miles on a horse. Connor originally had figured the guy for a Texas transplant who'd spent too much time herding cattle before moving here to The Edge of America. Then another customer had filled him in on Brinks' backstory, explained that he walked that way because he'd been shot in the hip running from the police in Belize. He'd been down there two months, posing as a tourist, sipping margaritas and diving the reefs and chartering sailboats, until the FBI tracked him down to a bungalow on the sand.

Turned out Brinks was the lead suspect in an armored car heist in Phoenix, and his two partners in the robbery already had been nabbed and had fingered their pal Jimmy. The local *policia* knocked him down with two 9 mm slugs and then two U.S. Marshals transported him back to the states, where a jury of his peers pronounced him guilty. He did twelve years of a ten-to-twenty rap at a high-security federal pen in Texas, then served out his parole before ending up in Folly. Rumor had it he still had his share of the stolen loot, but no one had the balls to ask him. No one seemed to know his real last name, either. People just called him Jimmy Brinks because of the rolling vault he and his gang knocked over.

He was one mean-looking sonofabitch, and most people steered clear of him whenever he showed up. He was tall and rugged, his frame carrying solid muscle that did not know the meaning of the word "atrophy." His leathery skin seemed to be one large mosaic of scars from old stab wounds and gun fights and broken bottles. He seemed tan, but it was hard to tell if the color came from exposure to the tropical sun or just that his skin was aging poorly. He never seemed to shave but didn't really seem to grow a beard, either. Nor did he seem to have much of a fondness for showering. His hair was thick and at one time had been black, but now it just hung in silvery ropes from his head. And he could have benefited from seeing a dentist.

Jimmy Brinks sat down and plucked a toothpick out of a cup on the bar. Clooney was curled up in a corner at the far end, pressed against the deck railing, and now he raised his head and gave the man a slow once-over. He let out his customary growl—Clooney, not Brinks—then lowered his head back on his paws again.

"Double Jack," the ex-con snarled at no one in particular. "And put it in my glass, not one of them cheap plastic cups."

Connor said nothing, just poured a healthy dose of Jack Daniels into a glass tumbler that he kept under the counter just for him. He set it in front of Brinks and turned away before the man's breath overpowered him. Jimmy Brinks grunted something, then picked up the glass and downed half its contents. His eyes seemed to dance a second, then he finished the other half. He slid it back across the bar and said, "One more."

Connor refilled it and slid it back. "You get that foundation poured yet?" he asked, just to make conversation.

It was widely rumored that Jimmy Brinks was building a house on a parcel of mud he owned at the edge of the marsh, somewhere near a place called Stono Flats. Brinks reportedly had spent months clearing the land, and people had started taking odds on whether he'd actually ever break ground.

"Rebar went in yesterday," he grunted. "And who gives a shit, anyway?"

It was a rhetorical question—Brinks was full of them—so Connor didn't answer. Instead he went back to his work and started mixing a Midori martini.

Jimmy Brinks felt offended, and said so. "You always turn your back when a customer's talkin'?"

Connor knew the guy's style; knew he was more bark than bite. Still, Brinks had gotten into an altercation with a drunk tourist at a gas station not long after Connor arrived in Folly, managed to get off on self-defense. Witnesses said the tourist, who was too drunk to be driving the car into which he was pumping gas, landed the first punch, and Brinks had a fresh bruise on his face that caused the judge to let him off with a stern warning. Since then he'd been a good boy, but Connor knew the guy was a box of fireworks waiting for a match.

"Just bustin' my ass trying to keep everyone happy," he said.

Another grunt, followed by the distinct sound of a long sip of Tennessee sour mash. Then: "I know who it was shot up this shit-hole last night."

That got Connor's attention. He stopped what he was doing, turned, stared Jimmy Brinks square in the eye. "Is that so?"

"Figured that might grab your ear," Brinks said. He held his glass, slowly swirled the amber liquid in it. He sniffed it, savoring the aroma, but did not drink.

"You hear a name?"

"Alls I heard is he's a kid, no more'n sixteen, seventeen max. Lives somewhere over on Cusabo Gut."

Connor didn't know much about Cusabo Gut except that a number of locals lived out there in the trailers and rotting cabins along a narrow dirt road that meandered around the edge of the marsh. "The gut" was colorblind, whites and blacks and mixed families living side by side, minding no one's business but their own. Plus a few goats, chickens, and dogs of undetermined pedigree and parentage.

"You're saying this kid's disappeared?"

"What I heard," Brinks replied with another grunt. "But like the man says, he can run but he can't hide."

Connor almost said *I guess you'd know all about that*, but knew better. One thing he'd learned about Jimmy Brinks was that if you weren't one of his friends—and he couldn't think of anyone who claimed that distinction—it was best to keep your mouth shut about such things.

"Do the police know this?"

"As you might imagine, I'm not much into hanging with the local constabulary," Brinks said.

Connor edged closer to where Brinks was sitting and, keeping his voice low, said, "Why're you telling me all this, anyway?"

Brinks leveled a threatening glare at him; no one questioned his motives or actions. No one, not ever. "Cuz I know who you are," he finally said, his words coming out no more than a slick whisper.

"Is that a fact?" Connor wondered where the ex-con was going with this.

"Stone cold truth," Brinks confirmed, no question in his voice. "You're the guy that brought down that sonofabitch governor last year."

Connor just stood there and stared at him, at first not saying a word. He chewed his lower lip a second, then said, "Where did you hear that?"

"No better source than Google, man," Jimmy Brinks said. "You should see what sort of shit they got on you."

"You can't believe everything you read," Connor reminded him.

"Yeah, well, if even half of what they said about you is true, what I'm wondering is what you're doin' 'round this joint, shakin' up daiquiris and margaritas, when last night some kid took down one of your customers, right over there. Doesn't sound like the Jack Connor they said shot that lunatic right through the heart."

Brinks was known for being blunt but, ultimately, he was right. The psycho he was referring to was killed in the struggle for a gun, and even though the sheriff had desperately wanted to nail Connor's ass, the county solicitor determined he had acted in self-defense. But none of that mattered right now, causing Connor to shrug and say, "Whoever 'they' are, maybe they're wrong."

"And maybe I'm the Pope."

With that Jimmy Brinks stood up and made a show of slowly rolling his shoulders. Then he pulled out his wallet, mostly duct tape and ragged thread, and stuffed with old bills. Connor wondered if the serial numbers were sequential, maybe from a stash lifted from an armored-car job years ago. Brinks thumbed a ten out of his wallet, let it fall on the bar.

"Keep the change," he snarled. "And listen: no one else ever touches that glass."

"Not a chance in hell," Connor assured him.

CHAPTER 7

Next morning Connor was up before the scuba divers. Instinctively he checked his phone for any sign of a message from Danielle, then set it back on the night stand. Over eight months and not a word.

For the first time in over a year he went for a run, three miles on the hard sand of Folly Beach. Then he fed Clooney before the two of them headed up the street to Gilbert's for breakfast. The little chat he'd had with Jimmy Brinks the night before had kept him awake long after he'd closed up and cashed out, something just out of reach nibbling at his brain. Not that Brinks had said that much, but somewhere in his words, or between them, was something Connor's mind could not let go of.

When he finished his egg and cheese sandwich he sat there at the table, sipping from a cup of black Jamaican Roast. It was a strong brew, and it seemed to do the trick. Clooney curled up in a patch of shade, keeping a hungry eye on the last morsels of Connor's meal. Between the sun and the breeze and the caffeine, the cobwebs slowly cleared from Connor's brain and he began to plan out his day. That plan had everything to do with scratching an itch that just wouldn't go away, an itch that began when Tony Carerra had taken a bullet in the back and then had died on the way to the hospital. The itch ran contrary to everything he had promised himself he would never again engage in, and maybe borne out of a passive defiance to Danielle, who had made it clear that his quest for danger had nearly gotten her killed.

One of the perks of running The Sandbar was the parking space that came with it. It was located between the wooden pilings that supported the elevated drinking deck and allowed a potential hurricane storm surge to wash right through. As it was, Connor had to lock a chain from one pier to another when he backed his old Jeep Wrangler out of it, or else he'd find another vehicle squeezed into it when he returned.

It was Sunday and Connor knew that most of the locals soon would be heading out to church. That was the way of the world here in the Carolinas, Saturday sinners resting their tired backsides on hard wooden pews on Sunday morning, praying away last night's debaucheries.

He took Folly Road out of town, navigating the potholes and fresh road kill until he found the sign for Battery Island. He headed left onto a narrow two-lane strip of pavement, which got thinner and narrower with each subsequent turn. Eventually he ended up on a dirt lane that was barely two vehicles wide, identified by a weathered wood sign that read "Cusabo Blvd." The lettering was almost faded from too much sun, and Connor chuckled at the thought of calling this stretch of corrugated dirt a boulevard. Someone around here had a wry sense of irony.

He slowed the Jeep to a crawl, but the queasy look Clooney gave him from the passenger seat told him he was still driving too fast for the corrugated road. Another sign back at the last intersection told him it dead-ended somewhere up ahead, and now as he slowly made his way past rusted trailers and sunburned shacks and even an old school bus, he realized that Jimmy Brinks had not said where in Cusabo Gut the suspected shooter might be holed up. That left a lot of open ground, and Connor realized with a growing pit in his stomach it would take him hours to knock on all these doors. Especially if folks around here were part of the Sunday morning devotional thing.

A familiar riff of warning kept running through his head, telling him to turn around and go home. This was a matter for the police—local and state—and he had no business getting involved with it. He could think of a dozen reasons to listen to the voice of reason and just turn around, but some misplaced sense of personal duty superseded the cries of logic and common sense.

He pulled the Jeep to the side of the road and climbed out. Something dark and brooding told him he didn't want to be here, but there was a side of his brain that almost seemed on autopilot, pushing him forward. A man had died in his bar and the kid who probably did it likely lived around here. Simple as that; nothing more and nothing less.

Jordan James' advice to *leave it to the police* barely registered in his head.

Connor stood at the edge of the dirt road, studying a cluster of residences that he suspected were all connected by family blood that dated back many generations. The nearest house looked as if it might have been painted at some point in a bygone era, but over the years it had faded and peeled until now it mostly was the color of old oatmeal. It was a one-story cinder block structure with a covered porch in front and a yard full of weeds that served as the family junkyard: tires, an old sofa, paint cans, an antique wringer washing machine, a tricycle with no wheels all were being strangled by twists of vines and creeper.

"Stay!" Connor ordered Clooney, who responded with a wary eye that Connor had come to recognize as a look of canine concern. He patted the dog on the head, then poured some water from a jug into a dish on the floorboard far from the reach of the sun. Clooney gave him an appreciative tail thump, then repositioned himself on the small seat and lowered his head onto his paws.

Once Connor was sure his canine buddy was okay, he crossed the road and made his way up a dirt path to the sagging front porch. A wooden door with a large gash in the screen drooped on tired hinges, and a gecko was clinging to the unpainted frame. Connor pulled it open and knocked on a second door that was almost hidden behind it. Somewhere inside he heard footsteps, followed by the sound of latches and locks being turned. Finally the door creaked open about six inches and a face peered out at him.

"Who are you?"

The wary voice matched the face, a girl who looked about twelve, maybe thirteen. Very dark skin, short hair and round, inquisitive eyes that spoke of worry and apprehension.

"Good morning," Connor politely said to her, trying to get a sense of what lay beyond this girl in the darkness. "Are your parents home?"

"No, sir," she said, and she started to close the door.

He gently slipped his foot forward, preventing her from closing it completely. "They due back soon?" he asked her.

"They gone to church," she told him, but Connor sensed from the hitch in her voice that a house of worship was the last place anyone would ever find them. "Look, mister. I'm not supposed to talk to no one."

"All I want to do is ask you something, then I'll be gone," Connor assured her.

"Where you from?" she asked him. "Cuz you sure ain't from here."

"You ever hear of a place called Michigan?" he asked her.

"I go to school," she said, a touch of indignation in her words. "It's that place where the water's so bad it can kill you."

"That's Flint," he told her. "I'm from Lansing, where they build cars."

"What's your name?"

"Connor. Jack Connor." His words came out sounding like Sean Connery in an old James Bond movie.

He expected her to tell him her name then, but she didn't. Instead she said, "You a cop?"

"No, I'm not a cop," he told her. "I run a…a drinking establishment over in Folly Beach. What's your name?"

The girl opened the door just wide enough to slip outside, then closed it again and leaned against the jamb. She crossed her arms, trying to appear tough, but she hadn't yet mastered the look. "Em Lee, two words. Not Emily, like most people think. You run a bar?"

"That's right. A place called The Sandbar."

"Where that guy got shot the other night."

"That's right."

"So what you doing all the way out here?" she asked, doing a good job of bouncing the conversation all over the place. "The Gut, I mean."

Connor tried to study her without letting his eyes give him away. The last thing he wanted was for Em Lee to think he was some sort of pervert who liked to ogle pretty young girls. She was not tall, maybe five-three, and she was dressed in faded Levis cut-offs and a green halter top that suggested she was an early bloomer. She was barefoot and her breath smelled of cigarette smoke, and he felt a momentary sadness knowing that by the age of twenty she'd probably have a child or two glued to her hip.

"I heard someone out here might know something about what happened."

"Not me," she said, quickly shaking her head. "I think I better go now."

"What about your parents?" Connor pressed.

"My mom doesn't know nothing," she said. "You got some bitchin' tats."

"Thank you," he said with an appreciative smile. "You live here with your mom, just the two of you?"

"And Jesry. Like I said, they're both out right now."

"Who's Jesry?"

"My mom's boyfriend." The pitch in Em Lee's voice reflected a dynamic at work here that did not sound right. In fact, it sounded far wrong, but Connor decided to let it pass. For now. "And like I said, I ain't—*I'm not*—supposed to talk to no one or see no one. Been grounded six weeks, all on account of that bitch Rosamund."

Connor wasn't about to venture down that path; wherever it led it had nothing to do with him. None of this did, and he only wanted to deal with one truth at a time. "And you don't know anything about the guy who shot the man in my bar?"

"Look—I really gotta go," she said as she quickly backed inside the house and—just like that—closed the door.

Connor waited on the porch while she fiddled with all the locks and latches inside. He considered knocking again, but didn't want to freak her out. Or push his luck. He turned and slowly retreated down the steps, then made his way back out to the road as he studied the next house up the road. Yep, it was going to be a long day, and probably a damned awful waste of time. But he had nothing else to do, and maybe—just maybe—he'd get lucky.

Luck didn't present itself for the next two hours, after he'd knocked on a couple dozen doors. At eight of them he found no one home, and he got a lot of doors slammed in his face. Four women invited him inside to chat, as did two men who didn't seem to mind that Connor had interrupted a baseball game on the tube. And no one seemed to know anything about anyone who might have gone into Folly Beach Friday night and pulled a gun on Tony Carerra, knocked him down with a twenty-two caliber bullet.

Not until he got to the lady with the Pomeranian.

Her house was tiny—the smallest along the entire road—but what it lacked in size it made up for in neatness. The place was impeccable inside and out: a small pink cottage, with two large windows flanking the front door. The weeds that passed for a lawn were closely mowed and neatly trimmed, while colorful bushes that Connor couldn't hope to identify were planted around the cinder block foundation. There wasn't a fleck of peeling paint anywhere, not a streak of dirt on the windows, not a spot of grease on the gravel driveway. A green anole that was clinging to the wall studied him with rotating eyes as he mounted the front steps, then scurried away when he knocked.

The woman who answered the door was as neat as the house, if not quite as trim. She wore a simple floral-print house dress, and a wide-brimmed straw hat covered her head at a slight angle. She flashed Connor a friendly smile of perfect false teeth and peered through the screen at him. He managed a polite grin and noticed that she held a tiny dog in her arms.

"Can't you read?" she asked him politely in an accent that hinted at her Gullah roots.

"Excuse me?" Connor said. It was not the greeting he had expected.

"I assume you're here to sell me something or preach to me," she told him. "So you must not have understood the sign."

He hesitated a moment, then looked at the cardboard notice that was tacked to the side of the door. *No Solicitors*, it read.

"Oh, no ma'am," Connor said quickly. "I'm not a salesman or a zealot."

"Thank the Lord," the woman sighed, giving him a friendly wink. Or was it just a facial tic? "She always provides. What can I do for you?"

"My name is Jack Connor," he explained, just as he had done at every other occupied house along Cusabo Gut Boulevard. "I'd like to ask you a question or two."

"I was wondering when the feds might step in on this, since the local cops 'round here don't know shit," she said. "And they don't care to know what I know."

"I have to tell you, I'm not a fed," Connor informed her.

She narrowed her eyes and studied him through the screen. Finally she said, "Maybe you are, maybe you aren't. Could be undercover, in those shorts and all that ink. Either way, I'd be happy to share some friendly talk with you."

She opened the screen door just far enough for him to barely slip through, then led him into the small living room that was impeccably decorated in what could only be described as consignment shop clutter. The sofa and love seat looked old but well-preserved, with a set of new red slipcovers to brighten the room. Tables seemed to be crammed everywhere, crowded with doodads and widgets and tchotchkes. An old television was tuned to a cable shopping channel, and the pitchwoman was hawking some sort of miracle skin creme.

"May I get you something?" she asked. "Coffee, tea, maybe some water?"

Connor had already accepted coffee at a half-dozen houses already, so he politely declined. A momentary look of disappointment registered on her face, but it passed just as quickly as she invited him to have a seat on the couch. Then she lowered herself onto the love seat across from him, easing her dog into her lap.

He waited until she appeared comfortable, then explained that he was there to find someone who might know anything about the shooting in his place of business in Folly Beach the night before last.

She mulled this over, said, "You mean that bar across from the beach, a block down from those ugly condos?"

"The Sandbar," he confirmed. "Have you been in?"

"That sort of place, it's not for me," she told him. No scorn or judgment in her voice. Then she leaned closer and studied his bare arms. "You sure do have a lot of tattoos."

"Reflections of old places and times," he said.

Fact was, Connor hadn't gotten any new ink since he'd been discharged from the Army and left Ft. Drum, not until he finished the V.A. program last winter. That day he found someone who branded his left foot with a red phoenix rising from the ashes, representing triumph over adversity.

"I just use my memory for that," she said. "Less permanent, and minimal pain."

He grinned at her, then said, "So tell me, just what is it you know?"

"Excuse me?" she asked, wrinkling her tired brow.

"You said the local police don't care to know what you know. And I was just wondering if that might include this kid they're saying pulled the trigger." He knew he was pushing her, but something was on her mind and he sensed she wanted to talk about it.

"They're saying that, are they?" She regarded him curiously, sizing him up before she said anything else.

Connor explained how he had heard that the police were set to arrest a kid from Cusabo Gut, if they could only find him. "I don't want to talk to him, ma'am," he assured her. "I'm just kind of curious what folks might know about him."

"And you're not government?"

"No, ma'am."

"Please...stop calling me ma'am," she scolded him. "My name is Helene."

Connor folded his hands in his lap and leaned forward, studying the dog in her lap. "He's a real cutie," he told her. He wanted to get on with this, but sensed she didn't like to be rushed.

"*She*," the woman corrected him. The dog was so small and fluffy it was difficult to tell the difference. "And she's been on this earth fifteen years, all of them good ones."

He glanced around the the confusion of knick-knacks and old photos, finally brought his eyes back to the woman sitting across from him. "How long have you lived in this house?" he asked her.

"Sixteen years," she replied. "Moved here when I married Henry and stayed on after he transitioned. He'll be gone now four years next month, God rest his soul."

"I'm very sorry," Connor said.

"Thank you," she smiled. She pursed her lips and closed her eyes, then finally opened them and said, "Justacious Stone."

"Excuse me?"

"That's the boy's name. Justacious Stone. He grew up down around Hollywood—the one just a few miles from here, not the one out west."

Connor knew Hollywood was a small town in Charleston County, located just south of Ravenel and north of Meggett. Mostly black, mostly blue collar, mostly rural. Which meant mostly poor. Just like so many other small towns scattered across the state.

"He moved here a couple months ago to stay with his aunt," Helene continued. "He'd got himself into some trouble, and his family figured there was less of it here in The Gut. Seems they were wrong."

"What kind of trouble, if I might ask?"

"That kid, he's a crack shot with a gun. He started by popping out porch lights, moved on to dogs and cats."

Connor nodded, figuring the kid had recently progressed to human targets. "Does he live near here?" he inquired.

The old woman nodded, started rocking in her chair again. "'Bout a half mile down the road there's this dirt drive, goes off to the right. Maybe a dozen people live down in there. Old trailers and campers, mostly. Young Mister Stone's been living in the green one."

"And you think he's the one who shot the man in my bar?"

"So I heard," she said. "And even at my age I can still hear a pin drop." She stood up abruptly, hugging her dog close to her chest. She'd told Connor what she wanted him to know, and now it was time for him to leave.

About a half mile up the road Connor found the little dirt drive, right where the woman with the dog said it would be. Except to call it a drive was being generous; it was little more than two dirt ruts carved by the wear of tires through the thick sweetgrass. Connor switched on the four-wheel drive, shifted into first gear, and started the bone-rattling journey through the dense brush. Clooney again shot him a *what the hell* look, but remained stoic as his master continued whatever foolishness he had up his sleeveless T.

A few hundred yards later the narrow track opened onto a clearing in which a half-dozen old trailers seemed to be returning to the earth. All but one were single-wides, paint faded from ears in the sun, corrugated siding rusting from rain and curling up at the edges from where nails had popped. How any of these structures had survived the wind and flooding of hurricane season was anyone's guess.

Connor pulled the Jeep in front of the only structure that could ever have been called green, an ancient camper shell supported on rusted stanchions that were embedded in the dirt. A flock of chickens squawked through the yard and disappeared into the overgrowth, and several large dogs that did not come across as friendly were hunkered down at one end of the clearing. Clooney eyed them suspiciously but clearly felt no need to cause a ruckus or start a fight. A feral-looking cat shot through the yard, its scrawny body easily slipping through the dense vegetation, but the dogs did not seem to care. At one side of the camper an old pick-up truck with faded, hand-painted camouflage was resting on cinder blocks, its wheels long ago removed. The vehicle was the centerpiece of a mass of oxidizing relics that also included an old oil drum with an outboard motor clamped to it, an aluminum boat with the bottom bashed out, and a copper-colored refrigerator tipped on its side.

Connor got out of the Jeep and cautiously made his way to the rear of the camper shell, where the door was located. He knocked gently, waited a couple minutes, then knocked again. He was about to give up when he heard footsteps inside, then felt an eye watching him through the dust- and grime-covered glass.

"Mrs. Stone?" Connor asked.

"Go away." The voice was that of a woman, but she sounded tired and old.

"Mrs. Stone," he said again. "I'd just like a minute of your time."

"I got nothin' to say, not to you or nobody," she growled. "An' that ain't my name."

"Is Justacious Stone your nephew?"

A silence followed, then the sound of a latch being turned. The door opened an inch, and he saw both a dark, worried eye and a chain holding the door to the jamb.

"I told you, I don' want to talk. Justy's my sister's boy, but neither of 'em's here."

It was not Connor's intention to bother this woman, who probably was exhausted by taking care of her nephew. Wondering how the kid could possibly shoot a man in cold blood and run away. But there was something about the whole scenario that bothered Connor, something he couldn't put his finger on. Not just yet.

"I understand, Ma'am—"

"So leave me alone, then." Another silence, this one marked by that single eye staring at him from behind the door. It didn't even seem to blink as it held its glare. "I don't want to talk 'bout that boy, you understand?"

With that she closed the door with a thud so firm it shook the entire camper. Connor stood there a minute, staring at it as he tried to picture a sixteen-year-old named Justacious Stone living with his aunt in this decrepit shell of a home. What had the kid done that had caused him to be sent over here to the middle of the Lowcountry marsh? *Popping street lights with a twenty-two, my ass,* he thought. Had the kid been into drugs? Guns? Gangs? Possibly all three, but it was hard to picture any of that going on out here.

Connor wiped a film of sweat from his forehead and turned to walk back to the Jeep, when all of a sudden he was hit by what felt like a locomotive and slammed to the ground. He crashed face-first into the dirt, tasting gravel and sand and blood. Probably from his nose, which throbbed as if it had just been crunched by Apollo Creed.

He started to scramble to his knees, just as a hand grabbed the back of his collar and hauled him up. Then he was whipped around, and he felt the barrel of a gun pressing up against the underside of his chin. For an instant all Connor could think about was that night a year ago when a homicidal dirtbag stepped out of the darkness and had done pretty much the same thing.

The same memory must have flashed through Clooney's brain, because without a moment's hesitation or any regard to what might happen in the next second, he leaped from where he had sitting in the passenger seat and launched himself at Connor's attacker. His teeth found purchase on an ear, and the man screamed as his head spun around. By that time Clooney's teeth had pulled free, along with a bit of flesh and cartilage, and the thug with the gun had it leveled at the dog's head.

"Don't you fucking dare!" Connor screamed at him.

The gunman looked at Clooney, then back at Connor, who had assumed the fighting stance he'd been taught in boot camp. Hand-to-hand combat was rare and discouraged when actually engaging the enemy, for the single reason that if you were that close to your opponent you were likely dead anyway. Still, Connor had been quick and wiry and had finished near the top of his class.

The thug with the gun studied them both, must have figured that if he shot the dog Connor would make his move. The man's left eye was bigger than his right, which had been partially closed by a scar that looked thin enough to have been carved by a razor blade. His skin was rough, his teeth only occasional, his nose twisted permanently to one side. His hair was wiry and black, styled with some sort of pomade, his eyes dark and full of rage. Connor caught a strong whiff of malt liquor on his breath when he spoke, mixed with something that smelled both sour and fried.

"You got no business here," he snarled as he finally lowered the gun.

"We were just leaving," Connor assured him.

"You lookin' for glass?"

Connor remembered one of the vets in rehab had used that term, meaning meth, so he quickly shook his head. "No. No drugs. Nothing like that."

Sour Breath stared at him, not making a move. Taking his time, thinking this through. Clooney was standing stiff and straight, the fur on his spine flared up, fangs bared. He licked the blood off one of them, and looked at Connor expectantly, as if he were waiting for a command.

"Like what, then?" the gunman demanded.

"It's not important."

"Everything happen out here's important to me. Got it?"

Stupid turf shit, that's what this was. And yeah, Connor got it. "None of that, like I said."

"I know what this is," Sour Breath said. "You're here about the kid."

That would be Justacious Stone, Connor figured. "Is he here?" he asked.

"Too late. Cops busted Justy, up at the Walmart. He's in jail." The guy wheezed again, an action that almost made Connor gag. "This don't involve you. You got it?"

"I got it," Connor said.

"I don't like mofos like you coming around my crib, where you got no biznass." He grunted, and his lip curled up in a snarl. "'Specially I don' like no one asking questions 'bout one of my bros."

As long as the guy was holding a gun, Connor wasn't about to argue. "Like I said, we were just leaving," he said. "C'mon, Clooney…load up."

Clooney seemed not to hear, keeping an eye on the man with the gun. Eventually he jumped back into the Jeep, where he scrambled over to the shotgun seat. Connor followed him, sliding behind the wheel and keying the engine to life. Then he clutched the gears into first, pulled a wide circle through the grassy yard, and headed for the dirt track that would take him out of this shit hole. Not looking back, or even venturing a quick glance in the rearview mirror.

He still half-expected the guy to shoot him anyway, just for the sport of it.

CHAPTER 8

When Connor got back out to Folly Road he turned right and headed back into town. The last street before the beach was Arctic Avenue, and he made a left turn and headed away from The Sandbar. The road was clogged with pedestrians barely clad in swim trunks and string bikinis, many of them hauling wheeled coolers toward the dusting of sand at the edge of the pavement. The aroma of sunscreen and ribs and barbecue hung in the air, and Clooney lifted his nose and seemed to savor every last scent.

A half mile later Connor pulled to the side of the road and parked in the shade of a live oak draped with Spanish moss. After months of wandering the beach he had discovered a length of sand away from the noise and bustle of town, where the water was deep and free of silt. Sure, there was a stretch of sand across the street from the bar, but there was always significant risk of being hit in the head with a volleyball or Frisbee. This secluded length of beach, however, rarely was occupied by more than a half dozen people, and it was easy to stake out a personal patch of real estate at the water's edge.

This afternoon there seemed to be only one other person basking in the tranquility, a woman who was sitting by herself far down the beach, gazing out at the gentle water. She was too far away for Connor to get a good look at her, so he paid her no mind. He'd already changed into a pair of swim trunks he kept under the seat of the Jeep, and he wasted no time wading into the water until he was up to his waist. Then he struck out from the beach, lightly kicking a course parallel to the shore as he kept an eye on for Clooney, who had eagerly followed him into the surf.

He tried to think as little as possible. That wasn't easy to do, particularly as he recalled his conversation with Em Lee that morning and the nagging feeling that something was not altogether right in her world. Then his monkey mind jumped to the woman with the little dog, and whatever motive she'd had for tipping him off to Justacious Stone. After that he leaped to the boy's aunt, living in a decrepit camper shell at the end of a dirt track, probably worried all to hell about what the kid had gotten himself into, and how he was going to get out of it. And then, more than anything, Connor thought about the barrel of that gun pressing up against his chin, the thug holding it telling him to get the fuck out and mind his own business.

Whoever the guy was, he was right: none of this was Connor's business. Whatever was going on here—whatever reason Tony Carerra had been shot—it had nothing to do with him. The local cops and SLED detectives were all over it and, if Sour Breath had his story straight, they'd already nabbed Justacious Stone and probably tossed him in a holding cell in the county jail. They were the ones who carried the guns and badges, while Connor ran an open-air watering hole just steps from the beach. There was absolutely no reason on earth for him to poke through this mess, and even Jordan James had told him to leave it alone.

In other words, case closed.

The sound of a low rumble cut into his thinking, and he lifted his head just enough to see a large twin-engine charter boat churning through the water about fifty yards away. There was no imminent danger from its props, and the captain standing at the wheel offered a casual wave to signal that he knew Connor was there. Connor waved back, but the relaxation he'd felt earlier had faded, so he began swimming toward the shore. Clooney eagerly followed him, dogpaddling through the light surf until his paws once again were able to touch the gritty bottom.

Connor toweled off, then settled down on a patch of sand. This stretch of beach was still empty, except for the same woman as before, who now was slowly walking along the lip of the sea. She was wandering slowly, her head down, glancing up at a gull wheeling through the sky above her, then down at her feet again. Something about her seemed oddly familiar, and when she lifted her face again, he realized what it was. *Who it was.*

Martina Carerra, Tony Carerra's widow.

She seemed to recognize him about the same time he noticed her, and she slowed her pace as she lowered her sunglasses to make sure her eyes weren't playing tricks on her. She wore a bikini top and a wrap-around skirt, and her hair was pinned up in a loose bun on the back of her head. She did not look as though she'd gone in the water, which meant she'd probably come down here just to reflect and find some solace in the sun at the edge of a lonely beach. Maybe unlock her soul and let the tears flow.

"You're...the bartender," Mrs. Carerra said as she approached him, her voice a sad mix of sorrow and embarrassment. "You drove me to the hospital."

"That's right," he said, standing up and offering her a damp hand. "Jack Connor."

She shook it lightly, then recoiled slightly at the sight of a tattoo inked on his hip. "Is that a gun?" she asked him.

"Glock nine," he confirmed. "Got it during boot camp, on a dumbass dare. And I have to apologize for just abandoning you at the hospital. You fainted and they...well, they wouldn't let you leave with me."

"Just as well," she shrugged a bare shoulder. "And I never got the chance to pay you for your efforts."

"No need, ma'am. It was the least I could do, considering."

Mrs. Carerra nodded grimly, glanced out at the water. "Tony and I came down to this beach the first day we got here, about this same time of day. We went for a swim, then cracked a bottle of champagne we'd brought along in a bucket of ice. It was so romantic—just the two of us: the beach, the waves, and two glasses of Mumms. And then, just as Tony started to make a toast, the bugs showed up and we had to high-tail it back to the house."

She flashed Connor a sad smile, and he suspected that behind those dark glasses she was pressing back a flood of tears.

"The mosquitoes are something fierce when the sun dips below those trees, there," he said lamely. Sometimes profound words are particularly elusive when they're most needed.

Mrs. Carerra gave him another nod, but he didn't think she really was listening. She was somewhere else, far away from here, trying to find some sense in a situation that didn't make any sense at all. Connor was all too familiar with the different emotions of loss, and he knew that right now she was overwhelmed by the raw knowledge that she would never see her husband again.

"Mr. Carerra said you were renting a beach house along here," he said, instantly wishing he hadn't.

She nodded, still lost in her grief. "Calypso Cove, right on the sand over there."

"I know the place," he told her, looking in the direction she was pointing. "The one with the pink roof."

"That's it," she replied. "It has an incredible view, and a gentle breeze all the time. And the lapping of the waves on the beach at night. Perfectly lovely."

And probably very lonely right now, too.

Just then Clooney wandered up and touched his nose to Mrs. Carerra's hand. She let him sniff so he would know she wasn't a threat, then rubbed the top of his head.

"This your dog?" she asked.

"Sure is," Connor replied. "Rescued him during the hurricane last summer. If you don't mind my asking, how are you holding up?"

She stopped scratching Clooney's head and gazed out at the ocean for a moment. "Last night was tough, and so was this morning," she sniffed. "I've been on the phone a lot, talking to friends and family, making arrangements, that sort of thing. It's helped keep my mind off...things. But after all that—well, I felt a need to get away from it all. Everyone telling me how sorry they are, asking me questions like how am I doing, how could this have happened, why would anyone want to shoot Tony. Eventually I'd had enough, so I came out here to go for a swim. Only as you can see, I didn't go near the water."

Connor wanted to say something to her, explain that everything was going to be all right, but sensed she would have cringed at the words. So he tried a different tack, saying, "I only spoke with your husband for a moment. Didn't take long to see he was in love with you."

"He was…the best," she agreed with a vague nod.

"Just so you know, your purse and credit card are under lock and key."

"Thank you. I'll drop by later and get them."

Mrs. Carerra stood there awkwardly for just a second, then flashed Connor a resolute smile and continued on her way up the beach. He watched her as she carefully stepped around the shell of a horseshoe crab that had washed up on the sand, then cut to the left and disappeared up over the dunes. Only after she was long gone did he and Clooney trudge back to where he'd parked the Jeep, the sense of calm he'd felt when he'd wandered down to the beach an hour ago now shot to hell.

He pulled into his parking space a little after four. The Sandbar was set to open in an hour and Sunday was Julie's night off, so he had to hold down the joint all by himself. After changing into a pair of dry shorts and a Sandbar T-shirt he restocked the coolers and made sure the shelves were supplied with enough booze to last through the evening. He really didn't feel like mixing drinks and making small talk for the next eight hours, but once the crowds started to belly up to the bar, he was able to purge Tony and Martina Carerra from his mind.

Just like every night Connor had a big run on painkillers and Bahama mamas, but mostly it was the beer that flowed freely and by nine o'clock he was beginning to worry that he might run out. Desmond Green was set to drop off his regular Monday delivery in the morning, but that wouldn't help him much tonight. He had two six packs of beer in his apartment fridge upstairs if it came to that.

Then: "Have you done your lime trick yet?" The voice came from behind him, and instantly Connor felt an errant tingle ripple up his spine.

"Miss Bay Breeze," he said as he reached for a plastic cup from a stack. He turned around to face her as he started to pour a generous dose of vodka.

"Good memory," she said, truly sounding impressed. She was dressed in white shorts and a pink shirt knotted at her belly button. Her hair was stuffed through the back of an Orioles cap and, even though Connor was a faithful Tigers fan, he had to admit it looked good on her.

"Missed you last night," he said. "Thought maybe you'd found a better place to quaff."

She shot him a strange look, then seemed to realize the word didn't come close to meaning what she imagined it did. "There is no better place to quaff in Folly Beach than The Sandbar," she said, and there was that smile again. "And no better bartender than Jack Connor. Just ask anybody."

"I'll take your word for it," Connor told her as he set her drink in front of her. "Are you with your pal Alfonse tonight?"

She shook her head. "No, I actually ventured out all on my very own." She dug a wad of bills out of a pocket in her shorts, dropped a five on the counter. "Will this cover it?"

For just a moment Connor thought about doing the "on the house" thing, but that might sound too obvious. If Jessica Snow was so into his beach bar and his magic, she was going to have to work at it. Besides, something she said was bothering him, and he decided to ask her about it.

"It's more than enough," he told her, ringing up her drink. "But tell me... how'd you know my name?"

The blanched look on her face told him everything: caught red-handed. She tried to hide her embarrassed grin, but he caught it anyway. So she 'fessed up, saying, "I asked around."

"You mean, 'who's the hunk who slings those wicked drinks at The Sandbar?'"

"Something like that, plus the tattoos," she admitted. "Anyways, it's a good name. Jack Connor. Cool but dignified."

"I can't take any credit for it," he said, matching her smile with one of his own. Then he got an order for two vodka margaritas, on the rocks, both with salt. "Don't go away," he told her as he picked up two large plastic cups and scooped ice into them.

She didn't move, and when Connor finally slowed down—two draft beers, two gin and tonics, and a couple more tropical trysts later—she was still there, nursing her drink.

Connor came back over to her, set a napkin on the bar and placed an olive in the middle of it. "All right," he said. "I have a trick for you. See those plastic swords there?" He nodded at the tray of small plastic picks he used to skewer all the pieces of garnish that went into the drinks.

"Sure," she said.

"Okay—I want you to pick up one of those swords and get ready to use it." She flashed Connor an odd look but did as she was told.

"Now—pay close attention as I fold this napkin over the olive, and then fold it again." He did as he described, and she followed his every move.

She looked bored and said, "So you folded the napkin over the olive. Am I supposed to be impressed?"

"If you wish," he replied. "Now, I want you to take that sword and poke it right through the olive inside."

She gave him another one of those odd looks, but then she did as she was told.

"Now—take another sword and do the same thing. Jam it right through the middle."

Again she did as he said, and then did it again, and again, and again, until there were five little plastic swords penetrating the napkin with the olive inside.

"Now I suppose you're going to have me take the swords out and show me that there are no sad little wounds in it?" she said, almost goading him.

"Well, let's try that." Connor removed the swords one by one, each time exhibiting a little magician's flourish, until there was only a small lump left in the napkin.

"Poor little olive," she said, in a mock whimper, her lower lip protruding almost in a pout.

"You think so?" he asked. "Take a look."

Again she flashed him one of those odd little looks, then picked up the napkin and unfolded it. Inside there was...nothing.

Jessica's bewildered gaze drifted from the napkin back to Connor. "It's gone!" she said. "How did you do that?"

"Magic," he explained. And with that he whisked the napkin and the swords off the bar and into the trash.

"But...I could feel the olive as I poked it with the swords," she said. "How did you do that?"

"The real thrill in life is not knowing all the answers," Connor replied with a wry grin.

She looked at him quizzically, wondering if he was playing with her or offering up a serious piece of bar philosophy. "Did you just make that up?"

"Saw it in a fortune cookie once," he said. "But it suits me just fine."

She gave him a roll of her eyes that said *I guess*, then moved on. "What I want to know is when you're going to do the lime trick again?"

"You see those limes over there?" he asked her, indicating a small pile of sliced wedges sitting in the garnish tray along with the olives and cherries. "That's all I've got till the next truck comes. So you're just going to have to do with the sword-through-the-olive thing."

"Well, I have to admit, it was good," Jessica said.

She said something else then, but Connor didn't hear what it was, because that's when Martina Carerra careened up the steps and into the bar. It had been hours since he'd last seen her, and now she was dressed in a bright yellow sundress with little tropical fishes on it, a rope belt cinched around her waist. She stood at the entrance, seemed to avert her eyes from the spot where her husband had been shot. Then she saw Connor standing behind the counter, talking to this young chick sitting on a stool, leaning close. She hesitated, then started walking uncertainly toward him. Over the last few months Connor had developed a pretty keen eye, and that eye had no problem realizing that Mrs. Carerra had been drinking—and her brain stem wasn't dealing with the alcohol very well. Still, she managed to make it over to where he was perched behind the bar.

"Good evening, Mr. Connor," she said as she steadied herself against the counter.

"Mrs. Carerra," he greeted her, dipping his head in a polite nod. Hoping she wasn't going to order anything to drink, because she wasn't in any condition to be served. "To what do I owe the pleasure?"

"I was...just in the neighborhood," she said as she placed her hands flat on the bar to make the world stop spinning.

"May I get you a cup of coffee?" Connor asked her.

Her mouth tightened into a frown and shook her head. "I really look that bad? Dammit. This is not the way...for a new widow...to act." She sniffled, then picked up a bar napkin and dabbed her eyes.

"What d'you say I call a cab, give you a ride home?" he offered. "On the house."

"Thank you, Mr. Connor. But I…already have an escort." With that she cocked her head at the Dodge Charger with the word "Police" stenciled on the side. It was parked down below at the shoulder of the road, lights on and engine rumbling. "That nice policeman, there…I can't remember his name—"

"Lincoln Polk," Connor helped her.

"That's it," she said, her words coming out slurred. "Officer Polk. A few minutes ago I was leaving another fine drinking establishment and he saw me getting into my car. The one my husband and I…rented it at the airport…when we got here. Anyway, that nice policeman said…it would not be a good idea…for me to drive. Gave me a choice between a lift…or a night in jail."

Connor's estimation of Lincoln Polk just went up a notch or two. "That was very kind of him," he said.

"I told him 'yes,' thinking I didn't have an option, and I got in. He asked me where…I was staying, and then I remembered why…I came into town in the first place. So here I am."

Jessica Snow shot him a curious glance from where she was sitting, an inquisitive look that said, *how well do you know this woman?*

"You know, you really have a… delightful place here," Mrs. Carerra went on. "Cocktails almost right on the beach."

"That's why it's called The Sandbar," Connor replied patiently.

She started to reply, but all that came out was a hiccup. Then she looked him in the eye, said. "The kid who shot my husband….the cops got him."

"How do you mean, 'they got him'?"

"They arrested him this afternoon."

"You got this from Officer Polk?"

She gave Connor the slightest of nods, then leaned across the bar as if she had a real secret to spill. "Said it was some kid with a strange name, began with a J."

"Justacious Stone." He said it more as a statement than a question.

"Yeah, that's it," Martina Carerra said. "You know him?"

"Not personally, but I've heard the name. Folly's a big place but a small town."

"Well, anyway, they nabbed him…buying Skittles at Walmart. The fucking bastard goes before the judge at nine o'clock tomorrow morning."

Her words hung there a second, followed by another hiccup, and then she turned to go.

"Hold on a second," Connor said, reaching under the cash register and pulling out her purse. "I believe this is yours."

Martina Carerra took the handbag, a full spectrum of pastels with a shoulder strap, then nodded and said, "Thank you for keeping it…in a safe place."

She flashed him a sorrowful smile, then turned and made her exit down the wooden stairs she had just navigated, a distinct lilt in her step. When she got down to the parking lot Connor watched as she slid into the police vehicle without a problem, then gave one last waggle of her fingers toward him.

"What was that all about?" Jessica asked when it was all over. She was rolling the remnant of the plastic cocktail straw in her fingers. "Do you know that woman?"

"Not really," Connor replied, casually wiping a rag across the bar. "She was in here the other night, when the guy got shot. Remember?"

"Should I?" Was this jealousy masked as curiosity, or was she playing games? "I've never seen her before in my life."

"My bad," he said, flexing his shoulder in a slight shrug. "For some reason it looked like you recognized her. She's the dead guy's wife."

"Is that a fact?" Jessica said then, glancing out into the night where the Dodge Charger had just been parked.

CHAPTER 9

When Connor enlisted in the Army, he'd grown accustomed to long days and short nights, sometimes getting no more than four or five hours of sleep at a stretch. He and his squad would slog through the desert in hundred-plus temperatures for twenty hours, then sack out on the hard, rocky soil and catch a couple hours of shut-eye before starting all over again at dawn's first light. Civilian life had changed that, and over time his body clock had worked back to seven—sometimes even eight—hours of sleep a night.

Danielle's full and unequivocal rejection had shattered all that. In the first months after she split, he would lie awake for hours, replaying that bloody night frame-by-frame in his head. Those images occupied the days and weeks that followed, Danielle's harsh words and unwavering insistence that they were finished as a couple. Rock bottom had come that morning he woke up under an overpass near the I-26 interchange out near the airport, his old Plymouth Fury convertible crunched head-first into a concrete bridge abutment. Miraculously he was not hurt, except for a scratch where his head had slammed the steering wheel, but he had no memory of what had happened or how he'd come to be there.

The cop who had awakened him with the glare of his Maglite proved to be another miracle, treating him with unlikely compassion when he learned Connor was a veteran who'd served in Iraq and had recently been swept up in a whirlpool of death.

"I'm taking you to the V.A. instead of Leeds," the officer had told him, beginning the process that landed Connor in the PTSD program in Georgia.

In any event, Connor had slipped back to only five hours of sleep, even on a good night, which meant that getting up at seven on a Monday morning was no big issue. He passed on his beach run but took Clooney for short a walk, then fed him and refilled his water dish.

Ten minutes later he was on the road, heading north toward Charleston. To be precise, the J. Waties Waring Judicial Center on Meeting Street, otherwise known as the U.S. District Court of South Carolina. A quick Google check told him that's where Justacious Stone was set to be arraigned at nine o'clock and, for an empty reason Connor still did not comprehend, he wanted to be there. He'd made a deliberate decision to drop the Carerra thing, but the moment his widow mentioned that "the fucking bastard" was going up before a judge this morning, Connor got it in his mind that he was going to be there, too.

He arrived early and joined the line at the metal detector. He asked one of the guards where Stone's arraignment was scheduled to be held, and after a quick check of a clipboard the man told him it would be in Courtroom B on the third floor. He followed a stream of men and women—most of them prospective jurors reporting for their civic duty—up the stairs, then found his way to the door that opened onto Judge Turpin's judicial realm.

Connor glanced around, half-expecting someone to ask him why he was there. But the only official-looking guy—probably a bailiff—was chatting with someone in a light gray summer suit, most likely an attorney. Connor slipped inside and took a seat on a bench at the back of the room and tried to make himself look as inconspicuous as possible. He took in the polished witness stand and jury box, the windowless walls painted a muted cream. A dozen suspects facing a variety of charges huddled in the front row of benches. Some of them were whispering to public defenders, some were crying to their wives or mothers, others were sitting with their arms crossed in defiance of the system that was blind to their street cred. Their dark eyes and arrogant sneers suggested they were familiar with this routine and didn't give a shit about what happened to them. What they seemed to be missing was that no one else did, either.

The bailiff didn't bring Justacious Stone into the courtroom until all other criminal matters had been handled and defendants dealt with. Many of the spectators had left the room as soon as the judge had sentenced their fathers, husbands, sons, and a few daughters. Some left in tears, some left with audible relief, and a few flipped off the judge and swore at him as they slipped through the unforgiving doors of justice. By the time young Mr. Stone finally was led into the courtroom there were only a couple of reporters and sketch artists lingering, all of them hungrily waiting for this morning's main event.

On the other side of the rail, studying a page of scribbled notes, sat the public defender whom Connor assumed had been appointed to Jones. The attorney—a young white man with washed-out hair and a beak of a nose—already had spoken for several other suspects that morning, but Connor couldn't recall how those cases had fared. The man was dressed in a wrinkled seersucker suit, pale blue shirt, a tie that had some sort of abstract, wave-shaped pattern running through it. He was holding a pair of glasses that never once got near his eyes, and Connor suspected they were simply a prop, something for his hands to do.

From his perch in the back of the courtroom Connor watched the public defender size up his latest client. Like the other prisoners, Justacious Stone was dressed in a gray jumpsuit that looked like it was from the one-size-fits-all rack. He was a little on the short side, no taller than five-seven, but what he lacked in height he made up for in weight. He wasn't fat, but there was a good deal of bulk attached to his bones. His hair was buzzed short, and his black skin looked as if it were pocked by scars from earlier encounters with sharp blades. Despite the coarseness of his cheeks he still looked all of his sixteen years. He turned around several times to flash a worried look at the woman whom Connor had met in the green camper, but her reproving glance made him turn away just as quickly.

Judge Turpin finally took up the matter of the State of South Carolina v. Justacious Stone and asked the defendant and his lawyer to rise. He looked out over his courtroom as if he were studying a congregation of followers which, in a way, he was. In fact, his black robes and furrowed brow made him look more like a preacher than a judge, and the dark scowl of his eyes seemed to hold a stern command over the spectators' gallery. Deep furrows etched in his forehead suggested he was not someone to mess with.

"Let the record show that public defender Bruce Skilikorn has been appointed to represent the defendant in this case," the judge said, glancing both at the bailiff and the court reporter. "Is that correct?

"Yes, your honor," the defense attorney confirmed.

"Then let us proceed," the judge continued. "Mr. Benton?"

Seated across the aisle from Jones and his attorney was the deputy prosecutor, who now rose from his chair and stepped forward. Like the public defender, he was white, and appeared to be savoring the publicity the case might bring him. His primary role this morning was to see that any chance of bail be denied and that Stone was officially charged with first degree murder.

"Jerry Benton, for the record, your honor, representing the state of South Carolina. I'd like to begin by reading the charges against the defendant, Justacious Stone, who is being charged as an adult in this horrific crime."

Judge Turpin drew his glance from Benton to the public defender and said, "Mr. Skilikorn, would your client like to hear the charges brought against him, or would you prefer to dispense with such reading and proceed directly with the hearing?"

"The defendant waives his right to a reading of the charges and requests that these proceedings be continued due to the fact that counsel has not had sufficient time to confer with his client," the lawyer named Skilikorn said.

"Very well, we will skip the reading of the charges. Also, your petition to delay the hearing is denied. We now will proceed directly to the matter of bail." Judge Turpin drew his weary gaze from the frustrated public defender back to the deputy prosecutor and said, "Mr. Benton, I understand that the state wishes that the defendant be held without bond because of the capital charges brought against him? Is that correct?"

"Precisely, your honor," Benton said. "Mr. Stone is a violent criminal who should not be released to the streets of this beautiful city."

"Objection!" the defense attorney barked as he jumped to his feet. "My client is as innocent as the day is long and, until the prosecution proves otherwise, he deserves to be treated as such. He also is a minor, and my client objects to his being charged as an adult."

"Overruled," the judge said.

"Your honor, Mr. Stone has lived in the Lowcountry his entire life," Skilikorn protested. "He is a senior in high school, he has a job, and he comes from an established family. I strongly urge you to..."

"The accused is known to associate with recognized gang members, and he has an established history of violence in this county," the prosecutor interrupted. "He is a significant flight risk, and we have strong reason to believe he will disappear if he is not remanded into custody. The people insist that bail be denied."

"Fuck you, and fuck bail," Justacious Stone suddenly snapped as he jumped to his feet, jolting the courtroom into a sudden bout of silence.

Silence, except for the judge.

"*Mis-ter Stone!*" he shouted, his booming voice loud enough to drown a thunderclap. "In my courtroom you will keep your mouth closed and communicate to me through your court-appointed attorney. Is that clear?"

"Fuck you. And fuck this shit. I already said I done it, so cut all this lawyer crap. Guilty."

"What!?"

"Guilty," the defiant young man repeated.

"You're pleading guilty to the charges filed against you?"

"Every single fuckin' one you got," Stone snarled, almost triumphantly. "Guilty, guilty, guilty, guilty, guilty..."

"Jim—" Judge Turpin glanced at the bailiff and a deputy standing against the courtroom wall. "...Please escort the prisoner from this courtroom and take him back to jail."

"Guilty, guilty, guilty..."

"And let the record show that the defendant has pleaded guilty to all charges."

"But your Honor..." Skilikorn protested.

"We're through here, counselor." The judge pounded his gavel on the bench loudly, then said, "The record will show that the defendant known as Justacious Stone has pleaded guilty to all charges filed against him by the State of South Carolina. I will take his words of admission under consideration and render my final decision on Thursday. Meanwhile, the bailiff will return the suspect to the county courthouse, where he will be held without bail."

And that was that.

Connor couldn't remember when he'd seen anything like it. Not on TV, and never in real life. Two minutes was all it took for the kid to try, convict, and all but execute himself. He thought about trying to corner Skilikorn outside in the hallway, but the public defender followed the judge into chambers and must have used a separate exit to slip out of the building. Connor waited by the courtroom door a good ten minutes, then gave up and started to wander down the corridor toward the stairs. Ahead of him he saw the woman from the green camper, weeping on the shoulders of an older woman. Connor hung back, buying himself some time by turning on the volume on his cell phone just to give let them get a head start down the stairs. Then the menacing hiss of a viper filled his ears:

"I told you, you come around again, you a dead man."

Connor wasn't even sure he heard the words correctly, not at first. They were more of a jeer than anything, delivered to his ear as he started down to the first floor.

"I'm talking to you, asshole," the voice said again, and this time Connor felt a hard object press firmly against his right kidney. "No, don't turn around."

Connor recognized the voice: it was the dickwad from yesterday, the one who slammed him to the ground as he was leaving Justacious Stone's place. "You make a move, any move, I blow a hole through your gut. Understand?"

"How'd you get a gun in here?" Connor asked him.

The thug chose to ignore him, instead saying, "I told you yesterday, I don't like assholes nosing 'round, asking about one of my brothas."

"I wasn't asking anything," Connor pointed out. The man's breath smelled of the same malt liquor and fried food as yesterday. "I was just watching the proceedings."

"Watching, asking, same difference." He dug the gun harder into Connor's kidney and twisted the barrel. It hurt like hell, but not as much as a bullet would.

Who the hell was this scumbag?

"You're not going to shoot me," Connor told him. "You wouldn't get ten feet before someone dropped you."

"That makes you the luckiest man alive," he snarled in Connor's ear. "Next time you'll be shrimp bait."

Connor had met self-assured shit-heads like this one before. False sense of power, figured they were running the show, never once realizing they weren't the least bit different from any other two-bit fish in a two-bit pond. Most times they were only as strong as the gun they held in their hand, and if this scumbag had actually managed to get one past the metal detectors, right now Connor wanted to ram it down his throat. Land a swift kick in his groin, too. Anything other than just stand there letting him call the shots.

"You sure have a strange way of looking out for your brother," he said.

"What the fuck you talkin' about—?"

"In there," Connor replied, cocking his head toward the courtroom. "Guilty, guilty, guilty. You tell him to say that?"

"One more word and I put a bullet through your ass," the dickwad said. "I'll be out of this joint so quick no one'll know I was here."

Connor was about to go for the gun when he heard footsteps approaching from behind. Suddenly the pressure eased up against Connor's kidney: this guy wasn't taking any chances.

"Next chance I get, you're dead," he whispered one last time as he turned and vanished, almost as fast as a lime at The Sandbar.

CHAPTER 10

The Charleston County Coroner's Office was located on Salt Pointe Road in North Charleston, about a half mile from the Al Cannon Detention Center on Leeds Avenue. Otherwise known as the county lock-up, which the locals simply referred to as Leeds. But Connor knew from previous experience that most of the real forensic work—a.k.a., autopsies—was performed by the Department of Pathology and Laboratory Medicine at the Medical University downtown.

Two phone calls told him the department subsection of Medical and Forensic Autopsy was housed in Room 281 of the main hospital, on Ashley Avenue. A pale man dressed in green scrubs was seated behind a desk when Connor pushed his way into the office suite, and he promptly explained that no one was available to talk to him. *Not now, not ever*, was the tone of his voice. He looked more like a lab technician than a receptionist or a doctor, a fact confirmed by the plastic tag pinned to his chest: Alan Harvey, LMT.

Connor explained that he was there to speak with whomever had performed the cut on Tony Carerra, who had died Friday night and likely had gone under the saw sometime over the weekend.

"That would be the director of the department," Mr. Harvey told him. "Linda Dillon. But she's in a procedure at the moment and can't be disturbed."

Connor assumed a "procedure" meant another autopsy. "I'm in no hurry," he said with a shrug.

"These things can take a considerable amount of time," Harvey replied, almost as a warning.

"No problem. I don't have to be anywhere until this afternoon."

So much for leaving the Carerra thing alone.

Connor took a seat in a chair that seemed to be designed more for budget than comfort. So did the entire room, in fact. The walls were white and sterile, the floor covered in industrial-grade linoleum that looked as if it were left over from the eighties. A small table next to Connor's chair was piled with magazines that looked as old as the flooring. He picked up a copy of *Men's Health* and browsed through it, then went on to *Conde Nast Traveler*, *Atlantic Monthly*, and *Sports Illustrated*.

Forty-five minutes and nine well-thumbed magazines later he looked up as Alan Harvey called out his name. "Dr. Dillon has a few minutes to see you now," he said without an ounce of warmth. "Please follow me."

Connor got up and trailed the lab tech down a hallway that was designed with the same sense of aesthetics as the waiting room. In other words: sterile white walls, stained acoustic tiles in the drop ceiling, flickering fluorescent tubes.

Linda Dillon, M.D. was sitting at her desk, and made no effort to stand up when Harvey showed Connor into her office. They shook hands and she waved him into a chair in front of her. The room was not large, but she had decorated it acceptably, mostly with photographs of reef fish and rainforest birds. Several exotic plants Connor did not recognize were arranged on a low table, and a large potted palm sat in a corner. A shelf unit set against one wall held an array of reference books that appeared well-used, evidently not there just for show. The desk was standard government-issue gun metal gray, the surface cluttered with manila folders, accordion files, and stacks of loose papers. On the wall were framed certificates that indicated she was co-director of the Forensic Autopsy Section, as well as medical director of Cytogenetics and Molecular Pathology. She also was a member of the American Board of Medicolegal Death Investigators, the American Academy of Forensic Sciences, and the International Association of Coroners and Medical Examiners.

Alan Harvey stood in the doorway with an uncertain scowl on his face until she told him that would be all. Then she said, "So—to what do I owe the urgency of this interruption?"

"It's strictly a business matter," Connor told her, not exactly answering her question. He guessed her to be in her mid-forties, an assessment based primarily on the few strands of silver that coursed through her otherwise dark, close-cropped hair. Her eyes were the color of caramel, and her upper lip carried tight, thin lines that seemed more the result of worrying than aging. She was well-tanned, probably the by-product of southern living, and she struck Connor as the sort of woman who enjoyed outdoor activities but probably didn't get to do as many as of them as she would like.

"First off, and let's get this straight from the beginning: I do not speak with the public. You are here because you caught me in a rare good mood, which is likely to change any second. People around here call me the Dragon Lady. They don't know that I know, but I do."

"I'll keep that in mind," Connor replied.

"And just to be honest with you, I don't expect this conversation to last very long."

"Duly noted."

"So what sort of business matter brings you to my door?" she inquired. "I know all the lawyers and detectives and funeral directors in this county, and you're not one of them."

"No, I am not," he said. "I run a bar in Folly Beach."

"And you're here wasting my time *why?*" Dr. Dillon was one guarded woman, and she seemed to take pleasure in the whole Dragon Lady thing.

"Last Friday night a man was shot in that bar."

The ME eyed him suspiciously. "You're talking about The Sandbar, I presume?"

Connor acknowledged her comment with a nod and said, "Correct. And I believe you've already made the victim's acquaintance."

The look of suspicion had not left her eyes, which remained fixed on his. "From what I understand the police have arrested a suspect," she said. "If you have any questions about the investigation, I suggest you speak with them."

"I've talked with them extensively," Connor said. He leaned forward in his chair, letting her know he wasn't about to let up. "I appreciate that you're a busy woman, and I'm sure you have your share of cranks who come in here looking for information they shouldn't have. Insurance investigators, private eyes, reporters. Someone is always looking for something, and you can't trust any of 'em."

"You speak the truth," she said. "Your candor has earned you sixty seconds. Starting now."

Sixty seconds was not a lot of time, but more than he'd hoped for when he'd walked in almost an hour ago. "Look...you don't know me. You have no reason to trust me. I have nothing personal to gain here, but I'm a curious man. I'm hoping you can help me figure out something about the shooting that's been bothering me."

Dr. Dillon leveled him with pensive eyes that filled her bookish, oval-shaped glasses. She picked up a pencil from the desk and started turning it over in her hand, then tapped the eraser on the metal surface.

"What's your interest, other than the fact that this guy died in your place of business?"

Connor could have split hairs here, pointing out the fact that Tony Carerra technically had died in the ambulance, not on the drinking deck at The Sandbar. But the clock was ticking, and it was an inconsequential point. So he got right to it.

"I want to know what the autopsy on Tony Carerra showed."

"Is this guy somehow related to you?" she asked. "Or maybe he owes you money?"

"No, nothing like that. I'd never met him before Friday night, just a few minutes before he was shot."

"I'll ask again: what's your interest in him?"

Connor had been asking himself the same question and had yet to come up with a clear answer. Carerra's death clearly was a police matter, and both the local cops and SLED had done their thing. The young gunman had already been apprehended, arraigned, and—faster than you can say *lethal injection*—had pled guilty to all charges. With absolutely no regard to how long he might be locked up, or what impact a conviction might have on the rest of his life. Connor had wondered if the shooting might have been some sort of gang initiation, that maybe Justacious Stone had tried to prove himself worthy of a Lowcountry version of the Crips and Bloods. Gangs were a way of life in every project or

Section 8 neighborhood, and just a year ago a maximum-security prison up in Bishopville had experienced a massive riot that left seven rival inmates dead, and a couple dozen more injured. Taking another man's life had almost become a rite of passage.

But there was another thing that bothered Connor, and he mentioned it now. "Look, Dr. Dillon. I spent sixteen months on the front lines in Iraq during the surge. I went through basic training, which included an intensive course in armaments and munitions. I've also seen battle up close, so I know what a gun can do, and what it can't."

The ME glanced at her watch, which told him she was still keeping time. "You're now down to thirty seconds," she told him.

"I had a question about the man who got shot, and whether the wound was consistent with the weapon that was used."

That seemed to get her attention, and she made an almost imperceptible move closer to listen more intently to what he was saying. "Please elaborate," she said.

Connor hadn't thought this all through, and small elements of last Friday night were coming back to him now. The position where Carerra had been standing, and the palmetto tree down below where the gunman had been lurking about twenty feet away. The pop of the gun that turned out to be a twenty-two, not exactly a large-caliber implement of death and destruction. A peculiar choice for a known gang member to use as a murder weapon, even though it had caused Carerra to bleed out in the back of the ambulance on the way to the hospital.

He told all this to the ME, which took him well past the sixty-second mark. By the end he figured she must have taken him off the clock, specifically when he said, "I just don't see how the man could have died."

Dr. Dillon again picked up her pencil and began fiddling with it. With many people this was an indication of anxiety, sometimes even foreshadowing a falsehood, but he read it simply as a way for her to construct her thoughts before she spoke.

"I shouldn't be telling you what I'm about to say," she finally told him. "In fact, I could get into a heap of trouble if it ever got out that I spoke to you about this case at all. *Any case*, in fact."

"But—" he prodded her.

"But there was one little element that I thought highly curious."

"Which was?"

She paused again, as if going any further would cause her to step across a line from which there was no going back. Then she said, "An inconsistency, actually. How much do you know about postmortem lividity and calculating time of death?"

As the former manager of Palmetto BioClean, Connor had been trained to understand the particulars about death scenes and dead bodies, decay and decomp and coagulation. He knew what blood could do when it seeped out of the body, and he'd experienced first-hand the infestation of maggots and other crawling critters that zeroed in on a body within minutes of it becoming a corpse. But most of the time the remains of the deceased had already been cleared away, and he and his team were only tasked with cleaning up the detritus. Even during his time in the Iraqi desert, the medics had been assigned to transport the bodies, which meant he'd never directly dealt with rigor mortis or putrefaction.

"I know it has to do with muscle stiffening and blood gases, that sort of thing."

"That's my big issue with television," Dr. Dillon said, shaking her head. She stood up, walked over to her window, adjusted the blinds so she had a better view of the brick wall across the way. "Postmortem lividity, or hypostasis, is when gravity settles the blood during the early post mortem interval. This generally becomes apparent within a short period—thirty minutes to two hours after death—and appears as a purple coloration, except where there's been what we call 'contact pressure.'"

She paused to give him time to understand what she was saying. "Got it, so far," he assured her.

"The degree of discoloration is very useful in determining time of death. Precision is hard to come by, except in the rare instance when a bullet stops a pocket watch, or something else clichéd like that. Anything else is more or less an educated guess, typically based on evidence collected at the scene. These things can include changes in the victim's eyes, temperature, rigidity, and decomposition of the body. You still follow?"

He nodded but said nothing, letting her continue.

"Now…putrefaction—the act of decomposition—begins at the moment of death, and usually becomes evident about twenty-four hours later. The skin starts to show signs of discoloration, especially in the lower abdomen and groin area. There are other signs that begin to appear within thirty-six hours, but they're not important for the matter of our discussion here. What is important—" She hesitated again, as if trying to make the final determination of whether she should share her hypothesis with a former soldier who now ran a beach bar "—is it appears in this case that there may be a discrepancy in the timeline of death."

"The timeline of death?" Connor repeated.

"An inconsistency between the moment when the victim was struck by the bullet and when he died," Dr. Dillon clarified.

Connor thought about what she was saying and flashed back to Friday night. No more than a half hour had passed from the time Tony Carerra had been shot and Connor had pulled his Jeep Wrangler in front of the E.R. at the Medical University. "You're saying the lividity and discoloration don't add up?" he asked.

"That's a piece of it," she said, her words sounding guarded. "And again, I shouldn't be mentioning any of this to you."

"But here we are."

She stared at him for a good ten seconds before responding. "What I'm about to tell you is…well, it's going to sound crazy," she said.

"That makes me your guy," Connor replied with a smile.

She smiled back, said, "The thing is, the victim—Tony Carerra—well, indications strongly suggest he did not die in that ambulance on the way to the hospital."

"I'm not sure I understand," Connor said. "I saw him being loaded into it."

"I've read the police report," the medical examiner said, nodding pensively. She picked up the pencil again, but this time started drumming on her desk, rather than rolling it between her fingers. "I know all the supposed facts, and I reviewed the statements from the med tech and the doctor who were riding with him. Still, no matter how I look at it, I keep coming around to one big contradiction."

Dr. Dillon fell silent, and so did the pencil. She appeared reluctant to take this conversation any further, mentally debating why she should share her secrets with this bald man with all the tattoos who had walked in off the street and started hitting her with questions. But Connor didn't want to let the moment slip away, so he decided to go all in on a hunch.

"How long do you think he'd already been dead?" he asked.

The question did not seem to shock her, which meant it was consistent with her own line of thinking. "Hours," she said simply.

"You're sure of this?"

"Lividity doesn't lie, Mr. Connor. According to my calculations, Mr. Carerra had been dead at least four hours—possibly as many as eight—before he arrived in the ambulance last Friday night."

CHAPTER 11

"Eight hours?" Connor stared at Dr. Dillon as if she had just sprouted a second head. "That's impossible."

"Four to eight," she corrected him. "And the evidence doesn't lie."

"But—"

"Don't even start. I don't understand it myself."

He took a deep breath, then massaged his eyes with his fingers. His sixty seconds had clearly extended into triple overtime, and he wanted to make the most of whatever time still remained. "You're sure it was Carerra?"

"We don't mix up patients here, Mr. Connor—"

"I know, I know," he said quickly. This wasn't making sense. Carerra had come into The Sandbar around ten o'clock and ordered two beers, then shared a few words about software and honeymoons. Twenty minutes later he was shot, and half an hour after that he had been pronounced dead. Four to eight hours after he'd actually passed away, if the ME was accurate in her assessment.

"Where's the body now?" he asked her.

"At Mrs. Carerra's direction it was sent on to a funeral home, where it's going to be cremated..." she glanced at her watch "...well, about an hour ago."

"There goes the evidence," he said dryly. "Have you talked to the med tech or the doctor that rode in the ambulance with him? Maybe they can give confirmation."

"That's another funny thing," Dr. Dillon. "I can't locate them."

"How do you mean?"

"Exactly what I just said." She founded more frustrated at the situation than tired of his questions. "The number the doctor gave when Carerra was wheeled into the E.R. is disconnected, and the ambulance seems to have vanished into thin air."

"What do you mean, 'vanished'? Ambulances don't just disappear."

"Well, this one did," she said, raising a single eyebrow. "The truck, along with the two EMT's who were in it."

"Did you mention any of this in your report?"

She sat back in her chair and folded her hands in front of her. Her mouth ticked up in a slight grin of resignation, and she said, "The police already have a suspect, who pleaded guilty. Case closed."

• • •

By the time Connor got back to Folly Beach it was mid-afternoon. Desmond Green had already made his Monday delivery, locking up after stacking every case of beer and rum and tequila in the store room. Connor checked the lock on the door, then retreated upstairs to his small apartment for a quick shower. A day in creased trousers and a button-down shirt always left him feeling sticky, and he wanted to wash the day away before putting in another eight hours behind the bar.

The splash of cool water felt good, and after toweling off he slipped into a clean pair of cargo shorts and a tropical shirt with The Sandbar parrot logo on it. He ran a razor over his head, then picked up his cell phone and dialed a number in his contacts. He paced the floor as he waited for the call to go through; finally on the fourth ring someone answered.

"Kat Rattigan," the voice on the other end announced. All business and right to the point, just as he had remembered her.

"Hey, Kat!" Connor hadn't really expected to get her, just make the call and leave a message. "Jack Connor here—"

There was a slight hesitation as the hard drive in her brain went to work, and then she said, "Hey Connor—long time no talk!"

"Way too long," he said. "So long, in fact, I wasn't sure this was still your number."

"I'm tied to it like a Siamese twin," she said. "Although I guess the word they use today is *conjoined*. To what do I owe the pleasure?"

Connor had met Kat Rattigan several years back, when he was working a job to recover something that had belonged to Jordan James. She was a private investigator who had been instrumental in helping Connor decipher a complex riddle that involved a young woman whom, he suspected, was now living in some distant banana republic that didn't have an extradition treaty with the U.S. More recently he had counted on her to conduct a search on a high-profile suspect that he couldn't trust to anyone else.

"I need a background check," he told her. "Thought maybe you could help me out."

"What do you need?"

Connor explained everything he was looking for, then waited for her reaction.

"Not a big request, but I'm a bit backlogged right now," she said. "How soon do you need it?"

"Yesterday, of course," he replied. "Feel free to charge me a rush fee if you need to. Can you do it?"

"Tomorrow's more realistic. I'll see what I can do."

When he finally came downstairs it was not quite five, but Jessica was already seated at the bar, a Bay Breeze set squarely on a cocktail napkin in front of her. She was deep in conversation with Julie, who was standing behind the counter emptying maraschino cherries into the garnish tray.

Starting early tonight, Connor thought as he wandered over.

"Mr. Jack Connor—so glad you could finally join us," Julie said when she caught sight of him. "Getting a little beauty sleep upstairs?"

He ducked behind the counter and flashed a knowing look Jessica's way. "She gets like this whenever she thinks she's overworked," he explained to her. "Like on those rare occasions when I show up a few minutes late and she actually has to do a bit of work around this joint."

"My ass," Julie said, emphasizing her point with a hand gesture known throughout most of the western world. "Without me, this place would go to hell on an oyster shell."

"Pearls of delusion," Connor replied. He picked up a stack of clear plastic cups and took a rough count. "And you, Miss Bay Breeze—what brings you into our humble establishment at such an early hour on a Monday evening?"

"Pre-dinner cocktail," she explained. "Alfonse invited a few colleagues up to Charleston, some hoity-toity place named Rhett's."

Connor knew the place, an upscale restaurant located in an historic house several blocks off Broad Street with only a handful of tables and a wait list of at least a month. He'd never eaten there, but the chef had gotten two stars from Michelin, which he'd heard was a big deal.

"They'll tell you to order the buttermilk fried conch, but don't fall for it," he warned her. "Go for the kiwi flounder instead."

Julie gave him a sideways glance, said, "Since when did you ever go there?"

"Never," he confessed. "But word gets around."

Connor then moved off, eyeballed the Coronas and Coors and Buds in the cooler, saw the supply was low so he went into the store room to get some more. When he came out five minutes later with two cardboard cases in his arms, he found that Jessica was gone, but he gave it only a moment's thought. He set the cases down, ducked back behind the bar, and started packing the bottles into every possible space in the cooler.

"I think she likes you," Julie said without turning around.

"She seems the type who likes everyone," he said, shrugging it off.

"No, I mean she *really* likes you," she insisted. "She told me to give you this."

Julie handed Connor a cocktail napkin that had some scribbling on it. He glanced at it and almost blushed at what she had written:

I'll be back for a nightcap…please save some of your magic for me.

"Well?" Julie pressed him.

"She's just a customer," he said. He folded the napkin and slid it under a bottle of Galliano. No one hardly ever ordered Harvey Wallbangers anymore, so he knew it would be safe there.

"Well, my advice is, whatever she's dishing out, sample with care."

"Thank you, Mother, for your concern," he told her, a sarcastic edge to his voice. "Now, if you don't mind, you've got a customer at your end of the bar. Several of them, in fact."

Julie made a clucking sound with her tongue and moved on down to the other end of the wood counter. An early bird couple had just settled in on the stools and they were eyeing the bottles lined up on the mirrored shelf. She took their order and went about making a pair of gin and tonics. Monday evening at The Sandbar had shifted into gear.

It wasn't much different than most nights, same pattern of customers, progressively more festive as the hours wore on. At one point a regular named Deke Diggerell—a.k.a. Digger—scooted up on a stool at the corner of the bar and leaned forward to catch Connor's ear. "Gimme a painkiller, heavy on the rum, light pineapple, no nutmeg," he said.

Digger was a creature of habit. He ordered the same thing each and every night, no variation on a theme, and usually put away a good half dozen by the time last call rolled around. Connor could tell he'd already consumed a few at one or more other fine Folly drinking establishments, but since he'd lost his license and now rode a scooter Connor wasn't particularly concerned. He fixed Digger's drink and set it in front of him, said, "Think maybe you should have a hot dog to go with that?"

"I know where they are," Digger replied as he took a long sip from his plastic cup. "Heard you were over in the courtroom today."

"Heard from whom?" Connor asked him.

"See that? You said 'whom.' Shows you know your grammar."

What that had to do with anything was beyond definition, but Connor had come to realize that Clemson Diggerell truly illustrated the adage, "you can't judge a book by its cover." Despite the well-worn T-shirt, blown-out flip-flops, and hair that hadn't seen a comb in days, Digger was an enigma. He'd been a well-rewarded trial attorney up in Richmond who collected millions from big tobacco until the day he just quit the law firm and bought a sailboat. Now he lived at the Folly Beach marina, offering tourist charters by day and drinking away whatever ghosts haunted him by night.

An order for a mango martini and a rum and Coke took Connor to the other side of the bar, but that didn't keep Digger from chattering on.

"I heard you sat in on the Justacious Stone arraignment," the aging lawyer said. "Word is, he just gave himself up. Pled guilty to everything they were going to hit him with. What I'm thinking is, whatever that kid got himself into, he's protecting someone."

"What makes you say that?"

"Three years of law school and thirty-one years of courtroom litigation," Digger replied.

"Do your sources say whether the cops know why he pulled the trigger?"

"The prevailing theory is, there was a traffic altercation earlier in the day," Digger replied, but his eyes seemed loaded with skepticism. "Road rage, maybe Carerra called him the N-word, or something like that."

"You don't buy it?" Connor asked, curious to hear the former trial lawyer's take on things.

"What—you think the kid was packing heat just in case he ran into Carerra?"

Connor shrugged as he wiped a rag across the bar. "Maybe he was packing heat because that's what he did," he said.

"Are you profiling him?"

"Just figuring if he took that shot, he probably had plenty of experience. Like, maybe someone had a score to settle."

Digger took another healthy hit of his painkiller, then said, "You think Carerra was knocked off by some wannabe gangbanger over an unpaid marker?"

"I like to keep my mind open to all possibilities," Connor told him.

"So what I don't get is why the kid pleaded guilty. That took the judge, the D.A., even his own lawyer completely by surprise."

"Maybe he wanted to ease his guilty conscience."

Digger snickered, then pushed his empty cup across the bar, indicating he wanted a refill. "Painkiller, heavy on the rum, light pineapple, no nutmeg," he said.

All evening long, every time a horn honked or a siren wailed over in the downtown area, Connor found himself glancing up and looking to see if the woman named Jessica might have meandered up the stairs into the bar. And each time he forced himself to push her out of his mind. If he'd leaped every time a drunk young woman had come on to him since he'd started running this place, he'd be a very tired man. He was smart enough to know that sampling the flavor of the day brought no lasting comfort, especially when the sun came up in the morning and the brain was having trouble getting last night's name right. Besides, he still wasn't at that point where he felt comfortable moving on. Danielle still invaded every waking moment, and many of those when he was still sound asleep. Sometimes he would dial her number, but hang up before hitting the last digit. He knew it was time to move on, forgive and forget, but the heart sometimes is slower than the brain. This was one of those times.

Besides, Jessica seemed to have more going for her than a lot of the other usual suspects who wandered—*stumbled*—up the stairs into The Sandbar. In fact, she had that *je ne sais quoi*—whatever that meant—and it wasn't just her maraschino lips or her sparkly laugh. He found himself thinking about her green eyes, the curve of her face, and the cut of her jib, so to speak. Also thinking that he'd better get his mind off her because Lincoln Polk had just walked in and was looking straight at him, coming over toward the bar.

"Mr. Connor," he said as he squeezed his way between a couple of customers. "Looks like business is a bit slow tonight."

"Blame it on the moon," Connor said, giving a nod to the nearly full orb that had risen over the water to the east. "To what do I owe the honor?"

"What? A friend can't just come in, have himself a drink in this fine establishment?" Polk said, a hint of a grin showing in his dark eyes.

"A friend is welcome here any time," Connor assured him. "But you don't drink."

"You right about that, my friend. But maybe I could get some of that guava nectar?"

"Couldn't make a proper rum punch without it. You want anything in it?"

"A little ice, maybe a piece of that mango, there," Polk told him, nodding at the garnish tray.

"Coming right up." Connor poured the policeman his drink, set it on a napkin in front of him. "On the house," he said.

"No can do," Polk said, reaching for his wallet. "Chief issued a new policy, no more freebies."

"Then think of it as one friend buying another friend a drink."

Polk considered this, figured it worked for him. He slipped his wallet back into his pocket, then picked up his plastic cup. "To friendship, then," he said, holding the cup in a toast, then taking a healthy sip that drained half its contents.

Connor knew Polk had come in for a reason, probably a follow-up on Tony Carerra. The police officer hardly ever included The Sandbar on his regular patrol, night or day, so he must have had a specific purpose for dropping by tonight. But his curiosity would have to wait, because just then a group of young men came up the stairs from the beach and stumbled over to the bar.

"Three cold brewskis," one of them said. He was wearing a Red Sox cap backwards, and if he was going for the cool customer look, he missed it by a mile. They were kids on the prowl, entertaining themselves with a prolonged pub crawl just in case they didn't get lucky. Which was becoming increasingly tonight, since they'd already consumed way too much to make them appear anything other than wasted. And that, Connor figured, might have been the whole point.

"You guys have IDs?"

The three young men were armed and ready, and Connor inspected all three licenses. "Where you guys parked?" he asked as he popped three bottles of beer.

"Don't have a car…my folks own a condo at Mariner's Cay," the Sox fan said, pronouncing it *key*. "But there ain't anything happenin' there. This is where it's at."

"How'd you get into town?"

"Uber," he said. "After what happened last time, my old man took the battery out of his truck."

Smart old man, Connor thought. He edged back down the bar to where Polk was sitting, his attentive eyes fixed on the boys.

"Those fellas, they're in no shape to drive."

"Good thing Daddy took the T-bird away."

Polk nodded, took another sip of his guava juice. Connor wanted him to get around to why he was there, but there was no point in rushing him.

"I heard you were up at the courthouse today," he finally said.

"Damn," Connor said. "Was I on the news tonight?"

Polk shot him an odd look but just sipped his drink.

"I woke up early, thought I'd see that fella, Justacious Stone, go before the judge."

"Figured as much," Polk said. "What d'you think?"

"You mean, do I think he was the kid I saw running up over the sand after Mr. Carerra got shot the other night? Yeah, I'm pretty sure he was."

"*Pretty* sure?"

"Like I already told you, it was dark, but the moon was almost as bright as it is tonight. Waxing gibbous, I think they call it, and only a few clouds. I think he might've waited until one of them blocked the light, then did his Usain Bolt thing. Besides, he already convicted and pretty much sentenced himself."

"Yeah…that's what's been bothering me."

"What do you mean?"

Polk said nothing for a moment as he finished his juice. Then he looked Connor straight in the eyes and said, "You see, whatever Mr. Justacious Stone must've been thinking, he signed his own death warrant."

"Maybe he figured if he copped to killing Carerra the judge would give him life instead of death."

"Maybe," Polk said. "But if that's what was going through his mind, it just doesn't make sense that he just went and killed himself tonight in his jail cell."

CHAPTER 12

Polk's words caught Connor by surprise, and he felt a sharp shiver rattle up his spine. Connor had seen the kid just that morning. *Guilty, guilty, guilty,* he'd cursed as he was led out of the courtroom.

"Justacious Stone is dead?" he finally said.

"Dead as that there bird," Polk said, nodding at a stuffed parrot that someone had left behind in the bar one night. Connor had kept it around for a few days in case the person came back for it, then propped it up on top of the cash register as a mascot.

"But…how?"

"Preliminary finding is he stabbed himself in the neck," Polk explained.

"With what?"

"That's the thing," the plainclothes officer said. "There's no sign of the weapon, and the whole jail's gone as quiet as a convention of mimes."

• • •

Jessica never showed, which may have been why Connor kept waking up every hour on the hour. Whatever the reason, he slept fitfully through the night, waking and dozing and waking again until the damned phone began to ring.

He grabbed it as he glanced over at the clock: seven twenty-two. Who would possibly be calling him at this hour? No one in Folly could possibly be awake this time of day.

"Yeah?" he said tiredly as he rolled back onto his pillow, thinking it had to be a marketing robocall.

"Jack Connor?" the voice on the other end asked. A woman's voice, and it sounded lot brighter than he felt at that very moment. "Did I wake you up after a rough night?"

"Who's this?" he replied, rubbing his eyes with the back of one hand.

"Your diligent twenty-four seven private detective," she told him. "Kat Rattigan."

That caused him to sit up, even though a large part of him wanted to roll over and pull the pillow over his head. "You're already at work?" he said.

"Crime never sleeps," she replied. "Nor do the creeps and lowlifes who commit them."

"Did you find what I asked for?"

"With a little help from the usual search engines, yeah. And I'll tell you, from what I can tell, I think you've stumbled onto something."

That caused Connor to blink the lingering grains of sleep from his eyes. "All right—you've got my attention," he said as he swung his legs over the edge of the bed.

"Thought I might."

Connor slipped on a pair of shorts and went out to the landing at the top of the stairs. Tuesday morning was just beginning to dawn over Folly Beach and the pelicans were already out, a squadron of them skimming just above the surface of the water in search of breakfast. A gentle rustling in the palmetto turned out to be Rocky, an ancient squirrel that lived deep within its fronds.

Just as Connor sat down on the top step, he heard the creak of a floorboard. Clooney lumbered out from wherever he'd been curled up inside and did a perfect down-dog yoga pose. During the hot summer months he tended to change sleeping locations throughout the night, usually settling wherever the floor was the coolest. And that usually meant the tile in the tiny kitchen off the equally tiny living room. Clooney now gazed at Connor with desperation, and a quick "go" followed by a hand gesture sent the dog bounding down the stairs to find a place to answer nature's call.

"First, I have to tell you this was not one of your regular searches," Kat Rattigan began. "This Tony Carerra character really had me going."

"That's why I called you," Connor said. "Tell me what you know."

"Okay." There was a pause on the other end, either for dramatic impact or to collect her thoughts. "First, my search turned up ninety-two Tony Carerras living in the U.S. Not that many when you think about it, and it was easy to narrow that down with the Visa number you gave me. Credit cards or social security numbers really eliminate a lot of busy work, if you have the right contacts. Which I do. So I ran the Visa and guess what—"

It was a rhetorical question, so Connor just let it dangle there.

"—The number belongs to a Mr. Tony Carerra of Biloxi, Mississippi. American Advantage frequent flier number HYE477. Total unused miles to date: three hundred twenty-eight thousand."

"Are these actual flown miles or credit card purchase miles?" Connor asked.

"That's the thing," the detective told him. "Almost all of them are real miles. But get this: all those miles have been accumulated over the past thirty-six months. Nothing before that."

"Any idea where he goes when he flies the friendly skies?"

"Wrong airline," Kat said. "But yeah, those flights are all part of the record. Which I'll get to in a second. But there's another question you should be asking."

"Which I'll assume I don't have to ask, on account of I just woke up and haven't had a chance to get a cup of coffee," Connor replied.

"Sleep is overrated," she said, a touch of cynicism in her voice. "Anyway, the real question is, 'what happened prior to thirty-six months ago?' Before Carerra got this Visa card?"

"He had a MasterCard?"

"No. He got one of those thirty-six months ago, too. Along with an American Express and a Discover card. The guy had great credit. And you know what else?" This time she didn't give Connor time to wait for an answer. "That's when he also got his driver's license and his passport. All of them applied for at the same time, within a two-week time frame. You know what I'm thinking?"

"Probably the same thing I'm thinking," Connor said, now fully awake and listening intently to what she was telling him. "But to get to your other question, I'm assuming this was Mr. Carerra's first driver's license, and his first passport."

"And his first Social Security card. Yesterday I called a friend at the IRS center up in Maryland, and she ran a check on Mr. Carerra's tax status. Guess what she found?"

"No tax records before three years ago?"

"Bingo. You can see where I'm going with this."

Connor took a deep breath. This was getting damned good, pretty damned fast. "Tony Carerra isn't Tony Carerra."

"Not before three years ago, he wasn't."

"So who was he?"

"I'm still working on that one," Kat told him. "But I can tell you that he's never been arrested, never gotten a speeding ticket, never even pulled a day of jury duty. At least not as Tony Carerra."

"What about those three hundred thousand air miles?"

"Right. I saved the best for last," she said. "In the three years since he received his American Advantage card, he made a bunch of trips to the Caymans, maybe a dozen to Nassau in the Bahamas, and three or four each to Nevis, Panama, and Belize."

"That hardly adds up to three hundred thousand," he pointed out.

"Oh, there's plenty more, places like Zurich and Geneva."

Connor thought on this for a second, then said, "What about Mrs. Carerra?"

"That's hard to tell, since I don't have any account numbers for her. They were only married a month ago, and only met a few months before that. And as far as I can tell she stayed home while her husband jetted off. Whatever Tony Carerra was into, chances are his new bride knew nothing about it."

Maybe, maybe not, Connor thought. He was about to thank her for all his help, let her get on with her day, when another question crossed his mind. "When you were doing your search did you happen to run a credit report?"

"*Please*," she said, sounding as if he'd just maligned her professional integrity. "In fact, I ran all three. They were spotless. Zero monthly balances across the board."

"No mortgage?"

"No mortgage, no debt. Except for the plastic, which he pays off every month, Tony Carerra is an all-cash kind of guy."

Connor felt a part of his brain already going to work on that, decided to let it do its thing at its own natural pace. "Sounds to me like he was a ghost," he said.

"If you believe in ghosts, which I don't."

Connor didn't either and started to tell her so, but then he heard some static on the other end and realized the call was lost. He didn't know if she'd simply hung up or had fallen into a dark cell phone hole of the Lowcountry, but she was gone.

He waited for her to call him back, but when she didn't, he figured he'd hear from her again when she had more to report. He remained out there on the landing, eyes closed as he listened to the sound of the surf tumbling on the beach in the distance. Clooney padded his way back up the stairs and flopped down at his feet on the landing. More noises were beginning to fill the morning as the town came alive, but Connor ignored them. He inhaled deeply, savored the aroma of fresh-brewed coffee drifting up from Gilbert's. He could have used a cup right then, but he was too lazy to move from his perch. His brain was wide awake now, but his arms and legs were still in need of sleep.

Connor didn't actually doze off, but he did let his brain wander through the information it had just downloaded. The implication of what Kat Rattigan had told him was clear, but it led to another series of questions. Tony Carerra seemed to have materialized out of thin air just over three years ago, complete with credit cards, passport, and driver's license. But where had he lived before then? What was his name, and why had he changed it? Connor remembered that Carerra had mentioned he was in the software business, but what exactly did that mean? Computer software was one thing, but it also could be a euphemism for just about anything. Drugs. Cash. Smuggling. Gambling. Human trafficking. All of the above.

He tried to step back mentally from what he knew about the man. After all, there could be a rational explanation for Carerra's sudden emergence from a shadowy womb into the real world thirty-six months ago. It wasn't difficult to make the mental leap to some sort of nefarious activity, especially when you looked at the facts surrounding him. For starters, Tony Carerra was dead. More precisely, he had been shot. He had been loaded into an ambulance and transported to MUSC in Charleston, and had passed away somewhere along the way. Fast-forward to yesterday morning when Justacious Stone abruptly pled guilty to pulling the trigger. Then, just hours later, Stone was found dead in his cell in the county jail. Add in the fact that Carerra very likely had died hours before he was shot on The Sandbar's drinking deck, the kill shot coming from a twenty-two caliber gun.

It was pretty clear that Carerra was not who he said he was. Either that, or someone else *was* Carerra. Which Connor found oddly intertwined with the idea that the Tony Carerra who was loaded into the ambulance was not the same Tony Carerra who ended up in the emergency room. And that was the part that he was having the most trouble with. Who was the real Carerra, or at least the Carerra who had gotten credit cards and a passport three years ago?

The refrain from an old rap song started thumping in his head: *Will the real Slim Shady please stand up?*

A tingling sensation began to swell in his right leg, and he realized it was falling asleep. He slowly rose to his feet, taking care not to stumble over Clooney's sprawled body at the top of the stairs. When he felt the blood return to his veins he stood there on the balcony, letting the stray bits of data cascade around inside his head like lottery balls, trusting them to pop around on their own until they yielded an answer. Or at least provided him a direction in which to go next.

Connor was about to duck back inside for a shower when his phone rang. For a second, he thought Kat Rattigan might be calling him back, but he didn't recognize the number so answered it tentatively. He was in no mood for timeshare pitches or credit card scams.

"Jack Connor?" a voice asked on the other end, tentative and unsure. "It's Leon, from Dublin."

Dublin was the nickname for the V.A. rehab center in Georgia where Connor had spent three weeks last winter, attempting to silence the ghosts that had followed him home from the desert. Leon Scott had been one of his two bunkmates, and the shudder in his voice suggested this was not a pleasure call. Still, he said, "Hey, man…what d'you hear?"

"Nothing good," the voice on the other end replied. "Gordo checked out last night, left no forwarding address."

Connor stood there in stunned silence and slumped against the doorjamb. *Checked out* was the term they'd used when one of their brothers-in-arms left the planet early. Five seconds passed, then ten, and eventually Leon said, "Connor? You still there?"

"Shit, man…yeah, I'm still here. Gordo? Seriously?"

Gordo was a fellow grunt who had come home from Afghanistan a few years back, a kid from Pennsylvania who had driven a beer truck until patriotic duty came calling. He'd signed up, gone to war, killed eleven insurgents no older than he was, and saw almost a quarter of his squad blown to pieces by IEDs and suicide runs. When he got home to his young wife, he couldn't escape the visions of nutcrackers that danced in his head, and eventually turned his arms into pincushions to ease the pain when it became too great. Last winter he'd seemed as if he'd beaten the depression and the addiction and the dependence, and he'd left the treatment program with a glint of hope in his eye.

"His wife called me this morning," Leon was telling him. "I hate to give you bad news like this, but I figured you'd want to know."

"Yeah, thanks," Connor replied, his mind all of a sudden drifting off to his own version of the desert, and the guns and bombs and destruction that always resided there. "Any word on how—?"

"Overdose," Jackson said. "Kelli—that's his wife's name—she said he's been flirting with death for months. She's working on a memorial service, up in Orangeburg where they lived. I'll text you the details when I get them."

"Thanks, man. I appreciate it."

"This really blows, you know?"

"Totally fucked," Connor said, then hung up before he could share the words he really wanted to say.

CHAPTER 13

An hour later Connor was in his Jeep, heading out along the northern stretch of shoreline toward Morris Island Light. A large cup of coffee jostled in the plastic holder next to him, each new pothole and asphalt patch splashing drips of Ethiopian roast on the floor. So much sand had accumulated down there since he'd bought the thing that it resembled a small beach itself.

As he headed out of town, he couldn't get Gordo out of his brain. The kid was part redneck and part Puerto Rican, and almost too pudgy to survive boot camp. Hence his nickname. Connor understood what he was going through, the cold sweats at night when the faces of the dead came calling, the uncontrolled panic when an unmarked van followed too close in traffic. The sudden backfire of a car, or a string of firecrackers randomly popping in the night, especially when it wasn't the Fourth of July.

Eventually Connor passed his favorite part of the beach, where he had run into Mrs. Carerra Sunday afternoon. Two hundred yards further up the road he pulled to the shoulder in front of a small house painted in a tropical palette of turquoise and violet and yellow, pink roof the color of bubble gum, palmetto trees and hibiscus lining the driveway. A hand-painted sign out front said its name was *Calypso Cove*. This was the house where Mr. Carerra had told him they were staying, and Connor was hoping that the new widow hadn't departed yet with her husband's remains for the long trip home.

The Jeep's tires made a sizzling sound on the gravel drive as he came to a stop behind a white rental SUV. He sat behind the wheel a moment, looking out at the sand and the deep blue water beyond. The house sat precipitously close to the shoreline, no more than twenty yards from the high-water mark, a temptation for any Atlantic hurricane. A small walkway led from the driveway through a jungle of canna lilies, salvia, and clematis, and as he climbed down from the Jeep Clooney side-eyed a disinterested look. Connor topped off the dog's water dish, then followed the walkway to a set of stairs that led to the upper floor. He hesitated briefly, then started climbing, rehearsing in his head how he wanted this to go.

At the top of the steps was a small balcony with a wooden door that opened into a screened gallery. It was early—too early for many folks whose inner clocks get time-shifted while they're on vacation—but then the aroma of coffee hit his nose. He knocked twice, then peered through the screen to catch any movement inside. His knocking got no answer so he did it again, waited one more time. He was ready to do it a third time when a voice called out, "Is somebody there?"

"Mrs. Carerra?" he said through the screen.

"Who is it?" Her voice sounded suspicious, and he didn't blame her.

"Jack Connor," he replied. "From The Sandbar in town."

There was a prolonged silence, then Martina Carerra wandered from the back of the house into the screened-in gallery that looked out over the beach. She came to the door and offered him a wary smile through the wire mesh, but she did not open it.

"What a surprise to see you again," she said. This time she wasn't wearing her shades, and he could tell it was too early in the day for the tears to have begun. "The only people who've come out to see me are cops and reporters. You already gave me my purse back, so to what do I owe the pleasure?"

"Well, Mrs. Carerra…" he began, then hesitated just a second. "The thing is, I hate to bother you, but there's something about the other night I'd like to ask you."

"Is that a fact." It was a statement, not a question. She continued to study Connor through the door, then pushed it open and said, "What the hell. I only ask one thing of you."

"That seems more than fair—"

"Don't agree so quickly," she said, almost scolding him. "Come inside."

She had just brewed a pot of coffee and was holding a fresh mug in both hands. She poured Connor a cup and topped off her own, then invited him to sit at a round table that overlooked the sea. She was wearing a pair of yellow shorts with tight creases and a floral-patterned silk top that looked like a garden of hibiscus. She'd casually swept her hair up on top of her head, where it was pinned with a wooden clip. She hadn't had time to apply any make-up, but from where he sat, she didn't need to.

Tiny waves lapped against the sand and a mild wind ruffled the fronds of the palmettos that had been planted at the edge of the dunes. Connor sipped his coffee, winced at the taste of vanilla and cinnamon, figured she must have ground her own beans at the specialty market in town.

"So, Mrs. Carerra…you said there was one thing you wanted to ask me?" he said when they were finally seated.

"It's nothing, really," she told him. "I insist that you stop calling me Mrs. Carerra. My name is Martina."

He nodded his assent and said, "Of course."

"I don't know if you knew this, but Tony and I were only recently married, so I haven't been Mrs. Carerra for very long. And now…it just doesn't seem right…" Her voice trailed off and she stared out at someone running through the waves at the lip of the beach.

"I understand," Connor said.

She studied him a minute, then said, "You were in the courtroom yesterday."

Her statement caught him by surprise, only because he hadn't seen her there. "I had to go to Charleston anyway, thought I'd look in on the proceedings," he explained.

She nodded, but Connor didn't think she bought it. "So, you know that kid pled guilty to shooting my husband," she said.

"He was rather vocal about it, yes."

They both sipped their coffee then, prolonging an awkward moment as Connor tried to figure out how to get to the point, and Martina Carerra wondering when he would.

"So why are you here?" she finally asked. "You said you wanted to talk about something from the other night."

Fact was, a number of things bothered him about the shooting, heightened by his conversation yesterday with the medical examiner. But he didn't want to get into any of that with Mrs. Carerra, plant the seed that he suspected there may be more to her husband's murder than met the eye. On the other hand, he didn't buy the story about Carerra's murder being a gang initiation thing, or that Justacious Stone had shot him over some traffic altercation. Or a racial insult.

Instead he dodged her question and just said, "Tell me about Tony."

"Tony?" She said the name as if she were trying on a dress that no longer fit. She took a deep breath and said. "What do you want to know?"

"I'm just curious about him," Connor said. "How you met, what he did, what sort of man he was."

She looked at him through narrow eyes that seemed unforgiving. "I know what you're thinking," she said warily. "You think Tony died because of something he did, or maybe someone he knew. But you're wrong."

"I'm not here to pry, or to accuse him—"

"Good, because there's no point," she told him. "He'd dead, and the little prick who shot him is behind bars. End of story."

It was obvious she didn't yet know what had happened to Justacious Stone last night in his cell. "One would think so," Connor said. "And I get the who, what, when, and where. But what bothers me is *why*. Specifically, why that kid shot your husband."

Martina took a deep breath, let it out slowly. She massaged the ridge of her nose with her fingertips, then looked up and shook her head. "Last Friday afternoon, the day of the shooting, Tony took the car into town," she told him. "He went to the market, mailed some post cards. He was driving along one of the side streets—narrow and clogged with cars—when all of a sudden, a little truck pulled out in front of him. Tony said he almost hit him and laid on the horn, and knowing Tony, he probably gave him the finger, too. Anyway, I think the driver of the truck may have been this Stone kid, and later he must've seen Tony go into your bar."

"You think he shot your husband because he flipped him the bird?" Connor wondered if she actually believed this to be true, or if she was just telling herself a story to give the murder a reasonable explanation.

She lifted a shoulder in a shrug, sipped her coffee. "That's the only thing I can think of," she said.

"Did you get a good look at him?" he asked her. "The shooter?"

"I wasn't in the car."

"I mean Friday night. At the bar."

She shook her head. "It happened so fast, and all I was thinking about was Tony."

"What do you remember about that night? When he was shot?"

She lowered her head into her hands, and for a moment he thought she was going to burst into tears. Eventually she looked up and said, "Not much more than what you already know. We were standing there, listening to the music, watching the crowd. Tony was leaning against the railing and I was standing next to him. He started to say something about maybe renting a boat so we could poke through the marshes or along the waterway, when I heard this loud bang. Before I knew what happened Tony was lying on the floor, and then I was kneeling there next to him."

Connor considered what she was saying. He'd seen and heard virtually the same thing, albeit from a different vantage point. The Carerras had been standing at the railing, just as she had said, and Justacious Stone had been no more than twenty feet away. "He was either a great shot, or a really bad one," he said.

"Whatever," she replied, suddenly sounding tired. "They arrested the guy, and he's already pled guilty."

"That's right, but there's something else now that doesn't ring true," he said. "Justacious Stone is dead."

A sharp look of puzzlement spread across her entire face, from her wrinkled brow to her narrowed eyes. She really *hadn't* known.

"He died in his cell sometime yesterday afternoon," Connor told her, then explained what Lincoln Polk had told him last night, that the kid had been stabbed with a missing shiv.

"What on earth...how could that be?" she wondered aloud, a look of horror in her eyes.

"Sounds to me like the kid had a price on his head," Connor said with a deliberate shrug. "He'd already opened his mouth in the courtroom, and maybe someone was worried he might keep talking."

"But...he was just a kid—"

"A kid who maybe knew too much."

"Too much about what?"

"Good question," he said.

She said nothing for a while, just gripped her cup in both hands while she studied the coffee gently swirling within. Finally she said, "And this ties in with Tony how?"

"Mrs. Carerra…Martina," he said, feeling his way through what he was about to tell her. "I really don't know what to think at this point. But I learned a long time ago never take to things at face value."

Another silence, but this time she was studying his face, not her coffee. "Who are you, really?" she said, adding almost as an afterthought, "Why are you here? I think I deserve the truth."

Now it was Connor's turn to study her. It was there in her tired eyes: a need to know what he was thinking, no more bullshit about him owning a bar and being a beach bum and all that. So he told her his story, or at least the *Cliff Notes* version—just enough to let her know why his interest in her husband's life went beyond popping a couple of Heinekens for him a few nights ago. He told her how at one time he'd tidied up death scenes for Palmetto BioClean and had pieced together a murder case that the local police had gotten wrong. Eventually he got around to his own heartache and loss, how his latest attempt at playing sleuth had resulted in his fiancé slipping her ring off her finger and hurling it across the room at him. His entire world had flipped at the poles and he'd lost all equilibrium, like an object floating aimlessly in a vacuum that was devoid of gravity.

Martina Carerra considered everything he told her, then said, "And all this leads you to think there's more to my husband's death than a case of road rage?"

"Do you?" he pressed her.

She rose from her chair, walked over to the front window and pressed her face up against the screen. She stood there for a long while, then turned around and glared at him, fury flaring in her eyes. "How could you possibly think my husband had anything to do with…with his own death?"

"I didn't say that," Connor answered quickly. "But I do believe it goes beyond a random act of violence."

She took a deep breath, wiped her forehead with a napkin. Then she folded her arms across her chest and studied him with a dark glare. "All right, Jack," she said. "What can I tell you about Tony? He was a good, decent, caring man who worked hard. He hardly ever drank more than a beer or two, was a good lover, made me laugh, held my hand, made me feel wanted and appreciated and not so alone—"

"I'm terribly sorry, Martina—this really wasn't a good idea." Connor started to rise from his chair, but she motioned for him to sit back down.

"You're right, but here we are. You want to know about Tony, so tell me what you're looking for."

Shit: this was not the way he wanted this to go. He looked into her eyes and said, "All I'm looking for is a little background. Where your husband came from, how long you've known him, how you met. That sort of thing."

She drummed her fingers on the edge of her chair. Was it nerves or grief? Maybe something more?

"We met three, maybe four months ago. Not a long courtship, I know, but it was one of those instant attraction things. I had gone into Staples, of all places, looking to make some copies and the machine jammed. He came over and fixed it for me."

"He worked there?"

She laughed. "No, he wrote software for a company that did a lot of subcontracting work. Government, small businesses, schools. That sort of thing. He was making print-outs of some sort of presentation."

"Did he ask you out?"

A smile crossed her face. "I gave him my card, figured I'd never hear from him again. But he texted me that afternoon, invited me to dinner. He picked me up and we talked the entire night. All the way through dinner, and all the way home. I'd never met a man who liked to talk like that, and not just about himself. In fact, he hardly said a word about himself the entire evening, which I remember thinking was refreshing."

"Was it love at first sight?"

"Close to it," she said, and Connor detected a note of sadness in her voice. "Part of his job required him to install the software the company sold, so he was always flying all over the place. When we got married, he promised me that when he was able to clear some time we'd get away for a week. Just the two of us. This was supposed to be that trip."

"What about before the two of you met?" he asked her. "Had he been married before? Did he have any kids?"

She shook her head. "Tony said this was his first time to the altar, but he admitted he'd been close once before. His fiancé died in an accident."

"What kind of accident?"

"I don't know. He didn't seem to want to talk about it, so I didn't push him."

"What about family or friends? Anyone from his past?"

She rolled her eyes just enough to show she was growing tired of his questions. "He said his mother was dead, his father was God-knows-where. He was born in Texas, lived in New Orleans for a while. Went to college there—Tulane, just before Katrina. He didn't like to dwell much on the past, said he was more interested in his future with me."

"So you have no knowledge of his life before the day you two met." It was a statement, not a question.

She shot him a frosty look. "That seems so impossible to you?" she said.

Connor could see it in her eyes: a brief flicker of anger. "This is not an interrogation, Mrs. Carerra. Martina. I just want to get things straight in my mind."

"Well, that's all I know, and a lot more than I wish to remember right now."

Now it was his turn to be silent. He had pressed this as far as he could, and he wanted to let the moment cool. Mrs. Carerra was still dangerously close to the precipice of grief, and he didn't want to be the one to push her over.

"I appreciate how honest and open you've been," Connor told her. "And if I've over-stepped...well, I apologize."

"No problem," she said. "But I'm afraid I'm just very distracted right now. I'm sure you understand."

He assured her he did and stood up to go. "When are you heading home?" he asked as she walked him to the door.

"Probably tomorrow," she answered. "There's still some legal matters I have to deal with, lots of red tape I never possibly envisioned. I'm not in any particular hurry to go home to an empty house."

Connor did not envy her for the upheaval she was going to endure over the coming months. "I'm sorry your trip down here didn't turn out as you had planned," he told her.

"Such is life," Mrs. Carerra said wistfully. She opened the door and held it for him as he stepped outside into the glaring sun. "I never thought I'd have to identify my husband on a cold steel table."

He stood there, not quite knowing how to react, then said, "Who made you do that?"

"The state cops. I think you call them SLED down here."

"I'm sorry you had to go through that," Connor said, his mind bouncing like those lottery balls all over again.

"It was difficult," she said as she wiped a tear from her eye. "But it gave me one last chance to say good-bye to him."

"And did you?"

"He looked so...so peaceful lying there," she said. "Just like he was sleeping."

Connor said nothing further as he continued down the stairs toward his Jeep. When he reached the bottom, he raised a hand in farewell, a wave she returned with a waggle of fingers before disappearing back inside the house.

CHAPTER 14

Fifteen minutes later Connor was sitting out on his landing, feet propped up on the rail, a bottle of cold spring water resting on the floor beside him. So was his cell phone. On his lap was an oversized book of black-and-white photos of Charleston, and on top of that was an invoice from the company that supplied the plastic cups and straws for the bar. The reverse side of it was blank, and that's what he was staring at now as he listened to the squawk of gulls lifting off from the dunes across the road.

His brain was at that familiar place where there were enough unconnected dots that he needed to visualize them in physical form. In the center of the page he wrote "Tony Carerra," and circled it. Next, in the upper left quadrant of the page he scribbled "Dr. Dillon," followed by the notation "victim deceased 4-8 hrs prior to accident." Connor then circled that entry and drew a line between the two names. He thought for a second, staring out at the ocean without really seeing it. Sometimes the mind needs to work just beyond what the eye can see, and that's what he had going on right now. Almost without thinking he wrote "Justacious Stone" in the upper right quadrant, along with the words "age 16, pleaded guilty, stabbed (killed?) in cell." He etched a dark line between him and Carerra, going over it several times with the pencil just to emphasize the connection between them.

Next, he moved to the bottom right corner of the sheet of paper, where he wrote "Martina Carerra" and connected her with a solid line to "Tony Carerra." He scribbled the words "positive visual ID night of murder?" and then, almost as an afterthought, he added "no history before 3 yrs. ago."

When Connor was finished, he looked at the bare diagram he had drawn. At this point it was simple, but he knew from previous experience that it would fill itself in as each new element came to light. Still, at the moment he was satisfied with what he was looking at. He studied each cluster of notes on the page, scribbling in some details or questions as he allowed his brain to sift through what he already knew or suspected. And as he did this, the thought became clearer and clearer: there was far more involved here than a random shot fired by a local 16-year-old kid named Justacious Stone.

Connor had no idea how long he'd been sitting there, but it must have been a while, because when he reached for his bottle of water it was warm. He checked his watch: almost one o'clock. He'd totally lost himself in the process, allowing his mind to spread out through the scenario like batter filling the crevasses of a waffle iron. Now, as he physically pulled his numb feet off the balcony railing and straightened his back, his phone rang.

He hadn't expected to hear back from Kat Rattigan so soon, but he recognized the number on the screen and quickly answered. "Hey, Kat…what's up?" he asked.

"What's up is I came across another thing or two on your Carerra pal—"

"You've already done more work on this than I asked," he said.

"Inquiring minds want to know."

Connor took a swig of warm water and said, "Fill me in."

"Okay, here goes. I called a friend at the South Carolina DMV, who talked to a friend of his at the Mississippi Department of Public Safety. I owe him big time now, which isn't necessarily a good thing. Anyway, seems Tony Carerra used legitimate birth records to get his Mississippi license three years ago. According to the certificate, Tony Carerra was born in Crockett County, Texas, thirty-nine years ago. Little town of Ozona, to be exact."

"Good work," Connor said.

"What did you expect?" Kat laughed. "But that's just the start. I had a hunch, so I made a call to the county records office out there and they dug up an old death certificate. You'll never guess who it's for."

"Tony Carerra. I'll bet he died in childbirth, or as an infant."

"Age ten, actually. Cause of death is listed as drowning. That was twenty-nine years ago."

"Ten plus twenty-nine equals thirty-nine."

"The man's a math whiz," she said. "And you'll never guess what else I found."

"Let me try." Connor could feel this one now; it was taking shape right before his eyes. "The last time anyone requested a copy of the kid's death certificate was…"

"…A little over three years ago," she finished Connor's sentence. "There's no record of where the death cert was sent, but you can figure it out."

"Carerra was a ghost," he said.

"We call them cut-outs in the business," she told him. "Look, Jack…when I found out about this kid, the young Tony Carerra, I called the police chief out there in Ozona. Figuring the memory of a small town dies hard. As it turns out, the chief's still around. I figure him to be sixty if he's a day, and man, does he talk like a Texas cliché on steroids. I explained that I was interested in Carerra and the circumstances surrounding his death. After all, it's a small town, and I figured everyone who lives there's got to know everyone else's business."

Sounded just like Folly Beach. "So what did you find out?" Connor asked.

"What I found is that Ozona is like a lot of other small towns across America. Lots of typical things happen, all the time. Car crashes, bar brawls, drug busts, all that shit. But the old chief, accent and all, he remembered something about Tony Carerra, after all these years."

"I'll bet the kid had a close childhood buddy."

"Damn!" Kat Rattigan sounded truly disappointed. "You've already figured this all out."

"I'm just making it up as you go," Connor said. "So go on."

"Okay, sure. And you're right. The chief, he's a career man named Holbrook, he was a beat cop on the force when young Tony drowned. He remembered it, 'cause everyone made such a big deal about it. Seems one day Carerra went hiking in an arroyo, flash flood came roaring through and swept him away. It was a local tragedy, especially since no one found the body for months."

"You mentioned Carerra had a close friend," Connor pressed him.

"Actually, you mentioned it, and I said 'damn,'" Kat corrected him. "But you're correct. He did have a friend. From what Chief Holbrook told me, those two kids were almost inseparable."

"Did your friendly local police chief remember this kid's name?"

"Not right away, but he called me back thirty minutes later," she said, sounding triumphant. "The boy's name was Daniel Parra."

"I'm sure young Tony had lots of childhood friends. What's so special about this kid that the chief would remember him?"

"Because he totally dropped out of sight not long after his friend drowned. His mother and father split up, and Daniel Parra and his mom left town. Moved to Louisiana, is what the chief said."

Connor recalled that Martina Carerra had mentioned her husband had lived in New Orleans for a time. "Did they suspect him in Tony's death?"

"The chief said there was no indication of foul play, so I don't think so," Kat told him.

He thought on this for a moment, then told her that Tony Carerra supposedly had attended Tulane University. "Don't suppose you could check that out?" he said.

He heard a voice in the background, the playful giggling of a child. "No problem," she told him. "I just want to tell you that whatever you're involved with, please keep one thing in mind."

"You're still on the clock?"

"Smartass," she quipped. "What I'm saying is, when a person pretends to be someone he's not and then ends up with a bullet in the back…well, just watch yourself."

"Thanks, Kat. But I really don't think this thing is that dire."

"All I'm saying is keep in mind what happened last time," she said, the words of impunity heavy in her voice.

He thought about asking what she meant by that, whether she was talking about that dark night in the pines on Pelican Creek. But the dead air that hit his ear indicated she'd already hung up on him, leaving him to ponder what she had just told him.

The afternoon was warm and Connor dozed off in the shade that had swept across his landing. When he awoke, the sun had moved further toward the west, and a thin film of sweat had formed on his face and neck. With all the speed of a banana slug he rose from his chair and went inside to find his keys. He refilled Clooney's water bowl and said, "Sorry boy, but it's too hot for you to come with me," then locked the door and headed down to where he'd parked his Jeep.

It was a quick ten-minute trip along the east shore road, and he pulled off the road into the same driveway in which he'd parked just hours before. He was hesitant to come back out there, but a question was burning a hole in his brain, and he knew he wouldn't be able to let go of it until he had an answer. And only Mrs. Carerra could provide it.

The first thing he noticed as he cut the engine was that the white SUV was gone. A sense of disappointment was overridden by anticipation as he got out of the Jeep. He glanced around, then climbed the stairs to the gallery and knocked, waited, knocked again. He peered through the screen as he'd done earlier, but saw and heard no one. He tried knocking one more time, waiting a good thirty seconds in case Martina Carerra was in the back of the house. When she still didn't show Connor finally turned to leave, and that's when he noticed that the nylon screen had been punched in just above the doorknob, leaving just enough room for a hand to squeeze through. He tried to recall whether it had been like that when he'd been out here earlier, but he wasn't sure he would have even noticed.

Connor reached through the screen and felt the knob turn easily in his hand. The house was located on a secluded stretch of beach, but it was right off the main road and an easy target for a quick smash-and-grab. He wondered if he'd stumbled upon something like that, and as he pulled the door open he again called out, "Mrs. Carerra?" Once more he waited for the slightest of sounds, but when none came, he stepped inside the screened gallery and eased the spring-loaded door closed behind him.

During Connor's last visit he and she had remained out in the sun-washed gallery. Now, as he again called out her name, he stepped through the French doors into what would be called a great room. The walls were painted in light tropical pastels—lilac, yellow, aquamarine—and the space was filled with wicker furniture with cushions designed around a tropical motif. A kitchen area was set off toward the back, with a central island separating it from the dining area, where six wooden chairs were pushed in around a matching table.

He slowly made his way around the room, picking up a three-ring binder that contained menus from restaurants throughout Folly Beach. Next to the telephone he found a pad of paper on which were scribbled a bunch of numbers, none of which made any sense to him. A tourist map of Folly Beach and the surrounding coastline had been unfolded on a cocktail table, and someone—Connor presumed it was Martina Carerra—had drawn a dark "X" on a low-lying island tucked into the marsh southwest of town. The Carolina Lowcountry was peppered with these little scrub-covered hummocks, most of them only a few acres in size and just a few feet above sea level, their shores defined by lazy rivulets and tidal eddies that wound through the salt water grasses and pluff mud.

The "X" had been marked on an island that was roughly shaped like an axe, with a long handle-like extension and then a bulky, squarish blade at one end. Connor studied the map closely, found some small print that said its name was Hatchitch Island. A quick calculation told him it measured about a half mile long east-west, and two hundred yards across at its widest point. The purpose of the "X" was lost on him, but what he found even more curious was that someone also had drawn a small circle on the map, just a couple blocks south of the main street that ran through town. Right across from the beach, at the precise spot where The Sandbar was located.

He set the map back where he'd found it and kept looking around. Just off the great room was the master bedroom, and it looked as if Martina had been interrupted while packing. Two matching suitcases were lying open on the bed, with hastily sorted piles of clothes lying next to them. But that was where any semblance of order ended, since the bedroom was a disaster area. Other clothes and shoes and swimsuits and towels were scattered all over the floor. A stack of magazines seemed to have been hurled into a corner, and it looked as if someone had pushed a pile of hardcover books off the nightstand. Similarly, a collection of shells appeared to have been swept off the top of the dresser across the room, with some spare change mixed in. And now that he took a closer look, it seemed as if the clothes on the bed had just been dumped there as if someone had been going through the open drawers. He stood there in the doorway, wondering whether Mrs. Carerra had thrown a fit of anger in here, or if there had been an argument? And if so, with whom?

Connor moved around the room slowly, taking it all in. He pawed through what was left in the open drawers, which wasn't much. There were two small closets, his and hers, one with its door wide open and empty hangers dangling from the wooden rod. Some T-shirts had been stacked on the upper shelf, along with a small back pack and a high-end digital camera. Men's and women's beach sandals—those that hadn't already been scattered around the room—lay on the closet floor, next to a steel safe that was bolted to the porcelain tile. The door to the safe was wide open, and Connor crouched down to look inside. He tried to figure out whether it had been pried open, or if it even had been used at all. That's when he noticed something flashy on the floor behind it, something that looked like the key that had fit the old attic door in Connor's childhood home up in Michigan.

He picked it up and turned it over in his hand. The key was about three inches long and a little more than a half-inch wide and appeared to be made from polished brass. It was heavy and thick, way too thick to fit into the slot in the attic door lock. Then he noticed a small notch where the circular handle met the base of the key, a notch just wide enough for his fingernail to fit. Acting on a hunch he gave it a slight tug, and out popped the flat plug of a standard USB flash drive.

Connor slid the slotted drive back and forth a few times as he looked at it more closely. It clearly was an external memory device, cleverly designed to look like a skeleton key. Maybe a cheap *tchotchke* of some sort, like a marketing token handed out by a sales rep. But the more Connor looked at it, the more he wondered what sort of information might be stored on the miniaturized drive that was designed to slide up inside the key, out of sight.

Without giving it too much thought he slipped the thumb drive into the front pocket of his cargo shorts and stood up. The principled side of his brain told him he should leave it where it was; whatever it contained could be evidence in a homicide investigation. He weighed that knowledge against his own curiosity about what was on it and decided no one would miss what they didn't know existed.

He started to turn around just as he sensed—rather than saw—a shadow move across the edge of his vision. But this awareness of motion came a fraction of a second late, as something hard came down on the back of his head, sudden and quick. Connor felt only a sharp, dull explosion in his brain as he pitched forward into the closet. A liquid dizziness swept through him as he struck the base of his skull on the corner of the safe and a heavy blackness engulfed his world.

CHAPTER 15

When he awoke his head was screaming with an explosive pain that pulsed from his crown to his jaw. His arm was twisted and his right ankle ached from where it had buckled beneath him. He felt a trickle of something sticky—probably blood—on his face, and a fleeting thought reminded him that if he was bleeding, he couldn't be dead.

Connor slowly pushed himself up off the floor. He massaged his forehead and the base of his skull and blinked himself awake—or at least back to a raw sense of consciousness. A sharp agony fueled a wave of nausea as vague questions struggled to form in his brain. Who had cracked him across the base of his skull? What had they used as a weapon? It felt like a nuclear tire iron, but more likely it was a crowbar or a baseball bat. Or maybe a boot. Whoever his attacker was, had he already been hiding in the house when Connor came in and started nosing around? Maybe a burglar, looking for cash and jewelry? He dumped that theory as soon as it crossed his mind, figuring this was much more complex than that, most likely connected to what happened last Friday night.

He wondered how long he had been out, and when Martina Carerra might return. A quick look at his watch answered the first part of that question, and the sound of tires skidding to a halt in the driveway outside filled in the rest. It was quarter to four, and the lady of the manor had just pulled up.

Connor quickly ran his hands over his clothes and face, hoping he didn't look too disheveled or bloody. He checked for the USB drive in his pocket, breathed a sigh of relief when he realized it was still there. That told him whoever had assaulted him either hadn't been looking for it, or just hadn't found it. Either way, he was struck by a quick moral dilemma: hang on to the skeleton key or put it back where he found it? But now was no time for a lengthy ethical debate; Martina Carerra had to have seen his Jeep parked in the driveway and would be coming up the stairs any second.

"Hello?" she called up from the driveway below.

Any sense of integrity slipped from Connor's brain as easily as it had appeared. He hurried out into the gallery and opened the front door. "Mrs. Carerra," he called down to her as she came up the walk with a reusable grocery bag in her hand. "I had to come out this way again, and remembered I had one more thing to ask you."

She looked up at him, removed her sunglasses. "Is that a fact?" she said.

"The door was open and I thought I heard you inside," he explained. "I'd just let myself in when you arrived; you must have been right behind me."

Martina thought about this, gave a resigned nod. What was done was done. She walked around to the foot of the stairs and started up just as Connor came down them.

"You say the front door was open?"

"Actually, the screen next to it was torn," he corrected himself. "Like I said, I thought I heard a noise, so I was going to take a quick peek in case someone was ripping you off."

"And no one was, I take it," she said, not doing much to hide her annoyance. Or was it suspicion?

"I wouldn't know," Connor told her. He didn't want to suggest that her place was a disaster zone just in case she had left it that way. But someone had been here—someone besides him—and that simple fact deserved attention. "I think you should call the police, and maybe let the property manager know they may need to install new locks and screens on the front door."

She stared at him, then nodded. "I'll do that," she said.

With that she brushed past him, up the stairs. She hesitated briefly at the front door and studied the ragged screen, then pushed it open and disappeared inside. For a second Connor felt guilty letting her go into the house alone, but he was sure that whoever had assaulted him was long gone. He also wanted to be on the road by the time Martina had found the mess in the bedroom and figured him for it.

Connor climbed into the Jeep, backed out onto the narrow shore road, and headed back into town. He parked in his space beneath the drinking deck and made his way up to the bar, where Julie was already slicing up fruit for the evening's cocktails.

"Well, well," Julie greeted him with a broad grin. "Look what the cat dragged in."

"Better late than never," Connor said, wincing at the pain that was still gripping his skull.

"Not if you're expecting a death row pardon," she said.

It took a second for that one to sink in; then he said, "Gotta go change into my barkeep's uniform. I'll be down in five minutes and make up for all my sins."

"Promises, promises," she clucked as he mounted the stairs to his attic apartment two at time.

He was true to his word: dry shorts, dry shirt, Sandbar parrot hat, worn with the bill in front, the way baseball players intended. When he came back down she nodded her approval, then slid a cutting board full of mangoes in front of him. "Have at 'em," she said. "It's your turn to smell like fruit cocktail."

"You're going to make someone a great mother someday," he told her as he picked up a paring knife and started slicing.

"Not in this lifetime," she laughed, with a bite that suggested she really meant it.

They set about their regular routines then, chopping, slicing, mixing, and pouring until about five-thirty. That's when Julie—out of the blue—announced, "He's back."

Connor wasn't really paying much attention, letting his mind travel over all the random info he'd picked up during the day. So she said it again, even louder this time, tugging on his arm.

"Who's back?" Connor finally asked, snapping his brain back to the present.

"Look over there—not now, just do it natural." She nodded her head toward the edge of the road where a dozen cars were parked off the pavement, even though the signs said not to do so until after six.

"What are you talking about?" he said. "I don't see anything."

"There's a man in that Tahoe over there, the dark blue one," she said, her voice just above a whisper. "He was parked there when I arrived, looking over this way. I gave him a hard stare and he took off, but now he's back."

"And this means what?" Connor asked innocently, although the hairs on the back of his neck had started to twitch.

"Well, maybe it means nothing," Julie said as her knife sliced through a mango and bit the cutting board beneath it. "But I grew up in Brooklyn, and whenever a car was parked out in front of someone's house with someone in it and the motor running, especially on a hot day like today, they weren't listening to a ballgame."

"So who do you think this guy is?" he asked.

"I figured you'd be on top of that one," she replied.

Connor gave her a sideways glance, but said nothing. Over the months he'd learned that Julie was like a dog that refused to let go of something it held in its teeth. He'd called her Spike just once, and she'd almost punched him for it.

And she was right: the blue Tahoe was sitting there with its motor running, which meant the AC was cranking. It stayed there for a good half hour, well after the first group of happy hour drinkers stumbled up the stairs and placed their orders. That was the beginning of the first wave, and things got pretty busy pretty soon after that, with a run on—of all things—banana rum punch. Whenever something like that happened Connor figured one of the party boats had been pushing a certain type of drink that day, and often the passengers—already half in the bag—would disembark with a taste for just one more. Either that or it was Jungian collective consciousness at work, something he'd heard about in rehab but dismissed as total horseshit.

Whatever it was, tonight he ran through his stock of bananas in near-record time, at which point mango rum punch suddenly became all the rage. Julie was down at the other end of the bar doing her "Name That Tune" thing, while Connor entertained his customers with a version of saw-the-magician's-assistant-in-half trick, only he substituted his last banana for the assistant. And by the time he had a moment to glance over again at the blue Tahoe, it was gone.

Several hours later, during a light drizzle that began a little after eight, Jimmy Brinks shuffled in and sat down on a lone open stool at Connor's end of the bar. He looked as if he hadn't shaved since the last time he'd been there, and it quickly became apparent that he hadn't showered, either.

"Double Jack, no ice," he grumbled as he settled into his seat. "In a glass."

Connor had the glass ready and waiting and poured a healthy measure of Tennessee whisky into it. He set it in front of the man, then tossed a couple of empty bottles into the recycle bin under the counter.

Jimmy Brinks took a long, slow swallow. He smacked his lips once, made a low grunting sound, then said, "Hook, line, and sinker."

Connor took his time responding, but finally turned around and said, "Say what?"

"I figured this one would reel you in."

"What're you talking about?"

Jimmy Brinks was not the sort of character you really wanted to encourage. He had a reputation for drinking too much and saying the wrong thing to the wrong people, which all too often ended up in broken bottles and furniture and teeth. Connor had made the mistake of engaging him only once and, from then on, had ignored any hooks that Brinks tried to bait. But tonight, for some reason, was different.

Brinks leaned forward, clamped his hand on Connor's wrist. "You drop enough bait in the water, you're bound to catch somethin'. Don't ask me how, but this I know."

Connor leveled a hard look at him, firmly pulled his wrist away. He leaned across the bar, until his nose was less than a foot from Brinks'. He caught a good whiff of sweat and body oil, but didn't let on. "And just what the hell do you think you know?"

"Enough," Jimmy Brinks growled, letting out a long, low belch. If anything, the man functioned at the basest level of crude. "For one thing, I know that Cecil Maines was out last Friday, fishing down around Hatchitch," Brinks said. "And I know he's pretty fuckin' afraid for his sorry-ass life right about now."

Hatchitch was the same stretch of barely elevated earth that had been marked with an "X" on Martina Carerra's map, the island of dredged pluff mud and oyster shells that Connor remembered was roughly shaped like an axe. Hence its name which, in the colloquial Gullah dialect, meant *hatchet*. Connor had encountered this Cecil Maines just once, remembering him as black guy with gold studs in his ears and 18 carat bling encircling most of his fingers. The story was that he was a local fisherman who supposedly knew all the best inlets and eddies to catch red drum and bluefish and shad. But he also owned a forty-foot cigarette boat with twin 350s hanging off the back, low and sleek and fast. Anyone who knew him would tell you he did not use the vessel for casual deep-sea fishing excursions.

"And why would that be?" Connor asked, maintaining a measure of tough-guy composure, but already realizing that Brinks was telling him something important, only doing it in his own way. "Afraid for his ass, I mean."

Brinks stared at his glass, didn't look up. Eye contact clearly was for losers. "That's the point—he ain't sayin' nothin', except that he was out there. And whatever he *did* see is causing him to shit grits and gravy."

That was an image Connor knew he could never un-see, so he said, "And you're sure this was Friday night?"

"My intel ain't ever wrong." Brinks lifted his shoulder in a shrug and picked up his glass. He drained the contents, then made a show of dealing a few bills onto the counter as he stood up. "Do with it what you will," he said as he shuffled off.

Connor kept his eyes on him until he slipped into the shadows and disappeared. Whenever Jimmy Brinks came into the bar, he made the local customers nervous, and he was one regular Connor wouldn't mind never seeing again. Of all the strange characters populating the streets of Folly Beach, this dude was one of the strangest.

Still, he wondered just what it was that Cecil Maines had seen out on Hatchitch Island. Except for one chance encounter, Connor knew the guy by reputation only. He was not the sort to set foot in a place like The Sandbar, and he'd only seen him on the streets a couple times. There was an unspoken speculation of Maines' illicit line of work, fueled by the lightning-fast nature of his boat. Rumor had it the feds were keeping a keen eye on his movements but so far had not been able to catch him transporting anything other than friends and his family, and an occasional cooler of red drum or flounder. But that didn't keep the D.E.A. guys from trying, and the prevailing wisdom said that one of these days their diligence would pay off. Until then, if something needed to be moved fast, without a trace, Maines was the man to see.

In any event, whatever he was doing out on Hatchitch Island was his own business, and Connor figured it was safer for everyone if it stayed that way.

A few minutes later when he had a spare moment he reached under the bar and dug through a pile of old marketing flyers that advertised everything from sunset champagne cruises to all-day scuba excursions. He finally found the road map he kept around for tourists who wanted to know how to get down to Kiawah or out to Fort Sumter. He opened it on the counter and ran a thumb from Folly down to Hatchitch, which was only about ten miles southwest of town as the crow flies. It was located at the edge of a broad sound formed by the Kiawah River, in a relatively isolated stretch of marsh that was well off the beaten path of most boaters and fishermen. Cecil Maines easily could have been out there the other night, doing whatever he was doing by the light of the moon.

Connor tipped his head upwards, as if some bit of wisdom was pasted on the spinnaker ceiling. Whatever it was—whatever Maines had seen—it had caused the guy to be, in Jimmy Brinks' words, pretty fuckin' afraid for his life.

CHAPTER 16

Martina Carerra dropped by the bar a little past eleven. She seemed tipsy again, and for a second Connor was worried about letting her loose on the road in her rental car. But she waved off his concerns and assured him she'd enlisted the aid of a taxi to take her back to the rental house.

"I'm going home to Biloxi tomorrow and I just wanted to thank you for everything you've done," she told him.

"No thanks necessary," he replied, his guilty mind immediately going to the flash drive he had shifted into the pocket of the shorts he was wearing. Wherever he went, it went.

She stood there a moment, not knowing what else to say, not appearing ready to leave. Then she added, "And just so you know, I did call the cops. Turns out there *was* a break-in."

"I thought something seemed wrong," he replied with a nod. "Did they send someone out to take a look?"

"In fact, they did. They dusted for prints, but it didn't look like they took anything. Oddest thing."

"Like the sign says, it's the Edge of America."

"Whatever that means." She inhaled deeply, let her breath out slow and measured. "Well, I guess I'd better be going."

Connor heard someone on the other side of the bar call for a couple of Coronas, but he sensed that this might be his last chance to speak with Martina. "Mrs. Carerra," he said, a hesitant hitch in his voice. "You mentioned the other day that your husband grew up in Texas. Do you happen to remember where?"

"Excuse me?" she said, wrinkling her brow.

"Texas," Connor repeated. "Did your husband ever mention a place called Ozona?"

"I wouldn't have a clue," she said as she turned to leave.

"He ever mention someone named Daniel Parra?"

That caused her to stop in her tracks and glance back at him. From the look on her face it appeared he'd hit a nerve. She stared at him for a second, then said, in a measured tone, "Good night, Mr. Connor." And with that she marched out of the bar, with a bit of a noticeable wobble.

Jessica Snow bumped into her at the entrance, but Martina Carerra hardly seemed to notice as she disappeared into the night. Jessica watched her storm out, then navigated her way up to the bar and wriggled onto an empty stool, making herself comfortable. Connor noticed she was alone tonight, at least for now. She was wearing a thin, gauzy beach wrap that barely covered the white one-piece she had on underneath. Her hair was piled loosely on the top of her head, with a few loose fly-aways poking out around the edges.

"Good evening, Miss Snow," Connor greeted her as he rested both hands on the counter. "And how are you tonight?"

"As perfect as perfect can be," she told him. "Have I missed your show?"

"I still have a few tricks up my sleeve," Connor said. "Next act in ten minutes. Meantime, may I get you the usual?"

She nodded, said, "What does it say about a woman when she has a regular drink at a beach bar?"

"Just that she knows what she likes."

He turned and picked up the bottle of well vodka, just in time to see Julie flash him the thumb-and-forefinger "O" sign for good luck. He felt his face go red, so he took his time mixing the drink, and by the time he set it in front of Jessica he had his composure back under control.

"Thank you, good sir," she said, stirring it with the plastic cocktail sword he'd put in it.

Just then a woman he knew only as Neptune edged up onto a stool and made herself comfortable. Mid-fifties, sun-scorched skin the color of an old baseball glove, hair that looked like it hadn't seen a brush in months. She was one of the usual suspects who frequented The Sandbar on an almost nightly basis, and Connor fixed her an apple martini, not too sour. He set it on the bar in front of her just as she began to shuffle a deck of miniature tarot cards.

"Good evening, Mr. Jack," she said as she took an immediate sip. It seemed to hit the spot, so she took one more. "Has anyone read your cards lately?"

It was a question she asked every time she came in, and he gave her his standard reply. "I'm afraid I'm not much into that woo-woo stuff."

Fact was, she reminded him of a fortune teller he'd met several years ago named Naomi Walker who, it turned out, also went by the names Alyson Anderson, Valerie Templeton, and Jennifer Drayton. It was a long tale, and part of a bloody backstory that he didn't care to dwell on because it also involved Danielle.

"Oh, you'd be surprised just what these woo-woo cards can tell you," Neptune said in her deep, smoker's voice. "Let's see what they say about you tonight." She began dealing them out on the counter in front of her, carefully studying each one as she turned it off the top of the deck.

"Tell me if you see anything truly amazing," he told her.

She didn't say anything, just continued dealing out the cards. The last one that turned up was an image of what looked like the grim reaper clad in black armor and riding a white horse. The word "Death" was printed at the bottom of the card.

"That doesn't look good," Connor observed as he wiped a spot of moisture off the bar.

"Heavens!" she said, which was the closest he'd ever heard her get to using a swear word. And with that she swept the cards into a pile and folded them back into her tiny deck. She looked visibly shaken by what she had seen and pounded the rest of her cocktail in one gulp.

"Another," she finally said, nodding at her empty cup. "Double the vodka."

Connor did as she asked and set the drink down in front of her. "What did those cards mean?" he asked, somewhat bemused at the reaction she'd had when she'd seen that last one.

"Death, destruction, and mayhem," she said, her voice hardly more than a breath. She took another hefty gulp of her drink and added, "I'd pay attention to what they're saying."

Just then a young couple made their way up the stairs and squeezed onto a couple of stools that had just opened up on the other side of the bar. They looked like young newlyweds on their honeymoon, and Connor guessed they were staying at The Tides, which turned out to be dead-on. They ordered rum and Cokes, and then the young husband asked him if he knew how to get out to Morris Island Light. Connor retrieved a map from under the counter and gave him careful directions, whereupon his bride thanked him and clinked her plastic cup against that of her new husband. Then she interlocked her arm in the crook of his elbow as she took a sip. *Yep,* he thought. *Definitely newlyweds.*

When Connor finally turned his attention back to Jessica, she already was halfway through her bay breeze. It was evident she'd been sitting there studying him, watching the bar, gazing out at the near-full moon rippling on the dark water beyond the sand. Listening to the faint sound of reggae drifting in from some other place a few blocks closer to town. Inhaling the aroma of jasmine drifting through the night on the tropical breeze. Enjoying herself, knowing Connor would get back to her when he had a moment.

Eventually he did.

"Ready for that trick?" he asked her as he came back to where she was sitting.

"I've been waiting, but patience has never been one of my strongest virtues," she confessed.

"Then prepare yourself for the most astounding illusion in all of Folly Beach," he said. He reached under the counter, his fingers fumbling for something, then brought his hand back out. He held it closed like a fist and said, "Any guess what I've got here?"

"A lime?" she shrugged.

What was it with this woman and limes?

"Nope, it's not a lime," Connor said. Then he opened his hand and set the object down on the bar.

She looked at it, her eyes widening as a grin formed on her lips. Its shape, size, and packaging was unmistakable. "A...a condom?" she stammered.

"Sealed tight, see?" he told her. "Now, I want you to pick it up, take a look at it. Go ahead... it's not going to bite you."

Jessica glanced from Connor to the wrapped condom, then gingerly picked it off the counter. She held the little cellophane packet in her hand with the tell-tale, circular form neatly tucked inside. Safely sealed, as he had said. She turned it over, studied the other side, then set it back on the counter. This time when she looked at him, he detected a glimmer of embarrassment in her eyes, maybe something more.

"So we're agreed on what it is, right?"

"Agreed."

"Okay, fine," Connor said as he plucked a cocktail napkin off a stack on the bar. He handed it to her, said, "Now I want you to examine this."

She did as she was told and handed it back.

"I'm going to use it to cover the condom, like this," he explained as he draped the napkin over it. "Now, I want you to wave your hand over it and say the magic word."

Jessica Snow glanced around her to see if anyone else was watching. So far, she was in luck. "Abracadabra?" she asked.

"No. Prophylactic Carolina hyperbolic magic."

"*Pro-phy-lac-tic Car-o-li-na hy-per-bo-lic ma-gic.*" She repeated the words slowly, one syllable at a time, giggling as she moved a hand a few inches above the napkin and wiggled her fingers. As if she truly had a magical touch.

"Excellent," Connor encouraged her. "Now...watch closely." And with that he pinched a corner of the napkin between his thumb and finger and yanked it away.

The condom was gone.

Jessica giggled again, even as her mouth dropped open. "Let me see that napkin—"

He handed it to her, watched as she examined it carefully. Then she handed it back to him, said, "So...are you going to make it reappear?"

"That's another trick altogether," he grinned, raising a single brow.

"Come on...you can't leave me hanging like this—"

"Have dinner with me tomorrow night, maybe I'll show you," he said.

She thought on this one for a moment, then nodded her head as her cheeks grew red. "I just fell for the oldest trick in the book, didn't I?" she asked him.

"Depends on whether you say 'yes,'" Connor said.

"You can get the night off?"

"I know the boss," he told her.

"In that case, I'm looking forward to it," Jessica told him. Then she did something with her eyes, raising and lowering her perfect brows in a Groucho Marx gesture. "There's just one thing," she said.

"And that would be?"

"Well…" she said slowly, a grin forming on her lips as she raised her cup to her lips. "I'm kinda curious to see whether this next trick involves your magic wand."

CHAPTER 17

Next morning Connor was up before the sun. A single broad streak of orange was smeared across the horizon, and the air held the scent of salt, diesel fumes, stale beer, and a thin aroma of citrus blossoms. Somewhere a pot of coffee was brewing but it was not Gilbert's, which Connor knew did not open until seven. He stood on his landing a moment, looking out at the edge of the sea, gingerly massaging the lump that still throbbed at the base of his skull. Clooney made no move to get up, so Connor descended the steps and crossed the road to the beach. When his feet hit the sand, he turned left and began running toward the landmark fishing pier that stretched out into the water. Then he heard a tiny voice say:

"Excuse me...Mister Connor?"

He wasn't even sure he'd heard the words, which sounded like no more than a whisper on the wind. Then he realized the voice was that of a girl, coming from the darkness near an empty PVC rack where kayaks and paddle boards would be rented out later in the day. The girl sounded timid and scared, and a bit nervous.

Connor stopped mid-stride and turned, saw her huddled in a clump of sea grass, her arms hugging an oversized T-shirt to her knees. He couldn't make out who she was, but she certainly seemed to know him. A quick uneasiness gripped him, then reason took hold: why should he be afraid of a little girl?

"Yes?" he said cautiously. "I'm Jack—"

"I saw you come down the stairs, and hoped it might be you," she told him, her dark eyes shrouded with fear.

He recognized her from somewhere, but he couldn't figure out just where. *Give it time—it will come to you*, he thought.

"Mr. Connor...you probably don' remember me..." she said, her voice shivering from anxiety. Certainly not from cold, since even at this hour the temperature was in the low eighties.

Then it all clicked. This was the girl he had talked to the other day at one of the houses out near Cusabo Gut. *What was her name?*

"Em Lee," she said quickly, as if reading his mind. "You were out at my place last Sunday." She forced a tight grin, and that's when he noticed the nasty bruise on the side of her face. Her skin was quite dark, but the bruise was even darker, and threatening to close an eye.

"Who did that to you?" Connor asked her quietly.

"My mama's boyfriend," she answered. Almost sounding embarrassed, as if it somehow was her fault. "His name's Jesry."

"And where is this Jesry now?"

"In bed with my mama."

Connor thought for a moment, wondered how she had come here all the way from her house, a crumbling house he remembered was the color of dried grits. Sagging steps, old tires and wheel rims in the yard. But it was a question that could wait, so he said, "I was just going to get some breakfast."

"I don't have any money," she confessed.

"Don't you worry about that," he told her. "You must be hungry."

She was, but trust was a tough shell to crack. "What about my eye?"

It's more than your eye, Connor wanted to tell her, but didn't. "No one will see it…and besides, it defines your beauty," he smiled. He extended his hand, which she shook tentatively. "Come on…I'm starving."

"But…I rode my bicycle." She pointed at a corroded pair of wheels held together by rust and a chain lying on its side in the sand. "Someone'll steal it if I leave it here."

Not likely, Connor thought, but instead he told her, "It'll be safe upstairs, in the bar."

She regarded him skeptically, but trailed behind him as he thumped the bicycle up the stairs and leaned it against the counter, which was still locked tight from the night before.

"No one will touch it here," he assured her. "I promise."

She nodded as he gave her hand a little squeeze, then let go. They sauntered up the street a couple blocks, propelled by the smells and sounds of the new morning. A block south of Folly Road he cut to the right and wandered through a dirt parking lot where an old shipping container was nestled against a clump of wax myrtles and flowering bottle brush. A pack of feral cats scurried for cover, and something large and menacing seemed to move in the undergrowth as they shuffled toward the old steel box that was set up on cinder blocks.

Fish Bones was neither a restaurant nor a food truck, but it did serve breakfast. The twenty-foot container was painted in bright pastels—pink, orange, and lavender—and was fitted with a propane tank and stove. An open-air lean-to served that extended from one side served as a crude but efficient dining shelter. A half dozen plastic tables and chairs were chained together like convicts on a hard labor gang, and hinged hurricane shutters were propped open by poles in order to keep a breeze blowing through, day and night. Inside, an old woman Connor simply knew as Jo-Jo was already at work scraping fried crud off the griddle.

"What are we doing here?" Em Lee asked, a tentative hitch to her voice.

"No one's going to see you," he assured her.

The girl eyed him warily but didn't argue. Connor invited her to sit down at one of the chained tables, then went up to a window cut into the side of the container and studied a brightly colored menu painted on the corrugated rust.

"Morning, Jo-Jo," he greeted the woman bustling about inside the container, now lining up bottles of hot sauce on the counter.

"Hey, Mr. Jack…you're up awfully early this morning."

"Got a few things to do, figured I'd drop in for the best breakfast in town."

"Didn't anybody ever tell you that only trouble rises before dawn?" she asked him. She was a tall, thin woman with pale, mottled skin that had been cracked and fried from the sun. Wiry wisps of gray hair hanging down to her shoulders, which were thin and bony. She could have been anywhere from sixty to eighty, a carefree remnant of the Summer of Love dressed in tie-dye and flip-flops.

"I'm just looking for the first worm of the day," he replied. "Don't suppose you've got any coffee brewing yet—"

She did, and she poured him a cup. "And how 'bout a smoothie for your friend over there?" Jo-Jo squinted at the girl, said, "Is that Em Lee Rollins?"

"It is," he replied, wondering how she knew the girl. "I think she's hungry."

Jo-Jo smiled, said, "Looks like she could use a bowl of shrimp and grits."

Connor told her that would be great and waited for her to fix the smoothie. Then he walked back over to where Em Lee was seated, her head propped on steepled hands. He set the paper cup in front of her and took a seat across the table. He waited until she took a sip, then asked, "How long has he been doing this to you?"

Em Lee was holding the smoothie cup in her hands, doing her best to hide the bruise to her eye and cheek.

"Just when he drinks," she said. "Thing is, he drinks a lot."

"Is it always this bad?"

"No, sir. This is the worst." She thought on that a moment, took another sip. "You know why he did it? Cuz I wouldn't go and fetch him his stupid beer. I was in my room, minding my business, and he was out in the front room, hollerin' at me. I told him, I'm not his slave."

"Where was your mother?"

"Working. She's a cook up at the jail. I guess that's where he gets it, cuz she does whatever he tells her. Cooks for him, cleans for him, empties the trash for him."

Connor stared into his cup of black coffee for a minute. Then he said, "Why me?"

"What do you mean?" she asked, a look of worry creasing her forehead.

"Well, don't get me wrong, Em Lee. But you came a long way this morning to find me. There's got to be other people who can help you."

"No one else gives a shit," she said. The defiant look in her eyes told him she wasn't the least bit apologetic for her language. "Girl gets beat up, people figure she had it coming. An' they don't want to cross the ghetto banger who done it. Besides, I like your cat, there."

She pointed at his right arm, where a tattoo of a black panther was snarling with menacing eyes.

He smiled at her and said, "Got that one a few years back, in Detroit."

"Reminds me of the movie," she replied, returning his smile. "Saw it three times in one day when it came out. Wish I could run away to Wakanda."

"Me too, some days," he assured her. He crossed his arms over his chest like the salute in the movie, and she did the same. He fell silent then, figuring there was no easy way to ask the next question. But there was no way he couldn't pursue the truth here.

"Has he ever touched you in other ways?" he asked, choosing his words carefully.

Em Lee glanced down at her hands, which she had folded on the table in front of her. "No," she said, her voice little more than a breath of wind. "Not really."

"I'm not sure what 'not really' means," he told her.

"Me neither." She giggled nervously, then sipped some of her smoothie. "He touched me one time, but I told him if he tried it again, I would chop the head off the toad while he was sleepin'."

"Recently?"

"You call last night recent?"

Connor took a deep breath and held it in his lungs. "Does your mother know where you are?" he asked her.

"My mother don't give a shit." Em Lee looked so young—he now guessed she couldn't be more than thirteen—it seemed almost shocking to hear her swear. "I had to get out of there, Mr. Connor. You see that, don't you?"

Yes, he most certainly did. But Em Lee probably had no idea how difficult things could get for her.

"Where's your father?"

She lowered her head again and said, "Doing five to seven up in Bennettsville."

Connor nodded, just as Jo-Jo walked over and set down two paper plates heaped with shrimp and cheese grits and fried eggs. From her apron she produced bottles of ketchup and Cholula sauce, then wandered off when he assured her that there was nothing else they needed. He dribbled some of the sauce on his eggs, then scooped a forkful into his mouth. Once he'd swallowed, he leaned forward and looked hard into her sad eyes. Some people were dealt such a miserable hand in life.

"Do you have any relatives you could stay with?" he asked her.

"I got lots of cousins all over the place, but they got their own shit going on."

"Anyone else?"

"I got an aunt up north, place in North Carolina called Bug Hill. She'd probably let me move in with her, at least for a while."

"What about your mom?"

Her lip started to tremble. "I can't go back there, Mr. Connor. Jesry'll kill me, and Mama won't do nothin' but watch."

Connor decided to let it go for a bit, and they finished breakfast talking about other things. Em Lee seemed like a bright girl with a lot of spark, but months of physical and mental abuse at the hands of a predator had drained much of her spirit. Getting the ogre out of the house would be the easy part; one call to Child Protective Services would take care of that. Extracting Em Lee from her mother's clutches might prove more difficult and painful, but the girl didn't need to know any of that just yet.

As they chatted, he got the distinct impression that no one had ever talked with this young woman as anyone other than a child. Teachers ignored her, neighbors were afraid of the man named Jesry, and her preacher was of the fire-and-brimstone angry God mindset. After she realized Connor wasn't talking down to her she began to open up. She talked about school, friends, television, music and, of course, the Black Panther—all the things that defined her life. By the time he paid Jo-Jo for the food it was as if he was her Uncle Jack and she was his niece, entering high school in the fall with a whole new life ahead of her.

The morning sky was beginning to take on a pale pink hue as they made their way back up the street. Feet that had been dragging before now seemed lighter, and the darkness in Em Lee's eyes had turned brighter. Connor watched her shuffle along, and suddenly he realized she was just a year or two older than his niece Lily would have been today, if she hadn't been shot that night at the convenience store.

Correction: *If Connor hadn't let her get shot.*

"I'm going to make a few calls, set you up with someone you can trust," he told her they walked back toward The Sandbar.

Em Lee nodded. She'd already confessed that she had no idea what she'd expected when she came to see him that morning, except that some inner sense told her it was either that or get beat up by a drunk scumbag. Everyone she knew was terrified of Jesry, and there was no one she could talk to about him. He was the king of Cusabo Gut and ruled with an iron fist and a car full of guns. She understood that Connor could only do so much, but anything was better than nothing. An hour ago she had been a scared teen-aged runaway, afraid of what lay ahead of her, horrified by the prospect of spending going back home. Maybe things wouldn't be quite so bad as she thought.

Halfway up the block Connor slowed his pace, and Em Lee slowed alongside him. Something seemed out of order here, but he couldn't immediately tell what it was. The street looked different than it had when they had walked past here a half-hour ago, and not just because the sun was raising the curtain on a new day.

Then he saw it: parked under a pindo palm at the end of the block was a dark blue Tahoe, with a rental agency sticker on the rear bumper. He was sure it hadn't been there before, when he and Em Lee had wandered past earlier, and while that alone wasn't enough to cause suspicion it was enough to raise a red flag in his mind.

He stopped there on the sidewalk and thought this through. His mind raced back to Iraq, when a dead dog lying on the side of the road could mean the difference between life and death. His squad leader was always telling them *trust your instincts,* and those three words had served him well during his time in the desert.

"Listen, Em Lee," he said, turning to face her. "I want you to do me a favor."

She eyed him warily. "Like what?"

Connor fished his keys out of his pocket. "I want you to take these, go up to my place—it's right up the stairs above the bar—and let yourself in."

"But where are you going to be?"

"There's something I need to check out," he explained. "I'll be up in five minutes."

"Is it something bad?" she asked, picking up on his vibe.

He didn't want to alarm her but the fact was, he didn't really know what this was. If it was anything at all. "Nothing as bad as you went through last night," he told her. "Just let yourself in, turn on the TV. I have a dog named Clooney, but all he'll do is lick you to death. I'll be up in two minutes."

She hesitated, then took the key ring and headed for the stairs that led up to the drinking deck. He waited until he was certain she could not see what was going on; then he ducked down and hurried across the street toward the Tahoe.

It looked like the same vehicle Julie had pointed out to him last night, parked at the edge of the shore road. He could see a person inside, slouched behind the wheel, apparently asleep. Connor crouched behind the SUV and took a photo of the license plate, then moved around to the passenger side and slowly inched forward. When he got to the front door, he raised his eyes just above window level and peered inside. The man at the wheel still seemed to be dozing, a good sign. He had a dark tattoo on his cheek, his arms were dangling at his side, and his head lolled back on his neck. But there was something wrong with this picture, and it took Connor a couple seconds to figure out what it was.

The sleeping man's eyes were open. And the tattoo was not a tattoo at all; it was a large hole torn crudely through the side of his face.

Connor inhaled a big gulp of air and stepped back from the car. *Holy mother of God,* he thought. The man was dead. Whoever he was, for whatever reason he'd been watching the beach bar, he was sitting here in this rental car with a hole through his brain. What the hell was going on here?

Since the Tahoe hadn't been parked here a half hour ago this had to be a recent hit, which meant the shooter very likely was still somewhere nearby. Maybe even watching him right now. A flicker of paranoia began to nip dangerously close at the back of Connor's mind: could the gunman actually be after him? Did he think Connor knew something he wasn't supposed to know? Had Connor stumbled across something the shooter was looking for? And if so, how did he know where Connor lived?

That's when he remembered: he'd just sent Em Lee up to his apartment to wait for him. And if the shooter had Connor in his sights, he might have gone up to his place to wait for him to return, maybe gun down the first person to walk through the front door.

Connor took off on a dead run, sprinting across the street and taking the stairs up to the drinking deck two at a time. He raced through the empty bar, then mounted the steps to his apartment as quietly as he could. When he got to the upper landing he slowed to a crawl, not sure what he might find inside.

The door was closed but not latched. He pushed it open, just far enough to see Em Lee standing in the middle of the room, a look of complete terror etched on her face. She seemed frozen in place, her eyes as wide open as they possibly could be, staring at something on the floor.

"Em Lee?" he said to her, softly.

She didn't move, didn't say a word. She just stood there, then pointed at something that was lying between the couch and the wooden table set in front of it. Connor hadn't seen it when he came in—he was too worried about the girl—but now his brain began to take in all the extraneous elements of this scene. Which meant that he now was able to see what she was gesturing at: sprawled on the hard tile of his small living room was the body of yet another man, a puddle of blood just beginning to form under him.

And Clooney hovering over him, drool dripping from his jowls, raw canine hunger in his eyes.

CHAPTER 18

Connor raced over to where Em Lee was standing, her eyes frozen in a look of chilled fear. He put a comforting arm around her, and that's when she felt confident enough to finally let out a piercing, ear-splitting scream.

"Em Lee," he said as he physically turned her away from the grisly visage of the dead man. "I think you should you wait outside—"

"No! Don't leave me alone!" she screamed. Damn, she had a voice on her. "It's Jesry, I know it. He did this. He came here to kill me."

For a second Connor wondered if what she was saying could be true, quickly realized it was just the raw panic of a terrified girl swept up in a vortex of personal horror. He was certain this had nothing to do with Jesry or Em Lee or her mother; the Tahoe across the street was proof of that. No, this whole scene was of an altogether different nature.

Connor shook his head slowly, then told her, "No, this wasn't Jesry, Em Lee. There's something else going on that has nothing to do with you."

She shot him a look, one that said she'd heard it all before and she knew when adults were bullshitting her. "You don't know Jesry," she insisted.

"No, and I don't want to," he agreed. Then he realized he was forgetting something here, something that could be important. "Did you see who did this?"

Em Lee flashed him a look that suggested he was crazy. "He was like that when I came in here," she said in a fluttery voice that meant she was trying to hold back a flood of tears. She was determined not to let him see her crack, much less cry. "Didn't see him at first, because of your dog. Whoever shot him…well, he was done gone."

"Well then, you see? If your mother's boyfriend had anything to do with this, you think he'd just come in and shoot a stranger, then beat it?"

"Maybe he thought it was you?"

Connor figured whoever had done this damned sure had thought it was him, but Em Lee's mom's boyfriend had not pulled the trigger. But that knowledge did not answer the immediate question, which was: Who was this guy, and what the hell was he doing here in Connor's apartment? Followed close behind by: who had shot him through the head? And then: who was the dead guy in the Tahoe down on the street?

Em Lee's snuffling turned into waves of tears as her resolve finally wore down. She may have been a tough girl, but even the sight of a man with a hole in his head was enough to break down the strongest defense. The sight of death still invaded Connor's dreams at night, even after all these years, so he could only imagine what it must have been doing to this poor girl right now. *Just wait until you try to sleep tonight*, he thought as he steered her toward the front door.

"You gonna call nine-one-one?" she asked him.

"Right now. Just sit tight."

Two minutes later the police arrived. Darnell Evans, one of the officers who'd shown up after Tony Carerra had been shot, was the first on the scene, and now he was looking down at the dead man, shaking his head. Evans was in his late twenties, with red, close-cropped hair and a pinched face that gave him a stupid, anguished look.

"You have any idea who did this?" he asked without looking at Connor.

"Not a clue," Connor told him.

"You recognize him?"

Connor gave the body another quick glance. The man was white, with poorly cropped dark hair that was matted with blood that was starting to dry in the warm, humid air. He was wearing white trousers and a black shirt with red flowers on it that screamed "tourist."

"Never seen him before," he replied.

Darnell Evans shit him an impatient frown, said, "Any idea how he got in?"

"Not a clue," Connor answered tiredly. "The door's always locked."

The officer grumbled something inaudible, then glanced over at Em Lee, who was sitting on the steps outside the front door. He studied her a moment, then looked back at Connor. "So where'd you get the girl?" he asked, the accusation in his words clear and distinct. "She looks what, thirteen, maybe fourteen?"

Connor fought off the impulse to wrap his fingers tightly around Evans' throat. "Give your imagination a rest," he replied. "Her name is Em Lee. I ran into her out on the street and bought her some breakfast."

"I know who she is, Mr. Connor," he continued. "Her mother works up at the county jail. How'd she get into town?"

"Her bicycle is downstairs in the bar," Connor replied. "Someone took a fist to her."

Officer Evans studied her and nodded. "She's going to have quite a shiner for a few days," he said. "Any idea who did this?"

Em Lee stared at the floor and didn't say a word. When the cop realized she wasn't going to rat anyone out, not even the bastard who'd struck her, he turned back to Connor.

"What do you know about this?"

"It's a matter for Child Protective Services," was all Connor told him. Anything Em Lee had told him was revealed in confidence, and he didn't want to break that sense of trust. What he really wanted to know, and figured they'd get around to at some point, was why this dead man was here in his apartment to begin with. He figured it probably had something to do with yesterday's attack out at Martina Carerra's place; maybe this was even the same guy who had assaulted him and then ran off. Maybe he'd figured Connor had found something, like the flash drive that he still carried in his pocket. Whatever the guy was looking for—however he'd figured out where Connor lived—he hadn't found it by the time he was killed.

Lincoln Polk showed up a few minutes later. Connor was glad to see someone he considered a friend, but he knew enough to leave Polk alone while he went through the routine of an official investigation.

"Anybody touch this man?" Polk asked, directing his question to no one in particular.

"No one laid a finger on anyone," Evans answered. "Isn't that right, Mr. Connor?"

The suspicious tone in his voice suggested he was still referring to Em Lee, but Connor let it go. "Evans is right," he said, ignoring the implication. "No one's touched him."

Polk nodded, opened his investigative kit and rummaged through it. He pulled on a pair of nitrile gloves, then took out two plastic bags and secured them over the dead man's hands. He inspected the hole in the back of the victim's head, then drew his glance back toward the front door, where a hole had been shot through the screen, between two louvered panes of glass.

"There's your point of entry," he said.

Connor had been so intent on wondering who the dead man was that he had completely missed the bullet hole in the nylon webbing covering the jalousie window. Now he simply said, "Whoever it was, wasn't messing around."

"You think this is connected to the Carerra thing?" Polk asked him.

"I really don't have a Goddamned clue," Connor said, answered slowly, almost forgetting until now what he'd seen down on the road as he was walking Em Lee back from Fish Bones. "But that's only half the picture."

"What's that supposed to mean?"

"Well, across the street you'll find a blue Tahoe," Connor told him, nodding his head toward the beach road. "You'll find another stiff chillin' out behind the wheel."

Just then two more investigators—a man and a woman from SLED—pulled up in a county car. Within minutes they began their own investigation Connor's apartment, collecting evidence, photographing both scenes from every conceivable angle, dusting the apartment and SUV for prints. Eventually a team of med techs removed both bodies to a pair of ambulances parked in the lot below the bar. A separate medical crew with its own ambulance took Em Lee up to

MUSC to be treated for her injuries and assessed for psychological trauma, from both Jesry's physical assault and walking in on the dead man. An advocate against any kind of domestic violence, Lincoln Polk promised he would do everything in his power to keep her there overnight, and Connor assured her that he'd drop by later to check on her.

Around eleven o'clock the last of the detectives left the scene and the news crews that had traveled down from Charleston were packing up their gear. Polk waited until the cameras and microphones were put away before he walked with Connor back to his apartment, where a length of yellow crime scene tape now stretched across the front door.

"You're not going to lock me out, are you?" he protested as he ducked under the tape and went inside. "I live here."

"We need to secure the scene of the crime for the next 24 hours," Polk said, confirming the bad news. "The bar can stay open, but you'll need to find a place to stay for the night."

Connor thought on this a second, decided not to press the point. The sight of the dead man and all that blood had drawn him back to a blown-out corner store in Kirkuk, waiting for the kid he'd just shot to exhale his last breath. That was the image that was etched the deepest in his memory, and now as he felt the rush of panic coursing through his nerves he began to wonder if he could ever spend another night in this place ever again.

"It's tourist season," Connor reminded him. "Town's booked solid."

Polk nodded pensively, then winked at him. "I'll see if I can pull a string or two," he said.

He stepped aside and dialed a number on his cell phone. Connor couldn't hear what he was talking about, and a minute later the cop hung up and turned back to him.

"You're in luck," he announced. "My cousin owns a place called Cool Sands up on East Erie. You know the guest cabins with the crazy murals painted on the side? One of 'em's vacant, on account it's not quite up to code."

"Not up to code?" Connor repeated.

"I asked her about that. She says it has to do with old wiring or something. It's safe, but since she can't rent it out, she'll let you stay there at the family rate."

"Family rate? What's that?"

"Free, numb nuts. And my cousin, she loves dogs."

"How long can I stay there?" he asked.

"As long as you want," Polk assured him. "Bernice—that's my cousin—she's got a real sweet tooth, so keep feeding her chocolate truffles and you'll get along just fine."

Connor nodded as he gazed out at the ocean, the water resembling a sheet of crumpled aluminum foil, sparkling in the midday sun. "Something about this whole thing is really messed up," he finally said.

"You know more than you're letting on," the cop said.

"Didn't start out that way, but one thing led to another."

Lincoln Polk nodded but said nothing for a minute as he watched a man and a woman lug a massive cooler over the dunes toward the beach. Then he said, "I figured as much, since you were in the courtroom Monday morning."

Connor knew it was time to come clean, so he inhaled a weary breath and told him about his search out at Cusabo Gut. He explained how the man named Tony Carerra hadn't existed until three years ago, when he'd assumed the identity of an old childhood pal. He conveniently left out his conversation with the medical examiner, the USB drive, and the map with the "X" on Hatchitch Island. And the circle drawn around The Sandbar.

"I'm beginning to think Carerra and Justacious Stone are just the center of a very big root system," he concluded when he was finished. "Like an ancient oak tree."

"You sure you didn't know this guy before Friday night?" Polk said.

"I swear on the souls of all my buddies who didn't make it home from Iraq."

"Have you talked to the SLED guys?"

"Not since the day after Carerra was shot," Connor replied, shaking his head. "Besides, they don't much appreciate civilians poking their noses where they don't belong."

"Hard to imagine why," Polk said, the sarcasm thick in his voice. "You think the guy in your place was trying to kill you?"

"Either him or the guy who shot him," Connor said. "Are we just about done here?"

"For now," the cop said.

"Please take care of that girl," Connor told him. "I promised she'd be safe from her mother's boyfriend."

"I have a little pull with the county on this sort of thing, so I'll make sure they hold her overnight. A social worker will contact Family Services and other agencies that deal with this sort of thing. The next few days will be tough on her, but she'll come out of this okay."

"Any problem if I stop by the hospital later to see her?"

"I'll put your name on the list." Polk said as he set down his cup of coffee, from which he'd hardly taken a sip.

"I really need to clean up the blood," Connor told him.

"Not until SLED clears the scene. That'll be tomorrow at the earliest, maybe longer."

Connor reluctantly shuffled into the bedroom, started stuffing his things into an old Army duffel bag. Since he'd already lost everything he owned during last year's hurricane, it wasn't much. When he was finished, he lugged it out to the front room, where Polk was finishing up another phone call.

"I gotta run," the cop said. "Looks like there's another incident out on the north shore, possible fatality."

"Do what you need to do."

"That's the job description," Polk replied. "Listen, Mr. Connor. Since we now have people dying in the streets, I've got to ask you to lay off this Carerra thing."

"This thing goes a lot deeper than you think."

"Don't tell me what I'm thinking, Mr. Connor," Polk told him, his friendly demeanor replaced with one that was all business. "I'm a lot smarter than I look, and I don't want any more people dead. Not on my turf."

CHAPTER 19

Thirty minutes later Connor's feet were propped up on the wood railing of his temporary digs at Cool Sands. The place was a small compound of a half dozen wood-frame cabins set in a grove of palmettos that gave the place a tropical feel. Each cabin was painted in bright Caribbean colors, with storm shutters designed to be locked tight across the windows in the event of a hurricane. Neat and trim, tidy to a fault, the place had been described in travel blogs as a romantic getaway, cozy and comfortable, tastefully decorated and nicely stocked with all high-end amenities.

Connor's quarters were another matter altogether. It was easy to see why the cottage—really more of an old storage shed with a small front porch—was not up to local code, and now available at the Polk family rate. One interior wall had recently been mended with a patchwork of drywall, the seams taped and sanded but not yet painted. Several of the wall sockets had the tell-tale black signs of sparking wires, and one electrical box was missing altogether. The ceiling sagged where water had leaked through the roof at some point in the past, and the shower in the bathroom looked to be fabricated from rusted tin. But the full-sized bed was freshly made up, a small wall unit churned out cool air, and the place was equipped with a small fridge and coffee maker. Connor had held up for sixteen months in the desert under much worse conditions, and as long as he had three hots and a cot, he was content.

He wiped a bead of sweat from his brow and balanced his old computer in his lap. He slipped the purloined USB drive into a slot, then waited for the File Explorer app to show him what was on it. He took a sip from the bottle of iced tea he'd bought from a vending machine in the small office, thinking what he really wanted was an ice-cold beer but immediately pushing that notion from his brain.

Connor had no way of knowing whether the key-shaped device had belonged to Mr. or Mrs. Carerra, or maybe even someone else. Theoretically it could have been gathering dust on the rental home's closet floor for months, but the painful lump at the base of his skull was telling him otherwise. Again he wondered whether his assailant had already been in the house when he arrived, or had he let himself in after Connor started poking around? Either way, if the guy had been there looking for something, instinct told him it was the digital drive that now was doing its thing in the laptop's USB port.

When the contents appeared on the screen Connor found four folders alphabetically arranged by the names "Banking," "Companies," "Investments," and "Supply Chain." He clicked on the top folder first, which opened to reveal a list of files that all carried an .xlsx extension. *Excel spreadsheets.* When he'd started his job at Palmetto BioClean he'd never seen a spreadsheet, so he'd bought one of those yellow guidebooks for dummies in order to learn the basics of accounting software.

Each file in the "Banking" folder again was arranged in alphabetical order, so he arbitrarily clicked on the top one, which was labeled CIBT0519. He recognized it as a standard commercial profit and loss statement that listed financial deposits, monthly earnings, and periodic withdrawals related to a bank outside the U.S. He closed out of it and opened several more spreadsheets, each of which corresponded to other specific numbered accounts and, as Connor clicked through them, he jotted down where they were located: Two each in the Cayman Islands and Belize, and one each in the Bahamas, British Virgin Islands, Nevis, Panama, Geneva, and Zurich. Each of the accounts seemed to loop into some sort of transactional network that allowed funds to be easily transferred from one financial institution to another.

All but one of the files in the folder was an Excel spreadsheet. The lone holdout was a document that contained the names of the same banks mentioned in the separate .xlsx files. Each of these groupings listed an online URL address, a numeric account number, and a user ID and password. Acting on a hunch he highlighted one of the web addresses and copied it into the browser's URL window, then waited for the free Wi-Fi to go to work. When it finally did, it opened a page for Guaranty Financial Trust, a bank that appeared to be registered in Nassau in the Bahamas.

There was a window asking for an account number, so he copied it from the Word document to where the cursor was flashing, then typed in the corresponding User ID and password. That launched a security page, and for a second Connor thought he might have hit a roadblock. Then he realized the page was only asking whether he wanted to change his security information right then, wait another six months, or remind him later. He clicked on that link, which made the pop-up fade away and then forwarded him to the online account itself.

Connor was familiar with online banking; he was a member of USAA and conducted his personal transactions either from his phone or his laptop. But the account he was looking at appeared nothing like his own checking account, which survived on week-to-week life support. In fact, he literally did a double-take when he saw the amount of the current balance at the top of the page:

$108,987,361.19

A shit-ton of money.

The folder labeled "Companies" was different from the first. This one contained dozens of sub-folders, each of which itemized small independent businesses, parking lots, strip malls, a chain of convenience stores, and even a string of churches whose denomination Connor had never heard of. Each of these enterprises made weekly cash deposits—always in amounts of under ten thousand dollars—into a network of small, independent banks and credit unions located in towns from New Orleans to Norfolk. These banks, in turn, made regular transfers to the ten offshore institutions in the "Banking" folder.

Connor thumbed the cursor down the list of files and randomly clicked on one labeled PCP0618.pdf. This turned out to be a signed application form for a new business account for Panama City Parking LLC at a Florida panhandle bank. The account had been opened nine years ago, and he cross-checked to ascertain that the number on the signed application corresponded to one of the accounts in the "Banking" folder. A correlative Excel sheet identified weekly cash deposits, followed by transfers to any one of the ten banks located in the Caribbean or Switzerland.

Just as with the "Banking" folder, the "Investments" files mostly were Excel documents. He double-clicked on the first file and found a list of assets that he didn't understand at first, but when he clicked on specific entries, he realized each item was a parcel of real estate. The file identified dozens of real estate properties that had been acquired along the East and Gulf coasts, from Virginia Beach to Miami to Biloxi. Each of these appeared to be generating rental income that fueled the bottom line of the worksheet. Some properties had been sold, some purchases were pending, and the proceeds from each sale were tallied in a separate column marked "Gain/Loss."

The "Supply Chain" folder was different from the other three. It contained several dozen secondary folders, each of which represented either a large city like Memphis and Miami, or smaller towns from Myrtle Beach to Gulfport. Compared to the "Investments" folder, these worksheets seemed to cover specific distribution and sales territories. A separate PDF of a map showed that none of these markets overlapped geographically, and such phrases as "proprietary rights" and "protected distribution" reinforced the idea that these were exclusive market entities.

A cursory glance through the spreadsheets told Connor that each territory was run by an independent franchisee, much like a chain of fast food joints or carpet cleaning companies. And along that same theme, each franchise made weekly cash deposits—usually several thousand dollars at a time—at the various businesses listed in the "Companies" folder that operated within its exclusive territory. There was no indication of what sort of business these regional franchises were conducting, or what product they might be selling.

Connor had watched every episode of *Breaking Bad* and had seen enough crime movies to know that ten thousand dollars was the magic number that alerted the feds to illicit activities. Now, as he scrolled through the transaction history, he found that each deposit was comfortably under that ten-thousand-dollar federal radar, and each was funneled through some sort of cash-oriented business.

There was no doubt in Connor's mind that he was looking at the guts of a complex and sophisticated money laundering scheme. The patterns in the distribution and banking spreadsheets suggested an intricate mechanism designed to absorb massive amounts of paper money and then cleanse it beyond any suspicion of the tax man.

So what kind of operation was Connor looking at? Instinctively his mind went to drugs,

which immediately took him to Gordo's death and the memorial service his wife Kelli was planning. Half the vets who'd been in the rehab program down in Georgia had fallen into the abyss of opiate addiction, and the relapse rate was high. Each man suffered his own personalized demons, and none of them was any further away than the next dark corner.

So yes, it was an easy leap of faith—and facts—to connect the dots to drugs. But maybe there were other elements involved, things like gunrunning, smuggling, even human trafficking. Connor had come face to face with remnants of the Dixie Mafia several years back, and he knew they had their fingers in just about every poisoned pie in the South, from counterfeit scratch-off cards to murder for hire. But he didn't think that's what he was looking at here; this seemed as sophisticated as any global enterprise, a real stretch for the shallow brain pans of those redneck knuckle-draggers.

Besides the four folders on the flash drive, there were a half dozen standalone files that were Word docs, jpegs, and PDFs. Connor clicked on one and opened a short letter addressed to a man named Luca Roos, who was identified at the top of the note as an investigator with Interpol in Zurich. *Interpol?* he thought. *What the fuck?* He scanned the note, which turned out to be a follow-up to an email request for an explanation into a wire transfer to a securities brokerage in Zurich. From the urgent tone of the message, Connor concluded that a large sum of money was involved and Carerra was inquiring whether Roos had been able to follow it through the networking maze of offshore banks.

A second Word file was a copy of an email exchange between Carerra and a person identified as Shelton, gender unknown. Beginning with the most recent entry at the top, it read:

Shelton: Everything's all set. Window is closing, so you must move fast. Neven suspects something is up.

Carerra: Let's do it.

Shelton: You're the boss. Just waiting for confirmation. Ready to go when you are.

Carerra: Not happening. You get files and me, or neither.

Shelton: We'll take care of that once we have the files in hand.

Carerra: Of course. I want a full digital paper trail, and the security we discussed.

Shelton: You have all records of transactions?

Carerra: All accounts frozen and assets on ice. Ready to pull the trigger, so to speak.

Shelton: Re: previous email, rest assured: we have you covered.

Connor re-read the exchange, this time from the bottom up, then checked the time and date at the top of the page. The final entry, made by Shelton, was sent less than seventy-two hours before Carerra was shot on The Sandbar's drinking deck.

Next, he clicked on a file labeled ARDeathCert.pdf, a two-page document he enlarged in order to read the fine print. It was a death certificate bearing the official seal of Dade County, Florida, for a woman named Aurora Santana who was twenty-eight years old when she died from "extreme multiple injuries." The certificate did not say how she received those injuries, but Connor noticed the date was just over three years ago.

He closed the file and opened the one below it, which was named "Cozumel03.jpg." When he opened it, he found a snapshot of a couple taken at an outdoor table in a tropical locale that, judging by the file name, was probably in Mexico. A man he recognized as a younger Carerra was wearing a loose-fitting black shirt unbuttoned halfway down his chest, while a woman in a sleeveless sun dress cut from a floral print was leaning her head on his shoulder. Black hair cascaded over her shoulders, and her creamy skin seemed to glow in the fading sunlight. Her dark eyes were intense and seductive, her smile tantalizing and alive. She seemed natural in front of a lens, and Connor briefly wondered if she had posed for the camera for a living. She could have been a model or an actress, or both; the woman was that stunning.

Both she and Carerra were sipping on straws that were immersed in a goldfish bowl filled to the brim with some sort of blue tropical concoction. They were smiling up at the camera, evidently lost in the moment and whatever they were imbibing. On the woman's ring finger Connor noticed a large diamond solitaire that matched the sparkle in her eyes.

She was a striking woman and there was no question that she had been an important part of Tony Carerra's life. From the death certificate Connor figured something horrible had happened to her, something he suspected might be at the root of everything that had occurred over the last five days.

The last file on the disk provided the missing link. It was an article from the digital edition of the *Miami Herald* web page, dated thirty-eight months ago. On a hunch Connor checked the date on the death certificate, found it was just one day before the newspaper story had appeared. When he scanned the headline he understood why:

Woman's Body Lands In Miami Backyard
Victim most likely fell from plane, police say

MIAMI – Maria Perez was hanging her wash out to dry Thursday afternoon when a loud noise in the corner of her yard startled her and caused her to trip over her laundry basket. When she went to investigate, what she found was enough to make her faint.

The Dade County sheriff says that what Ms. Perez discovered near her backyard fence was the body of a woman that somehow had landed in a bed of roses. While investigators are not exactly sure how the body got there, they suspect the victim—a young woman in her late twenties—apparently fell from a great altitude. Because there are no high-rise buildings in that neighborhood, it is suspected that she may have fallen from an airplane flying overhead, a source inside the department said. The dead woman reportedly had no identification on her body, which was fully clothed, a source told the *Herald*. Cause of death is being investigated and an autopsy is scheduled for this morning.

"This is a horrifying and grisly occurrence," Dade County Deputy Sheriff Philip Sanders said, noting that no one in the neighborhood remembers hearing any aircraft flying overhead prior to the incident. "We currently are working with all airports in the area to determine take-offs and landings, and the FAA is reviewing the flight plans of all aircraft that flew in the vicinity of the city on Thursday. But as of now, we have no idea who the woman is, or where she fell from."

Ms. Perez, who suffered a mild concussion when she fainted, told authorities that she remembers hearing a whistling sound just prior to a loud bang. "It sounded like a big bomb coming down," she reportedly told police. "Who could do such a terrible thing to that poor woman?"

Connor re-read the story, then studied the photo that accompanied it. There was no doubt this was the same woman as in the Cozumel photo: same dark hair, same eyes, same silky skin. Same smile. He closed his eyes and tried to picture the events surrounding her death, instantly wishing he hadn't. Aurora Santana had fallen from an airplane; there was no other explanation for how she got to be in Ms. Perez' back yard. But he also realized her death could not have been an accident; she must have been pushed. Which meant that she probably had been alive the entire time during her plunge. He tried not to imagine the sheer terror that must have filled the woman's mind as she plummeted toward the earth, but the image was too strong for him to dismiss easily.

As the Perez woman had wondered, who would do such a horrible thing, and why? What had this beautiful young woman done to deserve such a horrifying death? Again, the most obvious answer in Connor's mind was drugs, and everything that accompanied their mayhem. Dealers and junkies and gang-bangers all shared an inhumane lack of regard for life, preying on those who—for whatever reasons—had lost all measure of their own existence. The nightly news was filled with stories of psychopaths, scammers, and grifters who would say anything—do anything—to sell anything to just about anyone, and the trail of overdoses was evidence of their total lack of regard, or remorse.

Aurora Santana, he found himself thinking, turning the name over and over in his mind. *What was your involvement in all this, and what the hell happened to you?*

CHAPTER 20

Connor pulled the skeleton key out of his laptop, his brain racing with questions he wanted to ask Mrs. Carerra.

Leading off: what did she know about the network of illicit businesses and laundering operations Connor had just reviewed? He figured she'd deny knowing anything about it, but he wanted to gauge her reaction when he put the question to her. Next in line: Why was there a map in her rental house that marked an isolated, low-lying island five miles south of Folly, a map which also had Connor's bar circled in red ink? Both of these could be easily explained as points of interest that had been recommended to newly arrived tourists, but he'd stopped believing in coincidences at the same time he figured Santa Claus couldn't possibly visit all those houses in one night.

There was something else that didn't add up, something that had been bothering him since he'd dropped in on Mrs. Carerra at her rental house a few days ago. Something that only she could explain to him. Problem was, she'd told him she would likely be leaving town today, and since it was mid-afternoon, he figured she'd already checked out. He was probably too late to catch her, but if he didn't make the effort he'd never know for sure. He hated to disrupt the remainder of the afternoon, especially considering how his day had begun. But it was his night off and he had a date lined up with a woman named Jessica Snow in a few hours. He felt a little guilty leaving Julie alone behind the bar after the shooting that morning, but she'd assured him she could hold down the fort. He watched a pair of squirrels chasing each other around the trunk of a water oak in a ritualized mating dance, then closed his laptop and carried it back inside the out-of-code cottage.

Five minutes later he walked into the Cool Sands office and punched a silver bell on the counter. Several seconds later Lincoln Polk's cousin Bernice came out of a back room and flashed him a massive smile. She was a jolly middle-aged woman with a round face and eyes that sparkled even in the shade, and a multi-colored scarf was wrapped like a turban around her head. When Connor had checked in, she had apologized for the shabby condition of his room and assured him there was no threat of fire and it would keep him dry. She also had taken a liking to Clooney and had agreed to dog-sit for the evening, and now Connor now asked her if she would mind looking after him for a bit while he ran a couple errands.

"No problem, Mr. Jack," she assured him. "Him and me, we already got a thing goin'."

"I'll be back to feed him before I go out," Connor promised.

"Take your time. We're gonna be watching Dr. Phil."

Five minutes later Connor was driving out along the north shore road, hoping he'd catch Martina Carerra as she was loading her things into her rental car. Questions were still spinning in his head, and he was trying to form them into coherent thoughts that would make sense when he spoke with her. *If* he spoke with her.

But that was not to be. When he slowed his Jeep in front of the rental home, he felt his heart skip a beat. The white SUV Mrs. Carerra had picked up at the airport was gone, and in its place was the Palmetto BioClean truck. The rear doors were wide open, and bright orange traffic cones had been placed on the shoulder of the road behind it as a warning to drivers that people were at work here. To Connor the truck's presence meant only one thing: Lionel Hanes and his cleaning crew were at work inside the house. And since the company specialized in spilled blood, death and decomp had to be involved.

He took the stairs two at a time and made it just inside the front door when Hanes stopped him with a straight-arm right out of his NFL days. He was carrying a bucket of pink liquid, and a few drops splashed out as Connor came to a halt.

"Holy shit, man...did you catch a murder scene here?" he wanted to know.

"This is a work zone, bro," Hanes told him, trying to sound friendly yet firm. "You can't come in here."

Connor tried to peer past him into the shadows but couldn't make anything out beyond the screened porch. "C'mon, man...I won't touch a thing."

"You know how it is," Hanes told him. "No one except the team goes in or out."

"Yeah, yeah...I used to give the same orders. But *damn*...who died in here?"

"Don't know, and I don't care to know. All I was told was a woman was stabbed, bled out. Fortunately, it was a tile floor, and the grout was sealed. That's gonna shave hours off the job and save the insurance company some big bucks."

"When was this?" Connor asked, remembering that Lincoln Polk had gotten a call that morning about an incident somewhere along this stretch of road. "I mean, do you know when she died?"

"All I heard was the housekeeper found her this morning, and the cops were done a couple hours after that," Hanes explained. "That's when we got to work. What's your interest in it, anyway?"

"The woman who was renting this place...well, it was her husband's blood you cleaned up at my place over the weekend."

"Shit, man…is this another one of those fucked-up things you're always working on?"

There were lots of ways Connor could have answered, but instead he said, "It's me, bro. *Hanes*. Just give me five minutes."

"No can do, Mr. Connor."

Mr. Connor? What was going on here? "Sixty seconds, then. *Please*…I promise I won't touch anything, and I'll stay way clear of the blood."

Connor could tell that his old teammate hated to say "no," even though company policy insisted that no one other than trained employees could enter a clean-up scene. They'd literally worked over a hundred of these jobs together, mopped up gallons of blood, cleaned more flesh and gray matter off walls and ceilings than either of them cared to remember.

"Just this once," Connor pressed him. "No one has to know."

"Dammit, man," Hanes finally said, letting out a sigh of defeat. "Keep your hands in your pockets, and nothing leaves this place except your ass."

"I swear."

"You have one minute."

"I owe you."

The first thing Connor noticed was the victim had bled out in the great room, near the breakfast counter that was part of the open kitchen concept. He made brief small talk with Jenny while he studied the ceramic tile where the blood had pooled, an irregular pattern roughly six feet across. Because of the heat it had dried quickly, leaving a crusty line around the perimeter of the stain the BioClean team was working on. Connor didn't recognize the third member of the team, a young deer-in-the-headlights rookie who regarded him sullenly but said nothing.

Connor shuddered to think what could have happened to Martina Carerra. Had she been murdered by the same assailant who had whacked him over the head the afternoon before, or was someone else involved? The shooting in his own apartment just that morning—and the dead guy in the Tahoe—confirmed there was a lot more going on here than just the random murder of Tony Carerra last Friday night. Especially since Carerra didn't seem to be Carerra at all, and a flash drive found on the closet floor in this very house held the blueprints of a complex money laundering scheme.

Connor took a quick peek into the bedroom and saw that the mess he'd found the other day had been tidied up. In fact, the closet had been cleared out and all the scattered clothes and suitcases were gone. The bed was still unmade—Connor figured the housekeeper would never set foot inside that beach cottage ever again—but there was no sign of Martina Carerra's things.

Which meant just one thing: if that was not Martina's blood out there on the tile, whose was it?

Just as Lincoln Polk had said, Em Lee had been transported to MUSC in Charleston for observation. The nurse manager was reluctant to give Connor any information about her condition, except to say the staff was trying to contact a relative so that in the morning she could go somewhere—*anywhere*—other than home.

"No one goes in there who's not on the list," she told him. She was solid and sinewy, steel-gray eyes and red hair cut in the shape of a bowl. A name tag identified her as Penny Cooper, RN. "And it's a very short one."

"Please check to see if I'm on it," he persisted.

She regarded Connor's full range of body art and shaved head with skepticism, then said, "And your name would be?"

"Jack Connor."

Nurse Cooper must have memorized the very short list, because she didn't even glance at it when she said, "I'll need to see some I.D."

Connor showed her his driver's license and asked, "How's she doing?"

"Aside from complaining about the food, she's been pretty quiet," the nurse replied as she inspected the I.D. carefully. She eyeballed him again as she handed it back, then said, "You can go in."

He pushed the door open and stuck his head into the room. Em Lee was lying in the bed staring at something on the television that was affixed to the far wall. It was one of those mind-bogglingly bad courtroom reality shows, some young woman yelling at her former boyfriend about stealing her car and wrecking it. Em Lee turned her head when she heard the door click shut, then smiled weakly as Connor approached the bed.

"Thanks again for breakfast," she told him, trying to force a smile to her lips.

"Jo-Jo makes the best grits and eggs," Connor replied. A chair was set at the edge of the bed, so he pulled it closer and sat down. "How are you feeling?"

She glanced past him to the closed door, then relaxed. "I'm good. Do they really have a guard out there?"

"Just some pretty tough nurses you wouldn't want to cross," he assured her. "No one's getting in here who shouldn't be."

She thought for a minute, then asked, "So why am I here, anyway? I'm not sick."

"Think of it as a place to sleep without worrying about getting beat up," Connor told her. "Officially you were admitted for observation, at the request of the Folly Beach P.D."

She considered this, seemed to accept it. "What happens to me now?" she asked.

He really didn't have a clue, but didn't want her to know that. "A lot of legal stuff, mostly," he told her. "Tomorrow when you get released from this place, you'll be met by a representative from Child Protective Services—"

"I'm not a child," she said, an indignant pout slipping into her dark eyes. "I'm almost fourteen years old."

"Maybe, but in the eyes of the law you're still a minor. And fortunately, there are laws that protect you against the kind of abuse you've been experiencing."

She thought about all this, seemed to digest it. Then she said, "So I meet this person. What happens then?"

"A judge will get involved and there'll probably be a hearing of some sort, other legal stuff. Meantime you go into temporary protective custody."

"Temporary, like in a *foster home*?" Em Lee asked incredulously.

"Hopefully only for a few days, until they can place you with your aunt. If she agrees that you can live with her, and the judge approves, that's about it."

She considered all this for a few minutes, weighing all the natural objections an almost-fourteen-year-old girl could imagine. "I can live with that," she finally said. "Anything is better than going back to my mama and that prick. Sorry."

"No problem," Connor grinned.

"She called me, you know. My mom. She said I had to change my story or Jesry was going to leave her."

"And what did you tell her?"

"I said that would be the best thing ever happened to her, and besides, he'd probably be going to jail anyway. Then she called me a bitch and a liar, and hung up."

Wonderful, he thought. The woman was so much in need of a man that she either refused to believe her daughter, or wanted her to lie just to maintain a sick *status quo*.

"You think he will?" she asked. "Go to jail?"

Connor had no clue how the system worked, but if it was anything like the V.A. it was slow and frustrating. Still, he wanted to give her some hope on which to hang her future, so he said, "That depends on what the judge thinks, and whether he—or she—decides there are grounds to prosecute. Most of them don't take kindly to child abusers."

Em Lee looked ready to object again to his reference of her as a child, but realized he meant it only as a legal term, not an insult.

"Have you talked to your aunt?" he asked her.

"Yeah, I told her 'bout Jesry and everything that happened this morning. She was horrified that I coulda been shot."

"Did you talk to her about spending some time with her?"

"Oh, sure. 'Any time,' she said."

Connor wondered if her aunt realized this would be more than just a casual weekend visit. "Well, that's a good sign," he assured her.

They made small talk after that—what living in a town called Bug Hill would be like, making new friends, going to a new school—and then he got up to go.

"Am I ever going to see you again?" she asked.

"Count on it." He squeezed her hand, then slowly let it drop to the bed. "You take care now, Em Lee," he told her, then turned and walked out of the room.

He made his way back to the nurse's station and stood there until he attracted the attention of Penny Cooper, R.N. "You keep a close eye on that girl in there," he told her. "She's got a good, long life ahead of her."

Bright strokes of orange and red streaked the sky as Connor walked back to the parking garage where he'd left his Jeep. A pink contrail creased the darkening sky and he watched the tiny speck of a jet race southward. He took the stairs to the second level and started to climb into the driver's seat when he heard a shuffle of feet behind him. He whirled around instinctively and saw a large man coming toward him.

"Jack Connor?" the man said. His nose was large and flat, and his hair was cropped close to his head. He had a coarse, rugged face, with a thin line that stretched from his left eye down his cheek. He wore khaki trousers and a light blue shirt that looked as if it had been folded, wrinkled, and unfolded too many times. But it wasn't the wrinkles that attracted Connor's attention; it was his hands, which he couldn't see because they were thrust deep in his pockets.

"Who're you?" Connor snapped, instinctively bracing himself for a fight.

"Relax," the man said, removing his hands from his pockets. "David Landry, U.S. Justice Department. You got a moment?"

"I was just getting set to drive home," Connor explained. "It's been a long day."

"I know. I read the report."

"You been following me?"

"Let's just say I know who you are. And I have a few questions for you. Can I buy you a beer?"

"We can talk right here."

David Landry considered this, gave a slight shrug. "Whatever smokes your bacon," he said.

"You have I.D.?" Connor asked him.

The man from the Department of Justice seemed put off by the question, but was duty-bound to produce his badge and I.D. card. The photo looked enough like him, but there was no way of knowing if it was a forgery. Then again, if he was anything other than who he said he was, he could have killed Connor by now.

"Satisfied?"

"For now," Connor said. "What can I do for you?"

David Landry took out a pack of cigarettes, offered to share, but Connor shook his head. "This is a hospital," he said. "Smoking's not allowed anywhere on the grounds."

The federal agent ignored him as he plucked a smoke out of the pack. He stuck it between his lips but didn't bother lighting it. "I've checked around," he said slowly, the cigarette bobbing up and down as he spoke. "You seem to be asking a lot of questions about Mr. Carerra."

"I'm a questioning sort of guy," Connor replied with a shrug.

Landry said nothing for a moment as he cupped his hand around the cigarette and lit it with a disposable lighter. He took a puff, inhaled deeply, let out a cloud of smoke. Then he said, "So maybe we've got something in common."

"Look," Connor said tiredly. "It's been a long day, and there's somewhere I have to be. Whatever you want to ask, get on with it."

Landry leaned against the Jeep and stared up at the garage ceiling, reflecting on something he clearly wasn't revealing. He was silent another second or two; then, without even looking at Connor, said, "I want to know who you think took that pot shot through your window this morning."

"You and me both," he said.

"So you don't know who killed your John Doe?"

"He's not my John Doe."

"A man with a gun sneaks into your apartment while you step out for breakfast and someone else just happens to plug him through your kitchen screen? You're telling me you don't know who he is or why he did it?"

"Nope," Connor said. "Just like I don't know who the dead guy was across the street in the car."

Landry plucked the cigarette from his mouth, shot him a dark look. "You don't seem to know much about anything—"

"Looks like you and I have something in common," Connor replied.

The fed regarded him with a deep frown and shook his head. "Look, Jack. In case you haven't noticed, a crime has been committed here. You go any closer to this case than you've already been, you're obstructing the investigation."

"As far as I can tell, there is no investigation," Connor replied. "All I'm hearing is that the local cops say a kid named Justacious Stone shot Tony Carerra. The kid confessed, and now he's dead. Case conveniently closed, except a lot of people still seem to be dying."

"Don't play dumb with me," Landry sneered with contempt.

"Who says I'm playing?"

The G-man scowled at him, obviously not in a joking frame of mind. "I can make you reveal what you know, if it comes to that—"

Connor was losing his patience, but he still was doing an admirable job holding on to his temper. "I'll tell you what I've already told the cops: I went out for breakfast. I ran into a young girl who asked me for help. I told her I'd make a call or two, see what I could do. On the way back to my place I noticed a blue Chevy Tahoe and felt something was a little out of place. Call it intuition or battlefield instinct, whatever. I sent the girl up to my apartment, and when I arrived a few minutes later I found a dead man lying on my floor."

Landry snickered and said, "I think we can find a judge who'd like to hear what a prepubescent piece of jail bait was doing in your apartment at six-thirty in the morning."

If Connor were a stupid man, he'd have swung at him then and there, but he kept his cool and simply climbed behind the wheel. "I think we're done here," he said.

"You know what, Connor?" Agent Landry took a half-step closer but not close enough to get completely in his face. "You think you're some hot-shot former Army grunt who solved a couple murders and made a few headlines. You figure maybe you can run a bar that will help take your mind off what you did over in Iraq, all that PTSD bullshit. Maybe take your mind off your girlfriend, who dumped your sorry ass when she saw you for what you really are. That's right, *hombre*—I know all about you, and you're way in over your head here. You're drowning in sewage and you don't even know it."

"Thanks for the analysis," Connor said, doing his best not to rip this Justice Department asshole a brand new one. Instead he keyed the engine to life and shifted into reverse. "And now, if you don't mind, my hot-shot attitude and I are expected elsewhere. Good night, Mr. Landry. *Sir!*"

CHAPTER 21

An hour later Connor was seated across from Jessica Snow at Tortuga Verde, one of Folly's more fashionable—a.k.a. pricey—restaurants. Unlike most of the local joints that served up massive platters of ribs and pulled pork and oysters, the menu was a spiced Latin take on a variety of surf and turf dishes. Cubano shrimp, habanero chicken, lime-encrusted swordfish. Set a block back from the beach in a walled courtyard, the intimate restaurant offered a choice of either being seated indoors or *al fresco*. The night was warm but not hot, so they elected to enjoy the ocean breeze and the rustling palmetto fronds, fused with the fragrance of summer jasmine and sweet alyssum.

His original plan was to pick Jessica up at the Tides, but since it was only a four-block walk to the restaurant they decided to meet there instead. He still drove the Jeep and parked it at the edge of the road, just in case the night yielded some magic of its own and they went off in search of a secluded stretch of beach. *Be prepared.*

The maître d' seated them at an intimate table in the corner of the courtyard, recited the specials of the day, and took their drink orders. Now, as Jessica sipped a pink bay breeze and Connor cooled his hands around a bottle of beer, night was coming quickly. A wash of orange and red was painted across the sky, and a blinking light heading in a northerly direction caused him to think of his family up north, or what was left of it. His ex-wife was remarried, his father had passed away years ago, and his sister now lived in Reno. Only his mother remained in the row house in Lansing where he had grown up and worked the General Motors line alongside his old man for a few years. Then he'd let his little niece get gunned down at the Mega Gas down the street, his fault because he'd taken his eyes off her for thirty seconds while he filled out a Powerball ticket. Her blood was still on his hands, and that tragic night had been like the first crack in a windshield that quickly dissolved into tiny stars of glass.

"I wonder what the cold people are doing tonight?" he pondered out loud.

"It's August everywhere," she reminded him as she raised her glass to her lips. "But this is Shangri-La."

She leaned closer and seized him with eyes that seemed greener tonight than the limes that had brought them together in the first place. Her hair hung loosely around her shoulders, framing her gentle cheekbones and supple lips. She was dressed in a light strapless thing that looked like a garden of summer flowers, and when she leaned over the table her low-cut neckline transfixed him. She let him enjoy the view for a moment, then straightened her back.

"They say it's hard to improve upon paradise," Connor told her. "But—" He gazed deep into her eyes so there would be no mistake what he was talking about "—whoever they are, it seems they're wrong."

Jessica seemed to blush, but there was no embarrassment in her eyes. They both suspected where this was going—where *they* were going—but getting there was half the fun. Maybe more. No need to rush a good journey when the destination is mutually assumed.

He caught her looking at the ink on his arms just as she said, "So tell me… what's your story?"

"Are you talking about the tattoos or the beach bar?"

"The whole picture. I know you didn't grow up here, so how did a human canvas like you come to be slinging drinks in paradise?"

"You make it sound like a Jimmy Buffet song."

"All that's missing is the cheeseburger," she said. "C'mon—out with it."

"It's a long story, and there's no *Reader's Digest* version."

"Are you planning on going anywhere soon?"

She had a point, and the last thing he wanted was to cut the evening short. So much promise, and all things that are worthwhile take time. Connor figured there were two ways he could go here: he could be as vague about his past as possible, or he could dig into his bag of memories and let them all out. He'd suspected this moment would come at some point during the evening, but now that it was here, he was still at a loss. There was a difference between how much she wanted to know, and how much she *needed* to know.

In the end he told her almost everything. He started with the murder of his niece, how his life had taken a nose dive and led directly to his tour in Iraq. That segued into the story of Eddie James and everyone else who was blown up when the suicide bomber rammed his van into their Humvee. Next came his own injuries and lingering PTSD that followed him home from the war, the affection for gin that sometimes got the better of him, all the risks he'd taken and bullets that almost killed him. He judiciously left out anything that had to do with his tendency to poke his nose where it didn't belong, which alternately had landed him in jail, the hospital, and the lonely-hearts club. He also omitted any mention of the name Danielle, since this was a first date and bringing her into the conversation was certain to spoil the evening.

"I am…so sorry," Jessica said when he finished. He wasn't sure, but he could swear he saw a little tear in the corner of her eye. "Not about your whole life, of course. Just that…I had no idea—"

"The past is what brings us to where we are," he said with a shrug. "You can't change what has already happened, but you can focus on what you have here, and now. At least, that's what the V.A. shrinks kept hammering into us in group. Still, it's hard to live by words alone, especially when you're in the middle of a total mental eclipse."

"These shrinks…have they ever asked you why you keep putting yourself in danger?"

"If you're military, it's expected," he told her.

"But you're a civilian now."

"Hoo-ah!"

She stared at him over the lip of her glass for a minute, then said, "Is that supposed to tell me something?"

"As they say, objects in your rearview mirror are larger than they appear."

Jessica was still staring at him, her eyes locked on his. Then something in her mind seemed to click and she said, "I remember that thing with the governor last year. Wasn't it on *Dateline*, or something—?"

"They did a story," he admitted. "It wasn't very flattering, and there was a lot of death and controversy surrounding the whole thing." And Danielle had wanted nothing to do with it—*or him*—once it was all over.

"Looks like you came out of it okay."

"Not without a lot of help from Uncle Sam," he said. "It's still one day at a time."

"What about beach fever?" she asked as she shifted her glance to a gecko that was clinging to the stone wall. "Don't you ever feel the need to go someplace with department stores and multiplex cinemas?"

"Charleston is twenty minutes away," he explained with a shrug. "The number one tourist city in America. Best of both worlds."

"I don't think I could do it," she said, shaking her head. "I mean, I love the surf, the sun, the sand—all the wonderful 's' things in life. But I don't think I could ever give up walking down Madison Avenue, or going to the theater, or browsing through the galleries in SoHo on a Saturday morning."

"So…the lady finally gives up a little info about herself," he said.

"What are you talking about?" she replied, with mock indignation.

"All I know about you is you like vodka drinks and magic tricks," he told her. "Otherwise it seems there's a side to Jessica Snow that doesn't get out very often."

"That's absurd. Go ahead…ask me a question—"

Connor thought a moment, said, "We'll start with an easy one. What do you do when you're not browsing through galleries in SoHo?"

"A little of this, a little of that," she replied.

"Any chance you might provide some details with that evasion?"

She raised an eyebrow, then sighed. No getting around it this time. "Well, there's not much to tell. Not even *Reader's Digest* would be interested. But since you've been honest with me, I guess it's my turn to tell all."

He shot her a look as if she was going to spill some horrible tale about a secret life.

"No, I'm not a high-end escort or a stripper," she continued, giggling nervously. "In fact, my life is pretty boring. I work for a company that publishes travel books. A lot of travel books. And I get paid to go to different places, check out restaurants and resorts, write them up. Incognito."

"You call that boring?"

"Most times, yes," she replied. "A lot of these places, if they know who I am and why I'm there, they roll out the red carpet hoping to get a good write-up. Which completely defeats the purpose. What I'm looking for is how they treat the average Joe. Or Jane."

"Do you review beach bars, too?"

Jessica raised a lone eyebrow at that. "It's been known to happen on occasion, but don't worry. From what I've seen, The Sandbar is a lively nightspot with great drinks and magical fun. Emphasis on the magic. Plus, it has a very accommodating bartender who takes great care of his customers."

"Do you subtract points if one of those customers gets gunned down in plain sight?"

"We try to overlook local nuances, unless they become a common occurrence," she said with a wink. She took a long sip, savoring the aroma as it trickled up her nose like flowers opening on a spring morning. "The other night, that was a first for me. I've never seen someone die before."

"Not something you ever get used to," Connor told her as he gazed into her eyes.

"People make a regular thing of dying in your bar?"

"Tony Carerra was the first, at least that I know of," he replied. "But sixteen months in Iraq was a different matter entirely. And what do you say we forget about the other night and move on to this one."

"A marvelous idea, Mr. Connor," Jessica agreed. "To the here and now, and the living."

They clinked glass again, and he gazed over the top of his bottle at this woman who was studying him so intently. He felt a momentary pang of guilt as he wondered where Danielle was at that very moment, but he managed to dispel the thought with another sip of beer.

"So—what do you know about this Carerra guy?" she asked him then.

"I thought we were talking about the living," he pointed out.

She nodded, a thin smile forming on her lips. "Then let's talk about his wife," she said. "She seems to like your bar. Or maybe it's not just the bar."

Connor grinned then, too. "She left her purse behind Friday night, and she came in to get it back," he explained. Not wanting to go into the fact that Martina Carerra very well might be dead as well, something he hadn't had time to confirm before his dinner date with Jessica.

"You're sure there isn't something else?"

Connor couldn't read her here, couldn't tell if she was being obtuse or just playing with him. "Her husband's been dead for what—five days?" he told her. "His ashes aren't even cold."

"Some women are funny that way," Jessica observed. "But I'm just messing with you."

He found he was losing himself in her eyes, almost didn't hear his own words as they came out: "Well, then...tell me about your pal. Alfonse Romano."

"Well Mr. Connor," she said in her best Scarlett O'Hara accent. "Do I detect a touch of jealousy?"

"Curiosity is more like it," he replied. "I just want to know where...things stand."

"Between him and me or you and me?"

"All of the above."

Jessica giggled, then gently set her glass down. She leaned forward, folded her hands in front of her, said, "Alfonse is a colleague, Jack. We work together. And sometimes our work means we travel together. And when we travel together, we sometimes go out on the town together. But that's it."

"So what about you and me?" he asked.

"That's what this evening is all about, isn't it?"

"Yes, and I seem to be screwing it up," he confessed. "I'm a bit out of practice."

"Practice can be overrated," she assured him. "It's getting to Carnegie Hall that really counts."

Connor wasn't quite sure what she was talking about, but he let it go. They made polite small talk for a while, Connor asking her all the requisite questions: Where was she born, did she have any brothers or sisters, did she enjoy living in New York? He signaled to the waiter for another round of drinks as she explained she was raised in suburban New Jersey, had attended New York University in Manhattan, worked in marketing for a while before landing her current gig. She launched into some tales about traveling around Europe—Paris was beautiful, Venice was romantic, the food in Tuscany was to die for. Connor didn't ask her the question that was really on his mind—had she been traveling alone or with Alfonse?—as she recounted her tales of adventure. And none of that mattered, because tonight she was sitting across the table from him, and the evening was theirs and theirs alone.

The waiter arrived with their entrees and also produced a bottle of California merlot, from which he painstakingly removed the cork. He did all the proper things with the wine, then offered a taste to Connor. He passed the honor to Jessica, who proclaimed that it was full and fruity, with just a hint of oak. In other words, quite drinkable. He poured a full glass for each of them, then politely excused himself to the kitchen.

Jessica picked up her glass and started to swirl it, then hesitated and reached across the table. "Here's to keeping the eye on the road, and focusing on the here and now," she said.

"To the here and now," he repeated as he touched his glass to hers. "And here you are."

"Here *we* are," she corrected him.

Later: Jessica Snow was attacking her key lime pie with a vengeance—*limes again, he noticed*— while Connor was inhaling the aroma drifting up from a cup of decaf. A single malt Scotch had tried to tempt him, but the moment had come and gone without incident. He watched as she slipped a forkful of the creamy desert into her mouth and ran her tongue over her lips, licking away a wisp of green syrup that had been trickled on it.

She looked up from her plate and cracked an embarrassed smile. "I don't normally eat like this," she whispered, a little wistfully. "But this is out of this world."

"Finest in Folly Beach," he agreed as he sipped his coffee.

"You've had it before?" Jessica asked.

"I'm not talking about key limes," he told her.

She giggled again, conscious of his glance and enjoying every minute that it lingered on her. During dinner they both found themselves leaning closer over the table and talking less and less, until very little ended up being spoken at all. Now that the meal was drawing to a close neither of them was in any hurry to push the evening toward its grand finale. That seemed almost a foregone conclusion, so there was no rush.

There was very little to say after that. Connor paid the check while Jessica finished the last of her wine, then walked her outside to the street. He'd parked the Jeep half a block away, but decided not to mention it, figuring the coming moments would evolve as they were meant to. The evening had grown dark and a galaxy of stars had winked on across the heavens. A distant light was blinking steadily in the constellation of Orion, another plane taking people to a different here and now.

They kissed once at the side of the road, under the spreading limbs of a live oak draped with tufts of Spanish moss. Soft and tentative at first, then harder, with more passion as the inhibitions fell away. Connor pulled her close, felt her body against his as he ran his fingers through her hair, and she took his face in her hands and kissed him again.

"It's a long walk back to my hotel," she told him when they finally parted lips.

"Your chariot awaits," he said, gesturing toward his Jeep with a sweep of his hand.

"This is yours?"

"Such as it is," he replied as he helped her up into her seat. No way was he even going to suggest they go to his place, a surefire way to force a definitive end to the evening in one quick move. He walked around and climbed in next to her, traded one more kiss before he pulled out onto the street and pointed the vehicle toward town.

When they arrived at the Tides, he took her arm in his and walked her across the parking lot to the lobby. She snuggled close to him, even though the night was warm, and once or twice she rested her head on his shoulder. Off in the distance he could hear the sound of the water lapping at the sand, the same sound he heard every night when he was drifting off to sleep, only now it suddenly took on a romantic tone. One more kiss in the elevator—this one on her forehead—and then they were standing at her door.

The moment of truth.

In the end, Jessica made it easy on him. She turned to face him, kissed him lightly on the lips, then eased back a few inches and held his eyes with hers.

"You have to come in and show me how that magic trick of yours ends," she said.

"The pleasure is all mine," Connor grinned.

"I sure hope not," she shot back.

She moved first, which did not surprise him. Nor did he mind; he found assertive women attractive, particularly those who also knew how to be delicate and feminine. Jessica Snow certainly fit all these categories, so when she closed the door and turned to press her lips to his, he was not disappointed. They touched lightly at first, barely more than a spark. She placed her hands on his collar, gently running her fingers over his shirt as she tasted him with her tongue. Connor responded by touching one hand to either cheek and pulling her toward him. She reacted with a low purring sound, then slipped her arms around his neck. She eagerly pressed her body against his and held him tightly, as if she was afraid a marvelous dream might end if she let go.

He had no intention of letting that happen. He ran his fingers down her neck and shoulders, trickling them over her bare shoulders. Then he touched them lightly to her breasts and felt her entire body sigh in his arms.

She led the way to her bed, her lips fixed to his as they edged into the darkness of the room. Then she slowly began to kiss his chin, his neck, his hands, his shirt, his bare chest as she unfastened the buttons. She looked up at him as he grasped the thin fabric of her sundress and gently pulled it over her head. She held on to him seductively for a moment, then raised her arms and allowed him to remove the rest of her clothing. She wore nothing underneath except a pair of thong panties, which looked anything but comfortable. He lowered his head and ran a tongue over one breast, then drew it gently over to the other, each time lightly imbibing a faint taste of salt. Then he buried his head against her soft skin and nuzzled her with his hair. He ran his hands up the back of her legs, letting his fingers explore as they went, and he thought he felt her skin quiver at his touch.

She had her first convulsion standing in the darkness of her bedroom; a second one came not long afterwards, when Connor lowered her to the bed. He had to clasp a hand over her mouth, out of consideration of her neighbors and concern for the late hour. Then, when she was done with this round, he allowed her to envelope him once more, eventually finding release as he lay on his back in the waning moonlight, watching as her body rose and lowered, rose and lowered, ever so slowly, over his.

It didn't take very long.

Connor awoke several hours later to find he was alone. He'd sensed Jessica's absence in the darkness before he reached out, felt for her body where he had remembered it had been when he'd drifted off to sleep. He lay there a moment, breathing easily, not thinking much of anything except how he didn't want to move, didn't want to do anything that might disrupt the warmth that was still tingling at the ends of his nerves. The glass slider leading out to the balcony was cracked open and a gentle breeze was oozing in through the drapes that neither of them had bothered to close. In the distance he could hear the gentle lapping of water on sand, but otherwise the night was quiet and still and dark.

For a moment he thought Jessica must be in the bathroom, but the door was wide open and he could see she was not there. This puzzled him for a moment, and then his mind snapped past the point where he was more awake than asleep. He sat up in the king-sized bed, blinked his eyes rapidly as they adjusted to the dim light, then swung his tired legs to the floor and stood up. He pulled on his trousers and found his shirt in a mound on the floor.

The digital clock on the nightstand told Connor it was ten minutes past two. He reflected on that a moment, his first thought being that by now Julie had closed up and the bar was locked down for the night. Earlier, he'd felt a touch remiss for not stopping by after dinner to see how business had been, considering the events of that morning. But Julie was a big girl and The Sandbar was in good hands. There was no reason for him to go nosing about where it wasn't needed, especially when he'd had other things on his mind.

His mind quickly returned to where Jessica might have gone, why she had left him alone in her room. What was she up to and when was she coming back? He had a fleeting thought that Alfonse Romano somehow might be involved, but quickly forced that idea from his mind. He pushed the glass slider open and walked out onto the small balcony, but there was no sign of her down at the pool, either. He peered through the darkness to see if he could catch her wandering along the sand, but he saw no movement at all. He gave her another few minutes to return to the room, but when she still didn't show he slipped on his shoes and headed down in the elevator. She wasn't in the lobby, and the restaurant and bar had long since closed. Not knowing what else to do he made his way through the parking lot to where he'd parked the Jeep.

Perplexed by Jessica's disappearance and operating out of habit, he started the engine and headed back toward The Sandbar. Julie very likely had already closed the place down, but he didn't want to go back to his converted garden shed at Cool Sands. Not yet. The night was warm and still, and the lingering aroma of barbecue and boiled shrimp from earlier in the evening still hung in the air. Off in the distance a stereo was thumping out a steady reggae beat, Bob Marley partying from the grave. The Jeep's headlights filled the roadway ahead and caught a possum as it waddled into the underbrush. The pavement itself was slick from a squall that must have moved through earlier and dumped some rain before moving on.

As Connor drove through town, he noticed an orange glow low in the sky down near the beach. His first thought was that somewhere a party was lasting too long into the night, but as he got closer, he sensed it was far more than that. Something was very, very wrong. The tops of the palmetto trees were pulsing red and blue, and the orange hue he'd seen seemed to be dancing against the black sky. He slowed as he drove up the street, realizing now that the red and blue lights were coming from emergency vehicles, but the flickering orange remained a puzzle until he spotted Folly's two fire engines blocking the intersection directly ahead of him.

Connor cut the engine and jumped out of the Jeep, then ran the rest of the way up the street toward The Sandbar.

Or what was left of it.

CHAPTER 22

The entire structure was engulfed in flames, tongues of fire lapping hungrily at the night. A small army of volunteer firefighters was unloading water through a hose, but there was no point. The blaze was too large and the hose too small to make much of a difference.

Connor slowed to a stop just a few yards from where the steps that led up to the drinking deck were now just smoldering chunks of blackened wood. A wall of flames was devouring the counter, the stools, the floor, the spinnaker ceiling. Bottles of booze exploded under the plywood cover with a fiery whoosh, fueled by the alcohol inside.

He moved just close enough to feel the intense heat on his face, then backed off a few steps. He didn't even see Lincoln Polk standing under a scorched mangrove tree until the cop said, "Stand back, Mr. Connor. Nothing you can do."

"But...*the bar!*" Connor choked, the smoke heavier near the flames. "I have to save it."

"Too late," the policeman said, his low, steady voice equal parts empathy and authority. "It's gone. Now they're just trying to save the buildings next door."

Connor glanced up to where the stairs led to his attic apartment, saw that it was totally consumed by the ravenous flames, as well. "I can't believe this is happening—"

"Sorry, man," Polk said, shaking his head. "Good thing you moved your stuff out."

"Yea...good thing."

Connor was going to say something more, but he suddenly felt everything drain out of him. He was not a man prone to showing his emotions, but at that particular moment he felt a flood of them, mostly fronted by anger and fear. Anger at whoever had done this to The Sandbar, relief that by a simple twist of fate he hadn't lost everything he owned as he'd done in the storm last year. He also felt a profound fear that someone could have been injured in the fire, or worse. He closed his eyes as he felt an inner weight drag him down, and he slumped against the tree next to him. He took a deep breath, let it out, then forced himself to open his eyes and look again. Yeah, it was real, all right. Too damned real.

Finally he turned to Polk and said, "What the hell happened?"

"Looks like it started up there, on the steps up near your front door." Polk glanced past the immolated crime scene tape to the top of the charred stairs that led up to the landing outside Connor's apartment.

"But…how?" Connor asked. "What caused it?"

"Too early to tell," Polk told him. "But the fed man will want to talk to you, I'm sure."

"What fed man?"

"That one," Polk said, gesturing with his chin at a man dressed in khaki trousers and a wrinkled, light blue short-sleeve shirt.

Fuck! Connor thought. Agent Landry. What the hell was *he* doing here?

"I think he's with the FBI or DEA," Polk added.

"Justice Department," Connor corrected him. "We've already met."

"Well, he thinks he's in charge." Polk turned toward Connor, a look of relief in his tired eyes. "You want to know the truth, I thought you coulda been in there."

"You kicked me out, remember?"

"I know you better than you think. Anyway, I'm glad you're okay."

"That makes two of us."

If Agent Landry was relieved to see that Connor's body was not among the charred ruins, he didn't show it. He was standing at the perimeter of the fire scene, watching the firemen battle the flames. He stood with his hands in his pockets, his eyes showing no expression other than concentration, like an impassive football coach standing on the sidelines while his players did what he expected of them. Eventually he edged over to where Connor was standing and took up residence about two feet away.

"As you can see, the building sustained considerable damage," the fed said as if he were narrating a training film.

"What the hell happened?" Connor demanded.

"We're still trying to determine that," the federal agent answered abruptly. "I thought you might be able to help us."

"I wasn't here. I just got back…"

"Where were you?"

"Not that it's any of your business, but I was at the Tides," he said.

"Do you have a witness who can vouch for you?" Landry said, his voice expressionless.

"Do I need one?" Landry didn't respond and they both stood there, not saying anything for a minute, so Connor asked, "Any idea what started the fire—?"

"All we know so far is that there was some sort of a pop," the federal agent answered with a shrug.

"What do you mean, a pop?"

"We have two witnesses, a couple here from Atlanta on vacation, who say they heard something that sounded like a gunshot." Landry nodded in the direction they were standing, some ten yards down the sidewalk. "Then a moment after, a big whoosh of flames."

"Someone set this," Connor said.

"The man's a genius," Agent Landry said, his face expressionless like a marble bust. "Maybe the dead guy over there on the stairs did it."

"Dead guy?" Connor felt that old icy chain dragging up his spine. "What the hell are you talking about?"

"Right there," Landry said, pointing with his chin. "Because of the heat we can't get close enough to move the body, but we believe that may be his car parked over there. You recognize it?"

Landry pointed beyond the charred ruins to where a new Ford F-150 quad cab dually was parked at the edge of the shore road. It was wrapped in a custom purple that glowed under the orange flames, and on the passenger door Connor could see a picture of a scantily clad woman with oversized breasts. He had seen the truck around town and, while he'd never once said "hi" to its owner, he knew who drove it. So did almost everyone in town. The custom purple matched that of his high-speed cigarette boat.

"We're running the plates right now," Landry added.

"Don't bother," Connor told him. "I know who it belongs to."

Lincoln Polk, who had been standing off to the side, flashed Connor a worried look, a look he returned with a carefree shrug.

"I thought you might," Landry said.

Connor didn't like the sound of what the federal agent was implying but chose to ignore it. Instead he said, "His name is Cecil Maines." *And why the hell he showed up at my door in the middle of the night I haven't a clue.*

Landry seemed to recognize the name. "You're sure about that?" he said, glancing again at the crisped corpse on the wooden stairs. The glow from the flames gave an orange tint to the agent's face, which was glistening from the sweat caused by the rush of heat.

"I'm sure that's his truck," he confirmed. "But I don't know if that's his body."

"Leave that to us," Landry said. He ran a hand across his brow, wiped it on his trousers. "How do you know this Mr. Maines?"

"I don't. I've seen him around town a few times; hard to miss the truck."

"Let me get this straight," Landry said. "One of the top gang-bangers in all of Charleston comes calling on you in the middle of the night, gets himself shot and cremated in your place of business, and you don't know why?"

"Nope. Like I said, I didn't know the man."

"But you know his truck."

"It's his calling card," Connor replied.

Landry gripped his right index finger with his left hand and cracked the knuckle; then he proceeded to slowly do the same to the rest of his fingers. "You seem to be pretty popular with people you don't know," he eventually observed.

"Meaning what?" Connor asked, studying the flames that only now were beginning to lose their battle against the Folly Beach fire battalion.

"Meaning that less than twenty-four hours ago a man was shot to death in your apartment, and then this Cecil Maines—who you say you don't know from Adam—burns up right outside your door. Pardon me if I'm more than a little curious at any connection that might tie these two events together."

"If you're going to cuff me, go right ahead."

"Look, Connor," Landry growled. "This is not an interrogation, and you are not a suspect. But take a look around. You know what I see? I see a building that's in ruins, with a bad-ass drug dealer fried extra-crispy on the stairs. How he died is obvious, but why is another story. It's my job to find out, and whatever you might be able to contribute to the cause would be most appreciated."

"Like—?"

"Like anything that could help me figure out what the hell is going on. Do you hear what I'm saying?"

"Loud and clear," Connor said. This conversation was getting old and a swarm of thoughts was buzzing around in his brain like bees drawn to a new queen. "But I'm afraid I'm not going to be much help right now. It's late, I'm tired, the bar just burned to the ground, and my head hurts."

"Sucks to be you." The sarcasm in Landry's voice was thick, like drive-thru ice cream. "Tell me what you know about Cecil Maines and I'll leave you alone until morning."

"You probably know more about him than I do." Connor's head really was hurting, especially where it had connected with something hard and fast and very painful the other day. "Rumor is, the guy is—was—a drug runner. A transporter more than a dealer. From what I hear he was fast, slick, and very smart."

"Not smart enough," Landry said, casting a glance at the man's charred remains.

"Everyone has his limit."

"And tonight he just drops by your place unexpected?"

"Like I keep telling you, I don't know anything about that," Connor said. "You ask me, someone must've used some kind of highly flammable accelerant."

"No shit," Landry said, picking at something that may have been stuck in his teeth. "What's your point?"

"My point is, I think they were trying to cover something up."

"They?"

"You mentioned there was a pop that sounded like a gun. I wouldn't be surprised if Maines got himself shot, and the fire was set just to hide it."

"That's why we do autopsies," Landry quipped. He plucked his finger from his teeth and examined the nail. Nothing. "Look, Mr. Connor—go home to Cool Sands and get some sleep."

How do he know about that? he thought but did not say. "Where I'm headed now," Connor told him instead.

"Make sure you get there," Landry replied with a sideways glance, not trusting him for a second. "Don't you even think about messing around in this."

"Not in a million years."

"Good. Because if you ask me, Cecil Maines was not the target tonight. I think there's someone in this town who wants you dead."

CHAPTER 23

After Landry moved on, Connor lingered a bit under the scorched palmetto. When he'd first seen the remnants of what appeared to be Cecil Maines' body lying on the charred stairs, his mind had flashed on Julie and whether anything had happened to her. He felt guilty for putting her in charge of the bar for the night, then quickly realized that the fire most likely had been started long after she'd closed down for the night. But he'd put that those thoughts out of his mind when he realized her VW bug wasn't parked in its usual place, and had gone home before the blaze had begun. He considered calling her, but if she was already in bed, he didn't want to hit her with the hard news tonight. She'd hear what had happened to The Sandbar soon enough as it was.

Eventually he decided it was time to make himself scarce. Wisps of smoke still curled up from the smoldering embers, and a team from the coroner's office was attempting to get close to what remained of Cecil Maines. The glowing embers from the fire caused his mind to flash on the horrors he had witnessed in Kirkuk, a visual montage of sights and smells and sounds that had become deeply etched in his brain.

That line of thought led him to remember the phone call he'd received the other day, Leon Scott telling him that Gordo had checked out permanently, no forwarding address. Another one of his buddies was gone, not someone he knew from his own time in Iraq, but a fellow traveler who had fallen into a pit of desperation. A hole from which he had not been able to crawl out.

Just as quickly as he had beamed back in time to Iraq, Connor now found himself back in the present, his mind massaging the nagging question: *who the hell did this?* Was it someone connected to the John Doe who had been shot in Connor's apartment, or maybe the dead man in the blue Tahoe? However it went down, the triggerman could be out there right now in the darkness, keeping Connor in his sights, waiting to get a clean shot at him. But why? What had he learned—or found—that had caused all this grief?

The flash drive, of course. That's why Connor had been cold-cocked on the head out at Martina Carerra's place, and that's what the man who'd broken into his apartment had been looking for. Then he'd met up with the mushrooming end of a lead slug, one that most likely was meant for Connor.

None of which answered why Cecil Maines had come to The Sandbar tonight. Jimmy Brinks had mentioned that Maines had seen something out on Hatchitch Island that had scared the shit out of him the night Tony Carerra had died, something he definitely did not want to talk about. Had he come by the bar to tell Connor something? Possibly, but that seemed out of character of a Lowcountry gang-banger with a private cache of guns whose speedboat could outrun anything owned by the feds.

All of this told Connor that drugs were involved. The local news reported almost daily on random shootings and busts from North Charleston to Walterboro, almost all of it gang-related. None of these thugs paid any mind to the collateral damage their actions might cause; if six people had to die just to take out one target, that was just a matter of being in the wrong place at the wrong time. A few stray lives were insignificant compared with the dollars that were at stake. Which meant that whoever was targeting Connor didn't give a shit about who else might get killed. A job was a job and nothing else mattered, which was probably how Justacious Stone came to be standing under this very same palmetto last Friday night.

And then ended up shanked in his cell.

Connor's mind drifted to Jessica, wondering again where she was and why she had disappeared. Had last night been just a notch in her lipstick case, or was there more to it than that? He pulled out his cell phone and started to dial her number, then realized she'd never given it to him. All their contact had been at the bar, and now even that was gone.

As Connor slipped his phone back into his pocket, he figured he ought to call Julie, let her know what had happened to the bar. But it was the middle of the night and there was no point in waking her up just to tell her that her job had just gone up in smoke. That truth would hit her soon enough.

All of a sudden, he felt very exposed, sensed he was being watched by whoever had botched this job. Whoever had set the fire probably was lurking in the darkness, lining up a red laser dot on the back of his skull. Connor took one more look at what had been The Sandbar, then walked back up the road to where he'd left the Jeep. He climbed behind the wheel and sat there for a minute while he tried to figure out what to do, where to go. Finally he started the engine and pulled forward, past the last emergency vehicles that remained at the scene.

The sensible thing would be to go back to his cabin at Cool Sands and dredge a few hours of sleep out of what remained of the night. But at the end of the block Connor made a left turn so he could circle back through town. As he did, he caught sight of a black four-wheel drive SUV—he couldn't make out what make or model—parked at the edge of the road. Behind the wheel he noticed the shadow of a large man, his skin almost as dark as the car, watching him through the driver's window. There was a vague familiarity about him, but it was too dark and Connor was too preoccupied—and tired—to make any connection. Whoever the man was, he didn't shift his dark, sunken eyes as Connor drove past. A cigarette dangled from his lips; it didn't move, either.

Five minutes later Connor was heading out of town, comforted by the knowledge that Lincoln Polk's cousin had agreed to watch Clooney for the night. Except for the emergency crews that were cleaning up the ashes and soot, Folly Beach was still asleep. A gentle wind was blowing in from the south, and along the sill of the marsh a necklace of white lights glimmered from boats gently rocking on the water. The night was dark and still, a black canopy strewn with constellations of stars, obscured here and there by the occasional passing cloud.

Keeping one hand on the wheel he massaged his temples. The initial shock of finding the bar engulfed in flames had yielded to a very raw anger that someone would have had the balls to do this. If they were trying to get him to back off, they sure as hell had no idea what made him tick.

Besides, this was not about backing off; it was about silencing him permanently. Connor was certain of it. He also was certain that whoever was behind this entire scenario was not some two-bit player, and somehow Tony Carerra was mixed up in all of it. And now as he thought about it, as he let all the pieces slide into place, he suddenly knew where he had to go.

Over the past few months Connor had heard that Jimmy Brinks lived amidst the mosquitoes and marsh flies in an area known as Stono Flats. It was a soggy patch of pluff mud and old oyster beds that stretched along the shore of the Stono River only a foot or two above the high-water mark, and during a moon tide much of it disappeared with the rising current. The area definitely was on the endangered list for climate change and shifting sea levels, but no one who called the place home was inclined to believe—let alone understand—that sort of shit. Pricey seven-figure McMansions with long docks and boat lifts had been built on pilings less than a mile away, but no one dared venture into The Flats without a pair of hip waders and a good excuse for being there.

Brinks had picked up an acre of prime mud for not much more than the cost of the old houseboat that sat on it, and over time he had cleared the lot in preparation for building. Connor had never been anywhere near it—he'd never had the need— but rumor had it that Brinks lived in the boat with two large dogs that guarded his share of the armored car heist. That same rumor speculated that the money was stashed somewhere in the hull, or maybe in a watertight vault buried in the muck. Connor had heard the stories and had listened with amusement when they were being told, but he was quite certain that Jimmy Brinks' money—if any of it was left—was nowhere near his scrappy marsh-front lot.

Even though it was well past midnight, that's where he decided to go. Whatever Cecil Maines had told Brinks might shed some light on what the hell was going on. Brinks generally kept to himself, which made Connor curious why he'd dropped into the bar a couple of times recently. He usually came into town only when it was absolutely necessary, which seemed odd since the few times

Connor had spoken with him—always at the bar—he seemed to know just about everything about everyone.

Connor followed Folly Road a few miles out of town, then hung a left onto a narrow chip-seal road that was scabbed with asphalt patch. The night was darker along here, the moon and the stars blocked out by the thick vegetation choking both sides of the road. The Jeep's headlights bounced off the deep green undergrowth, picking up the gleaming eyes of some sort of critter hiding in the brush. The pungent smell of pluff mud invaded his nose, and a gentle spritz from a passing cloud dampened the windshield for just a second, though not enough for him to even hit the wipers.

He first noticed the vehicle behind him when he headed into a sharp curve. Its headlights were off, but he could see the glow of moonlight reflecting off the tinted windows fifty yards back. A jolt of adrenaline shot into Connor's bloodstream and he settled his foot a little more firmly on the accelerator. The Jeep fishtailed slightly as it surged into the bend, and he had to fight the wheel to keep it on the road.

The curve was more of an elongated "S" formed around a drainage culvert that emptied into the marsh. Jeeps are not known for their responsive handling, and Connor had to ease up on the gas until he hit a straight stretch again. Then he pushed the pedal down to the floor, just as he caught the glint of light off the pursuing vehicle's roof navigating the very same curve.

Then the headlights came on, removing any doubt of what this was all about. Connor could almost feel a red laser dot fixing on the back of his head. Any second now his skull might explode, and he would never even hear the crack of the gun. Instinctively he touched his foot to the accelerator as edged the wheel to the left, then to the right. Tires chewed on gravel as the Jeep wobbled on the narrow shoulder, but Connor kept swerving from one shoulder to the other, making it difficult for his pursuer to get off a clean shot. He goosed the gas a little more, then hit the brakes at the very last minute as he raced into another series of sharp turns. He glanced into the mirror and made out the distinctive tubular grill of a Land Rover—the rugged Defender model, black over black, with tinted windows and darkened rims. The same vehicle he had seen parked at the side of the road when he had left the fire back in Folly Beach.

All of a sudden, a star pattern etched the Jeep's windshield, a web of lines spreading out from a small hole in the center. At the same time there was a loud crack, and Connor barely had time to register what had happened as the glass dissolved into a torrent of diamond. The shooting had definitely begun.

Again, he twisted the wheel and swerved from the left shoulder to the right. The Jeep's fender glanced off something that looked like an old refrigerator, killing one of the headlights. Connor pulled the vehicle back onto the road just as another bullet cracked what was left of the windscreen. Another shot slammed into the roll bar just behind his left ear. He glanced up at the rearview mirror, which thus far had survived the barrage of shots. The Land Rover was right on his ass now, no more than fifteen yards back, and he could see a man holding a large pistol out the driver's side window. Connor swerved again just as he heard the smack of lead on steel; another shot had missed. Almost subconsciously, he found himself clearly aware of two things: the man was trying to kill him, and Connor was dead if he didn't do something now.

Up ahead he could see another sharp turn that led away from the marsh. He knew Jimmy Brinks lived out here somewhere, but he was not familiar with the terrain and had no idea what lay ahead. Then his lone headlight caught a hand-painted street sign that gave him the option of turning left toward Stono Flats or hanging a right back toward Folly Road. Either way his Jeep was no match for the Land Rover that was clinging to his ass; one of those bullets eventually would hit its mark.

Just then an old pick-up truck charged up the road from where the sign said, "Folly Road 3 Miles." The truck's headlights were off, making it only a shadowy ghost in the darkness. Connor's first thought was that this was an ambush, but then—almost too late and with no time for mental follow-through—he recognized the make and model of the pick-up. *Shit,* he thought as he grasped the situation and swerved as far to the right as he could. The dark truck bore down on him, then spun sharply to the opposite side of the road and raced past.

The truck and the Land Rover appeared to be on a collision course, but at the last moment the black Defender veered far over to the shoulder. Almost immediately the driver realized he'd whipped the steering wheel around too far and too fast, but his corrective move came too late. The rear of the Land Rover began to fishtail; then, almost as if the view slowed down frame by frame, it flipped sideways and rolled like a barrel until it collided with a large propane tank that had been abandoned in a mound of oyster shells.

The explosion came next as a rush of gas vapor ignited. The flames intensified and the glow began to brighten the night. A startled heron lifted off from where it had been sleeping in the marsh, offering a rude honk as it glided away. For a moment Connor thought he saw a man inside the vehicle trying to scramble out from behind the wheel, but he couldn't be sure. Then the fire grew too fierce and all he could do was imagine the horror that was unfolding within.

"Get out," a voice yelled as the pick-up quickly backed up and slipped alongside the Jeep. The glow of the fire cast an orange hue to the leathery face that was looking at Connor through the window on the passenger side. "Bust your tattooed ass...now."

"Dammit, man—where the hell did you come from?"

"I heard what happened to Cecil," Jimmy Brinks said. "Figured some major shit was starting to come down."

"I owe you one," Connor said as he took a breath—he had no idea when he'd taken his last one—and wiped an arm across his forehead.

"Yeah, you do," Brinks assured him with a raspy growl. "Now get in the truck."

"I can't just leave my Jeep—"

"You can report it stolen in the morning," Brinks told him. "No questions— just get in."

Connor hesitated only a second, then did as Brinks ordered. He slipped out of the old Wrangler, climbed into the passenger side of the pick-up.

Brinks said nothing as he gunned the engine, backed the truck into a narrow pull-out, then reversed direction. Connor stared straight ahead but said nothing as he tried to find a shred of sense in what was going on. They rode in silence a few seconds, then Connor glanced over at the old armored car robber sitting beside him.

"You saved my life," he said.

"Didn't start out that way," Brinks grunted. "Alls I did was drive into town to check on Cecil. Poor bastard."

"So, how'd you know?" Connor asked. He cocked his head backward, indicating the burning Land Rover. "About all this, I mean."

"I passed you as you drove out of town. Then I saw that shithead, Jesry Freeman, right behind you."

"Jesry?" Connor said.

"High-rollin' gangbanger, locked in with some bad dudes."

"You heard this from Maines?"

Jimmy Brinks looked over at him with a scowl, said, "Don't ask questions. Too late for that sort of thing."

Connor glared at him, said, "Like I said, thanks for saving me back there. And I'm sorry 'bout your friend. But I've got other things on my mind right now, so lay off the tough-guy shit and either tell me what you know or let me out right here."

"What, you're gonna walk home?"

"It's only a few miles to the main road. I can get a ride from there."

Brinks thought on this a second as he gnawed on his lower lip. To the east a faint glow was beginning to seep into the black sky, and he took that moment to change the subject. "Sun's gonna come up soon."

"Happens every morning," Connor grunted as he leaned back in his seat.

They came to another fork where the road split one more time, but this time there was no sign offering driving directions. Brinks shifted into low gear and headed left, the nearly bald tires slipping on slick mud.

"Where're we going?" Connor asked, breaking the silence.

Jimmy Brinks looked at him but offered nothing.

"I said, 'where're we going?'" Connor repeated.

"Jesus, man—I heard you," the ex-con said.

"Then tell me where the hell you're taking me."

"My place."

Connor eyed him, but only for a second. "What the hell for?"

"It's where I live," Brinks explained shortly. "And I got something to give you."

CHAPTER 24

The rumors about Jimmy Brinks' dogs were true, except there were three of them, not two. He described them as "pedigreed hybrids," each of them a mix of various breeds and all three long in the tooth. Two of them roamed free on the patch of land that ran from the dirt road to the marsh, while the other was chained to a post at the far end of a clearing, near an old flat-bottomed houseboat that looked as if it had floated right up onto the mud. The hull appeared to be constructed mostly of fiberglass patchwork and paint, hardly seaworthy, and Brinks had somehow managed to haul it up onto cinder block pilings that, over, time had sunk unevenly into the odorous sludge.

Two plastic Adirondack chairs sat on a small patio fashioned from moldy pavers that looked as if they'd been scrounged from an old building site.

"Have a seat," Brinks grunted, nodding Connor into one of them.

"I really need to go—"

"I'll make some coffee," Brinks said, ignoring him.

Now that the new day was dawning Connor realized he really didn't want to be there. In fact, what he really wanted was to get up and get back to his cabin at Cool Sands. But he had questions about Cecil Maines, and he knew Jimmy Brinks had some answers. Brinks also had said that he had something to give him. In any event, a cup of any kind of strong coffee sounded like a damned fine idea right about now.

"One cup," Connor said.

"Don't do me any favors."

Still, Brinks scrambled up a rickety ladder to the boat's deck and disappeared inside. Connor glanced around, studied the tethered dog, wondered how long the chain was. All three beasts were eyeing him now, and they seemed to have the same nasty temperament as their owner. He did his best to ignore them as he tentatively sat down in one of the plastic chairs. He stretched his legs out in front of him, tipped his head back and soaked in the deep purple sky overhead. A few large puffy clouds drifted lazily from the east, momentarily covering the face of the moon.

Off to Connor's right was a mound of concrete rubble, large fragments of cement that had been hacked into chunks the size of firewood. Behind this, a stack of pressure-treated floor joists was set up on cinder block pilings, alongside a pile of marine plywood. It looked like Mr. Brinks finally was starting to build his dream home.

He thought about what Brinks had told him, letting the pieces slip more firmly into place. First up: Jesry Freeman. Jesry wasn't a common name, so he figured he had to be the boyfriend of Em Lee's mother. Connor also was willing to bet that Jesry was the guy with the gun who'd confronted him outside Justacious Sone's aunt's house out on Cusabo Gut and, later, at the courthouse. Probably shot and killed Cecil Maines, too, before chasing Connor on Ossituh Road just now.

Could Jesry Freeman have been the gunman who had fired a shot through Connor's screen yesterday morning? Possibly, but not likely. Even less possible was the idea that he'd offed the driver of the Tahoe outside the bar. That just didn't make sense.

Just then Brinks came back out of his land yacht carrying two mugs of coffee. He navigated the ladder down from the deck, then came over and handed one to Connor.

"Never mind the mess," he said. "I ain't got around to carting off the pieces of the old cistern yet."

"No ground water out here?"

"Too salty. Anything drinkable comes right from the sky."

"You bust it up like that?" Connor asked, sipping his coffee. It was strong but good.

"Easier than it looks," Brinks shrugged. "Back in the day a lot of concrete was mixed with salt water, no rebar. Crumbles real easy. Don't take much to knock it down."

Connor nodded but said nothing, just stared eastward toward a faint crease of dawn on the horizon. In the growing light he could see a lone egret perched on its spindly legs, waiting for an early breakfast to swim by. The definition of patience. Neither he nor Jimmy Brinks said a word for a good five minutes, Connor resting his brain from the shitstorm he'd downloaded over the last few hours, Brinks giving him time to work it all through.

"So, what's the deal with Maines?" Connor finally asked. "Why'd he come to my place?"

Brinks slowly swirled his mug and pondered the ripples within, then said, "The deal is, Cecil Maines was out here, earlier tonight, still spooked about what he saw out on Hatchitch last Friday night. This is a guy who's got a house full of guns, an armed posse guarding his ass, and an ego larger than his dick."

"I assume that was an impressive thing," Connor said dryly as he took a sip of coffee. "He tells you what it was that spooked him?"

"Just that he saw something," Brinks explained. "And then the night before last some dude with long hair came 'round his place wavin' one fucking big gun, as Cecil told it, sayin' he was already a dead man."

"My guess is, Maines probably got that a lot," Connor pointed out.

"The man did have his enemies," Jimmy Brinks agreed. He was using the toe of his sandal to draw an arc in the sand that dusted the concrete pavers. "But this time was different, he said."

Begging the question, which Connor supplied: "Why is that?"

"'Cause this long-haired guy with the gun, Cecil said he'd seen him out on Hatchitch. And he was sure, when he looked the guy in the eye, that the fuck-head knew he'd been there."

Connor considered this, then said, "This 'fuck-head'…did Cecil tell you exactly what the guy said when he showed up at his place?"

"That's the thing. Cecil wasn't the type to pay it no mind, but this time he remembered every word. Like it was more than a threat. Something like, 'You were out there that night, you saw what went down. Time comes, I'm gonna blow a hole through your spine.'"

Something about what Jimmy Brinks was saying rang true. "Did Cecil say if he knew this guy?" Connor asked.

The corner of his mouth turned up in a lopsided smile. "Yeah, he knew him."

"So why didn't he take him care of him then and there? Way you say it, Cecil Maines had a regular National Guard armory at his house."

"That's what I asked him when he showed up. But he didn't want to talk about it, 'cept for one other thing."

Yet another question waiting to be begged. "And that thing is?" Connor asked.

"Jesry Freeman dropped by his place this afternoon. Yesterday now, I guess."

Connor stared at him but said nothing.

"So Jesry's all hopped up on something, some kind of pharmaceutical, and he's wavin' a gun around. And he says to Cecil, 'you're dead, man, and so's that mutha-fuckah white man, runs that bar.'"

"Think he meant it?"

"What do you think?" Brinks said simply.

Another silence, another couple minutes ticked by. Then Connor turned toward the ex-con, looked at him over the rim of his mug. "Back there on the road, you said you had something to give me."

Brinks' head dipped in an almost imperceptible nod. "Yeah, I did," he said in a voice that sounded as if he'd get around to it sooner or later.

"Not to be rude, and thanks for the coffee and helping me out earlier, but do you think maybe we can get to it so I can be on my way?"

"You in a hurry?"

"Day's almost here, and it figures to be a long one."

Brinks nodded again, rocking in his plastic Adirondack chair to some secret rhythm in his head. Then he balanced his mug on a chunk of concrete next to him, and slowly rose to his feet. He pulled something out of his waistband that was hidden by his loose-fitting shirt and hefted it in his hand.

It was a gun. More specifically, a Glock 9 mm semi-automatic with an extended clip.

"What's this for?" Connor asked in an impassive voice.

"A lifeline," Brinks said, handing it to him.

The last time Connor had held a gun in his hand he'd winged a crooked DEA agent, total self-defense, do-or-die. "I don't need it," he said.

"The fuck you don't," Brinks snorted. "How many times you almost get killed the last couple of days?"

Brinks was right; Connor had already done the math. If you counted the blow on the head at Martina Carerra's place, the magic number was three. At least that he was aware of. "I figure, with this Jesry Freeman out of the picture, I'll be okay."

Brinks cracked a disgusted grin and shook his head. "Jesus, you really are one dumb sumbitch," he said. "You think the storm is over because that shit-for-brains is dead?"

No, Connor did not. But he wasn't about to let on what he really *was* thinking. He turned the gun over in his hand, then handed it back to Brinks.

"Thanks, but no thanks."

Brinks hesitated, then tossed it on the ground at his feet. "Tell you what. You want the gun, take it. You don't, leave it there. I'm goin' inside, and when I come back out, I want you gone." He started off toward the houseboat, didn't look back as he muttered, "Jesry Freeman was right: you *are* a dead man."

Connor took off not long after that. He hiked three miles to Folly Beach Road and waited close to a half hour before an old surfer dude with gray hair and a shark's tooth on a gold neck chain came by in a rusty Kia and gave him a lift. Ten minutes later they were in Folly Beach, where Connor thanked him for the ride and made his way down the road to charred remains of The Sandbar.

In the dawn of a new day it didn't look better or worse, just different. Last night the flames had been racing through the wooden walls and floor timbers, devouring everything in their path. What the fire itself hadn't consumed; the water hoses had destroyed. Broken glass was everywhere, and the melted cash register and scorched beer coolers looked like burned-out remnants from a war zone. The plastic chairs along the rail now resembled candles that had melted into puddles of wax. The Dacron spinnaker that shaded the bar from the sun and kept the sudden rains out was hanging from its aluminum frame in blistered shreds.

The stairs leading to the apartment were totally gone; only the risers remained, and they looked ready to collapse at the slightest breeze. All signs of Cecil Maines' immolation had been cleared away, and a new strip of yellow crime scene tape was the only hint of color against the mass of blackened timbers.

"I told you those flaming tiki torch drinks would be the end of you," came a voice from behind him. It belonged to a local named Derek Smyth, and as

Connor turned around, he heard the click of a digital camera. "Alcohol serves as a great accelerant."

"Alcohol had nothing to do with what happened here," Connor said to the editor and publisher of the *Folly Beach Wave*. The *Wave* was a free weekly advertising rag that mostly focused on local fishing tournaments and sandcastle contests, and tended to ignore high crimes and misdemeanors of any kind. The less the tourists knew about the seamier side of town, the better.

"Relax, Jack," Smyth said, placing a hand on Connor's shoulder. He was a tall, scrawny man with thinning gray hair and pale skin that seemed to hug the bones in his jaw. He wore an orange shirt with a purple Clemson tiger paw, and a black fedora hat with a white band was perched on the top of his head. "I've already read the police report. I know you had nothing to do with this."

I wouldn't be so sure about that, Connor thought, but instead asked, "You writing a story about the demise of The Sandbar"

"You've sure had a run of bad luck," Smyth pointed out, not really answering the question. "First the shooting last weekend, then yesterday, and now all this."

"Yeah, well let's hope bad luck runs in threes," Connor said. "You're actually doing some investigative work for a change?"

"This week's paper's already at the printer," Smyth said, dodging the question.

"Then what's with the camera?"

"I belong to a couple of online image libraries," he said with a shrug. "Figured I could upload a few shots of the damage in case other papers wanted them."

"Profiting from the misfortune of others."

"A buck's a buck," Smyth replied with a wry grin that was nowhere close to apologetic. "And for what it's worth, I hear the mayor is convening a special meeting with the police chief today. Local businesses are worried that this sudden wave of murders might give Folly a bad name. I'm surprised he hasn't called you."

As far as Connor knew, only close friends and business associates knew his cell number, and he aimed to keep it that way. "Haven't heard from hizzoner yet," he said. "Besides, whatever is going on, I'm sure no one has anything to worry about."

"Really? After what happened to your place, here?"

Connor had no witty reply so he kept silent and closed his eyes, hoping Derek Smyth would be gone when he opened them. No such luck.

"Seems to me The Sandbar is in the middle of all this," Smyth pressed. "Four men already dead, and then the fire. Even the murder at that house out on the shore road ties in, since it's where the first dead guy was staying."

There was no point denying the connection, and Connor was curious what the cops were saying about the deceased woman out at the place called Calypso Cove. The same woman whose blood was being cleaned up by Lionel Hanes and his BioClean team when he dropped by just yesterday afternoon. So, he said, "Have they identified the body?"

"Dunno," Smyth said, offering up yet another shrug. "You know me—yard of the month and the town's best fish tacos are my beat. Do you mind if I get a couple more shots?"

"Shoot away," Connor replied. "Everyone else seems to be."

By now the fire had drawn the gapers and gawkers, locals and tourists alike. They were standing around the perimeter of the ashes, clicking their cell phones and capturing video that no doubt would be posted on YouTube and Facebook within seconds. As they pointed and clicked and theorized about what had happened, Connor picked up snippets of what was being said: "...*Suspicious origin...*" "...*Burned to a crisp...*" "...*Who would do such a thing...?*" "...*Fourth murder in less than a week...*" They were the same things he was asking himself, but it was clear that these tourists weren't even close to knowing what this was all about.

What Connor didn't yet realize was that neither was he, but he was going to learn, as they say, right quick.

That's when Julie arrived on the scene. She drove an old VW bug, light yellow where the rust hadn't consumed the old steel body, two hubcaps missing. She swerved onto the shoulder across the road from the bar and was on her feet almost before it stopped rolling. She was dressed in cut-offs and a faded k.d. lang concert T-shirt, and was carrying her flip-flops in her hand. She hesitated a moment as she stared at the charred rubble, then saw Connor standing there and came racing up to him.

"Jack...thank God you're okay!" she gushed, throwing her arms around him and burrowing her sobs into his shoulder.

"Why wouldn't I be okay?" he asked her when he finally managed to push back an inch or so.

"I heard someone was killed in the fire. On the steps leading up to your place."

Connor forced a smile and said, "You know you shouldn't believe everything you hear."

"You mean...no one died?"

"No—you got that part right," he explained. "But it obviously wasn't me."

"Obviously," she said. "But if it wasn't you...who was it?"

He lied, telling her that he didn't know if anyone had identified the body yet, that this was a matter for the state cops. They commiserated over a menu of questions, like "who could have done this?" and "how did it start?" and "is it a total loss?" Then he brought the subject around to what she—Julie—was going to do, now that her place of employment had burned to the ground.

"I'll figure something out," she replied. "Where's Clooney?"

"He had a sleepover," he said, not wanting to get into the last twelve hours. Not yet, at least. "Let's go get a cup of coffee at Gilbert's."

Julie sniffed back another tear as they walked up the road in the direction of the strong coffee that was just beginning to hit the morning air. She began bombarding Connor with more questions about how the fire might have started, whether someone had set it deliberately, might it have anything to do with the shooting last Friday night or the guy who was found dead in Connor's place just yesterday morning. He told her he'd give her whatever answers he could, just as soon as he had some caffeine in his bloodstream.

"In that case, you can start by telling me how your night with your lady friend went," she said as they headed up the wooden steps into Gilbert's. "The palmetto telegraph is buzzing with rumors."

"I plead the fifth," he replied.

When Connor got back to Cool Sands, he collected Clooney from Bernice, who said he was the first bedmate who didn't hog the entire mattress in years. She'd fed him and made sure he'd answered the call of nature, and Clooney seemed content and relaxed. Maybe it was all the time he'd spent watching *Dr. Phil*.

As he headed up the walk to his cottage, he found Lincoln Polk sitting in a chair on the small porch. He was the last person Connor wanted to see, but he'd expected the cop would show up, sooner or later. Sooner seemed to be his custom.

"Officer Polk," he said, flashing him a broad smile as he fished through his pocket for the key. "What a pleasure to see your face first thing in the morning."

"Good day, Mr. Connor," Polk said, a dour look in his eyes. "It's good to see you, I must say."

"Considering the alternative, I second that emotion," Connor agreed. "But that's not why you're here."

"No, it is not." Polk shook his head, then glanced at a housekeeper getting ready to clean a nearby cottage. She seemed to be minding her own business, but you could never be too careful. No telling what else might be buzzing around the palmetto telegraph. "Do you mind if we take this inside?"

Connor took his key out of his pocket and unlocked the door. He held it open, inviting the cop inside, but Clooney pushed his way past them both and bolted for the bed. Despite its sad state of disrepair, the cabin already felt like home and he was glad he'd been forced to move in yesterday. He knew it seemed trivial—especially for a veteran who had seen far worse in the course of war—but he hadn't been looking forward to moving back into an apartment where a man had died just yesterday. Now that was impossible, and he felt a sense of relief. As long as Bernice's "family rate" held up he could settle in, find another job at one of the dozens of bars in town, and get on with his life.

He apologized for not having any coffee, but Lincoln Polk told him thanks, he was only going to be there for a minute or two. He sat down in a chair by the window, while Connor sat on the edge of the unused bed. The cop obviously had something on his mind, and he waited for him to come out with it.

"We found your Jeep last night," he said, no pretense or small talk.

This was going to get dicey right away, but Connor decided to play it cool. He'd forgotten to report it as stolen, and now it was too late.

"Hey, man, that's great," he said, not sure his words came out as convincing. "After the fire I went looking for it, but it was gone."

"You're saying someone stole it?"

"I don't know what happened to it," Connor lied. "I think I left the key in it. Where was it?"

Polk took a minute to consider what Connor was telling him, then said, "Sheriff deputy found it, out near Stono Flats."

"Where's that?"

"Near the Stono River, about seven miles from here. As the egret flies."

"How in God's name did it get there?" Connor asked.

Polk was studying him carefully now, checking his eyes, reading the fine muscles in his face. Looking for a sign of what was really going on here, having a good hunch what wasn't. "Looks like someone used it for target practice," he replied.

"Shit. First the bar, now my Jeep—"

"That's not all of it," Polk said. "Just a few yards away from it we found a Land Rover, nothing more than a charred hulk. Inside was a dead man, extra crispy."

Connor did his best to act both confused and surprised, but he doubted he was going to win an Oscar. "This dead man—any idea who he was?"

"The vehicle was pretty well burned up, but since the victim was sitting on his wallet when he died, his license was only singed around the edge. Poor bastard was Jesry Freeman."

"Jesry? I know that name—"

"You ought to. He's the boyfriend of the mother of that girl you were with yesterday. Em Lee."

Connor turned and gave Polk a long look, then shook his head. "This doesn't make sense. None of it."

"You're right about that," Polk agreed.

"You think he had anything to do with the fire, or how my Jeep got from here to there?"

"Don't know, but he had a gun," Polk observed idly, as if he were commenting on the weather. "Thing is, it looks like he took a bunch of shots at your car. You know anything 'bout that?"

"Nothing," Connor lied again, lifting his shoulder in a defense move. "In fact, I don't know what I know anymore."

Polk rose from his chair but made no move to leave; not yet, at least. For a moment he appeared deep in thought, then said, "You don't seem surprised by any of this."

"Nothing surprises me about this place," Connor said, patting Clooney on the head. "Nothing and no one."

"Ain't that the truth." Polk looked at him, did a thing with his eyebrow, raising it as if making a point. "Just when you think you've seen it all, got the whole world figured out, suddenly you're surprised all over again."

After Polk left, Connor booted up his laptop and carried it back out onto the small front porch. He sat down in his favorite chair and opened the web page for the *Post and Courier*, the local Charleston daily, and scanned the headlines. He found what he was looking for halfway down the page and clicked on the link.

Folly Murder Victim Identified As Former Nurse From Akron

Police have identified the body of a woman found in a home in Folly Beach yesterday as Roberta Tucker from Chillicothe, Ohio. Tucker was found unresponsive on the floor of a rental home on the north shore of the popular beach town yesterday morning, and emergency medical personnel were unable to revive her. Charleston County Coroner Helen Price confirmed Tucker's identity and said an autopsy to determine cause of death has been scheduled for tomorrow.

Ms. Tucker, the victim, reportedly pleaded guilty eight years ago to four counts of check fraud, and subsequently served eighteen months for embezzling from the assisted living facility where she was employed as a registered nurse. She also was charged with writing false prescriptions for controlled substances, but that charge was dropped as part of a pre-arranged plea deal. Since her release from prison she had been working as a cashier at a restaurant in her home town of Chillicothe, but several family members said they hadn't seen her in several weeks.

State Law Enforcement Division investigator Andrew Dodson said in a prepared statement that the suspect in Ms. Tucker's murder is still at large, although they have interviewed several witnesses and are pursuing all leads.

Connor was both shocked and relieved. He'd fully expected the dead woman to be Martina Carerra but—unless she was using an assumed name—he was wrong. The color photo accompanying the article confirmed this, since it showed a woman who looked nothing like Tony Carerra's widow. The old mug shot depicted a pale woman with dirty dishwasher hair, square chin, a belligerent scowl in her dark eyes that said *I piss on all of you*. Plus, the markings on the chart behind her indicated that her height was five-feet-four, a good three inches shorter than Mrs. Carerra. Unless she's had complete facial reconstruction and some magician had physically lengthened her legs, this woman was not her.

But Connor recognized her anyway. The mug shot was old, and the lighting was bad, with a slightly green hue cast from the fluorescent lights he imagined had been flickering overhead. But those eyes, the broad nose, and the mole on her right cheek had not changed over the years.

Roberta Tucker had been in The Sandbar last Friday night, when Tony Carerra had been shot in the back. In fact, she was the woman who stepped forward, claiming to be a med-surg doctor who had called nine-one-one. She had ridden in the ambulance with Carerra to the hospital, then had disappeared when Dr. Dillon had tried to find her.

And now she was dead.

CHAPTER 25

Connor had just closed his laptop when his cell phone rang. He doubted it was the mayor inviting him to his emergency city council meeting, and he had yet to hear from Jordan James. That was a call he was dreading, but one he knew he eventually would have to take.

But this call was not from either man; instead, it was from a 517 area code he remembered but hadn't seen in many years. He stared at the number on the screen, trying to figure out who it could be, but he couldn't think of anyone up in central Michigan who would want to call him, much less know where the hell he was.

"Hello?" he said, tentatively, the hairs on the back of his well-inked neck standing at attention.

"Jack? Is that you?"

Holy shit, he thought as his mind bounced around like a ball in a pinball machine. The voice was the same, but different: a woman's voice, calm and soothing and comforting, yet cracked from age and corroded from nicotine. It had been seven years since he'd last heard it, accusing and filled with darkness, but it seemed more like a lifetime.

"Mom?" he replied.

"Jack," his mother said again, this time more of a weary sigh. "You have no idea how hard I've tried to find you."

Connor was at a loss for words. Alice Connor had made it clear long ago that her son was no longer welcome in her life, not after his actions had directly contributed to the death of his niece. Definitely not after his marriage had fallen apart, his sister had moved to Reno, and his father had died. In some bizarre cosmos of her own creation, his mother had laid the blame for all the ills of the Connor family directly at his feet, setting in motion Jack's visit to the Army recruiter who was more than happy to welcome him into a new tribe.

"Good to hear your voice, Mom," he told her. He knew if she had tried so hard to find him there had to be a reason, and she would get to it in her own way.

"You live in Charleston now?"

"Been here for a few years," he replied. "Ever since I got out of Iraq."

There was a long silence then, and for a few seconds Connor thought the call had been dropped. Then his mother said, "They finally caught the guy."

"Who's they?" he asked. "What guy?"

"Turns out you were right," she continued, as if she hadn't heard his questions. "Sonofabitch was white, lived about two blocks from the Mega Gas, stoned out of his gourd—"

"Mom...Mom," he said. "Slow down. What are you talking about?"

"I'm talking about the bastard who killed Lily," she said, snapping at him before calming herself down. "Sorry...I didn't mean to yell. I know it's been years, but they finally nailed his murdering ass. When they arrested him, he denied everything, but the cops leaned on him hard and eventually he fessed up."

Connor wondered how hard they'd leaned on him, figured the harder, the better. "He admitted he killed her?"

"Yep. It was a long time ago, but he remembered everything. Said he needed money for his next fix, or whatever you call it, and he went to the gas station that night to get some quick cash. You remember—"

Yeah, Connor remembered. How could he ever forget? He'd been distracted while filling out a Powerball ticket in the back of the store and didn't see his niece as she ran toward the check-out counter with a container of her favorite ice cream in her tiny hands. A masked gunman had been in the process of robbing the place and her squeals of delight startled the thug and he pulled the trigger. The bullet had pierced her head like a Halloween pumpkin, and she had fallen face-first on the dirty linoleum floor. The Lansing police had rounded up the usual suspects, eventually pinning the murder on a black guy named Lester Veris, even though Connor insisted the gunman was white. Veris ended up getting shanked in the county jail where he was being held pending trial, and both he and the case died a convenient death. Connor had dutifully assumed responsibility for Lily's death, and the rest of his family had eagerly piled on the guilt-driven pig-pile.

"How did they catch him?" Connor asked her, a sudden emptiness numbing his heart.

"This guy—a real scumbag named Jason Something—a couple weeks ago he tried to jack a car at a gas station near the university," she told him. "He fired two shots at the driver but they both missed. Anyway, the police ran ballistics, and the computer matched them to...to the same gun that killed Lily."

"I don't know what to say, Mom," he told her, and he really didn't. Arresting his niece's killer didn't change the fact that she was dead, nor that Connor's negligence had contributed to her death.

"I just thought you might want to know," she said. "Closure, and all that."

Closure. He'd heard that word a lot, first when Dr. Pinch tried to free him from the chains of his war guilt, then later when he'd solved the murder of a former lover whose body had been left in a Charleston gutter. Most recently during the V.A. program in Georgia where the shrinks and group sessions stressed the need to check all baggage at the door. It was one of those nebulous words that promised the curative benefits of healing, but which often yielded ambiguous results.

"We'll have to catch up one of these days," he told her, not wanting to sound as if he were trying to give her the bum's rush.

"Maybe you could come home for Thanksgiving."

Connor couldn't tell if she was serious, or if this was one of those things people talked about but ended up not doing. Still, he said, "I'd like that."

He'd barely ended the call when his phone rang again, and now he figured it was either Jordan James or his mother calling him back. Turned out to be neither, as he recognized the number as Dr. Dillon's cell phone.

"Good morning, doc," he answered.

The medical examiner got right to it, and she seemed genuinely concerned. "I just now heard about the fire last night," she said. "For a second there I thought I might be seeing you on my table."

"Yeah…seems a I dodged a bullet," he replied. "Literally."

"For what it's worth, I'm truly sorry about what happened. Both for the victim and the bar. This whole thing."

"Me, too," Connor said as he watched a blue-tailed skink scurry across the porch. "I'm still having trouble believing it."

"Sounds like you've been a busy man."

"More than you know."

He briefed her on the fire, insisting that he didn't have a clue why Cecil Maines showed up at his door in the middle of the night. He skipped past his evening with Jessica Snow, the dinner and everything that came after, as well as his car chase and his visit with Jimmy Brinks out in Stono Flats.

"I know you called me for a reason, but what can you tell me about the dead woman who was found at the beach house down here?" he asked her when he was done.

"Why do you ask?" she wanted to know.

"That was the place where Tony Carerra and his wife were staying. It has to be connected somehow."

"Damn." Dr. Dillon was quiet for a moment, then said, "I'm out of the loop on that one. I didn't see any link, so I punted the cut to Frank. He's one of my associates. The report should be ready this afternoon."

"No big deal," Connor told her. "I'm assuming you didn't call just to say 'hello.'"

"In fact, you're right. I wanted to fill you in—at great risk of losing my job, I have to remind you—about the guy who was shot in your apartment."

"You did the autopsy?"

"That's the thing," she replied. "They took the body."

"What do you mean, took it?"

There was another short silence, then: "I had both of them on my schedule— the victim from your place, and the one from the SUV. Then these two suits came in waving a wad of federal papers, saying something about 'homeland security' and a bunch of mumbo-jumbo bullshit. Before I knew it, they were wheeling the two bodies out. They drove off in a black van."

"Did one of these suits go by the name Landry?" Connor asked.

"Don't think so…it was a man and a woman," she said. "Anyway, the papers he showed me said they could take them, and who was I to argue? I had two other stiffs waiting for me in the drawers."

Connor thought on this a minute, then said, "These papers. Did they give the names of the victims?"

"That's the first thing I checked. Victim number one, the man who got shot in your apartment, was IDed as Luca Roos. Victim number two, who was found in the Tahoe and whom the prelim ballistics show was killed by the gun found with victim number one, went by the name Arnold Shelton."

Another tumbler fell into place as Connor remembered that the name on the email string he'd found on the flash drive was Arnold Shelton. "What about Cecil Maines?"

"I was coming to that. His flash-fried parts went straight to the feds this morning, as well."

"Jesus…sounds like they're scrambling all over this—"

"Like rats gone wild," she said. "Look—I gotta go. Some poor stiff the feds don't seem to give a damn about is waiting for me. Just thought you'd like the update."

Connor hung up and sat there with his feet propped up on the porch railing, working on his next step. Now that he had a good idea where this was all headed, he went down to the homey front office and begged another night's stay out of Lincoln Polk's cousin. Bernice said she was truly sorry about what had happened to the bar and hoped it would be rebuilt soon, then dug through a pile of papers on her desk.

"See this?" she asked him, holding up a yellow form. "It's a notice from the planning board saying that cabin you're in ain't going to pass inspection anytime soon. That means I can't rent it out until it's up to code."

"You're booting me out?"

Bernice clamped her hands to her ample waist and rolled her eyes at him. "You think I'd do something like that, Mr. Jack? What I'm saying is, you can stay there as long as you want, but I can't collect a penny from you."

"I can't just stay here for free—"

"We'll work something out," she assured him. "Linc, he tells me you're a good man."

"Much appreciated," Connor said, wondering else what the cop had told his cousin.

Bernice offered him that big smile, then leaned across the registration counter and propped her hands on the polished wood surface. "Is it true what happened to Jesry Freeman, got himself burned to a crisp?" she asked him in a conspiratorial voice.

"Did you know him?" Connor could tell she had been a real beauty when she was younger: large eyes the color of dark chocolate, smooth skin, high cheeks and a long neck. She had added some serious middle-aged girth over the years, which she barely hid with a cotton dress that looked as if it came from Africa.

"Never met him, but the guy had a rep. Liked the ladies."

Connor was thinking about what Em Lee had said about her mother: *She does whatever he says. Cooks for him, cleans for him, empties the trash for him. Whatever.* "The real love 'em and leave 'em type?"

"Leave 'em all beat to hell, is more like it, judging from what he did last night before he got torched."

The question hung there, just itching to be asked, so Connor obliged her. "Just what did he do?"

Bernice's eyes lit up, as if this was what she'd been leading up to all along. She leaned across the registration desk and lowered her voice a notch. "What I hear is Jesry went to his old lady's house last night, got word her little girl had run away," she said. "Cops found the mom this morning with a busted knee cap, couple of cracked ribs, both eyes swollen shut. Poor woman was too banged up to get to a phone, just lay there all night until the police dropped in to tell her what happened to her boyfriend."

Some boyfriend, Connor thought.

• • •

Jessica Snow's room looked different in the daylight. For starters, she was not there. No green eyes, no cherry lips, no hair hanging to her shoulders in the dim light of the lamp beside the bed. No strapless dress, either, although that had come off within moments of entering the room last night.

Now the door was wide open and the draperies that covered the glass slider had been pulled open, letting in the glare of the July sun. A young woman from the housekeeping staff came out of the room and stuffed a mound of sheets into a bag in her laundry cart. As she removed a stack of clean linens she glanced up at Connor, but said nothing as she disappeared back inside the room.

He stood there a moment, then poked his head through the open doorway. The first thing he noticed was that Jessica's suitcase was not where he'd seen it last night on the floor. He stepped further into the room, took a peek in the bathroom, saw that her perfume and soaps and toothbrush and moisturizer all were gone. The closet was empty, as well.

"May I help you, sir?" she asked him. Heavy Latino accent, tentative, bordering on the edge of fear.

Until Connor heard the woman's voice, he was not fully aware he had edged so far into the room. But now, as he stood there in the doorway—the housekeeper standing warily on the other side of the bed—he realized he had ventured farther than he was welcome. He backed up, raised his palms in the air to show her he meant no harm.

"I'm sorry, ma'am," he said. "I was looking for the woman who's staying in this room."

She flashed him a sudden look of relief, said, "She checked out this morning, sir."

"Checked out?"

"Yes, sir. You can ask at the office, but my print-out says she's gone."

Connor glanced around the room, realized what the woman said was true. Jessica Snow definitely was gone. Sometime last night she'd slipped out of bed and disappeared into the night, and since then she'd come back and left for good. He thanked the young girl for her help, gave the room one final glance, and took the elevator down to the lobby.

The round-faced clerk at the front desk confirmed what the housekeeper had said. His name tag identified him as Regis, and after conferring with his computer he said, "I'm sorry, sir, but it appears that Miss Snow left us this morning."

Connor considered this a moment, then said, "What about Alfonse Romano?"

"Let me take a look," Regis said, and again his fingers attacked the keyboard. After a moment his shoulder flexed in a slight shrug, and he said, "I'm sorry, sir. Same thing. Mr. Romano checked out just after eight o'clock."

When Connor arrived back at his Cool Sands digs, Jordan James was waiting for him on the front porch. He was clutching a double gin martini, straight up, two olives, and watched silently as Connor wandered up the short path toward the non-code guest cabin. The cocktail had come from a portable bar he kept in the trunk of his Bentley, and the ice with which to chill it probably came from the rusty machine outside the office.

"Good to see the reports are true," he observed as Connor mounted the brightly painted wood steps. Clooney had accompanied him to The Tides, and now he attacked his water dish with a vengeance until half the contents had splashed on the deck.

"Good afternoon, sir," Connor replied as he lowered himself into the other chair on the porch. He turned so he could see his boss—his *former* boss, given the circumstances. "And what would those reports be saying?"

"That you're still in one piece."

"A shitload better than the alternative," Connor said as he lifted his feet and rested them on the porch railing. "I'm sorry, but I haven't been able to check on last night's receipts. The safe is supposed to be fireproof—"

But Jordan James stopped him right there, raising his hand like a traffic cop stopping cars at an intersection. "The money doesn't matter," he said, and the heavy tone in his voice indicated he meant it. "Your safety is all that counts right now."

Connor had never really been able to figure this guy out. Their history dated back years, to that day in the Iraq desert when the suicide bomber detonated his Ford Econoline van just as it collided with the Humvee Connor was driving. Both vehicles were blown apart on impact, and when the dust and smoke had settled several of Connor's buddies lay bleeding out in the blistering sun. Eddie James by far was the worst of the injured, but Connor managed to stanch the flow of blood where the kid's arm had just been severed. He'd also suffered a severe cranial breach—that's how the Army doctor classified it later at the hospital in Germany—and Connor had kept it clean by wrapping it with strips torn from his shirt.

"I'm assuming you have insurance," Connor said.

Mr. James studied him over the rim of his martini and said, "Not for you to worry about. I'm just concerned about what you're going to do."

"One day at a time," Connor replied, recalling the recovery steps that had been driven into his brain in rehab. These days they applied as much to trauma and stress as they did to booze and pills.

Mr. James lifted the glass to his lips and took a healthy sip. "Well, you can't be a bartender forever," he pointed out after the gin had washed down his throat.

"It's been less than twenty-four hours, sir," Connor said. "I haven't had a chance to think that far ahead."

"I get that. I just want you to know I'm here to help you when you need it. Job, place to live, whatever you need. Whatever caused that fire, it wasn't your fault."

Don't be so sure, Connor thought. *I sure as shit kicked a couple yellowjacket nests the last couple of days.*

Instead, what he said was: "I appreciate you saying that, sir. And when I figure out what comes next, you'll be the first person I call."

Not quite true, but close enough for the time being.

CHAPTER 26

Ten minutes after Jordan James packed up his portable cocktail lounge and drove off in his Continental W12 with burled walnut dash, Lincoln Polk knocked on the door. Connor and Clooney had gone inside, where the distressed air conditioner made the room feel only slightly cooler than it did out on the porch. He'd only slept only a few hours in the past twenty-four, and exhaustion had overcome him while he was outside listening to his former boss.

"Mister Connor...you in there?" Polk called as he pounded on the door for the third time. "My cousin says she signed you up for an indefinite stay."

Connor was already on his feet by now, and he turned the latch and pulled the door inward. Clooney glanced up with a wary look, but he recognized the cop at the door and dropped his head back to the floor with a thud.

"Can you come back later?" Connor said, no subtlety or finesse in his voice. "I'm trying to sleep."

"I apologize for waking you up," Polk said, eyeing the dog on the floor. "This'll only take a minute."

"And just what is 'this'?"

"One quick question, then I'm gone."

Connor let out a heavy sigh and said, "Whatever I can help you with. You want to come in?"

Lincoln Polk firmly shook his head, said, "I know how Bernice hates her electric bill, so I got a good idea what it feels like in there. Like I said, I'll be quick." He shifted his weight to his other foot and fixed his eyes on Connor. "Do you know a beach house out on East Ashley called Calypso Cove?"

"There's a lot of houses on the beach up there," Connor replied, buying time for his brain to sort this through.

"I'm talking about the turquoise one with the pink roof," Polk clarified for him.

Connor made a show of cocking his head, as if trying to figure this out, then brightening as if a light bulb had gone off in his head. "That's the place where Carerra and his wife were staying," he said. "You even gave her a lift home a night or two later."

Polk was nodding now, but Connor couldn't tell if he'd jogged the cop's slow memory or if he'd known this all along. "One and the same," he said.

"So, what about it?" Connor asked.

"Can you explain what you were doing out there?"

"I'm not sure I'm following what you're saying—"

"Your prints were all over the place," Polk told him. "You want to explain to me how they got there?"

Connor figured his prints were still in the system from the bogus drug wrap several years ago. He pretended to think on the cop's question a second, then said, "I went out there a few days ago. That night she staggered into the bar and you drove her home I gave her back her purse, but I forgot that I still had her husband's credit card from the night he was killed. He'd told me where they were staying, so I drove out there to give it back."

"And Mrs. Carerra—she invited you inside?"

Connor nodded, impressed with how genuine his story was sounding. If he stayed close enough to the truth, he could avoid talking about how he had searched he place, found the flash drive, and got whacked on the head. "We drank coffee in the screened gallery, and then she asked me to help look for something in the house."

"What kind of something?" Polk asked.

"I thought this was going to be a quick question," Connor reminded him.

"Semantics. What did she want you to help her find?"

"Well, that's what was kind of odd. She said she was looking for a book that her husband had, but couldn't find it."

"And you helped her look for this book?" Polk pressed him.

"For a couple minutes, but I told her I couldn't stay," Connor explained. "I have no idea if she ever found it."

Polk seemed to think this through, nodded as if he accepted it. Or at least believed it could be true. "Which means you could've touched a lot of surfaces," he said.

"All over the house. Is this about that woman who was killed out there yesterday?"

"What do you know about that?"

"I was driving up to Morris Island and saw my old company truck parked outside," Connor said. "Palmetto BioClean. They clean up death scenes. Later I saw the story online and put two and two together. For a second, I thought maybe Mrs. Carerra had died, but the picture on the paper's website didn't look like her."

"That's right—it wasn't," Polk said. He said nothing for a bit, as if searching his brain for any further questions, then added, "Well, that's it, I guess. How's my cousin treating you?"

"Nothing could be finer, considering," Connor said. Now it was his turn to think, and as the cop turned to go, he said, "What do you know about Hatchitch Island?"

Lincoln Polk cocked his head at the question and turned back to face Connor. "Well, that's pretty much out of the blue," he said. "Why do you ask?"

"Actually, Mrs. Carerra mentioned it when I was out there that day," Connor lied. "She wanted to know what I knew about it."

"What did you tell her?"

"Just that I thought I'd seen it on a map, somewhere down near Kiawah Sound. I asked her why she wanted to know, just like you did now, but she changed the subject."

"Well, you got it pretty much right," Officer Polk said. "Hatchitch is a lump of scrub about a half mile long and a foot or two above high tide. Nothing more than mud and muck and old oyster shells. The Gullahs called it *Hatchitch* because that was their word for hatchet, which I guess it's supposed to be shaped like. But the government had a different name for it, one you don't see much on maps anymore."

"And that would be?"

"Skeleton Cay," the cop said, pronouncing it *Key*. "Named for all the bones that were dug up there after the civil war. Some sort of burial ground, former slaves or Indians. Native Americans, I mean. No one knows for sure who they were, and there wasn't any money for archaeologists to figure it out. Anyway, the government owned the land for decades, used it as an encampment during both world wars. The Army Corps actually built a bunker there in the forties, to monitor the presence of German U-boats. The place was sold in the sixties, and now it's private."

"You sure know a lot about the place," Connor said.

"My daddy used to talk about going out there when he was a kid, spent the night once. He swore there were old ghosts that belonged to the skeletons, chased him from one end of the island to the other. He never went back."

"And you don't know who owns it now?"

"Nope," Lincoln Polk said. "Just someone who has the money to waste on a useless lump of mud in the middle of the marsh. I think the bunker's still there, but that's about it. Just sludge and stink and old oyster shells."

Plus, whatever it was that Cecil Maines happened to see out there, something that scared the living shit out of him. Something that ended up getting him killed and grilled up like a brisket of beef.

"I don't know if hearing from you out of the blue is a good thing or a bad thing," Dr. Pinch said as Connor shifted his weight in the tired leather chair that faced him across the bare coffee table. "How long has it been?"

"Eight, nine months," Connor guessed. "And I think me being here is both. Good and bad, I mean. But mostly good."

"Still, something caused you to call and see if I had any cancellations."

There was a time when Connor had met with the V.A. shrink in his drab, colorless office once a week, and he'd never looked forward to it. Avoided it like the plague, and sometimes he just blew off his appointments without a second thought. The walls were white and stark, framed certificates in cheap black frames, and scholarly books jammed into a pair of cheap wood grain bookcases. The last time he'd been here a withering ficus tree had been dying in a dark corner, but now it had been replaced with a large putted cactus. Probably didn't need as much watering as the ficus, he figured.

"I got a call the other day," Connor said slowly, not really knowing how to get into this.

"Grim news?" Dr. Pinch ventured.

"How'd you guess?"

"I don't usually see a lot of joy and laughter come through that door," the psychiatrist observed.

Career military, Pinch was large a large, muscular man with thick arms and an even thicker neck—the result of vigorous workouts in a home gym. In stark contrast, his legs were withered and lifeless, made that way by a bullet that had severed his spine during the final days of Desert Storm. That incident, and his subsequent recovery, initially left him bitter and angry, realizing he was bound to a wheelchair for the rest of his life. That was almost three decades ago, and during the intervening years he'd managed to offset the resentment and outrage by earning a medical degree that now helped other vets deal with their own scars.

Connor nodded at what Pinch had said and looked down at his hands. "Last winter I was having a hard time, totaled my car under the 526 overpass out near the airport," he eventually said. "I went into rehab in Dublin and got my head cleared out."

"How clear?" Pinch asked.

"I still jump at the sound of a car backfiring, if that's what you're asking. But I sleep well, and my dreams are mostly good. I don't look over my shoulder in Publix anymore, and I'm able to compartmentalize what I did and what I saw over there. That was a big word the docs kept using: *compartmentalize*. Anyway, at the program there was this guy, one of my roommates, he came back from Afghanistan with a shit-ton of pain. Doctors gave him meds to deal with it, and he got hooked. Damned opioids took over his life. He was there in Dublin because his wife and booted him out, told him she wasn't going to walk into the house one day and find him dead in the bathroom, a needle hanging out of his arm."

Dr. Pinch studied him but said nothing, as if he knew where this was going.

"So, Gordo—that's his name—he went into the same program I was in. He tried, he really did. He always talked in group, he started working out, did whatever he could to turn his life around. The doctors put him on Suboxone, and that seemed to work. His arms cleared up, and so did his outlook. It was like a red light changed to green. That last day, at the end of the program, I thought he was the one who stood the best chance of all of us to make it."

"And then the other day you got a phone call—"

Connor dipped his head in a nod, closed his eyes. When he opened them, he said, "Thirty thousand," his voice almost a whisper.

"Thirty thousand what?

"That's how many veterans OD'ed last year. More than twice as many than all the U.S. soldiers who were killed in that fucking war—*in just one year.*"

Pinch leaned back in his chair, seemed to rock back and forth in place. "I came close to being part of that number," he replied. "I can't tell you how many times I lay in my bed in a dark room, praying a nurse would squeeze just enough extra juice into me to put me over the top. Put me out of my misery."

"Morphine?"

"Pretty standard back then."

"How long did it take?" Connor asked him.

"How long for what?"

"To stop thinking like that."

"An eon," Dr. Pinch said. "Maybe two. Re-entry is one of the hardest things you'll ever come up against."

"We've been talking about re-entry since my first visit here," Connor reminded him. "I don't think re-entering is the problem."

"No?" the V.A. doctor said. "Care to enlighten me?"

Connor chewed on his lip a second, then took a deep breath as he folded his hands across his chest. "The other day, when I heard about what happened to Gordo, I started thinking about that word. *Re-entry.* As if coming back from the war is like astronauts dropping out of orbit and drifting back to earth. I get the parallels, but it's really all wrong. Because those astronauts, they're not up there shooting at people who don't want us in their country or getting shot at for the very same reason. They're not getting their arms and legs and nuts blown off. They're not dealing with bloody images burned into their eyeballs, things they've seen and done and wish like hell they could forget, but can't. Up in orbit you see Earth from a distance, this big blue ball of continents and clouds, and it all seems so peaceful. Noiseless. But close-up...well, when that van carrying a hundred pounds of C-4 comes barreling at you, what happens next is anything but quiet. So, you see, coming home from the peace and quiet of space is nothing like crawling back from the battlefield, your mangled body bloodied and bandaged, and your mind in ruins."

Dr. Pinch held his gaze on Connor for a long moment, then said, "You are not your friend, Jack. Gordo's demons were his, and yours are yours. We each have our own set of circumstances that we bring home from war, and you can't carry his troubles on your shoulders. Whatever guilt you may feel for what happened to him is not on you."

"But that's just it, Doc," Connor replied. "You see, I'm not feeling any guilt. Something tells me I should be, but I'm not. Grief, yes. Definitely that. Failure, possibly, for not doing something to help him. And absolutely a lot of anger, because of how this whole war thing sucks and we all know it, but the machine just keeps rolling along. I feel all that...but no guilt."

"So why are you here, Jack?" the shrink pressed him. "What's eating at you so much that you had to come see me with almost no notice, even though you've always hated this place?"

Connor took a deep breath, let it out slowly. "Maybe to thank you. I'm not sure. You see, when I first came in here, I was a real mess. I don't have to go through it all; your notes are all in that file in your lap. But I was royally screwed up in my head. I couldn't sleep. I couldn't function while I was awake, and I took a job that reminded me of death and dying every day. I couldn't shake the images of me in the blown-out rubble of that market, waiting for the kid I'd just shot to die. But a funny thing happened as I waded through all that shit."

"Funny?" Dr. Pinch asked him.

"*Weird* funny, not *ha-ha* funny. Like I said, I sleep pretty damned fine. And when I dream, it's about things that might happen, or I wish would happen, not what *did* happen. I figured out that I don't need to clean up blood every day just to realize I'm alive."

The V.A. shrink leaned back in his wheelchair, a lone finger tapping on the manila folder in his lap. The one that read "Connor, John H." on the tab. Seconds ticked by, then even more seconds until finally he said, "Welcome home, Jack. It's good to have you back."

CHAPTER 27

Later: a brilliant sunset soaked the sky with all shades of orange and purple and red. The wind was light and from the south, and the aroma of jerk chicken and spicy wings lingered in the air. Somewhere—*everywhere*—a mix of blues and jazz and bad karaoke was defining the rhythm of the night, with an underlayer of hard rock thumping from one of the clubs.

After leaving Clooney to watch *House Hunters* with Bernice, Connor rode Em Lee's old bicycle south out of town. Five minutes later he was at the Folly Creek Marina, where a friend of his kept a simple Carolina skiff with a small outboard clamped to the stern. The friend was a guy named Jimmy Page, no relation to the legendary front man and founder of Led Zeppelin. In fact, *this* Jimmy Page owned a place called Jimmy's Buffet, a booze-and-blues bar locally famous for its pour-your-own drinks. In a different lifetime Connor had played congas there with a reggae group known as the Jamaica Jerks and, while that era came to a close well over a year ago, the two rival bartenders remained friends. Even if they did compete for the same customers every night of the week.

Jimmy Page on several occasions had told Connor he could borrow the skiff anytime he wanted to drop a hook in the water, but neither of them ever expected any follow-through. Still, Connor knew where Page kept the key, and he was surprised to find that the engine started right up. The marina was almost deserted, and the few live-aboard yachtsmen partying in their own boats were too busy with tumblers of rum and old nautical tales to notice him cast off. He kept the single piston just above idle as he motored out past the outer boat slips, then pushed the throttle forward when he hit the open creek. The engine immediately responded with a deep growl as the propeller bit into the water, cutting a path through the dark water toward the river. The rhythm of town faded into the night behind him, and now all he heard was the whine of the motor and the slap of the water against the flat hull.

Lights were winking on to the south like clusters of diamonds along the distant shore. He kept the skiff to the leeward side of Bird Cay Preserve, steering a more westerly course that took him through the broad sound where the Stono and Kiawah Rivers met. As the evening deepened from peach to violet to indigo, a canopy of stars emerged overhead, blocked here and there by patches of thick clouds lumbering across the sky.

He held a steady course as he studied the map with a flashlight, weaving through the tidal tributaries and rivulets that traversed the marsh. More than once the skiff dragged on oyster shells, and as it glided through the dark water, he could hear critters of one sort or another rustling in their hidden thickets.

Eventually Connor came to what his old tourist map told him was Hatchitch, aka Skeleton Cay. It stretched about eight hundred yards from tip to tip, with a hatchet-shaped bulge at the southwesterly end. Connor had Googled it before he'd left Cool Sands, the satellite view indicating a small dock protruding a few yards into the river on the far end of the island. Stealth was critical tonight, however, and the tourist map told him there was a small indentation on the westerly side of the island where he might be able to bring the skiff ashore. He eased the throttle back until the engine was humming just above idle, then steered toward the tip of what would have been the tip of the hatchet's handle. Sure enough, as he came around the spit of land, he saw a tiny inlet in the moonlight: dark, calm, and cloaked by dense marsh grass.

He nudged the boat up onto the pluff mud and found the shoreline clustered with shells and stray bits of ocean-going flotsam. Connor used his LED flashlight to spot the best place to beach the it, then cut the engine and tipped it up out of the water. He climbed out over the bow and dragged the skiff up onto the shore far enough so that an outgoing tide wouldn't take it for a ride. Another boat had already been dragged up onto the mud, a small outboard that barely seemed seaworthy. Except for a of couple drab orange life vests it was empty, and the engine was cool to the touch.

It took him a moment to get his bearings. In the dark, Skeleton Cay looked to be largely covered in scrub and grasses and low trees, the type that tolerated saltwater and periodic moon tides. Connor had no idea what species they were, but they had grown thick along the shore and for a minute he wished he'd brought a machete with him. Since Connor didn't yet know what he was looking for—only that he was looking for *something*—he swept his light against the brush to see if there was a way through it.

There was. A narrow path bad been cut through the underbrush, leaving a gap just wide enough for a person to squeeze through. Connor picked up a stick and used it as a blind man would use a cane, sweeping it from side to side as he started along the dark trail.

It followed a straight line for about fifty yards, and in the scrub on both sides of the trail he could hear the rustle of creatures that didn't want him there any more than he wanted to be there. Eventually the path ended at a muddy clearing, flat and wide and wet. In the darkness Connor could make out a small masonry hut with a rusted corrugated roof that sagged on one end. As he started toward the building, he kicked something, saw it was a small smudge pot set in a slight depression in the earth. It still had kerosene in it, and the wick looked as if it had been burned recently. He considered this, then continued to walk the perimeter of the clearing. Sure enough, there was another smudge pot, and another, and another. Ten of them in all, carefully arranged in a circle some thirty yards across. A landing pad, it seemed, just about the right size to accommodate a private helicopter.

Maybe you did see something out here, Cecil Maines, he thought.

Connor made his way over to the old building, which he now could see was constructed from cinder blocks and mortar. It was about fifteen feet square, with a rusty tin roof and unpainted wooden shutters locked tight over the windows. A heavy door fashioned from large pressure-treated timbers was held in place by iron hinges and a makeshift latch. He swung the latch out of the way and pushed the door inward on a pair of rusty hinges.

He flicked on the flashlight again and played the beam along the walls and the floor. The air was hot and thick and stale, with a faint acidic odor that he recalled from somewhere but could not identify. He edged into the center of the room and slowly drew the light in a lazy arc. Along the far wall the beam fell on a long work table, upon which were stacked some plastic crates and a tool kit. The table's surface was unpolished wood and it had a dark stain on one end. Flecks of color—he presumed it was paint—were spattered everywhere. Underneath the table was a clear plastic tarpaulin, wadded up into a massive clump, and next to that was an empty five-gallon fuel can. Connor bent down, unscrewed the cap, took a whiff: kerosene again, just as he'd smelled in the smudge pots that lined the clearing.

He turned around, aimed the flashlight behind the door, found another stack of crates. They appeared to be new, and when he opened one, he found it packed with beans and tomatoes and pears, bags of rice and pasta, tins of condensed milk, jars of applesauce and peaches. Two of the cases contained jugs of purified water, another held bottles of South African Petite Syrah. Whoever had stored all these supplies apparently planned on staying for a while.

Connor drew the light over the walls and across the ceiling, but that was it. He clicked it off, backed around toward the door, started to pull it closed behind him when his foot struck something soft on the floor. He hit it with the beam, found a balled-up piece of cloth that had been kicked up against the doorjamb. He bent down and picked it up by one edge, saw it was a dirty shirt, light blue with a pattern of red and yellow flowers on it. Puffs of thread bloomed where several buttons had popped off, and a pocket had been partially shredded, leaving a line of stitches behind. That, and a ragged hole the size of a quarter crudely torn through the shoulder. Around the fringe of the hole was a dried substance the color of old bricks. Dried blood. Connor let it fall back to the floor, wondering if this had anything to do with what Cecil Maines had witnessed out here. Or at least thought he had.

Outside, a white glow was beginning to seep into the eastern horizon. The moon was starting to rise, and as it did the surrounding foliage appeared backlit against the night. Connor quietly slipped out of the hut and stood there at the edge of the clearing deciding what to do next. He'd come out to Skeleton Cay not knowing what he'd find, and now he had no idea what he'd found. Or what it meant.

He had a choice now: explore some more or go back to the skiff and get his ass away from this little island. All he knew about the place was what Lincoln Polk had told him: it was privately owned and had an old Army bunker on it somewhere. Ghosts of old skeletons roamed the place at night, and from what he had seen in the concrete hut there were people out here. He was flying blind, not knowing how—or even if—all this tied in to Tony Carerra. Or, for that matter, the dead man named Shelton, or the fire at The Sandbar that had killed Cecil Maines. One way or another it was all connected, and Connor figured that the people who'd been doing all the killing were pretty damned good at it.

Fifty yards further the full face of the moon now was visible above the horizon, casting long shadows over the scrub and brush. Connor stopped a moment, took a look around. A sense of self-preservation told him nothing was happening out here tonight, that it was time to turn back. But there had been no logic in any of this from the beginning, yet there had been plenty going on.

Somewhere, not far off in the distance, he heard a noise. It was hard to discern above the wind whispering through the sweetgrass, but he was sure he'd heard it: a low scraping noise, the sound of something—*someone*—scuffing along the trail. He heard it again, a little louder now, the sound coming with the wind, approaching him from further up the path. Definitely the sound of feet shuffling through the dirt. And now that he really listened, he could tell he was hearing two sets of footsteps coming toward him.

Connor quickly retreated back down the trail to a gap that disappeared into a thick clump of marsh grass. He ducked into the darkness and crouched down just as the footfalls came around a bend. They were accompanied by a pair of hushed voices, belonging to a man and a woman, just barely audible above the crush of the wind. What they said sounded something like:

Him: "…totally unprofessional conduct…"

Her: "…no knowledge of it at all…"

Him: "…could have screwed up the whole operation…"

Her: "…it was totally off the clock…"

Him: "…when this is all over…"

Then they were gone, but not before the shockwave hit and Connor realized that, somehow, he'd missed another angle all long. His eyes lingered on the silhouette of the woman as she and her companion skulked down the path toward the clearing. Then, when they were both out of earshot, he said out loud— but quiet enough so only he could hear— "What the hell are Jessica Snow and Alfonse Romano doing out here on Skeleton Cay?"

Connor used his shirttail to wipe the perspiration from his face, then stood up and edged back to the trail. He listened for the sound of other people approaching, heard nothing as he studied the filtered shadows. Off in the distance he thought he heard a sharp noise—*the sound of a door slamming?*—then silence again. He waited a good thirty seconds before hitting the trail again, the unmistakable sound of Jessica's voice echoing in his brain. Knowing now that he'd been used, tricked, and tossed away; realizing also there was still something missing, something that was lurking just out of reach.

Connor could see he was approaching the far end of the island, where it widened to a couple hundred yards across. Staying inside the shadows of the rising moon he made his way along the path, occasionally making out the tracks of a sneaker or a boot. Then a cloud that had blocked the moon lazily slipped aside, and in the resulting glow he spotted a large mound of earth about fifty yards in the distance. It rose a good twenty yards upward from the scrub-bound terrain and was flat at the summit as if a giant knife had sliced off the top.

Connor moved cautiously along the trail, ready to slip into the brush again if he heard another sound. The path curved around the base of the mound, and as he followed it, he saw the massive concrete bulwark that marked the entrance to the old military bunker. This was the fortress Lincoln Polk had told him about, created by the Army Corps of Engineers to keep an eye on Nazi submarines during World War II.

Connor was familiar with these bunkers. A handful of them dotted the northern end of Sullivan's Island, where he had lived until the vicious surge from Hurricane Eleanor swept his ground-level apartment out into the marsh. One morning months before the storm he had been returning from his regular run on the beach and had cut inland, detouring down a quiet side street that ran parallel to the sand. That's when he came across a man in cut-offs and no shirt, power-washing the concrete entryway to something that looked like a doomsday shelter straight out of *James Bond*.

The man with the power-washer was named Frederick Lane, a retired executive for a soft drink company in Atlanta. He'd bought the decommissioned fortress years ago because it reminded him of the stories his father had told him about the bunkers his father had stormed on D-Day in the cliffs above the Normandy. He confessed that he'd acted on a whim and had absolutely no idea what he was going to do with the place, but a more unique home could not be found along the eastern seaboard.

Since Connor was a war veteran, Lane proudly offered him a quick tour of the place. It was hot and stuffy, and the concrete walls seemed to bleed dampness, but the man seemed not to notice. "You can see right here that once these doors are barricaded, nothing can open them," he'd said, ignoring the palmetto bugs scurrying across the floor. "They're water tight, so unless the waves are hammering directly on them everything inside stays dry. In fact, during Hurricane Hugo back in eighty-nine I'm told not one drop of water got in."

He went on to explain the vast size and construction of the bunker. The reinforced concrete walls were ten feet thick in places, and the bulge of earth contained four thousand square feet of useable space. Mr. Lane had partitioned the area into four bedrooms, a kitchen, living room, and three bedrooms, with a thousand square feet left over. A crude internal stairway led up to the reinforced gun turret at the top, where he had built an outdoor kitchen with pergola and hot tub.

What Connor was looking at now, out here on Skeleton Cay, was slightly smaller but no less impressive. The front doors were made of heavy steel that, when opened, could probably accommodate a full-size automobile. Concrete stairs led up the outside of the earthen bunker to the truncated top, which seemed to be framed with more concrete. Connor guessed that was where the old gun would have been bolted during the war, even though the island was more than a mile from the open ocean and any shot would have to go directly over Kiawah.

He studied the configuration of concrete, steps, and trails, then slipped back down the path a few yards. His mind kept going back to Jessica—Alfonse, too— trying to figure out just what side they were on here. But there was no time for that now, as he heard more voices drifting out into the night. He didn't recognize them, couldn't make out what was being said, but he knew someone was very close and, it seemed, very angry.

Connor crouched in the darkness at the base of the bunker and surveyed the scene. He had a better view here; the moon was growing brighter, illuminating the concrete cupola at the top. He couldn't make out the details, but whoever owned this place had renovated the existing space into a hilltop terrace with a three-sixty marsh view. He assumed it was connected by internal stairs—or possibly even an elevator—that led to the reinforced living space within. From where he was hiding, he couldn't get a good look at what was on that terrace or how it was laid out but, as he was studying it, a man came into view and leaned on the massive railing that encircled it.

The man stood there in the moonlight, holding something in his hand. In the glow of the moon Connor could tell it was a highball glass, with some sort of liquid in it. He wore white trousers with a yellow button-down shirt that was not tucked in. He took a sip, then said to someone who had not come out on the terrace, "I'm tired of waiting, dammit. I want this done now." His words were thickly cloaked in a foreign accent whose origin Connor was unable to place.

There was a response from someone out of view, a woman, but Connor couldn't hear what she was saying. Whatever it was, the man on the terrace snarled, "Well, now that he's awake he's got twenty-four hours. If he doesn't come up with something by then, kill him." Then he stalked off into the darkness to a part of the terrace that Connor couldn't see.

Whatever breeze had been blowing earlier seemed to have stopped, and now the only sensation he felt was a constricting tightness in his heart as he studied the bunker house. From what he could tell there was just the one double door, with the stairs that climbed up the side of the mound to the top. Because it was night he couldn't see where the stairway connected to the terrace, nor did he know how many people were out here on the island. Four that he had counted so far, but he assumed there had to be more. Whatever was going on, it required a lot of planning and manpower to carry it out. With everything he'd said to Dr. Pinch earlier, he'd conveniently left out the part about jumping into the deep end again, and the more he thought about it, the more he realized the stuffed shirt named Landry was right: he was in over his head in sewage.

Taking care to keep out of the direct moonlight, Connor edged back along the narrow trail toward the clearing—and the strip of mud where he had beached his boat. It was time to return to Folly and get Landry in on this.

All of a sudden, the night seemed deathly quiet. Not a screech of a heat bug, not a breath of wind, not the rustle of a single blade of marsh grass. He stood there a moment, listening for a sound, but there was none. Way off in the distance the thrum of an engine out on the water chugged along on a nighttime passage. That was all.

Then a voice behind him called out, "Freeze, motherfucker. Hands on top of your head, or I ventilate it."

CHAPTER 28

"Are you the brains behind this sorry-ass outfit, or just following orders?"

Connor's question was met with a stony silence. He couldn't see the man's face: the bastard was behind him, prodding him sharply in the kidneys with the barrel of his rifle, driving him forward along the trail. He twisted his hands against the rope that now bound his wrists.

"My guess is this is about drugs, maybe guns. Am I close?"

Still no comment, just another stab in the back. He winced from the sharp pain; the man with the gun had jabbed him in the spine after forcing him to lie face down in the dirt, and the tissue was still tender. Plus, he felt stupid for letting himself get caught so easily, not even putting up much of a struggle. Then again, how was he going to put up a fight against a man who was holding an AR 15 and seemed itching to use it?

"Here's what I think this is all about," Connor continued, figuring the man might crack him in the back again, but probably wouldn't shoot as long as he was talking. He kept scuffing along, scanning the dark trail ahead for anything that might shift the odds a little closer to his side. No dice.

"What I figure is, Carerra was doing a little double dealing," he went on. "Moving a whole lot of cash from one bank account to another, maybe skimming a little off the top. And whoever he took it from wants it back—bad enough to do a lot of killing to get it."

"Shut the fuck up."

At least Connor got a response this time, even if it was followed by a solid dig into his kidney. The pain seared through his back and he stumbled, then slowly picked himself up and began to turn toward the asshole with the gun.

"Face forward," the gunman said. "Keep moving."

Connor did as he was told, said nothing for a good sixty seconds. His face was bruised from where he'd hit the dirt, and he probed his mouth with his tongue. All his teeth were intact, but he still tasted blood.

"Tell me one thing," he finally said. "Why'd you use a 16-year old kid to do your dirty work? Is your own aim really that bad?"

"You are so fucking stupid," the man with the gun said, an ominous tone in his voice.

Then everything went dark, except for the flash of pain that started at the base of his brain and spread through his entire skull.

He awoke in the dark. The back of his head pounded like a pile driver, and for a minute he thought he might be blind. Even the blackest of black sometimes has a touch of shadow to it, but not this place. *Wherever this was.* If his hands hadn't been tied behind his back, he still wouldn't have been able to see them. Tied pretty damned tight, too. He was able to move his fingers, but he didn't think he could feel them. Plus, he was wet, sitting in a good six inches of water. It was warm, mid-eighties, just like the ocean this time of year. It also smelled brackish, as if it had been sitting there for quite a while.

Then Connor heard a noise, a little splash in the water, and he realized he was not alone. A childhood of horror movie memories swept over him and he tried not to think about what was in there with him. He figured he was in some dank dungeon, maybe in the bowels of the concrete fortress he'd seen earlier. He tuned an ear to even the faintest of sounds, then felt something crawl out of the water and touch his knee. He jumped, hitting his head on the low ceiling, sending whatever it was back into the water with a splash. The sudden movement sent a wall of pain through his skull, and he winced as he tried to push it down. Then he heard another sound, this one familiar from his childhood in Michigan, and the throbbing pain suddenly was diluted by a sense of overwhelming relief.

It was the croaking of a frog. Several frogs, in fact. Hardly something to worry about, and it told Connor something else: he was in an old cistern. He had no idea where, but most likely still on Skeleton Cay, and possibly not locked away in the depths of the bunker house after all.

Despite the pain in his head and wrists, he knew he wasn't in any immediate danger of drowning. Even if a rain gutter was still connected to the cistern, it would take days of steady downpour to fill it up. That was the good news. The bad news was that he didn't think he had days, much less hours, to get out of here alive. Over the past week he'd seen how these people operated, and one more dead body wouldn't mean shit in the long run.

Connor pushed his way through the water from one end of the cistern to the other, calculated it was about eight feet from side to side and twice as long. A thick layer of slime coated the concrete walls and base. He tried to stand up, found that the concrete top was only five feet from the floor. From what he could tell, there was no one else in here with him, except for the frogs, and there only seemed to be a few of them.

They came for him some time later. He heard someone unscrewing the bolts that held an iron lid in place, heard it scrape across the flat masonry top. Then a beam of light stabbed the darkness, bouncing off the black, glistening sludge.

"Okay, motherfucker." The voice belonged to the gunman who had marched him up the trail. "Time to go."

Connor remained where he was at the far end of the concrete tank. When he didn't move, a hand reached down through the hatch, and a flash instantly lit up the inside of the cistern. There was a loud retort, followed by the sound of a slug smacking into the cement wall. Connor waited for the bullet to ricochet, but nothing came.

"Bust your ass or I'll bust it for you!"

Reluctantly Connor moved toward the open hatch and rose to his feet. The man with the gun reached down, grabbed him by the rope that bound his hands and yanked him out. The pain was excruciating but he was almost too numb for it to register. He sat there on the edge of the concrete a minute, waiting for the agony to subside, but the man with the gun was in a hurry.

"On your feet!"

Connor stood up and immediately was prodded in the back to get going. He took a cautious step, then another, not sure his legs could support him, not wanting to know what would happen to him if they did not. He was outdoors and it was still dark, but hours later. The moon had traveled past the apex of the night sky and was now beginning to descend into morning. The new day was just a few hours away.

He was prodded and pushed down a path—he couldn't tell if it was the same one as before or not—and several times he lost his footing. Each fall brought another stab of the gun in his back, and a hell of a lot more pain. Eventually, Connor was led to the large steel door he had seen earlier that night and was pushed inside the massive bunker. He found himself in a cavernous room fashioned from poured concrete, the ceiling reaching a good twenty feet high. Several low-wattage bulbs gave off a dim spray of illumination, and the man with the gun turned off his flashlight. The walls were unpainted and covered in large smears of black mold; this definitely was not a family room designed for socializing. Connor could make out a handful of doorways, but they were closed off and he had no idea where they might lead.

The gunman nudged Connor toward an arched doorway that led from the cave room to a set of steep metal stairs. There seemed to be five steps, then a landing, then five more steps that culminated in another landing. Five more steps, one more landing, another five steps, and so on.

"Up," the man ordered him.

Connor started climbing, his muddy sandals making a clunking sound on the metal grating as he went. The same dim bulbs were positioned along every other short flight, strung together with old electrical conduit. He went up, right, up, right, up, right so many times that he lost count. Eventually he came to another doorway that opened into a room about thirty feet square, with a ceiling fashioned from rough timbers and weathered shiplap. An array of recessed lights gave off a low, subdued glow, and illuminated a collection of framed paintings of old ships. The wall across from him opened out onto some sort of terrace that was built on the bunker's flat summit, and a steady breeze was blowing in from the marsh. Two ceiling fans helped push the air around.

The room was furnished in a hunting lodge motif, with a half dozen animal heads mounted on the walls. Twin leather couches faced each other, a hand-carved burlwood cocktail table set between them. At the far end of the room, facing the terrace, was a large leather chair. Next to it was a table with a cell phone on it. Connor could not see who was in the chair, but from where he was standing, he could tell it was occupied.

The man with the gun shoved Connor further into the room and waved him into a chair that had been covered with a towel. Despite the fact that he was soaked, he was glad to have the chance to sit. He glanced at the profile of the man in the leather seat and quickly determined he was the person he'd seen out on the terrace earlier.

The man slowly turned and regarded Connor pensively, studying him with cold, steel-gray eyes. "You are either a very brave or a very stupid man," he said in a throaty accent that sounded Russian, maybe Eastern European. "Sometimes it's hard to tell the difference."

Connor said nothing as he assessed the man in the dim light. His hair was bushy and gray, with a slightly whiter beard and mustache. His forehead was leathery and wrinkled, with a long, angled nose and eyes that seemed to harbor deep secrets from the past. He looked oddly familiar, but Connor couldn't immediately place him.

"You recognize me, don't you?" the man asked him.

"Like I'd recognize a hemorrhoid."

A grunt came from the man's throat, low and guttural. "I was in your bar just about a week ago," he said. "An enjoyable place, but I hate plastic cups."

"Glassware shatters, and liability insurance is expensive," Connor said. And now that he'd had a few seconds to think about it, he was able to place him: *The most interesting man in the world*, who had been standing by the railing, a Scotch on the rocks in his hand. Just as he was holding now. "You were there just moments before Tony Carerra was shot. Johnny Walker black."

"Good memory," the man said. "For the record, my name is Marco Neven." He watched Connor to see if the name registered.

"And that's important why?"

The man flashed him a tight smile and took a sip from his highball glass. "It helps to know who you're up against," he said.

"Where'd you get that accent…Walmart?"

A small frown wrinkled Neven's forehead as he glared at Connor. Then he said, "Since you ask, I'm from Zagreb. That's in Croatia, where we know a thing or two about killing."

"That's what we have something in common," Connor said with a painful shrug. "I did my time in Fallujah and Kirkuk."

"Yet I'm sitting here, drinking my Johnny Walker Black, and you're there with your hands tied."

"The night is young."

Neven glanced at the man with the gun and said, "Farris—can you believe this fool?"

"Stupidity comes in all sizes," the man who now had a name—*Farris*—replied.

"Seems to me we're both in a bit of a bind," Connor said, trying to ignore the AR-15 that was pointed at him.

"Excuse me?" Neven lowered his glass and stared, a glint of amusement in his eyes. "Have I overlooked something?"

"A team of federal agents is about to descend on your beautiful island here," Connor bluffed. "They know about your helipad, and when they land your game is all over." It was a lie, but it was the best he could do.

Marco Neven turned back to his gunman. "Farris, have you seen any sign of feds on the radar?"

"No, sir."

"Any helicopters or speed boats in the area?"

"Nothing."

Neven smiled smugly, then turned his attention back to Connor. "You see? No feds, no rescue. Which translates to shit out of luck." He seemed to ponder what he was going to say next, then nodded slowly to himself. "Let me explain this as simply as I can, Mr. Connor, so we don't go through a lot of pointless questions later. I am a very rich man. I like money. Money likes me. You might say it seeks me out."

"Sort of the way flies seek out shit."

Neven ignored the remark. "Someone has stolen some money from me. A very large sum of money. Money, I intend to collect."

"Tony Carerra," Connor said. "But you know him as Daniel Parra."

A spark of respect crept into Neven's dark eyes. "Very good," he said. "Some years ago, Parra came into my employ. I trusted him. I let that motherfucker become part of my family, and I thought of him as my brother." He glanced over at Farris, then returned his eyes to Connor. "But trust is a very...how do you say...*capricious* thing. It takes such a long time to earn, and just a few seconds to destroy."

Connor looked for even a flicker of emotion in his leathery skin, but there was none. Like a true sociopath, Neven had perfected a face without expression. "So, this is all about money."

"Everything is about money," Neven finally responded. "The earth's axis is greased with it. Some of us just develop a greater awareness of this fact than others."

"And it doesn't matter how much you get, or how you get it."

"Mr. Connor," Neven sighed, sadly shaking his head. "I am a businessman, just as you are. We both provide a product, and people buy it. Supply and demand. It's their choice, and we profit from it."

Connor had already figured narcotics were involved, one way or the other, so he said, "Let me guess: your product is meth and crack."

Another large smile formed on Neven's face and he let out a snort. "Everyone and his toothless sister can cook meth," he replied. "And crack ties you in with the cartels. I'm not into blood sports."

"Could have fooled me, with all the bodies you've left around town."

"You're pretty blunt for a man who's about to die."

"I've been to war, stared down both ends of a gun," Connor replied, trying his best to sound indifferent. "My luck should've run out a long time ago, so I figure I'm living on borrowed time."

Neven took a long sip from his cut crystal tumbler and said, "That is a fact, and your debt is about to be called."

"Sooner or later we all meet the same fate." Connor figured his best chance at staying alive, at least for the foreseeable future, was to keep this Croatian sociopath talking. "Since it seems I was wrong before about your line of work, my guess now is you're into opiates. And all the dead souls that go with it."

"People are going to do what they're going to do."

"A lot of those people were friends of mine," Connor told him. "Served their country and came home to nothing but pain."

"That's the job description," Neven said in an apathetic voice that made Connor's blood simmer to the boiling point. "And anyway, you're off by a Mississippi mile. Sure, my business started with pain pills, mostly hydrocodone. A lot of people want to take the edge off their lives, smooth things out. And there was a ready-made market. The drug companies got doctors to hook their patients on things like Percocet and Percodan and OxyContin, created my future customer base. Things were going pretty damned good for a while, until the feds started cracking down on manufacturers and pharmacies. It got harder to get your hands on the real stuff, and the consumer moved on to a harder and more direct product."

"Heroin," Connor identified for him.

"Ain't America great?" Neven said with a tight smile. "White collar or blue, it's the drug of choice."

Despite what Connor had told Dr. Pinch earlier, the image of Gordo lying on his bathroom floor with a needle in his hand pushed him right to the edge. "I am so fucking going to kill you—"

"Don't count on it anytime soon. And anyways, just so you know, there's not enough margin in any of that shit anymore to generate real cash flow. The real money is in additives, if you know what you're doing."

"Additives," Connor repeated.

"I shouldn't be telling you this, but you'll be dead soon enough," Neven told him. "I'm talking phenethyl propionyl anilino piperidine, but that doesn't run off your tongue quite as easy as 'fentanyl.'"

"A hundred times more potent than morphine," Connor said, everything now coming together in his mind. Half the patients in his V.A. program at some point had been hooked on heroin, much of it cut with some degree of fentanyl.

Gordo was just one of the latest casualties of a national epidemic and, from the sound of it, a lot of it came from this smug sonofabitch sitting in his fortified home on a soggy hummock in the middle of a Carolina marsh. "And fifty times stronger than heroin."

"Cheap to make, enormous demand, huge margin. Capitalism in its finest form."

"Except for one thing you didn't count on," Connor pointed out.

"And that would be what?"

"Tony Carerra froze you out." Bringing it around to why Connor was really here. "Locked you out of all your tax-haven bank accounts."

Just then he heard footsteps coming into the room, padding across the tile floor. Curiosity seized him but he couldn't twist around to see who it was. Then a voice said, "For someone with such good instincts you sure are one dumb fuck."

At that instant, any hope Connor may have had of leaving Skeleton Cay in one piece drained from his soul. He closed his eyes, as if hoping that when he opened them all this would go away, that he'd be behind the bar at The Sandbar making limes disappear. But he knew that was not going to happen, and when he opened his eyes, he found Special Agent David Landry standing in front of him.

"I figured you for a douchebag, but I didn't know how big," Connor said.

Agent Landry rolled his eyes as if he were bored. "I'd expect something a little more creative from you," he said.

"It's been a long day."

Landry shrugged, continued the bored attitude. "Just so you know, I ran into your policeman pal earlier tonight," he said, drawing out his words slow and easy. Taunting him. "Seems you left him a voicemail before you came out here. Unfortunately, he ran into me before he took action."

"You son of a bitch!" Connor seethed, trying to keep his temper in check. "You don't give a shit how many people you kill—"

"Give it a rest, Connor," Landry sighed. "Your friend will pull through, but just barely."

That did it. Connor pushed up from his chair, started to leap for Agent Landry, but one smack from the butt of Farris' gun and blackness once again engulfed his world.

Back in the cistern, back in the dark. Only this time there was a stream of light coming through a hole in the far wall. Two holes, in fact, about two inches in diameter. Overflow vents, probably the way the frogs got into the water tank. And excess water got out.

Connor's wrists still felt pinched; the rope was still there, still tight. But at least now his hands were tied in front of him, not stretched behind his back. Something to work with, however slight it may have been. He reached up, tried to massage the base of his skull. But when his fingers touched the tender tissue, he sensed a wave of nausea rise up inside, so he let it go. He closed his eyes, forced the agony to go away. It didn't work.

Mustering every ounce of energy that remained, Connor sloshed through the dank water toward to the far end of the cistern. The overflow drains were set just a few inches below the concrete ceiling, so he had to stand on wobbly legs in order to peer out. Not much to see, other than a clump of scrub about four feet away. He moved his eyes to the other hole, found the same thing. Scrub, and more scrub. But at least there was some fresh air, however slight.

He noticed one other thing: the old drains were no more than six inches from one end to the other, meaning the concrete wall of the cistern was no more than half a foot thick. He sank back down into a crouch, realizing there was no way he could chisel his way out of there. Also knowing he was dead unless he came up with a plan. He sat there a moment in the near dark, saw a flicker of light reflect off the blinking eyes of a frog.

Eventually Connor worked his way back to the other end and felt along the cistern wall where it met the ceiling. After a few minutes his fingers found the iron lid Farris had used to haul him out. He braced his feet and hands and pressed up against it with all his strength, but no luck. It was bolted tight.

Connor turned around, started to lower himself into a crouch again, when he saw it. Would have missed it, in fact, if he hadn't been looking at just the right place at the right time. A little spot of light—he was certain it wasn't a frog this time—halfway along the cistern wall, about a foot above the water line. He looked again but this time couldn't see it, and for a second, he thought his eyes had been playing tricks on him. But he scrambled his way back through the water to where he thought he'd seen it, just to make sure.

It took Connor a good five minutes, but he finally found what he'd seen before: a hole blasted clean through the concrete. And from the feel of the rough concrete, it was pretty recent. New, in fact. And then he figured it out: when Farris came to get him last night, he'd lowered his gun through the hatch, fired a shot into the dark. Connor had expected the slug would bounce off the walls, but instead it had embedded itself in the concrete.

Correction: it had bored a hole clean through it.

That's when Connor remembered what Jimmy Brinks had told him about cisterns just yesterday morning: "Back in the day a lot of concrete was mixed with salt water, no rebar. Crumbles real easy. Don't take much to knock it down."

Connor fixed an eye on the fresh hole, looked through it. It was no more than a half-inch in diameter, and the slug seemed to have slammed into a particularly soft patch of decaying cement. Even more amazing was the fact that the hole itself seemed no more than four inches through-and-through.

That gave Connor an idea, one that logic immediately told him wouldn't work. There was no way he could bust through a concrete wall, no matter how thick. He was not a Marvel superhero or a cartoon sailor who had just devoured a can of spinach. But then he thought about the alternative—staying there in the dark with the frogs, waiting to be executed—and he knew he had no choice. So, he inched back through the muck to the other side of the cistern, mentally trying to figure out the best way to play this.

In the end he just put his whole body into it, slogging through the water from one side to the other and slamming his shoulder into the cement wall. A jolt of pain shot through every inch of his frame, and the wall held. *This is friggin' stupid!* he thought as he backed across the cistern, and again threw his weight against the wall. *Idiot!* Again. *Damned fool!* Again. But on the fifth try, he thought he felt something give. Just a little shudder, maybe a little snap inside—or could that have been his shoulder? Either way, he gave it another try, then one more. And then an incredible thing happened: a crack began to form in the cistern wall. Just a thin line of light, about ten inches long, but enough to let him know this was working. So, he backed off one more time, drew up every ounce of strength he had, and threw himself as hard as he could against the concrete wall.

Damned if it didn't fall away.

CHAPTER 29

Connor's hard labor and bruised shoulder had caved a four-foot hole in the side of the cistern. A torrent of water spilled out, along with several wide-eyed amphibians. For a second, he worried that Farris might have heard the collapse of concrete and would come running. *No time to linger*, he thought as he slipped through the ragged opening and scrambled over the chunks of concrete and muddy rubble.

He glanced around, realized the cistern was located in an area that served as a dump. Corroded machinery, an old toilet, rusted stove, an old propane grill, even an air conditioning compressor were scattered about. The place was a veritable landfill, if there'd actually been any land to fill.

What caught his eye was an old roto-tiller, the kind his mother had rented one summer when she'd gotten it into her head to turn their small backyard into a vegetable garden. It was beyond repair, but the spiral blade that once cut through the soil was still intact, although it had rusted beyond any practical use. Connor wasn't looking for anything practical, however; all he wanted was something sharp and jagged enough to slice through the ropes that bound his wrists.

Sixty seconds later his hands were free. Crouching as low as he could, he set out in the direction of where he had beached the borrowed skiff. He inched his way through the thick vegetation until he arrived at the path he'd used last night. It was morning now, and he could see the houses of Kiawah Island across the sound to the east. Close enough to identify tiny specks that were windows, way too distant to attract attention. He kept expecting Farris—maybe an entire army of foot soldiers—to descend upon the cistern, find out he had escaped. But as the seconds ticked by and no one showed up, he figured maybe he'd gotten away clean. Not for long, of course—it was a small island and sooner or later Farris would show up to fetch him or kill him. For now, however, he was free.

He kept an eye open for even the slightest movement, tuned his ears to the thinnest of sounds. Nothing. For some reason he was struck by a momentary pang of loneliness, and his mind jumped from one mental frame to another: Clooney, the burned-out bar, Jessica Snow *right here on Skeleton Cay*. Agent Landry and an arrogant motherfucker named Marco Neven. Tony Carerra collapsing to the floor after being shot by Justacious Stone, Martina Carerra and Jimmy Brinks and a USB drive in the shape of a skeleton key. And, as he gazed out at this view of the marsh and the ocean beyond, he suddenly realized that he'd gone a full night—and a slice of the next day—and Danielle had not been part of his thoughts.

Which, of course, made him miss her even more. He missed her deep blue eyes, her loving smile, her fondness for dirty martinis in the evening on the small patch of lawn behind his old apartment that had been washed away in the hurricane. Even missed how she had called him "the last true gentleman in all of Charleston" at the close of their very first date, when he had opted not to invite her back to his place for an intimate nightcap that might lead to breakfast. Too soon, and too much unfinished business in both of their lives at the time.

He indulged the memories a moment, but now was really not the time for that. She'd left him high and dry because of the very thing he was doing now, going off half-cocked in search of...*in search of what?* Nothing, except the very real likelihood of his own death.

Fifty yards further along the trail Connor came upon yet another narrow path. Wary about using the main route back to the boat—he'd already been burned by his own stupidity—he chose to follow this new course, see if it might be more protected. He no longer had his map, but he knew he was on the far end of the island, a good distance from the patch of muck and oyster shells where he'd left the boat. Of course, if one of Neven's men had had found the skiff he was probably shit out of luck, but he decided not to dwell on that. He was a half-full kind of guy, not half-empty.

Two minutes later he spotted a small building tucked in between two twisted cypress trees that somehow had found reason to grow out here. In fact, he almost missed it as he picked his way along the narrow trail. What gave it away was the corrugated tin roof that had turned to rust over the years. He was less than twenty yards away when he heard a voice, muffled and thick, just barely audible inside the structure. Then the door opened, and the voice suddenly became clearer, and Connor realized it was the man named Farris.

"One hour!" Farris snapped at whoever was inside.

The response came back muffled and tired, something like "Fug you."

Farris responded angrily, but from the flurry of words that followed all Connor could make out was "...get it done."

And then: "Ub yers."

A short silence followed. Then Connor heard a dull thud that sounded like something hard hitting something soft, followed by a low groan. Then Farris said, clearer this time, "You screw with Neven, she dies."

Connor peered over a clump of wild goldenrod, watched as Farris pulled the door closed and marched down a path in the direction of the bunker house in the distance. He wondered what this outbuilding was—*maybe an old Army ordnance dump?*—and remained hidden in the scrub until he felt it was safe to come out.

Then he crept down to the concrete structure and pushed the door inward on rusty hinges.

"I said, 'fug you!'"

"Quiet!" Connor snapped in a low voice as he closed the door behind him.

There was a short silence, then: "Who the fug are you?"

"A friend, Mr. Carerra," Connor replied. "Or should I call you Daniel Parra?"

"Whoever you are, leave me alone," Carerra said, his voice little more than a loud whimper. He was lying on a filthy mattress on the floor, several stained pillows tucked under his head. "I've had enough of Neven and all you dirty bastards."

The man obviously was in a lot of pain. A week ago, he'd been shot in the shoulder and had lost a lot of blood, and from the look of things no one had much cared about his health since then. His upper torso was wrapped in strips of old bedsheets, and a red stain beneath his right shoulder indicated that blood was still seeping from where Justacious Stone had put a bullet through him. Both of his eyes were blackened, and he had deep purple bruises on his face and jaw. Similar markings were on his hands and arms. Neven's thugs clearly had beaten him severely and often over the last few days.

"I'm here to help," Connor said as he moved away from the door, nearer to where Carerra was lying.

"Sure, you are," Carerra snarled, turning his head away.

"My name's Jack," Connor assured him. He moved closer and studied Carerra, looking like a doctor trying to make a visual diagnosis. "I'm going to get you out of here."

"You and whose army?" Carerra hissed. Still, there was a spark of interest in his eyes, a glimmer of hope that suggested he wanted to hear more.

Connor glanced around the room: it was about ten feet square, dark gray walls and matching floor. Mold and mildew seemed everywhere. Hardly an antiseptic environment, but Connor figured Neven didn't give a shit about Carerra's long-term prognosis. There were no windows and no fan, which made the place feel like blast oven.

"I know about the money," he said.

"What the fug are you talking about?"

"Over a hundred million dollars, last I saw," Connor relied. "Of course, it's probably gone up a mil or two since then, with the interest and all."

Carerra looked at him differently then, studying him as if he was searching his brain for some long-lost scrap of data that was eluding him.

"What did you say your name was?" he finally asked.

"Jack Connor. A week ago, you came into my bar with your wife and ordered two Heinekens. Then you got shot."

The spark of recognition jumped a synapse, and Carerra rolled his eyes. "You are one crazy bastard, coming out there—"

"Tell me about it."

The sudden sound of footsteps outside the guest house made them both freeze. Then Carerra mouthed the words, *behind the door.*

Connor ducked into the corner just in time. The footsteps stopped, the deadbolt turned, the door creaked open.

"Neven moved up the deadline," Farris snarled. "He has travel plans."

"How the hell you 'spect me to finish, you keep interrupting?" Carerra replied, sounding parched and in pain.

"Not my problem. Just do what he wants, or your lady gets it. You understand?"

"Martina's got nothing to do with this—"

"Tell it to Neven," Farris jeered. "Helicopter's coming in thirty minutes." He marched out of the room, yanking the door closed behind him.

Connor and Carerra waited for Farris to move out of earshot; then Connor said, "We have to get you out of here."

"Forget about me," Carerra said, sounding helpless. "You've got to save Martina."

"You first, then we find her."

"But I—"

They both heard it at the same time: more footsteps outside, the deadbolt turning once more. Connor ducked behind the door one more time as it burst open and Farris came back into the room.

"One more thing—" Farris barked, his gun aimed straight at Carerra.

Without hesitation Connor leaned all his weight against the door, slamming Farris against the jamb. He let out a squeal of pain, and Connor knew he only had a fraction of a second to gain the advantage here. He pulled the door open a few inches, then slammed it once more against Farris's arm. That elicited a louder scream as Connor reached out to grab the gun from his hand, but Farris wasn't about to give up that easily. He threw all his weight against the door and flung it open, sending Connor spinning back against the moldy wall. All in one motion Farris crashed into him, pummeling Connor first with a right hook to the gut, then a left jab to his jaw. Connor ducked at a third blow aimed at his throat, causing Farris to smash his fist into solid concrete, causing him to yell "fuck!" In the same fraction of a second Connor managed to slip his finger through the trigger guard, and he squeezed off a single round. The bullet struck Farris in the left ear, and his life was gone before the slug emerged from his right temple.

Connor watched him crumple to the floor, feeling an odd mix of relief and fear as he watched the blood pool on the tile floor. Before today he had killed three men in his entire life—two in the war, and most recently the psycho who had ambushed him on that dark road in the woods a year ago. He still didn't feel good about any of it, but right now all that mattered was he was alive, and so was Carerra. He could dwell on it later, if his luck held out. For now, he just had to make sure there *was* a later.

"Damn, that was good," Carerra said. "Were you a cop in a former life?"

"U.S. Army, second brigade combat team," Connor said. He moved over to where Carerra was stretched out on the bed. "Can you walk?"

"Barely, but better than they think. Bastard shot a good chunk out of my shoulder."

"Any idea how many of Neven's men are on this island?"

Carerra thought for a minute, then nodded toward the body on the floor. "There's Farris, there. And Landry. He's DEA, been working both sides of the fence a couple years now. Some other guy I only saw once, never got his name. Dark hair and a ponytail. And there were two black dudes, too. One of 'em, I think they called him Jesry, but I haven't seen him in a day or two. The other one they just called Maines."

Damn! Connor thought. *Cecil Maines was part of this.* That's what he was doing out here last Friday night, and why he'd gotten spooked. Probably didn't realize what he'd gotten himself into until it was too late.

"Jesry and Maines are dead," he told Carerra. "Which is what we're going to be if we don't get out of here."

"What's your plan?"

"For neither of us to die." Connor popped the magazine out of Farris' gun and inspected it—just the one bullet missing—then jammed it home again. He tucked it into a pocket in his cargo shorts and said, "Try standing up, see if you can make it to the door."

He helped Carerra to his feet, but just barely. He was wearing a pair of boxers and a white T-shirt. "I think I can make it, but I'm going to need my shoes, there."

Connor retrieved them and helped him on with them. "This whole thing was all about moving money around, right?"

Carerra said nothing as he slipped his foot into one shoe, then the other. He couldn't bend over to tie them, so Connor did it for him. "What are you talking about?" he finally asked.

"I found your flash drive." Connor put an arm around Carerra's waist and helped navigate him around Farris' lifeless body. "The one shaped like a skeleton key. Seems a lot of people are dead because of that money."

"These are truly fucked-up people," Carerra told him. "And can we save the interrogation until we're far away from here?"

As it turned out, Carerra was one rugged son-of-a-bitch. Connor didn't comment on it until they were far from the concrete hut, working their way along the trail and staying as far from the fortified bunker as possible. Progress was slow, but fifteen minutes later they had found a spot to catch their breath in the dense brush. Unless Neven had dogs—something Connor didn't want to think about—they were in pretty good shape. Especially with Farris dead.

"You're in over your head," Carerra said as they rested in the shade.

"You think?"

"This is personal between Neven and me."

"Me too, now. But yeah, I kind of figured it might be more than just business."

Carerra wiped a tired arm across his brow and shaded his eyes from the sun. "Neven and I go way back, to when he was just a two-bit hustler in Mobile," he said. "He was a small-time thug back then, slipped out of Croatia during the war and moved in with his uncle who'd come over years ago. He started out running meth and weed along the Gulf, from Pascagoula to Pensacola. But over time he got more ambitious and aggressive, and started moving pills. Lots of pills. Millions of pills, from Miami to Atlanta to Norfolk."

"You worked for him?"

"I was what you'd call his bag man, at least in the beginning. He didn't trust any legit bean-counters, so I kept his books. Neven started making so much money I had to find creative ways to stash it, keep it hidden from the IRS."

"Offshore banks, real estate, cash businesses," Connor said.

Carerra nodded, then winced from a sudden stab of pain in his shoulder. "At some point, around four years ago, I got this sense that the feds had their eyes on him. *Us*. Clicks on the phone, ugly Detroit sedans that kept showing up where they shouldn't be. Then I started thinking with my third leg and fell in love."

"Aurora Santana."

The look of fury in Carerra's eyes suggested he would have clamped his hands around Connor's throat, if he'd had the strength. "Where did you get that name—?"

"The flash drive you left behind in the rental house."

Carerra said nothing after that, not for a good twenty seconds. Then he took a deep breath and slowly let it out. "I didn't know it at the time, but she was undercover with the IRS criminal task force," he said with a sad sigh. "I fell for her hard, thought she was the love of my life. Wife, kids, picket fence. The whole cliché. I had no idea who she was, or what she was doing."

"But Neven did," Connor pointed out. "That's why he pushed her from the plane."

Another silence followed, and Connor was starting to get nervous. The more time they stayed where they were, the greater the chance that Neven or his men would find Farris' body and come looking for them. But Carerra was on a roll, and Connor didn't want to stop him.

Eventually Carerra lowered his head in an imperceptible nod and said, "Until that day I'd never given one thought to what I was doing, where my life was going. I worked for one of the biggest drug traffickers in the U.S. and I didn't care, as long as the money kept flowing. But that day—" His voice trailed off for a minute, then picked up again. "That day I vowed to myself that I was going to bring that bastard down, if it was the last thing I ever did."

A sharp wince told Connor that Carerra had done enough talking, at least for now. "Let's save this for later," he asked. "How're you holding up?"

"I'll make it," Carerra grunted. "We need to find Martina."

Connor nodded and peered through the brush, trying to get a fix on where they were. Skeleton Cay was not a large island, and he didn't have a clue where Neven could be holding Martina Carerra. "Did they give you any idea where she might be?" he asked.

Carerra shook his head as he dragged himself down the path. "My guess is, he's got her in that old concrete fort, maybe in one of the bedrooms."

"We can't just shoot our way in there with one gun," Connor pointed out. The scrub on both sides of the trail was thinning, and he realized they were nearing the chopper landing pad with the smudge pots he'd seen last night.

"If they find out I'm gone they'll shoot her," Carerra said.

Just then, as if to emphasize the point, the sound of a gunshot rang out, followed by a second. A rapid volley of shots followed, and Carerra and Connor both scrambled for cover. The gunfire continued intermittently for about ten seconds, then stopped.

"Holy mother of God," Carerra whispered from where he had landed in a prickly tangle of Carolina briar. "They've killed her."

"I don't think so," Connor said in a hushed voice, for the first time feeling a slight ray of hope. His brain flashed back to his days on patrol in Fallujah, but only for a second. "Those shots came from down there—" He nodded toward the landing area "—and the bunker is back that way. Besides, that was more than one gun. Sounded more like a whole platoon."

Carerra appeared to think on this, realized Connor was probably right. The shots had come from the direction of the clearing.

"Who do you think's down there?" he asked.

"Hell, if I know, but I'm going to check it out."

"I don't think that's a good idea—"

It wasn't, but that had never stopped Connor before. He wriggled back out through the brush and inched his way along the trail until he had a view of the clearing through a clump of bushes. What he saw caused him to freeze: Agent Landry was lying near the center of the makeshift helipad, a gun at his side. From the looks of things, he'd caught at least one round right in the face.

Another man was lying half-in, half-out of the doorway of the old storage building. He wasn't moving, either, and from where Connor was crouching, he could see a dark pool beginning to form in the dirt beneath him.

Connor didn't move for a good thirty seconds. He felt Carerra's eyes on him but didn't dare look around, didn't dare say anything until he was sure all was quiet.

"What do you see?" Carerra finally called in a low whisper.

Connor raised a finger, indicating for him to be silent. Then he moved forward, leading with Farris' gun, cautiously working his way around the edge of the clearing. He kept an eye on Landry but realized the agent wasn't going anywhere. Then he drew his glance to the man lying in the doorway of the outbuilding, and figured the same thing. Both were dead.

Taking one slow step at a time Connor made his way around the perimeter of the landing area. From the look of things these two men had managed to kill each other, but he was taking nothing for granted. As he approached the masonry structure, he lowered his body into a crouch, sweeping the brush with his eyes for any flicker of movement, any hint of a sound. The wind was blowing away from the bunker house, but Neven must have heard something.

Connor edged up to the side of the building, holding the gun steady in both hands. He hesitated, then peered around the corner at the man lying face down in a patch of crimson mud. But it wasn't so much the blood in the dirt or the blowouts in the back of the head that sent the shiver rattling through his nerves. It was the fact that he recognized this man.

Alfonse Romano.

Connor inched forward slowly, looking at the blood and brains oozing out of the man's skull, while keeping an eye on Agent Landry lying out there in the middle of the landing pad. He crouched over Romano's body, just as a voice from the shadows inside the building snarled, "Freeze, you sonofabitch. And drop the gun."

CHAPTER 30

"Do it nice and slow," the voice continued as Connor stood there, his body frozen, just as he'd been asked.

"I'm dropping it," he said. He recognized the voice, of course, again thought *how the hell is Jessica mixed up in all this?* He let the gun slip from his hand, said, "Just don't shoot."

There was a short silence, then: "Do I know you?" Her voice sounded strained, as if spoken through clenched teeth.

"Are you talking in the Biblical sense?" He had his back to the door so he couldn't see her in the shadows, but he was operating on the belief that she wasn't going to just shoot him then and there. "You slipped out of bed early yesterday morning, and I haven't seen you since."

Another pause, then: "Jack?"

"Was it as good for you as it was for me?" he asked.

"Jesus Christ, Jack. Get in here." A short silence. "I've been hit."

"I'm picking up my gun."

"Leave it."

He picked it up anyway, then slipped through the doorway past Romano's body. Jessica Snow was huddled in the far corner of the room, between the work table and the wall, gripping a powerful-looking semiautomatic in her hands.

"Put that down," Connor said, more of a request than an order.

She stared at him in disbelief, slowly lowered the gun to her side. It was then that he noticed the wound in her upper left arm, bleeding but not gushing, and a red bloom high up on her right thigh.

"Man, you really got nailed."

"It's not as bad as it looks."

"Right…just a flesh wound. You need to see a doctor."

"I'll live." The quizzical look returned to her face and she said, "What the hell…what are you doing out here?" She winced, and Connor realized she was in great pain.

"Tracking down a customer who ran out on his tab," he said. "What's your story?"

Jessica looked away, her eyes falling on Romano's body in the doorway. She seemed to think for a moment, then looked up at him. "He's dead, isn't he?"

Connor nodded, wondering what the hell was going on. And waiting for her to explain.

"*Sonofabitch*." She took a breath, picked something up from the dirt-covered floor and handed it to him. It was her federal badge. "I'm with the U.S. Marshal's Service. So is…*was*… Alfonse. I trusted him, the bastard."

Connor studied the badge, did a double-take. "This says your name is Lisa King."

"It's my name," she said, offering him a contrite smile.

"So, no restaurant reviews or foodie blog?"

"I was under full cover," she explained. "What can I say?"

"You can start by explaining why your partner is lying there with a bullet in him."

"I shot him."

"You *what?*"

"He pulled his gun on me," she told him. "I had no choice."

Damn, Connor thought. *Just when he'd thought he figured this all out.*

"You're really a fed?"

"Witness Security Program," she said.

"Holy shit. Do you mind telling me what the hell is going on?"

Jessica closed her eyes, and for a second Connor thought she might black out. Then she opened them to thin slits and said, "Tony Carerra—a.k.a. Daniel Parra—contacted us four weeks ago, said he had information that would put one of the biggest drug dealers in America in jail for half a dozen lifetimes."

"Marco Neven."

"How do you know him?" she asked, flashing him an accusatory look.

"Met him last night, not long after I saw you and your pal, Romano, on the trail."

She blinked at that, then shook her head in disbelief. Or was it confusion? "DEA and IRS had been after Neven for years," she said, neither confirming nor denying what Connor had just said. "It was a no-brainer."

"So Carerra just happens to turn up in my bar, along with two U.S. Marshals and the guy he's trying to nail?"

"One Marshal, one traitor," she corrected him. "It's complicated, and I don't have time to fill you in."

"Just tell me one thing, then," Connor said. "Did you think I had something to do with all this? Is that why you cozied up to me at the bar? And got me into your bed?"

She winced at his words, or maybe it was just the open gunshot wounds. Then she said, "Tony Carerra—*Daniel Parra*—picked your place to meet with us. Very public. We didn't know why, and with these things everyone's a suspect, until they aren't. Alfonse and I got there first to scope out the place, see if he might've been playing us before we made any kind of deal. He'd never met us, so we went in undercover."

"I don't recall there being any covers at all the other night in your room," Connor pointed out.

"Like I said, it's complicated." She squeezed her eyes shut, trying to kill the fire that was sizzling in her arm and thigh. "Our plan was to pull him in and get him in front of a judge."

"Except Alfonse was playing both sides."

"Stupid me. Now I have nothing, Carerra's dead, and my career's toast."

"Carrera saved all his records on a flash drive," Connor told her.

Jessica's eyes darkened and she said, "What do you know about that?"

"Banks, shell companies, money laundering—it's all there," he confirmed.

Jessica grimaced again and Connor could tell her condition was worsening. "You've seen it?" she asked.

"Makes for fascinating reading," he replied. "And don't worry...it's all safe." Which was true, as long as old cistern water hadn't damaged it.

"Where?"

"Later," he told her. "Nothing matters if we die out here."

"I need that drive—"

Connor drew his gaze to where Romano was lying in the doorway, wondered just how much he could really trust this Jessica Snow. "Do you have a cell phone?" he asked her.

She shook her head. "No signal out here."

"You must have some sort of back-up—"

"We were working a joint op with that bastard Landry," she explained. She made an effort to stand up, but she had no strength in her leg. "He used us to get to Parra, except it turns out Alfonse knew about the cross all along. *Sonofabitch.*"

Connor thought on what she said, sensed another chunk of the game fall into place. "When Carerra got shot, you just stood by watching him bleed out in my bar." Connor said. "That's pretty harsh."

"We didn't expect that, and he wasn't in the program yet. We couldn't expose ourselves to Neven, not with him standing right there. This was supposed to be a quick in-and-out op, but all I did was get my witness killed."

"No, you didn't," Connor told her. "He's very much alive. But he needs a doctor."

She opened her eyes, gave him a sideways glance. "You've seen him?"

"Better than that," he said. "He's waiting right on the other side of the clearing."

"He...you...I don't believe you."

Connor tightened his lips in a thin grin and said, "Frankly, my dear, I don't give a damn."

She blinked and lowered her head, then asked, "How do I know I can trust you?"

"I could ask you the same thing," he replied. "Besides, you trusted me enough to sleep with me."

"I can explain—"

"Later," he told her again.

Things moved fast then. Connor left Jessica where she was and hurried back across the makeshift helipad, picking up Landry's gun in the process. Unless he'd emptied his clip, it might help them get off the island. Then Connor retreated back up the trail to where Carerra was hiding in the brush.

"Jesus, Connor," Carerra wheezed. "Took you long enough."

"There's two dead, one wounded," he explained sharply. "I think you know a couple of 'em."

Carerra shot him a confused look, said nothing.

"Alfonse Romano and Jessica Snow."

"Never heard of 'em."

"U.S. Marshal's Service?" Connor reminded him. "Witness security program? Does any of that ring a bell?"

By the look on Carerra's face, it did. He was silent a moment, then said, "They're dead?"

"One of 'em is, the other's going to be if she doesn't get help real soon," Connor explained. "We've got to get you both out of here."

"Not without Martina," Carerra protested.

"I'll do what I can. But first, you move. *Now!*"

Carerra actually gave it a moment's thought, then sighed and said, "All right... lead the way."

Connor helped Carerra stand up, then gave him a shoulder to lean on while they made their way to the edge of the clearing. Neither said a word as they passed Agent Landry's body in the middle of the clearing, but Carerra took a hard look as he staggered past. By the time they got to the cinder block hut he was visibly tired and collapsed to the concrete floor as soon as they slipped inside.

Jessica looked at him, registered a look of anger on her face. "Mr. Parra," she said at length. "So nice to finally meet you."

Carerra said nothing, just let out a low groan as a wave of pain engulfed him.

"You hanging in there?" Connor asked Jessica as he crouched between them.

"Better than he is," she said, nodding at Carerra.

He studied her, saw a woman who was trying to hold on to consciousness despite her injuries and her pain. "I'm going to get both of you out of here, but right now I have to leave you."

She nodded, made a motion with her head that meant "go."

"How many rounds are left in your gun?"

"A few," she said. "I'll be okay."

"I'm sure you will, but I still want you to take this." Connor handed her the gun he'd taken off Farris and said, "I know you won't hesitate to use it."

"You're sure you trust me?"

"Don't have much choice, do I?"

"But you'll need a gun—"

"I've got Landry's. I'll be fine, and I'll be back here as soon as I can." He turned and walked back outside, shielding his eyes from the sun. Mostly wondering how the hell all this was going to play out.

His plan was to get down to the beach, take the skiff over to Kiawah and call for help. If the skiff wasn't there, maybe the other boat he'd seen last night would start. Jessica Snow and Tony Carerra both seemed to be on death's doorstep, and he needed to get them some help. Problem was, even if the plan worked, it would take hours. And hours might prove to be too late.

Against his better judgment, against every cell of logic in his brain, he changed his mind. Farris had told Carerra that a helicopter would be arriving soon, presumably to whisk Marco Neven off the island. It would be landing here in the clearing, and if Connor somehow could get the upper hand with Neven maybe he could co-opt that flight.

He made his way across the makeshift helipad, stopping beside Agent Landry's body to rummage through his pockets. He already had the man's gun, but figured Landry was the sort who carried two weapons—his primary, and a back-up. He was right: tucked into the pocket of Landry's khaki trousers was a small, snub-nosed revolver with five rounds in the cylinder. Not much stopping power, but if Landry felt safer carrying it, so did Connor. For a second, he thought about what Jimmy Brinks had said— "Jesus, you are one dumb sumbitch"—and in retrospect he had to agree. He slipped the gun into his pocket, then started up the trail that led back to the bunker house.

Two minutes later Connor was hiding behind the same clump of brush he'd used last night. The bright sun overhead limited what he could see of the terrace at the top of the giant earthen mound, but the daylight provided a clear view of the surrounding terrain and the stairs rising up the outside of the berm. He estimated there were sixty steps in all, winding upwards around the outside of the man-made knoll. The massive steel doors through which he had been led last night appeared to be shut tight, so the stairs provided the only way in. There were countless problems with this plan, the most obvious being that he would be in clear view of anyone down below on Skeleton Cay during his ascent, or looking down from the top.

But it was his only option, and he was out of time. Without thinking twice, he made a run for the steep stairs and began to take them two at a time, mentally dodging imaginary bullets during the entire climb. The terrace at the top was larger than he had figured last night, fashioned to house the gun turret back during the war. At the far end was the room where Connor had been prodded last night to meet with Neven, the large doorway now open to the heat of the summer morning.

When he arrived at the top, he hesitated a second to determine his best course of action. He still had no idea how many armed men might be lurking about, and he didn't want to find out. Farris, Landry, and Romano all were dead, but there could be others. Connor was too smart to think Neven would surrender without a fight, which was why he'd figured on a different course of action. What he really wanted was to use the phone that he had seen on the table beside Neven's chair last night, although he doubted it was still there. It had been one of those larger Android devices, and he assumed it went wherever Neven went. Plus, its presence told him that—unlike Jessica Snow's phone—it picked up a signal out there. Farris had taken Connor's phone seconds after he'd assaulted him, and Landry didn't have one on him, either.

Just then the man named Marco Neven stepped out onto the terrace and wandered over to the concrete wall. He was only five yards from where Connor was hunkered down on the stairs, and he could tell Neven was furious, flailing his arms as he yelled at someone Connor could not see.

"I don't give a damn anymore," he cursed in his thick accent. He kicked at a wicker chair, sent it skidding across the patio. "I'll find some other software hack who can take care of it. I just want that man dead. No one fucks with Marco Neven, you hear me? No one!"

At first Connor thought Neven had been yelling into a phone, but then someone inside the adjoining room said something and Neven turned around. Connor couldn't make out what the person inside was saying, but whatever it was, Neven didn't take it lightly. "The only thing keeping him going is the Goddamned fentanyl, and that's got to be wearing off. I need Landry. *Where the hell is Landry?*"

Then the person who had been talking to him from inside glided out onto the terrace and walked over to him. It was a woman, and she lovingly put an arm around him. Neven spun away and snapped, "Not now, you whore" before he stormed to the far end of the terrace.

"Take it easy, Marco," Martina Carerra said, her voice soothing and tender as she stood there looking at him, his rejection rolling right off her.

Martina Carerra? Connor thought

And then, in an instant, it all made sense.

"Don't tell me to take it easy," Neven barked at her. "That man double-crossed me, and I want him dead."

"Just give him time. Landry said someone changed the passwords and Danny can't access the accounts."

"Who the fuck would know how to do that?"

Ooops, Connor thought as he was overcome by a momentary pang of guilt.

"I don't know," Mrs. Carerra said. "But if anyone can find a way to get into those banks, it's my husband."

Neven stood there gazing out at the marsh, then turned and looked at her. "Come here," he told her, holding out his arms.

She walked over to him, wrapped her arms around him as he leaned down and planted his lips on hers. She responded by reaching up, drawing his face tightly to hers. They kissed for what seemed like forever, until finally she pulled back. "Let's go inside," she said.

He hesitated, still holding her in his arms.

"Let me help you relax," she told him. "Take your mind off things."

"The chopper arrives in fifteen minutes—"

"Then we'd better hurry."

Again, he hesitated, then took her hand and led her across the terrace. He whispered something in her ear, and she gave him a playful swat with her hand.

"Not out here," she said. "Half those houses over there have telescopes."

Neven smiled, ran a hand through her hair, then took her hand and led her back inside.

Good old faithful Martina Carerra, Connor thought.

CHAPTER 31

Connor figured he had only a few minutes while the loving couple was indecently disposed. He waited a good thirty seconds, then edged across the stone terrace to the open doorway and peered inside. For a moment he crouched there, pressed up against the wall, listening for any kind of sound.

He pulled Landry's 9 mm out of his waistband and slipped into the room. He crossed to the chair where Neven had been sitting last night but, just as he'd figured, the phone was not there. *Shit.* He glanced around warily, reckoned the two lovers must have gone downstairs to where the bedrooms must have been located. He remembered that the steps were metal, so he probably would hear footfalls as they came back up. Still, he wasn't taking any chances, and several lives depended on him moving fast. His own included.

Neven didn't appear to be the sort of man who could be separated from a phone for long, and Connor didn't recall one being in his hands just now. That meant it must be lying around somewhere in this room, so he made a quick survey. There were lots of surfaces and he scoured everyone, finally felt a wave of relief when the sudden illumination of a screen caught his eye on the shelf of a bookcase. Connor moved quickly, grabbed the phone before the new message on the screen faded:

Reminder alert: Palmetto Avionics Reservation

helicopter en route. ETA 16 minutes

Connor knew from previous experience that Palmetto Avionics was a private aircraft charter agency located on Aviation Boulevard near the Charleston Airport. Neven was correct: the chopper would be there soon, which gave Connor an idea.

He "swiped" the message off the screen, then typed "911" into the phone's touchpad. Since Skeleton Cay was located out in the middle of the marsh, he wondered which police department would answer the call, but he didn't really give a shit. Even if a helicopter was due to arrive any minute, he needed back-up out here, *stat.*

He never got a chance to find out. The phone exploded in Connor's hand in the same instant that he heard the shot. A second later he heard another pop, felt a hot flame whiz past his ear as he instinctively dropped to the floor. Two more shots rang out, but by this time he was scrambling behind the leather couch. Not much cover, but any port in a storm. One more shot bounced off the flagstone floor just as Connor pulled the snub-nose out of his pocket. He'd set Landry's 9 mm down on a table when he picked up the phone, and he'd be committing suicide if he tried to go for it now.

"Give it up, Mr. Connor," Neven growled at him. "You move, you die."

Connor didn't respond, just tried to get a fix on the voice while calculating what sort of chance he might have of getting out of this. Not good, he decided. His hand was stinging from where the slug had torn through the phone, embedding fragments of plastic and glass in his skin.

"Put your hands up, slowly, where I can see 'em. You got that?"

Connor still said nothing, trying to sort out his options. The way he saw it there weren't many. Any, in fact. Of course, his prospects didn't improve if he gave himself up, so he stayed where he was.

"I am not a patient man," Neven barked. "You have three seconds, then I shoot. One…two…"

Connor raised one hand in the air, the one with the gun, and fired a blind shot over the back of the couch to where he guessed the fentanyl king was standing. A shot came back, followed in quick succession by two more.

"You motherfucker," Neven screamed. "You *die!*"

There was no point in wasting a breath, so he didn't. Instead Connor just raised the gun again and pulled the trigger, then launched into a quick forward summersault and grabbed the other gun from the table as he rolled.

A bullet ricocheted off the floor just inches from his shoulder. He scrambled back out of the line of fire, stretched out on the floor behind the couch with Landry's gun clenched in his good hand. He heard a footstep, really just a shifting sound on the tile, and realized that Neven was edging toward him. No more than ten feet away, coming closer. Unless Connor did something—something *conclusive*—he was dead.

Fighting every instinct in his body to stay put he raised the 9 mm above the back of the sofa, then emptied the entire clip in a blind rage of fire.

To Connor's surprise there was no return volley, no sound at all. Not for a good three-count, and then he heard the sound of Neven collapsing to the floor.

He waited another five seconds before warily inching upward and taking a look over the back of the couch. The naked body of Marco Neven was sprawled on the flagstone in a puddle of blood. A bath towel lay on the floor beside him. His gun was still in his hand, held out at an impossible angle, and Connor realized his arm had twisted out of its socket when he went down. The side of his head had collided with the floor, and a smaller stream of blood was oozing from his mouth. Connor had no idea how many times he'd hit him, but there was no question the sonofabitch was dead.

Connor listened for a sound from the stairway, but none came. He moved quickly but cautiously, stepping around the couch and kicking the gun from

Neven's hand. He'd seen enough movies to know not to leave it within the man's reach, no matter how dead he was. It skittered across the floor, stopped where the smooth floor met the rough flagstone of the terrace. Connor took one last look at the dead man, then started toward the stairs, leading the way with his good hand. The other hand hung at his side, blood still oozing from the shrapnel wounds, but not as rapidly as it had been.

He took a cautious peek down the dark stairwell, wondering where Martina was. She had to have heard the gunshots, but would she come up to investigate? He didn't like the idea of venturing down to find out, but Neven had destroyed the phone and he figured Mrs. Carerra must have had one, too. He took a deep breath, realized what he had to do. He started to take the first of several dozen steps down, when he sensed a slight shift in the light. He felt a bolt of pain erupt in his thigh at the same instant he heard the crack of a gun. *Fuck*, he thought. *Not again.* As he spun around from the force of the shot, he found Mrs. Carerra standing in the terrace doorway, the sheer, slinky robe she was wearing not distracting him from the pistol she gripped tightly in both hands.

Connor slumped against the wall, feeling the fangs of a dozen piranha biting into his arm. He glanced down, saw where the slug had torn into his black panther tattoo. Blood was trickling from the wound, which looked more like a graze than a hole.

"Just so there's no mistake, I could have put that through your eye at thirty yards," she told him as she took a step into the room. "The gun. Slide it to me."

Because of the pain Connor only guessed at what she was saying, but he set the gun on the floor and gave it a push with his foot. It slid about five feet and stopped. She eyed it, decided to leave it where it was.

"You know, Mr. Connor, I almost feel sorry about this. You were such a help in the beginning, that night you took me to the hospital. You had no idea what you were getting yourself into."

"You set me up."

She shook her head. "No, you offered me a ride. That wasn't part of the plan, but it got me away from the cops."

If Connor had the energy he would have nodded in comprehension, but the fury in his leg was sapping all his strength. "You work for Neven," he said.

Martina Carerra looked vaguely distant for a second, then returned to the present. "Daniel—my husband—was going to rat him out to the feds," she said. "Marco doesn't—*didn't*—like rats."

"That's why he killed Aurora Santana—"

"That whore was before my time, but yes. Daniel was madly in love with her, but Marco figured her for what she really was. Killing her eliminated his problem."

"It also turned Tony—your husband—against him," Connor said. "He dropped out of sight and plotted his revenge. The colder, the better."

Martina took another step forward, stared down at the lifeless naked body lying on the floor. "People never understood Marco," she said, a sadness in her voice. "He was a kind, decent man."

"Tell that to all the people he killed."

She snapped her head around and glared at him. Anger was beginning to take hold, and that was a dangerous sign. "They got in the way," she replied as she stared at Marco Neven's body.

"I have to say, you deserve an Oscar," he told her. "All that crying and whimpering, fainting at the hospital, even the red eyes. Total method acting. But you made one big mistake."

"I don't have time for this—"

"The medical examiner said you'd IDed your husband's body," Connor said, ignoring her. "That gave you away."

"Like I said, you should have stayed out of it."

"What you told me about how the two of you met..." His breathing was becoming tired and ragged. "Was all of that a lie?"

"Not that it matters, but after Aurora died, Marco spent several years searching for Danny. Eventually he learned he'd changed his name to Tony Carerra, and his people tracked him to Biloxi. He used me as the bait to reel him in."

"Why didn't Neven just kill him when he first had the chance?" Connor asked.

"Because Danny had hijacked his bank accounts, and he was the only person who knew the access codes. Marco is a very patient but persistent man, especially when a lot of money is involved. He trusted me, knew I'd be able to land Danny hook, line, and sinker."

"Yeah...I saw the two of you just a few minutes ago. Was that a sign of your trust or just another act?"

"I don't expect you to understand, Mr. Connor," Martina said as she edged around Neven's body, took a couple more steps toward Connor. "And enough bullshit. I really just wanted to thank you for your help before I blow your brains out."

"It was me who changed them," he told her.

"You did what?" she said, the gun aimed straight at him.

A spike of pain stabbed through Connor's arm and he winced. "I changed the passwords. That's why Tony—Danny—couldn't get into the accounts. I updated the user IDs and passcodes."

"You lie. There's no way you could have even known about that."

"I found the flash drive," he said. "In your house."

Mrs. Carerra shook her head rapidly, not buying it. "Landry and I already went through Danny's things," she said. "We looked everywhere."

"Obviously not," Connor replied, realizing now that it was probably Landry who had cold-cocked him that day.

"Don't fuck with me," she snapped, leveling the gun at him again. "Describe the drive."

"Shaped like a skeleton key," he told her. "Account numbers, spreadsheets, passwords—plus instructions on how to change them. If someone had a mind to."

Mrs. Carerra stared at him, clearly not knowing what to say. Not knowing whether to believe him or not, thinking that if he was telling the truth she still might be able to get to Neven's money. Even better, now that Neven was dead.

"How many banks?" she asked, testing him.

Connor thought about this, said, "Ten, mostly in the Caribbean, but two in Switzerland."

"I want that money," she told him in a voice that was cold and dark.

"I figured as much," he replied. Another stab of pain, another wince. "In fact, I was counting on it. So why don't you put the gun down—"

"I don't have time to play games—"

It was a partial statement that turned out to be dead on, because just then a single shot rang out and the took off the top of her head. Red and gray matter sprayed across the damp concrete wall just a few feet from where she'd been standing, and then her lifeless body folded to the floor. Connor had a vague sensation of motion, just a thin flicker of movement outside on the terrace as whoever had just fired the kill shot made his escape.

CHAPTER 32

Three months later, and Halloween was in the air.

Given any excuse for a rowdy celebration, Folly Beach plunged head-first into All Hallows Eve with a city-wide festival that welcomed revelers of all ages. The annual carnival for kids had been held earlier in the day with costume competitions, pumpkin carving parties, and food contests to see just how much shrimp and grits a southern belly could hold. Ghosts and witches and skeletons paraded through town, along with fire trucks and beauty queens and antique cars from times long gone by. One of these was an orange Camaro with a three-ninety-six V-8 under the scooped hood, causing Connor to offer up a fond smile as it rolled by.

Later, the party shifted to the beach and bars, with lots of dancing and drinking. It was the drinking part that interested Connor tonight, because The Sandbar was open again for business. Jordan James' contractors had worked faster than normal to put the finishing touches on the bar, and the kitchen suppliers had come down from Charleston earlier in the week to install coolers a new cash register. There was even a new hot dog cart and popcorn machine. The Planning Commission had refused to approve reconstruction of the attic apartment, but Connor was good with that.

The invitations to The Sandbar's grand re-opening had been sent out days ago, but the party was not exclusive. Anyone who wanted to stop in was more than welcome, and now—a little after nine o'clock—the crowd was spilling across the road and onto the beach. Connor was behind the bar, running through a half dozen new tricks he'd learned from an orderly in the hospital. Glass from the shattered cell phone had been driven deep into his hand, and Mrs. Carerra's bullet had taken a chunk of flesh out of his arm. Neither injury was life-threatening, but the E.R. doc insisted on keeping him overnight for observation. Once he was discharged, he moved back into his non-code cottage at Cool Sands and rode his bicycle five days a week to The Tides, where he mixed specialty cocktails at the hotel bar and gazed at the dark horizon beyond the sand.

Summer disappeared with Labor Day and the sun moved lower in the sky. A couple tropical storms crept up the coast but stayed a hundred miles out to sea. No hurricanes, which was just fine with Connor. Fine with Clooney, too, whose head was now resting on his paw, his eyes keeping a close watch on the bar's activities.

In the center of Folly a food festival was in full swing, and a steel pan band was drumming music into the night. A few people set off fireworks from the beach, the whistles and retorts of mortar shells echoing through the streets. At The Sandbar people were swaying and swinging to the beat of a new jukebox, many of them edging their way up to the counter to say "hello" and congratulate Connor on his recovery and grand re-opening. He sneaked a quick glance down the bar to where Julie was operating her new state-of-the-art triple blender, whipping up margaritas and banana daiquiris three at a time. She had spent the last four months pouring cocktails into real glasses at a rooftop bar in Charleston, and Connor wasn't sure she'd want to give up her posh surroundings to come back to work in Folly.

She'd jumped at the chance.

"Two rum punches and a Cheerwine," someone in the crowd called out.

As if on autopilot Connor set about making the drinks, dropped in two wedges of lime, then dispensed a measure of Coke into a third cup. He turned around, set them on the counter, grinned when he saw Desmond Green standing there with a very lovely woman and an equally pretty teenage girl.

"Evening, Mr. Connor," Green said, extending his hand and firmly gripping Connor's. Fortunately, it was not the one that still held fragments of glass from the shattered cell phone.

"Mr. Green," Connor greeted him, pumping his arm. "This must be your lovely bride you're always talking about."

Green's wife beamed and smiled at her husband. She truly was lovely, skin the color of a rich latte, dazzling dark eyes, black hair swept down over her forehead in a full wave.

"And I believe you already know Em Lee," Green said, handing her the Cheerwine.

"Hello, Mister Jack," the girl said, gently shaking his hand. "This place is *sweet*."

"I ever catch you in here, doing anything besides saying 'hi' to Mr. Connor, you're grounded for life," Green told her.

"Yes, Uncle Dez," she said. Sounding like she knew he was a pussycat at heart, but not ready to push the boundaries just yet.

"Uncle Dez?" Connor asked.

Green smiled a mouth full of teeth. "Em Lee's mama's sister is my aunt's cousin's niece," he said. "Or something like that. She's a good girl, staying with us now. I want to thank you for all you did."

"That's what friends do," Connor replied. "You come all the way down here just to trick or treat?"

"We're here to see you," Mrs. Green said. "Dez talks about you a lot, and I wanted to meet the man who saved my Em Lee."

"You doing okay?" Connor asked, turning his attention to the girl.

"Had to change schools a couple times, so I got off to a rough start," she told him. "But I'm doing better. I want to go to college so I can be a nurse."

"Good for you," he said.

"What happened to your panther?" she asked, pointing to where the nose of the black cat had been replaced with scar tissue.

"He met up with an enemy of Wakanda," Connor told her. Then he heard the words "two gin and tonics and a Corona" come from behind him, across the bar. "Be right back," he said, but when he returned two minutes later the three of them were gone. He tried to find them in the crowd, but the bodies were packed so tightly into the place that if someone fainted no one would know.

Not long after that the medical examiner surprised him as she edged through the crowd and used her arms like a snowplow to squeeze in between two locals. They made just enough room for her to slip through, then went back to arguing the playoff chances of the Carolina Panthers.

"What's good here?" Dr. Dillon asked while Connor vigorously shook a raspberry martini until it had a nice froth to it.

"How 'bout a corpse reviver?" he replied with a grin.

"Is that a thing?" she asked, not sure whether he was joking or not.

"Gin, Cointreau, absinthe, lemon, and a few other secret ingredients. Guaranteed to wake anyone from the dead."

"I get enough of that at the office," she laughed. "How 'bout a simple gin and tonic?"

That was easy. He mixed the drink and set it in front of her, then said, "What brings you to this neck of the woods on a Halloween night?"

"Getting a head start on the Day of the Dead," she said with a grin. "Plus, I heard that a certain beach bar had re-opened down here. Thought I'd stop in, pay the proprietor a quick visit."

Connor got an order for two mango rums and pineapple juice then, and when he got back to Dr. Dillon she was already halfway through her drink. They talked about simple stuff for a few minutes—the shifting weather, hurricane season, the reconstruction of The Sandbar—and then she leaned closer so no one could hear what she was about to ask him.

"This is probably not the place to talk, but I've been dying to know: whatever happened to Mr. Carerra? I heard there was talk of him going into witness protection, but then—*poof!*—he just faded like the closing shot of a movie."

"I heard the same thing," Connor replied. "I haven't heard from him since that day on Skeleton Cay."

He hated to lie to the medical examiner, but he'd been sworn to secrecy. Carerra had called him from an airport in an unidentified city three weeks ago, using a spoofed area code, and talked to him for all of five minutes. He'd thanked

Connor for saving his life, even if his evil, two-timing wife had been killed in the process. Carerra couldn't say where he was going, what he was going to be doing, or even if he would still be known as Carerra. Even though everyone high up in Neven's operation was dead, the feds still needed him to unravel Neven's web of bank accounts. So, he was being whisked away to some undisclosed location until they worked through all the numbers and a grand jury handed down whatever indictments might still be forthcoming.

Connor had pressed him about the night he was shot, how it all had gone down later out there on Skeleton Cay. Carerra had hesitated a moment, then gave him a truncated version of what had happened after he'd been wheeled inside the ambulance and it sped off toward the hospital:

"After I was shot, I was in a lot of pain and thought I was dying," Carerra had told him. "I'd heard enough to figure out the driver, a guy named McKay, was into Neven's local supplier for a lot of money. That skanky nurse who was posing as a doctor got him to make a detour and swap me out with some other poor sucker who was already dead. That dickhead who shot me had a real good eye, left me injured but not on the brink of death. They made the switch and then took the dead guy to the hospital, and the other medic in the ambulance delivered me to Marco Neven."

"On Skeleton Cay."

"That's right. Neven knew I'd frozen him out of his bank accounts, and he demanded I give him my passwords. I was in so much pain that I couldn't think straight, and by the time they started pumping fentanyl into my system the passwords wouldn't work."

"Because I'd changed them," Connor said.

"Right, but I didn't know that. And if you hadn't come along when you did, I'd be dead."

In the days after the "shoot-out on Skeleton Cay," as the news outlets were calling it, Connor had been visited by a long line of federal investigators. Men in black who levied all kinds of threats against him if he didn't tell them everything he knew. They talked about charging him in Neven's death, but Connor's attorney—provided by Jordan James, of course—reminded them that one of their own was at the center of all the carnage. Agent Landry was a black mart on them all, and the Justice suits backed down. Still, Connor coughed up the new user IDs and passwords he'd substituted that day that he'd accessed Carerra's flash drive— even though he could have played dumb and been over a hundred million dollars richer.

"Why such an elaborate ruse?" Connor had asked him on the phone. "Why didn't they just snatch you off the street?"

"If I disappeared people might start looking for me, but they figured no one would give a damn if I was dead," Carerra had told him.

"They figured wrong," Connor replied.

That was the last time Connor had spoken with Carerra, and he doubted he'd ever hear from him again. The Witness Security program had a solid reputation for hiding its wards deep in the American heartland, and Connor figured Carerra was probably balancing the books at a feed store somewhere in Iowa.

"You know one thing that's been bothering me?" Dr. Dillon asked now as she tipped her head back and pounded the rest of her drink. "Why that guy was in your apartment that morning, got himself shot."

"The guy with the weird name?" Connor asked.

"Luca Roos," she said.

"Turns out he was with Interpol, which was cooperating with our DEA to track Carerra's movements and the money trail from Neven's bank accounts in Zurich. He also suspected Landry was playing both sides, and probably had doubts about me, as well."

Connor had learned more than that, on the eight-minute helicopter flight from Skeleton Cay to the hospital in Charleston. The chopper pilot who had been hired to transport Marco Neven and Martina Carerra to their charter flight at the airport had taken off with Jessica Snow, Tony Carerra, and Connor instead. During those eight agonizing minutes Jessica had spilled a few details about what she knew, one of them being that Luca Roos had directly warned her about Landry, whose gun had been used to shoot both Roos and Arnold Shelton, the driver of the Tahoe.

"So, what was Roos doing in my apartment?" Connor had asked her.

"Carerra was shot in your bar," she replied. "You drove his wife to the hospital, and you were seen speaking with me several nights in a row. He probably figured you were right in the middle of this mess."

"So why did Carerra pick The Sandbar that night?"

"Turns out there's a Sandbar in Key West, or at least there was before Hurricane Maria hit," she told him. "It's where Tony—Daniel Parra—had proposed to his fiancé, Aurora Santana, before she died. I guess it was a sentimental thing."

"So, who was Arnold Shelton, the dead guy in the Tahoe?" Connor had asked her. "I found an email string between him and Carerra."

Jessica clearly had been lightheaded and going into shock, but she still managed an answer as the chopper landed at the medical university's helipad. It was the same answer Connor now told Dr. Dillon, minus the pain-induced cuss words.

"Carerra was a very thorough man," Connor explained to the medical examiner. "Not only did he alert the Justice Department here in the U.S. that he had the goods on Neven; he also had a back-channel with Arnold Shelton, a task force agent running back-up with Landry's unit. Just in case the thing with the feds went sideways, which it did."

The medical examiner took another sip of her gin and tonic in silence and considered what Connor was telling her. Another question appeared to be forming on the tip of her tongue, but then the cell phone in her purse began to ring. She plucked it out and answered it just as a young couple pushed their way up to the bar and ordered two pain killers. Connor dutifully threw a healthy combination of rum and a blend of juice into the mixer, then poured the concoction into a pair of cups and sprinkled a dusting of nutmeg on top. When he turned back around to say something else to her, she had disappeared into the night. The ME's empty cup sat on the polished granite counter, a ten-dollar bill tucked under it.

He glanced around to see where she might have gone, but all of a sudden a round of applause erupted throughout the place and the crowd began to part like the Red Sea. Standing at the far end of the gap of customers, near the new handicap ramp, was Lincoln Polk, a wide-brimmed hat jammed low over his ears, crutches tucked up under both arms.

"Mr. Polk," Connor called to him. "They finally let you out!"

Officer Polk had suffered gravely at the hands of Agent Landry. He'd endured four cracked ribs, two broken legs, a ruptured spleen, a shattered clavicle, several dislocated fingers, and a torn ear that had been partially ripped off. The doctors had repaired it all, including the ear, but that was why Polk now wore the hat. He'd spent ten days in Intensive Care and another four weeks in the hospital recovering from his injuries. Connor had dropped in to visit him once, but a lot of Percocet had been involved and Polk had not been very talkative.

"Mr. Connor," the cop now said as he slowly made his way up to the bar. He leaned his crutches against the counter, and a young lady in denim cut-offs and a tank top waved him onto her stool. "You're looking like the picture of perfect health."

"Nothing like you," Connor replied. He'd tried shaking hands with Polk during that last hospital visit, and suspected it was still not a good idea. "You've been the long way through hell and came back to the land of the living."

"Seen plenty of ghosts along the way, told 'em all to go pick on someone else," Polk said with a grin. "Can I get some of that nectar of the guava?"

"You can have anything you want, my friend," Connor told him.

They spoke for quite a while then, Connor taking frequent time-outs to blend a drink or pop a beer, but Polk was too comfortable to move from his seat. He hadn't been out on the town in months, and he was having a sweet time. After a few minutes he brought up Marco Neven, beginning with the embarrassing fact that none of the local or state cops had known that the southeast's most notorious drug trafficker was operating right under their noses out on Skeleton Cay.

"You think Jesry Freeman or Cecil Maines had any idea who they'd gotten involved with?" Connor asked him.

"They were part of his local franchise," Polk replied. "Lieutenants, captains, whatever."

"What still bugs me is why they had that kid—Justacious Stone—shoot Mr. Carerra. That was kind of a risky play, taking a shot like that."

"Not really. Word is, that boy had a calibrated eyeball, could place a bullet wherever he wanted at thirty yards," the officer replied. "He was already a triggerman for the Raging Beests, a heavy-duty gang out of Walterboro. Marco Neven heard of his skills, gave him a crack at the big time."

"And then killed him for his efforts."

"It's called 'loose ends.'" Polk took a long sip of his guava juice, then went on, "I know you've got a business to run, but can I ask you a question?"

"Fire away."

"Interesting choice of words," he said with a grin. "What I want to know is, who killed the lady—Mrs. Carerra—and saved your sorry ass?"

This question had come up a lot over the past four months, first raised by Jessica Snow in the helicopter, then by the FBI, then the DEA, then the state cops. Also, by the news media, which had been all over the story for days. All Connor told them—and all he truly recalled—was that Mrs. Carerra had lowered her gun just before she'd been shot, and he hadn't seen who pulled the trigger. It was the truth, but the nagging question still caused his brain to boil over in the darkest hours of the night.

"I really don't know," he told Polk now, shaking his head.

"But you have a pretty good idea."

"The bullet that killed her didn't come from any gun found at the scene. Whoever it was took one helluva shot from the terrace, then split."

Polk flashed him the same dubious look all the others had given him, and let a long silence emphasize his skepticism. It was Connor's story, and he clearly was sticking to it.

"That's hard for me to believe," Polk said anyway.

"You and me both," Connor assured the wounded cop. The truth was, he never got a good luck at whoever had taken that shot, and by the time Connor made his way back to the helipad the gunman had disappeared. Connor might have heard an outboard motor start up, but he was in no condition to go look. If he had any memory of what had happened, he'd filed it away as one of those "don't ask, don't tell" things.

They shot the breeze for a few more minutes, then Polk gingerly slid off his stool and explained that his presence was requested over at the town pier. The police chief was honoring him with some kind of medal for risking his life in the line of duty.

"I wish I could be there," Connor said, cocking his head at the thirsty crowd to silently explain why he had to remain behind.

"You've got a business to run," Polk told him. "Just wanted to stop by, see how things are going. Seems you're doing just fine."

"So are you," Connor said. "And if I didn't say it before, thanks again for all your help."

Polk looked Connor in the eye, said, "It's what a peace officer does, my friend. Except maybe next time you could be a little more forthcoming with the facts." He held his gaze for a second, then turned as the crowd parted for him one more time.

TRICK OR TREAT

Connor watched him until he disappeared into the night, then picked up a rag and absently wiped it across the counter. He couldn't help shake the thought that the events of last July easily could have landed Polk in the morgue rather than the ICU, and he was profoundly aware that his own actions—and inactions—had contributed to the cop's nightmare. Polk was right: if Connor had coughed up a bit more about what he'd known and suspected, the cop probably would not have suffered so harshly at the hands of Special Agent David Landry.

A jolt of guilt momentarily tugged him back home to Michigan, to how his inactions once before had led to the death of an innocent little girl. A murder that finally had been solved and, while not absolving him of any blame or responsibility, had brought a modicum of closure to his past. His mother had called him again when she'd seen his face on the network news, horrified that her son had almost died much the same way Lily had at the Mega Gas all those years ago. They'd talked a few times since then, and Connor had promised to come home in a few weeks, at Thanksgiving.

It was a promise he fully intended to keep, as long as Julie could hold down the fort while he was gone.

As if reading his mind, Julie squeezed behind him at that very moment and whispered in his ear: "You have to stop beating yourself up, Jack. Hard as it may be to grasp, the fate of the world does not rest on your shoulders."

She was right, of course, and Connor knew she wasn't just referring to Lincoln Polk. She knew more of Connor's backstory than he would have liked, and mincing words was not her style.

"You're saying I should have just left well enough alone?"

"That's something you're going to have to figure out on your own. But it might help if you weighed all sides of something before just jumping in head first."

"Meaning what?"

"Meaning a lot of people died."

"You think that's on me?" he asked her, partly because he was a bit peeved but mostly because he'd been thinking the same thing. He'd called Dr. Pinch about a month after the dust had settled, and the shrink had reminded him he wasn't responsible for any of the baggage on the luggage carousel except his own.

"That's the sort of question that can keep you up at night," she told him.

Sixty seconds later he was popping the caps off two locally brewed IPAs when he heard the words, "Double beefeater martini, exceptionally dry, two olives, straight up."

Intuition and instinct had told him this moment would be coming. There was no avoiding the inevitable. He handed the fresh beers to the man who'd ordered them, then turned to face Jordan James, who had pushed his way up to the new stone counter.

"Evening, Mr. James," Connor said.

"How many times do I have to tell you…first names only," the eighth-richest man in Charleston told him. He cast a quick glance at the throng of customers and added, "Halloween sure brings them out of the woodwork."

"It's been like this all night, sir. …I mean Jordan," Connor said as he carefully measured out the desert-dry cocktail and poured it into an honest-to-God martini glass. He dropped in two of the largest olives from the condiment tray, then placed the frosted drink in front of him.

Mr. James nodded at the gesture and said, "You going to join me?"

Connor reached to the back bar and picked up a half-finished glass of tonic water. "Rule number nine is, 'no drinking on the job,'" he said.

They touched glasses, took their respective sips, and then Jordan James got down to the real reason he was here. Same reason as the last four times he'd dropped in to see Connor since the bar had burned down.

"You ignored my advice and almost got yourself killed," he began. "But you also took down the biggest supplier of heroin and fentanyl in the southeast."

"You think it was worth it?" Connor asked.

"Do you know how many people overdose from opiates each day?" Mr. James asked him. "Over two hundred, just here in the U.S. *Two hundred every day*. Think of how many people are still alive—many of them former soldiers like yourself—because of what you did."

"I didn't know where this was going when I started," Connor explained to him, just as he'd done during those other visits. "I just wanted to know why a man was shot in my bar. *Your bar*, actually."

"And that's the real reason I'm here," Jordan James said as he took another healthy sip of his double martini.

"What reason would that be, sir?"

Mr. James scowled again at the word *sir*, but decided to give up on it. Instead he said, "Big changes are coming."

Alarm bells started ringing in Connor's head, and he said, "What kind of changes?"

Another sip of gin preceded Jordan James' response, which was, "I just sold this place."

"You...*what?*" Connor gasped, almost spitting out a mouthful of tonic water. "You just spent a ton of money rebuilding it."

"Most of it was insurance," Mr. James replied. "Thing is, a major chain in Atlanta saw the numbers and the location, made me an offer I couldn't turn down."

"Just like that?"

"I sign the papers tomorrow."

"But...why didn't you tell me?"

"That's what I'm doing now," Jordan James said. "Besides, this whole thing came out of the blue in the last week."

Connor felt a slow burn rising from within, and he took a second or two to extinguish it. Then he said, "So what happens to me?"

"Well, this company in Atlanta—I'm not at liberty to divulge the name, but you'll figure out who they are—their bartenders are known for their hot pants and tight tops."

"You're telling me I'm out of a job?"

"That's their decision, of course, but it's part of the change I mentioned." Mr. James took a long sip of his martini, then went on. "As I've always told you, I consider you family—and I always look after my family."

Mother of God, Connor thought. *Here it comes.*

"Now, I know you like your independence and autonomy. Self-reliance, and all that. But you've worked for me for a couple years now, and over that time I've watched how you pour yourself into your work. Whether it's bartending, cleaning up blood, or sticking your neck out when you don't have to, you get the job done."

"And get shot in the process," Connor reminded him.

"You do take unnecessary risks," Mr. James conceded. "Which does have a bearing on your asset value. But that's something we can work on, given the proper oversight."

Connor was silent a few seconds, figuring he was stumbling into some sort of trap. Eventually he said, "If this is about Citadel Security again, I've already told you: I don't want to be a rent-a-cop." Citadel was one of the many companies included in Jordan James' vast portfolio of local holdings, and Connor knew from past discussions that the firm had a multi-year contract with the port of Charleston.

"And like I've told you, that's not what this is." Jordan James finished his drink, slid the glass across the counter in search of another. "You know that problem you helped us with at the port last year?"

"Yeah...stuff kept going missing from containers," Connor said as he began fixing another desert-dry martini. "Last I knew you never solved it."

"The hurricane solved it for us. Whatever was going on stopped on its own after the storm blew through."

"So, what does this have to do with me?"

"You remember Gil Redman?" Mr. James asked.

"How could I forget him?" Connor placed the new martini on a fresh cocktail napkin and set it in front of his boss. *Former boss, and maybe future boss.* "He runs the company, and you had me speak with him a few years back."

"That's right," James said, savoring the scent of juniper berries. "He and I, we had lunch today. Finalized some plans for a new division of the company, and he suggested we bring you on board to run it."

Connor was momentarily saved by an order for a cosmopolitan and a painkiller, but when he turned back around Jordan James was still there. "What kind of new division?" he asked, knowing he was venturing into a mine field.

"You're aware I own a couple bail bonds businesses?"

"Among other things," Connor said. "I figure they must be pretty profitable."

"Most of the time," Mr. James replied as he sipped his drink. "But then, every once in a while, someone doesn't show up in court, and then our ass—my ass—is in a sling. Costs me big bucks."

Connor could see where this was going, couldn't believe he was even considering what the man was about to suggest. "You want me to be a bounty hunter?"

Jordan James cracked a knowing grin, said, "I want you to run our new bail enforcement agency, Jack. It's nothing like you see on TV. I mean, sure, there's a lot of footwork and persistence involved, and a lot of patience."

"I'm done with this detective bullshit," Connor told him, matter-of-fact. As if to emphasize the point, Clooney thumped his tail on the floor, although he didn't bother lifting his head. "It already cost me the most wonderful woman I've ever known, and I'm tired of hospitals."

Jordan James nodded at Connor's answer, as if he'd been expecting it. "I know it sounds risky, but I would never ask you to get involved with anything dangerous," he said. "You'd work from our local headquarters and oversee a team of contract agents. Rarely would you be in the field. Plus, the salary would be good. You'll get a bonus for everyone you bring back, and I'll give you a company car."

Connor didn't really know what to say, not just then. He realized the man was serious, also realized just how much he really liked working behind the bar at The Sandbar. But he couldn't see the new owners in Atlanta asking him to dress in a halter top and tight shorts, and now that he thought about it, he didn't really mind poking his nose in dark corners from time to time. As long as it didn't land him in the ICU, or worse.

"What kind of car?" he asked.

"I'll take that as a 'yes,'" Jordan James said as he drained the rest of his gin. "You're doing the right thing."

Connor started to object, his mind flashing on Danielle and what she might have to say about this whole thing. But she was miles away tonight, and she'd made her thoughts abundantly clear the last time they'd spoken. Besides, the eighth richest man in Charleston didn't get that way by taking "no" for an answer, and now he simply slid off his stool and tipped an imaginary cap on his head. Then he disappeared into the crowd, the words of protest still forming on Connor's tongue.

The Sandbar wouldn't have been the same without the woman named Neptune doing her tarot thing, and she had made sure she'd arrived early enough to get her regular stool at the corner of the bar. So far, she'd made it through five apple martinis without having to pay for a single one, counting instead on the generosity of the customers seated beside her. Now, as Connor checked to see if she wanted another, she inquired if he wanted her to read his cards.

"If memory serves me, the last time you did this all the cards told you was 'death, destruction, and mayhem,'" he reminded her.

"The cards didn't lie," she said.

She was right about that, but he sincerely doubted they had anything to do with any of that.

"Go ahead, good sir," she prodded him. "Shuffle the cards."

The cards were far too small to shuffle, and besides, he knew what Neptune was up to here. All it would cost him was another free drink, and then another one after that. He started to beg off, but then he figured it was Halloween, and mischief and magic were in the air. What harm could there be in a little tarot reading?

Connor spread out the cards in a pile in front of her, mixed them around, then collected them into a deck. "Okay—let's see what you've got," he told her.

Neptune slowly began to deal them out onto the bar as he mixed her another apple martini. When he came back, she had arranged the cards in the usual pattern and was studying each one thoughtfully. Then a slow grin formed on her lips, and she looked up at him. "Looks to me like Jack Connor has love and romance in his future," she said with a smile.

"Is that so?"

"Most definitely, see?" And then she proceeded to tell him about how the cards representing the Two of Cups and the Lovers both indicated a man and a woman coming together, heightened by the surface reality of the Magician. "That means love and romance, no question. And, it seems, some good old-fashioned lust, to boot."

Sometime later—how much later Connor didn't know—the crowd had thinned out. Music was still playing all over town: reggae and hip-hop and country and good old rock and roll, all layered atop the other. The aroma of fried chicken and barbecued pork hung thick in the air. So, did another very distinct aroma, but tonight the cops seemed to care less about that than they did on normal nights.

Connor mixed a couple of margaritas, set them down in front of a man and a woman in their early thirties who were talking about how they loved the beach life so much they were thinking about never going back to reality. Getting a business license and maybe renting bicycles on the sand. Knowing it was an impossible dream, but indulging themselves in the possibilities just the same. Then Connor felt, more than heard, someone scoot up on the stool behind him. He slowly turned, found himself looking into the dark, wrinkled eyes of Jimmy Brinks.

"Double Jack," he growled. "Put it in a glass."

Brinks' personal tumbler had been destroyed in the fire, but Connor made sure he had a new one under the bar on the slim chance that Brinks might show up again someday. He poured the glass full, set it on the counter in front of the leathery ex-con.

Brinks took a long sip, drained about half of the amber liquid down his throat. "*I don't need a gun,*" he murmured in an acerbic voice, almost too low for Connor to hear it.

"Say what?" Connor asked, as if he hadn't heard right.

"*I figure, with Jesry Freeman out of the way, I'll be okay,*" Brinks added, a smirk etched on his lips. "Like I said back then, 'you were one dumb sumbitch.'"

Connor realized Brinks was mocking him, getting on his case about the shoot-out. Not trying to be nasty, probably just trying to have some fun in his own warped way.

"I'm still here," Connor told him.

"Not without a bit of well-timed help," Brinks said, firing an imaginary gun made from his thumb and forefinger. He raised his glass almost in a silent toast, then tossed back the rest of the Tennessee sour mash. He set the empty glass on the counter, wiped his lips on his arm, and was gone. Just as fast as he'd showed up.

Connor picked up the tumbler and rinsed it in the sink, then set it back in its designated shelf under the counter. Tucked *way* in the back, hoping it would stay there for a long while. He wiped his rag over the counter, turned it over and did it again. He stood there a moment, seeing the replay of Martina Carerra's head exploding, then pushing it as far back in his brain as it would go. As far back as Jimmy Brinks' glass, under the counter. He didn't like feeling indebted to anyone, and certainly not to someone he normally wouldn't give the time of day to. Yes, the ex-con with bad teeth had been a one-man cavalry out on Skeleton Key, and that was a secret Connor would just have to live with.

He popped a couple beers for a man in a pirate's hat who had pressed his way through the crowd, then glanced out at the moon that was just beginning to peek above the lip of the horizon. The ink-black water was reflecting the bright lights of town and the intermittent roar of fireworks exploding in the dark night overhead.

Life doesn't get much better than this, he was thinking when his ears caught that distinct, sultry voice behind him:

"Hey, Magic Man…don't suppose you'd do that killer lime trick for me again, would you—?"

ABOUT THE AUTHOR

Reed Bunzel is a mystery writer, biographer, "media anthropologist," and president of Bunzel Creative Services, LLC.

The former President/CEO of an online music company (TheRadio.com), Bunzel also served as Executive V.P. of Al Bell Presents LLC. Previously, he was editor-in-chief for United News and Media's San Francisco publishing operations; earlier in his career he was editor-in-chief of Streamline Publishing's Radio Ink and Streaming magazines, as well as an editor at Radio & Records and Broadcasting magazine. Additionally, he served in an executive capacity at both the National Association of Broadcasters and the Radio Advertising Bureau.

A graduate of Bowdoin College in Brunswick, Maine, Bunzel holds a Bachelor of Science degree in Anthropology, cum laude. A native of the San Francisco Bay Area, he currently resides with his wife Diana in Charleston, South Carolina.